Benjamin McTish

And The Door Through
The Grandfather Tree

Benjamin McTish
And The Door Through The
Grandfather Tree

Book One

By
June M. Pace

Illustrations and Cover Art by June

Thornton Berry Shire Press
CA, 2015

Copyright TXU001786594

ISBN 978-0-9896464-0-6

Library of Congress Control Number 2013911770

I Dedicate this book to Ray, for his unwavering belief in me and this story, and for the countless hours of listening to me read out loud.

This book was written for the young at heart...for those of us who dare to be more than what we're told is possible.

CONTENTS

Chapter One

Mysteries

Well, that's very odd, thought Benjamin. He had never noticed the peculiar looking key, hanging from a very worn and tattered green ribbon, on the rusted nail in the garden shed before.

The garden shed was not a traditional shed in the least. Even though the walls were constructed from very old worn out wood, the interesting element was the solid glass roof. It was a very unusual version of a greenhouse, and the permanent home of the most rare and beautiful of begonias, grown by his grandmother Emmagene. It also doubled as Benjamin's secret hideaway.

The design was one of a kind built by his grandfather, Owen McTish, way back before Benjamin was even born. The wood came from an old abandoned farm on the outskirts of town. The remnants from the farm had sat in the big fields on the edge of the Gilley Forest for close to a hundred years or more now. The property was part of a long forgotten estate that had iron clad deeds and legalities making it impossible to tear down. Save for some wood that was sold off at auction *(which was now the main body of structure to the McTish garden shed)*, along with some rusted antique barnyard equipment, nothing had been touched in all these long years. The passed down rumors of the mysteries surrounding the Chickering farm was still local legend with all the residents, but especially with the children, in the small town of Grandlochcheshire.

And here he was now, sitting in the garden shed built of the same wood that had housed the infamous Chickerings all those long years ago, staring at a mysterious key.

Benjamin sat upright from his perch on top of the pile of burlap bags; that covered the mound of hay his grandmother stored in the shed for new seedling cover, and stared up in utter disbelief at the mysterious key.

His grandmother enjoyed the smell of fresh hay, as it reminded her of her youth on her family's horse ranch. This resulted in her always keeping much more hay than she truly needed under the burlap, making this a particularly cozy little spot for Benjamin to lounge about. As an added attraction it also happened to be in direct sight of the door and proved to be the perfect lookout for any uninvited guests.

Benjamin whipped his head around quickly and scanned the shed for any movement. *Nothing out of the ordinary, no one else around, no sounds of any kind...hmmm.* He sat still and stared into the air before him, searching for an answer. After a moment he continued his survey around the room.

The light coming in from the glass ceiling was soft and dark grey as it was about to rain again. This added a touch of anxiety to the moment, as Benjamin's all too familiar feeling of questioning arose. Everything appeared to look the same as it did every other day that he could remember...*except for that confounding and peculiar key!* The hairs on Benjamin's arms stood straight up and a flush washed over his entire body and he *knew* something big was about to happen.

For as long as he could remember, it seemed Benjamin had the ability to know things that other people never realized. He knew secrets about people, their inner workings, even before they knew about it themselves. It wasn't like he could see dead people, or tell you what you had hidden in your pocket, or anything like this, it was more about *sensing* things. He had gut feelings, but in a bigger more expanded way. He was rather good at telling you when your Aunt Gertie was going to show up at your door, or where to look for the lost cat.

However, he was *really* good at knowing if something was significant or not, if something needed a further or deeper exploration.

It had always been this way for Benjamin. When something was about to occur he had a warning it was coming. The hair on his arms stood up and an extremely powerful tingling from the bottom of his toes would rush up over his body. His heart would pound and a little sweat would instantly gather on his face and neck. His breathing would speed up and his eyes would widen in anxious search of the source of his alertness. Many times these sensations came with lightning rapid visions and sounds. And always attached to these pictures was a deeply felt emotion clinging along for the ride.

The Key.

Benjamin hesitantly turned back around slowly, like he was moving through thick syrup, and stared at the hanging piece of tarnished metal that seemed to be calling him. He had a very uneasy feeling about this key. In all his years of living with his grandparents he had never seen it dangling in the shed. Nor, in fact, had he seen its equal or anything remotely close to this anywhere in the whole of the household.

He estimated the key was somewhere around nine inches in length and looked as old as the hills...*Or the Gilley Forest*, came the distant thought to Benjamin. He shook the dreamy moment from his head and realized he needed a closer look. He could tell it was designed with marks that he couldn't make out from where he was sitting.

An impending alarm flooded Benjamin's mind as he began his slow concise descent off the mound of burlap covered hay. He inched his way toward the foreign old relic. The key with a worn out tattered green ribbon to match, that hung from an equally rusted old nail pounded soundly into the beam of the garden shed, that was home to Benjamin McTish and all that he knew.

As Benjamin approached the key he couldn't take his eyes off of it. It was like a magnetic beam was pulling him closer and closer to his target. Benjamin reached up on his toes and removed the key from its mysterious home on the old nail. The weight surprised Benjamin, he hadn't expected it to be as heavy as it was. He turned it around and around in his hands, studying every line of the intricate design. Then suddenly, by accident, he noticed that at a certain angle when he looked at it almost sideways there appeared to be...*words!*

Words and symbols in some kind of extraordinary language that Benjamin had never seen before. Benjamin's heart started racing and his breathing grew louder. His eyes widened and he quickly took the key over to the potting bench in the middle of the shed. The table stood immediately under the huge expanse of window ceiling and in between two other tables that were filled with pots and dirt. He laid the key on the top near the corner, in the strong growing light of the imminent storm.

The eerie cast that the light makes when it is so bright, yet dark at the same time, gave illumination to the key on the bench's edge. The table was a perfect height for Benjamin to scrunch on down with his hands on his knees at eye level with the key. He marched back and forth, squatting and repositioning himself for every possible discoverable view of this curious relic, without actually touching it. This small, yet significant, distance gave solace to Benjamin as he went deep into dissecting thought.

Just as he was about to pick up the key to examine it closer for details, the door of the shed flew open. A burst of exuberant and animated voices came at him so fiercely that he jumped from the sudden fright, scratching his shoulder on the edge of the table behind him.

"Blast it!" he groaned.

Quickly recognizing the voices of his two best mates, Annabel and Mathilda, he grabbed the key with stealth speed and put it in his pocket. He pulled his jumper over the protruding end to hide it and turned around to see what the commotion was about.

There was Annabel in her familiar flower-printed rubber rain boots and her younger sister Mathilda in her ever more familiar lavender tutu, with today's addition of a yellow, red and green plaid rain slicker and hat. All her wild orange curls were peeking out everywhere around her face and she held something tightly in her closed up fist.

"Hiya Benjamin! What're ya doing?" asked a particularly bubbly Mathilda.

4

"Oh, nothin much. Just hanging out, waiting for the rain to quit," he said, attempting to mask his guilt at hiding something from his friends.

"What's up with you Benjamin, you look like you're in trouble or something?" asked Annabel.

"Yeah, like you just ate the big fat canary or somethin," added Mathilda.

Benjamin's guilt almost spilled out, when a humongous thunder bolt exploded just above the garden shed, illuminating the sky in a bright white flash.

"Holy Cripes!" squealed Mathilda from fright. Shocked nearly out of her socks, Mathilda's clenched fist opened, and the three gum balls that had been held prisoner loosened their stickiness in slow motion and fell to the ground; leaving dots of candy flavored red, green and white imprints on her sweaty palm. When she caught her breath she looked back down at her outstretched arm and held her stiff sticky little rainbow colored hand open, like it was something defective and unattached to her, "Oh man! I can't believe I dropped those. I been savin them for two days now. What a waste of good candy," said Mathilda mournfully as she bent down to pick up the compost ladened confection.

"It's probably not as bad as you think tike, let me see if I can wipe them off," said Annabel. Just as Mathilda was handing the gum balls to her sister another crack of lightening burst over their heads. Everyone flinched and ducked.

"Bloody hell!" yelled Benjamin, "That was a good one."

"I'll say! You think this glass roof will hold up Benjamin?" asked Mathilda nervously.

The three small friends looked up apprehensively.

"Well, it's been here for a really long time. I think it's strong enough to last a rightly bit longer," offered Benjamin.

They all stood and watched as the rain poured down in buckets on the glass roof of the McTish garden shed, while they chewed on gum balls.

The Wickcliff girls were the most truest and best mates that Benjamin ever had, without exception. It had been almost a year since he sat in his bedroom

5

window and watched in curious amusement as the moving van unloaded the entirety of the Wickcliff belongings into the two story cream house with the forest green trim, next door to his grandparents.

Benjamin had come to live in Grandlochcheshire with his grandparents when he was almost nine. Because of the deep commitment that each of his parents held for their profoundly important work, and the time it took away from them as a family, Owen and Emmagene agreed without hesitation to have their only grandchild come live with them.

His father, Avery, was a marine biologist who was on the ocean most of Benjamin's youth. He was the lead scientist in a small group of sea worshipping comrades who's important global research was privately funded. No one knew the waters of the planet like Avery. He had a deep passion for every facet of study involving the ecosystems of ocean life. This path had consumed him even as a young boy growing up in Grandlochcheshire.

He would ask questions of everything, and read as much as he could get his hands on. Even at a young age he was capable of grasping the deeper complexity of science. Unlike most of his classmates it was second nature to Avery. He simply understood how things worked. He *felt* how things worked.

Then during his college years he met Gwyneth, who was his match, equal in every way possible. They had the same passion for life and study and fell deeply in love. They were married before their final year at the University and had Benjamin two years later.

Gwyneth was a botanist and just as dedicated to her work as her husband, if not more. She had an air of worldly excitement about her that held Benjamin in deep awe. Gwyneth was at the top of her field by the end of her studies at the University of Dorstanton. Respected globally for her unparalleled understanding of ancient and obscure flora, and all things to do with their biology; she was one of half a dozen on the planet who knew what she knew. She would be heralded off in a corporate jet to some exotic spot on the globe to study a newly discovered orchid or rare berry fruited shrub. Her discerning and expert knowledge gained her access to the most coveted research areas on the earth. Deep into the Amazon jungles of South America, or the Asian Rain Forest, where secluded indigenous tribes and Shamans guided her through ancient rituals. Steeped in other worldly tradition, using sacred plants found only in that area of the world, Gwyneth learned from her mentors.

She had written books and theses, and had projects funded by huge global corporations. She was brilliant and full of life, and Benjamin thought she was the most beautiful woman he had ever seen. Her family being from the North, closer to the Scottish boarder, gave her that old English country-shiny clean skin, with tiny freckles and bright green eyes. Her long strawberry blond hair swirled about in the air and surrounded her head like a halo when it was windy outside. Benjamin dreamed of her hugs...and her smile.

His parents both came to spend time in the McTish household as often as time would permit. Little by little the time span extended from weeks to months, until it finally became years. Neither he, nor his grandparents, had heard from either Avery or Gwyneth for almost three years. The unexplained coincidence of both parents remaining at large was unfathomable to the entire McTish family. Benjamin's heart was silently torn in two, and he kept this ache to himself.

There were several instances when Benjamin said something to his grandparents in passing about some random occurrence, that apparently only he had witnessed, and they simply stared at him; not certain what to make of his observations and predictions. This made Benjamin very uncomfortable. So he became a bit of a loner and stayed in his room most of the time, sitting on the bay window seat watching life pass by on the road down below.

Then there were the days he spent lying on a pile of burlap in the garden shed staring up out of the wondrous window into the sky, and imagining a life with his parents by his side once again.

Until one summer day, when he was thirteen, as he watched from his window seat while the new neighbors moved in, did his life change.

He sat silently as he witnessed the large boxes being carted out of the moving van and brought into the two story cream house with the forest green trim. As dark wooden chairs with colorful floral printed cushions passed by his view, Benjamin sat motionless. Only his eyes moved back and forth, like a large clock ticking in the foyer. Table tops and bed frames were leaned up against the porch wall, as the two burly moving men had a very animated discussion about who would lead up the staircase and who would carry the brunt of the load, and why. Suddenly a commotion was beginning to pull at Benjamin's attention. He was jerked out of his detached observation of the movers when he heard someone shouting "Cub-by. Cubby come here."

Within moments a huge golden retriever came bounding across the front yard. Benjamin sat up and took notice immediately. He turned his head in the direction of the stirring of activity that was apparently spilling out from the family SUV that had parked along the curb in front of the house. The ruckus was quickly growing in decibel until he heard the very boisterous high pitched squealing of what could only be called...*girl noise*. *Crikey*, thought Benjamin, *girls, and not one but two.*

He first took note of the little one that he guessed was younger than himself by at least three or four years. She had the most wild kinky curly bright orange hair that completely framed her little round face. She was an explosion of color. Benjamin's eye brows quickly slid up his forehead with piqued interest. She was wearing a baby pink ballet tutu, beat up bright green high top sneakers with glittery purple untied laces trailing behind her, and a plastic rhinestone tiara mixed in with her russet tangle of curls. And she was eating the biggest cookie he had ever seen.

Hmm, this is intriguing, he thought.

Then came the older one. Benjamin calculated her to be closer to his age. This girl had short dark hair with long bangs that nearly covered her eyes. She had a sleeveless green, orange and brown striped frock on. She wore faded worn out red leather cowboy boots that were a little too big on her; creating raspy noises on the pavement as she shuffled along. And then something that one does not see in Grandlochcheshire, she was sporting a baseball bat perched upon her shoulder; with a mitt dangling from the end that swung back and forth as she walked.

Blimey, must be Americans, thought Benjamin, *Okay, it's official...this has definitely gotten interesting.*

He got up on his knees in the window seat and pressed his nose, forehead and palms to the glass to see where they all ran off, as the front yard was now quickly void of all activity almost as suddenly as it had begun. He couldn't get a good view into the back garden from where he sat, although the upstairs windows were almost equal to his. He could spy the movers in their unending battle about where things went and why. He could hear everyone shouting and laughing. He could hear the girls running up and down the stairs giggling, and all the ordinary commotion of a family moving in...*a family*, thought Benjamin sadly for a moment.

Too caught up in the flurry of activity and newness of everything happening so quickly around him, and all the questions he had, Benjamin hopped down off the window seat and headed out of his room to investigate further.

In a flash his antennae went up and he got the distinct feeling that things were about to change in his life in a big way. The hairs on his arms were tingling and Benjamin smiled as he bounced down the stairs and out the front door.

Chapter Two

The Nanny

"Bellie what do you think will happen tomorrow? Tell me again, what a nanny does."

"I don't know Tildie, mom says she's going to help around the house because Da has so much work to do. A nanny helps with the kids mostly, she's like a babysitter who lives with you," replied Annabel.

The Wickcliff girls had come to call their father da because Annabel; also referred to by her baby sister as Bellie, only spoke in one syllable words as a toddler. Instead of *dada* like most infants, she said simply *da*. No matter how persistent aunts and uncles, the grocer, or complete strangers were at attempting to coax the other da out of her, it was not to be. So the Wickcliff girls had come to call their father da. A term he had grown to cherish with all his heart.

Edward Wickcliff, an energy technologies engineer, born and raised in Grandlochcheshire, was set to begin his new position at the Dagwood Corporation home offices in Callum. Edward had been living in America while working at the sister corporate offices of Dagwood for a little more that a decade. Edward enjoyed his work tremendously and had a great admiration for the company and the work they produced. So when he was approached almost twelve years before, and asked if he would be willing to transfer to the States to head up a team in the globalization of Dagwood, and the advancement of this important energy research, Edward could not say no.

This is where he first saw Claire, on the second floor of the twenty-seven story building in the heart of the city. Every day for a week, at precisely eleven-thirty, Edward would jump in the elevator and head down the twelve floors, landing him at the corporate accounting offices. There he would stroll the hall waiting to *'accidentally'* run into Claire as she did her daily rounds of paper shuffling between offices. It didn't take a genius to catch onto Edward's obvious attraction to Claire. Claire had become keenly aware of Edward's stratagem by day three, making certain her lipstick was fresh before making her rounds. *Well, two could play this game.*

When Edward finally had the courage to introduce himself to Claire, it was like a lighting bolt ran through them and they fell instantly in love. Much to the surprise of their colleagues, they were married within six months. They began their family by the end of their first year of marriage with the birth of their first daughter Annabel.

The plan had always been to someday return to the little town of Edward's upbringing, Grandlochcheshire. Not only was it the neighboring city to the corporate offices belonging to the company that Edward had given a majority of his career to, but it was home to his heart as well. Claire only wanted to be where Edward was, and if that meant moving back to the home of his childhood, then move she would.

Edward's new boss Braxton Dagwood, the heir apparent to the family company, had a different way of running things than the elders before him. Dagwood was a very old English family that had a very old English name. The lineage origin of the name Dagwood literally meant, *Luminous Forest*, a source of great pride and honor to Braxton Dagwood, the youngest son of Nathaniel. In the meantime, things were changing in the company and it was finally time to bring Edward home.

It may have taken a bit longer than the Wickcliff's had originally planned, but it seemed they had arrived at that precise moment they had dreamt of for so many years.

The family now included another daughter, Mathilda, and a rather large golden retriever named Cubby. Relocating across the Atlantic and establishing a new way of life for everyone was exciting and scary, as well as a huge undertaking. However, bringing the girls back to the place that was home for Edward, that could offer them the same simple pleasures of life that he had been privy to in his youth, was a tremendous sense of joy and accomplishment for him. The five Wickcliffs *(Cubby included)*, were beginning a new adventure in the perfect little country town, on the outskirts of the big city that backed up against the Gilley Forest, known as Grandlochcheshire.

Because of Edward's newly expanded duties with the Dagwood Corporation, and the amount of time he needed to settle in; plus the addition of an unfamiliar city to the rest of his family, the parental Wickcliffs decided some extra help around the house would be the added relief they required. So everyone was waiting with increased anticipation for the appearance of Mrs. Longpotts, the new nanny, who was due to arrive the next afternoon.

The next afternoon had indeed arrived itself, and with it came a taxi and the anticipated delivery to the Wickcliff residence. While the girls were busy in deep exploration of all the nooks and crannies of their new home, they heard the sound of a car pulling away and ran down the stairs as the front bell rang. Claire opened the door and in the bright sunlit background stood the silhouette of the woman who would *(at the time no one could ever have suspected)*, forever change the lives of every resident in the two story cream house with the forest green trim. The girls stood motionless halfway down the staircase as their mother closed the door behind Myra Longpotts, better known as Mrs. Longpotts, the nanny. There was an air of authority about her and a riddle to her face all at once. She stood five feet two inches in her grey and white lace up spectator shoes.

She looks like something from a fairy tale, thought Mathilda, "Cool," she whispered.

Even though it was the middle of June, Mrs. Longpotts wore a lightweight khaki raincoat with a sheer pink and red patterned scarf around her neck. She carried a large over sized satchel that looked like it was made from some old chenille bedspread of mostly yellow and coral roses. The thick leather handles were worn and faded down to a slight tan, almost colorless. A stranger couldn't have guessed her age, and in the eyes of her new charges she appeared ancient.

Mathilda and Annabel looked at each other with bated breath and wide eyes full of curious anticipation. They turned back to further study the diminutive woman standing in the entry way, who was now staring with great intent up at them! Knocked off guard for a moment, they just simply stood exchanging quizzical glances until Claire broke the silence, "Let me take your things Mrs. Longpotts," she said as she gathered the nanny's coat and bag, and invited her into the kitchen for some iced tea. Before she walked down the corridor she turned and made a funny face up at the girls while she ushered Mrs. Longpotts along. The girls giggled and ran quickly down the stairs following the lead to catch up with the conversation.

The next few days went off without a hitch. Everyone was pulling themselves into the rhythm of their new lives in the small English town. Annabel was tending with great seriousness to her room set up. Everything had a place to Annabel....and everyplace had a thing.

Her father had hung her perfectly clean white book shelves above her desk and now she was arranging her array of supplies accordingly.

Even at thirteen years of age Annabel was a student of knowledge. She was a voracious reader and loved a good story filled with clues and puzzles. She was drawn to ideas that made her look at things from every side. She had an unconventional thirst for learning something new. She loved to write. She loved taking notes and making lists. Lists were big with Annabel.

In the mud room, just off of the kitchen, hung a large wax board that she updated on a regular basis with the entire school year of activities, from soccer practice *(football here in England)*, to teacher conferences. The whole family's personal schedules, from dance class to dentist appointments were maintained. This was a huge undertaking that Annabel reveled in. She had five different color markers to represent each member of the Wickcliff household *(Cubby included, he needed shots and baths after all)*, and their corresponding chores, meetings and commitments.

A really good day for Annabel was when Claire would take them to the office supply store. To Annabel it was like being in a giant candy store filled with every confection a child could dream of and Christmas morning all rolled into one. Pencils of every shade, erasers in the cute little shapes of fruit, like a bunch of cherries or grapes. Every size sticky note pads in more colors imaginable, purple being her favorite bar none. Binders that had pockets to store specific separate notes, or special papers, and zippered transparent compartments that carried anything her little heart desired.

She also had a special knack for making up fun stories off the top of her head to tell her baby sister. Who would of course howl with glee whenever the fairy princess road off on the back of the dragonfly; after stealing away with the coveted sugared berries the farmer's wife set out to dry.

Then, of course, there was Mathilda. Mathilda marched to her own beat. She was everything opposite of her big sister. She was fearless and creative and loved a good adventure. Mathilda made the best out of every situation.

Mathilda had two serious loves. Not counting the irrepressible love she held in high esteem for her sister Annabel, as this love was the biggest her heart could hold. This was capital L Love. Every single part that was Mathilda worshipped her big sister, the kind of worship that a single day has for the sun when its heated glow breaks through the darkest of clouds after the bleakest grey wet winter storm. This kind of admiration and devotion is sacred and untouchable...and in a class all of it's own.

Besides this Love, however, Mathilda had two serious passions in her life which she shared as flagrantly as a ten year old fearless little girl was wanton to do. One was her love of music. All music. Old music, new music, rock, country, show tunes, it didn't matter she loved it all. She would sing along uninhibited in the car, without a care in the world. At home she would blast CDs in her room while she mimicked the movements of the idols she saw on videos. She would stand on the little low lawn table in the backyard and belt out a rendition of her favorite ballad with all the theatrics of a super diva, while Bellie sat and cheered her on like her own personal little groupie.

Mathilda was all things musical and entertaining. And she honored this love by wearing tee shirts that illustrated her favorite music icon images. Most days she wore these paired up with her infamous tutus. She had countless tutus that she owned in a multitude of colors. Mathilda wouldn't be caught dead without her tutu at a special occasion, as dance ran a very close second to her love for music. She personally believed them to be the identical feeling. Music, singing, dancing, it all felt pretty much the same to Mathilda. She simply embodied a tiny, orange haired, pile of natural talent.

But Mathilda's second love was butter and bread...toast in particular. Sweet salty greasy yellow butter puddled deeply into every crater of her toasty brown English muffin *(crumpets here in England, her new favorite word)*, then topped with her favorite strawberry preserves. Although sometimes she preferred plum, either way, this was sheer heaven to her.

On this particular summer morning she had her fresh hot toasty muffin while she was sitting up on the high blue stained barstool at the kitchen island. She had her favorite sunny yellow napkin; with the orange, pink and white daisies, spread out on the shiny dark granite counter top, open and ready to catch any loose remnants of richly golden soaked toasty crumbs that might escape her bite. She placed her elbows on the surface of the cool granite and held her drippy muffin in both hands equal to her lips. Abruptly interrupted by a peculiar sound, she held her position and took a quick look around the kitchen. Pulled out of her buttery reverie, she felt like someone was watching her. Then from behind her she saw a shadow darting off down the hallway wall. *Mrs. Longpotts! Of course, thought Mathilda with a shrug, what an odd duck she is. She makes me feel....squiggly.*

Assured that she was now utterly alone to indulge her senses, Mathilda turned back towards the prize in hand. As she readjusted her seating, she glanced up at the window shade that hung perfectly silent beneath the dark blue and claret striped valance above the large kitchen window. She took a moment and watched as the fiery bright sparkle reflections from the crystal star *(that hung in the window)*, had a ballet dance around the kitchen walls. Bright rainbows of color floated across all the surfaces surrounding her. After a small minute of

15

wonder, Mathilda let out a tiny sigh, looked back down at her patiently waiting butter drenched muffin and took a big bite.

Chapter Three

A Message From Mrs. Longpotts

Benjamin had been keeping a low profile for a couple of days while observing his new neighbors activities from between the Rhododendron hedge that separated the two properties.

When he first came down the stairs after watching the family move in two days earlier, he thought he would just go up and introduce himself. Why not, the girls were close in age and they seemed pleasant enough from a distance. He convinced himself that there was nothing wrong with girls as mates...*really*. And at this point a mate that lived next door and just happened to be a girl was one more mate than he had anyway. Furthermore, the idea that they were American was seriously enticing, as Benjamin had not really known anyone outside of Grandlochcheshire.

As he headed out the front door and turned in the direction of the neighboring house, his inner voice turned up the volume and began nagging at the back of his brain. He instinctively began to slow his stride and his momentum, until finally he just stopped cold in his tracks. Dead cold in fact. He stared off in the distance for a minute with acute concentration, listening to any sound that would guide his trepidation, but he just couldn't seem to put a handle on it. He came back to himself with a deep breath and decided to go off to the side yard, where he stood in the background and watched the bustling of activity going on next door. He sat hypnotized for hours just observing.

Then, on the second day of strategic surveillance, as he sat crossed legged beneath the tall flowering shrub eating an apricot, a very unexpected addition to his investigation presented itself in the form of a very peculiar woman. A most miniature of women at that, just stepping out of a taxi. Something about her presence in particular made the hairs on his arms go completely wonky....*what's this?* he thought, *this is different.*

His alertness became fully astute and he came to full attention. Mechanically he got up onto his knees and backed up further so as not to be seen. However, as he peered out between the branches and leaves, beyond all odds, this tiny wisp of a woman turned and looked straight at Benjamin's hiding place in the shadow of the bushes. He could swear she had even looked him right in the eye! He stumbled backwards a bit and sat dazed from the strange impact this action had on him. *How on earth could she even know I'm here, let alone look straight at me!* Benjamin's entire body was tingling and energized from head to toe. His now sweaty strands of hair were sticking to his forehead, and his heart was racing and pounding a furious beat in his brain.

Then Benjamin's sixth sense kicked into full throttle.

Within a breath, the extrasensory slideshow in his mind flashed with rapid blurry edged images and sounds....*first came a dark shadowy entrance into a broken down barn, and the distant echo of a single overwhelmingly melancholy voice singing ....then came a thick, lush wooded forest...trees and more trees surrounding him.* Instantly a great sense of urgency flooded Benjamin as he gleaned an image of *a towering and majestic ornately crafted wooden door....*until finally, *a dark menacing chill, like the swoosh of a black cloak, crossed his view...*and then the weirdest sensation ever, was the undeniable and overpowering scent of roses!

And then it all stopped.

Benjamin attempted to gain control of his senses as he wiped the sweat from his forehead with the back of his arm. He quickly attempted a dizzying search with his eyes and mind back to the tiny odd woman, who he located as she was just gaining entrance through the front door of the cream colored house next door. The fragmented images lingered and buzzed around Benjamin's head like a honey bee searching for nectar.

When Benjamin's surroundings in the side yard came back into focus he suddenly remembered what had initially sent him into his trance. The alarm grabbed him and he stood up and took off full speed for the garden shed.

Once inside Benjamin felt safe. He began unconsciously to pace back and forth, attempting to make sense of what had just transpired beneath the Rhododendron and the glance from the mysterious visitor next door. He went over every minute detail in his mind. *She looked right at me...I know she did!* insisted Benjamin's inner voice. *How could she know I was there? No one could see me in the shadows of the trees...no one!* argued Benjamin as he continued to dissect the mystery. And with this internal dialog more and more detail began to reveal itself to him. *That voice! That strange sad voice, singing that peculiar old song. It was like something from...what?...an old story...no, it was more like from another time...olden times....and it was off in the distance, like someone had turned the volume down, but is was clear and I heard it. And that forest, all those giant thick trees. It was moving so fast past us, it was like we....wait, WE?.....Who the bugger is we? Who is US?* thought Benjamin with unnerving surprise, *We?...Bloody Hell!*

Benjamin felt weak.

It was like we were running through this place and time was really important. There were others besides 'us' who were helping...no wait, not helping, more like...like tracking!....tracking our moves...and there was a game, or a match...no, no, not a match, but something like clues that needed to be done in order, an important order...like.... "Like an Exam!" he shouted out loud, and that door, that massive brilliant door!

Benjamin's breathing grew hard and audible until he was almost panting. He put his hands to his face then in a flash everything stopped moving and became profoundly sharp and clear. He stood still in the center of the shed and suddenly his eyes grew as big as saucers. The anxiety began to creep up from the bottom of his feet and touched on every bone, nerve and organ in his body. He flipped his head upward and stared out the sky window. A small moan escaped his lips as he realized that what he profoundly heard echoing in his brain, was the unquestionable and unmistakable resonance of the thick and deliberate cry.....*Help*. Then the over powering scent of roses filled the air around him, and with that Benjamin lost all feeling in his legs and he fell straight to the floor like a wet rag.

After several moments of sheer terror, Benjamin sat up and managed to drag himself over to the burlap pile, climbed up to the top and let his emotions spill. He couldn't even begin to fathom what all of this meant. He had never experienced anything remotely of this magnitude with his *special talent* before. He laid on the pile drenched in sweat, and fear, and attempted to catch his mind before it left him completely. As his heart rate slowly began to pace back in time with his breath, he stared up at the clouds above him. His body still energized with the pulse of his adrenalin, began to lull him into a daydream, as the anxiety began to calm. He eventually closed his eyes and fell into a deep sleep. The reflection of the hot sun pouring out from behind the light airy clouds held the tiny beads of perspiration on his forehead while Benjamin slept. Without effort, or time, Benjamin's mind found a lovely simple little vision to center his internal attention on.

He found himself...*sitting in a tiny wooden boat gently rocking on the bluest green water that one could ever imagine, dream or otherwise. The sky was crystal clear and bright and there were dozens, if not hundreds of tiny bubbles in the air floating about. Benjamin looked out across the expanse of the sea and everything remained calm. Even the bubbles didn't disturb Benjamin, it was a dream after all, and such things are possible and acceptable in dreams. Then he looked down into the transparent aqua water that allowed him to see clearly below for at least ten feet or more, and there he caught the split second image of something swimming past in the shade of the swaying boat.*

No alarm came to Benjamin's dreaming mind...*as he scooted to the edge of the boat to take a closer look at his shadowy company. Within moments the creature made his circle around the little wooden craft again, and this time Benjamin got a perfect look at his guest. Why it was nothing more than a cat fish!*

At least that is what Benjamin told himself...*After all it was a fish, because it had scales and fins and was swimming beneath the waves. And he surmised it was a cat fish in particular because, well, it had a black and white stripe tail, pointed ears and whiskers, just like a cat. So what else could one deduce?* As far as Benjamin's inner self was concerned, his peaceful sail on the perfect water with the cat fish riding the current along beside him; and bubbles filling the air, all made perfect sense in this lovely holiday from visions of broken down barns and ghostly singing....*and We.*

Then something started to nag and tug, and began to peel at the corner of this blissful dream, We....*WE were running.*

The feeling of serenity that had covered his dream only moments before, began taking on a more ominous tone. It started to creep up around the edges blocking out the sun, until it was nothing more than darkness, a storm that surrounded Benjamin in his once safely lolling haven.

The waves grew more aggressive, and the sound of the water slapping up against the tiny craft began to raise anxiety in Benjamin. And without warning a huge CRACK! of thunder smacked the air with such a full force, the smell of electricity singed the sky.

Benjamin sat back down onto the deck of wood and hugged his knees close to his chest. The unnerving fear rose up in his throat and he could taste the bile. Hot tears formed in his eyes and blocked out any visual detail before him. But he knew what to expect...he saw it all so perfectly in his mind's eye....SHE was here! Somehow she had found her way into this quiet place and was coming for him, then the swoosh of the black cloak filled his view and Benjamin awoke with a start.

He stared up out the sky window and felt detached from his body. He put his hands up in front of his sweaty face and wiggled his fingers to bring back the sensation that he was alive and well, and in his grandparents garden shed. When he was certain he was indeed in the shed, he bolted straight up and looked around quickly to see if he could trace any remnants of the dream. Everything was as it always was. Except now there was a powerful hidden source of energy pulling him unwillingly into something beyond all perception.

21

Benjamin knew he needed to get to the bottom of this situation or he would go completely mad from the fright alone. He needed to take serious action, immediately. He jumped down off the burlap covered hay and went back into the house and up to his room. Once inside he took out his binoculars, a notepad and a clock, and planted himself in front of the window that looked almost directly into the second level of the cream colored house next door. He instinctively knew he needed to take steps to understanding what he was being shown, and what he was meant to do with the knowledge once he gained it.

First things first. Who was this strange woman and what did she have to do with the new American neighbors?

Benjamin sat and watched the still house for the rest of the afternoon. It was like any other day on any other road in any other part of Grandlochcheshire. He saw the girls out in the back garden for a bit running about with Cubby. Then they sat huddled together in the far corner of the garden whispering to each other in a very animated way. He wondered what their urgent secret was. He felt certain it had something to do with the miniature *Mac Lady*, as he was wont to refer to her. *I mean really, who wears a Mac in the middle of June anyway?* thought Benjamin. Is she a visiting Auntie maybe or a family member? For some odd reason he just didn't think so. Well, whoever she was Benjamin was not about to find out at the present moment, as he suddenly realized how incredibly hungry he was. So he decided to follow his growling stomach and abandon his post, heading downstairs to the kitchen.

There he found the plate still left from lunch that he had never eaten. He immediately devoured the entire meal, grateful to his grandmother for saving it. He grabbed some juice and another apricot from the fridge and headed back upstairs. He was more than determined to find some kind of clue that would lead him to any explanation of the very unnerving experiences of his day.

As the sun left the sky and the switched on light illuminated the internal activity of the house next door, Benjamin's heart jumped as he finally caught his break.

It was six thirty-eight, and for the first time since the Mac Lady looked at Benjamin earlier that afternoon, she had appeared in his sight once again. This time she was following the Mrs. of the house about, going along in and out of all the rooms on the second floor. She even opened the linen cupboards and checked in the wash closets. *Blimey, what the heck does this mean?* wondered Benjamin. And at that precise moment he heard a car door shut and swung his attention down to the pavement where he watched the girls running to greet their father. There was so much commotion around this activity that Benjamin could only pick out a few phrases and key words.

"The new nanny... Da, wait...see her!   She's the tiniest...wearing a raincoat..did you know...called a Mac..in with mom right now...come see for yourself Da"

"So that's it. She's the new nanny," said Benjamin with a spark of enthusiasm. He felt a tremendous accomplishment at this bit of extracted information. At least now he knew who she was and why she was next door, and proceeded to jot it all down in his notes.

What he didn't know was how she had known he was in the shadows and why he received the myriad of pictures and information that was blasted at him from her stare; because that is precisely what Benjamin believed had indeed occurred. This was new territory for Benjamin. He had learned to live with his abilities to *see* things and receive messages in the form of quick mental images...but nothing of this caliber had ever crossed his path.

Try as he might he couldn't ignore the small voice tugging at his thoughts....*What about the dream?* When he allowed himself to feel what this could actually mean he froze in mid gulp of juice, and his heart began pounding once again. Benjamin thought for a moment, there was something in that mental space that felt...*real* to him. It's like sometimes in a dream when you actually know you're indeed dreaming. But this was even deeper than that.

Benjamin was beginning to feel that what he had experienced was...*a premonition.* He was starting to believe that these sounds and smells and feelings were based on some sort of future act, something he hadn't yet lived. This reality put his mind into a severe mental panic. Benjamin's heart started pounding again, and he began to tremble. He looked straight out into the air in front of him and suddenly it became completely clear to Benjamin. The instant realization was all encompassing and he was now certain without doubt, that whatever, or whomever, this dark cloak of power was...*it was coming for him*...and the people closest to him.

His body in complete panic and shaking, Benjamin slammed his eyes shut and wished with every ounce of his being for the sound of his father's voice to appear. He repeated to himself, over and over, "I need you now, please, I need you" and wished hard, like it was something physical pouring out of his cells. Hot tears filled his aching heart and streamed down his face.

Suddenly, he opened his eyes fully expecting to see his father standing there...but there was no one...nothing. Benjamin found himself extremely and utterly alone....*and terrified*.

Well, nothing like a cloak of darkness to get one's heart a pumpin, I always say.

Dunston Tibbets, The Keeper of the Books

Chapter Four

The English Boy and the American Girls

Mathilda was sitting at her play table, which had been converted into a perfect depiction of the proper English tea table, with all of her favorite stuffed animals seated as guests. Her giant stuffed giraffe, who was now adorned with a flower rimmed hat perched high upon her head, sat opposite her. Mathilda loved a good tea party and now here they were living in *Jolly Ol' England,* the original home of tea time. She was in little girl tea party heaven.

As it turned out Mathilda was really quite okay with this extravagant move from America, and had taken to it so far like a duck to water...*or a pond.* Mathilda just loved that coming from America to England was referred to as *"crossing the pond".*

Of course it had only been a few days, but she thought she was going to like it here just fine. She was already learning all the new slang, well, new to her anyway. Her father still used the typical words, like *loo* and *telly,* and truth be told, he stilled cussed up a good one when he needed to, *Bollocks!* being his favorite. But actually living here in the culture made it all so real to her. *The English have so many funny ways of saying things,* thought Mathilda, "What about Crumpet?" she had said to Annabel, "It's just the weirdest thing ever

Bellie, after all it's England, why don't they call it a English muffin *here?* Isn't that the weirdest?" This just made her laugh and laugh, and Bellie had to giggle right along with her, after all she did have a valid point.

She was singing along with her favorite CD from The Blue's Billies and breaking up a butter soaked Crumpet to share with all the members of her tea party, when she heard a strange repetitive noise from outside. She attempted to ignore it the first couple of times, but when it persisted she decided to go investigate the source.

She looked out the front window that faced the road and didn't see anything unusual. So she ventured over to the side window and looked out to see Mrs. Longpotts down below in the side yard whacking the hand knotted antique rag rug with a tennis racket *(or at least that's what it looked like to Mathilda)*, while it hung on a clothesline *(although she had never really seen a clothesline before either)*. Giant tuffs of dust flew off the rug into the air around Mrs. Longpotts, who was holding her nose with her other hand. The dust and old dog hair puffing off the rug was swirling about and disappearing almost instantly into the ethers above the nanny's head. Mathilda had never seen anyone doing this and got another good giggle from the peculiar English activities and habits.

While she chuckled to herself she happen to glance up at the house next door. Much to her surprise she saw a boy in the window directly across from her looking through binoculars down at Mrs. Longpotts. "Oh! Well how weird is that?" she said to the room. She hadn't seen any kids around the neighborhood in the past week that they had been living in the cream house with the forest green trim. Mathilda was elated. "Wow, a actual English boy, how cool," and she began waving her arms about attempting to get his attention. She looked like an airport runway flag man, without the flags. When that didn't work she began to hoot and holler, hoping that would get him to look her way.

When all of Mathilda's commotion became louder than the noise Mrs. Longpotts was making on the beaten rug, the nanny turned and looked up at the window. She saw Mathilda in her funny frenzy and traced her attention straight across the side yard and over the tall hedge to the window in the neighboring house where Benjamin was presently sitting. The same Benjamin that was looking down at the nanny through a pair of binoculars.

When Benjamin saw the nanny turn to look straight up at him and then smile, he nearly felt his heart completely stop! He fumbled and dropped the glasses and stood back from the window to break the contact before any of the dark visions began to revisit his mind. He suddenly became aware of all the shouting and looked up and saw Mathilda waving frantically at him.

"Boy, hey boy, over here," she called.

"Blast it!" mumbled Benjamin, "Now what do I do?"

All the jumping and shouting attracted Annabel from her own room to head out in search of all the excitement. She walked into Mathilda's room and witnessed the bobbing of orange curls and butterscotch tutu tulle bouncing up and down. Caught up in the commotion, she ran to the window to see just what had her baby sister so wound up.

"Tildie, what the heck are you yelling about? Between you and Mrs. Longpotts I couldn't keep my mind on my book."

"Oh Bellie, look, there's a boy next door...a really truly English boy, can you believe it?"

Annabel looked out the window at the boy standing back a bit in the shadows and blinked, "Wow, where did he come from? I haven't seen anyone since we got here, except that old woman in the overalls in the back yard the other day."

"Me too Bellie, not a single girl or boy in all these days. And here he is right next door to us. Isn't this cool? I'm going to go meet him, wanna come?" inquired Mathilda.

Without taking her eyes off of Benjamin, Annabel asked, "What was he doing up there anyway, how did you see him?"

"Oh, he was watching Mrs. Longpotts in his spy glasses and I saw him so now I want to go say hi up close, I never seen a real English boy up close before," said Mathilda.

"What are you talking about, his spy glasses? Watching what? And what do you think da is anyway?"

"Well, he's not a boy that's for sure," said Mathilda with a laugh in her voice, "Come on Bellie, let's goooo, I want to meet him now," whined Mathilda, as she grabbed her sister by the arm, swinging her around and dragging her out the bedroom door. Annabel let her sister pull at her, all the while building her argument as to why they shouldn't go.

"But maybe he doesn't want to meet us, why haven't we seen him before now? And what the heck was he watching anyhow...us? You think maybe he's creepy or something? Maybe he's a weirdo or a *pervie* or something. I don't know Tildie, I think we should just go get mom first."

But Mathilda would have none of it, and within moments they were tearing out the front door and on their way around the Rhododendron barrier between the two houses.

Benjamin stood like a stone statue for what seemed an eternity, then alertness caught him as he heard the traveling voices of the girls heading towards the front door downstairs. His cover had been blown. The nanny had caught him right between the eyes as it were.

"Sod it!" he blurted out with force. And before he had a chance to have another single thought, first came the ringing doorbell, followed quickly by the voices of the girls echoing throughout the house. In turn came his grandmother's voice calling for him to come downstairs.

"Well, it appears I'm to meet the Americans...finally," he said as he took a deep breath and secretly hoped that when he looked at either of the girls in the eye that everything stayed sunny and bright. Benjamin turned around, gave himself a quick shake to regain his grounding and headed down the stairs to meet up with his destiny.

He had no idea that his path was to be forever bonded to these two quirky little American girls standing in his grandparents living room.

Chapter Five

An Introduction From Dunston Tibbitts

Oh Me! Well, that Mrs. Longpotts is surely an interesting character to say the least. She even makes me a tad bit nervous, I don't like people staring at me. And I must say the wee one has my propensity for sweets as well. I am very partial to strawberry cupcakes, truth be told. Oh Me! Here I am talking about something as personal as cupcakes and I haven't even introduced myself. Simply put, I'm none other than Dunston Tibbitts, the Keeper of The Books. And I shall be your narrator for a small bit of this journey, keep you in the up and up as it were. Filling in a few of the blanks so to speak.

I make my home, and my life's work, in the World Library of Identity. Actually, truth be told, I am in charge of the whole thing...kit and caboodle, as they say. My position is passed down from father to son, generation to generation. The Tibbitts have a very long lineage dating back before the one hundred and two year Targanoe war, that ended with the heads of each clan putting their mark to the Treaty of Allegiance in 684. Putting a final kibosh, as it were, on the many years of discord and territory conflicts between all the clans of the Gnomes.

For more than three thousand years now, we have lived within a highly evolved, synchronistically aware and peaceful world, with the honor to uphold our sworn and solemn oath to protect the Heart of the Planet at all costs...be it life or liberty. We are in a land unlike any other, the breathtaking underground world of beauty, my home, Coranim.

Oh Me!...yet again, I have completely forgotten to explain....I say, sometimes I think I would leave my noggin sitting on a book stool if it weren't attached to my shirt collar....Ha! Anyway, The World Library of Identity is just that. Every being on the planet has a book with the recordings to the entirety of ones life, beginning to end....already finished more or less. Plain and simple. Now you see clearly why all the hoopla and ritual surrounding the passing of duties from generations to endless generations. The title of Keeper of The Books is a very important and sacred position. There is none other like it in the whole of the world...of course there isn't! I mean to say, really, how could there be?

The library must be kept protected and safe at all times...not that anyone has ever attempted to infiltrate or misuse the library...but one never knows does one? The minute you slack off and turn your back something always happens, at least that's the way I see it. And of course all the notations and Remakes that must be entered and dated. Remakes are a serious business. They don't happen often, but when one does present itself it must be accomplished with the utmost of earnest integrity and absolute correctness. Can't be making mistakes with a Remake in someone's life I tell you.

The most prevalent Remake is the one of high evolutionary choice. Everyone has a choice to evolve, whether they see it as a choice or not. Nothing happens by chance. It's a very serious business this keeping track of ones life...or should I say, EVERY ones life! Oh Me! Never the fuss..I mean to say, that is the nature of the work that I do of course. Oh, and all the Magic involved...ah Magic, now that's an interesting subject. Yes, indeed I say, Magic always has a way of remaking things.

Oh dear, I suppose I have gone on long enough now about myself, although a topic I do enjoy, HA! I dare say, I believe it is time to get back to Benjamin and see where this journey is taking us....sounds intriguing doesn't it? We shall *open his book at the point we find ourselves now....always good to start with the present.*

Chapter Six

A Map

It had been close to a year now that the Wickcliff girls had begun their inseparable relationship with their *really and truly English boy* neighbor, Benjamin McTish. They had become the three Muskydeers *(Mathilda's mispronounced version of Musketeers, which was a huge laugh and of course it stuck)*, and were rarely seen one without the other.

Benjamin's grandparents were relieved that their grandson's solitary little world finally had mates to cheer him up. And of course Claire and Edward were thrilled that the girls had chosen someone as kind and well mannered as Benjamin to spend their days with. His knowledge of the area was enough to help keep their offspring occupied while they continued in their extravagant procedure of settling into a new home, new job, and a new country.

Benjamin had shown Annabel and Mathilda around their new school and introduced them to some of the other kids. Although he really didn't know many of his schoolmates, he found that most were simply elated to make the acquaintance of such vibrant and loquacious spirits from the US of A *(actually, truth be told, he found that he had become a bit of a rock star to his classmates now from his budding friendship with the quirky Wickcliff girls)*. He didn't seem to mind that he wasn't such an outsider anymore. This attention was way better than the emptiness he felt for so many years just living the motions of someone with a life. It had been he and his grandparents now for almost four years....the last three without one word from either his mother or his father. The pain was brutal, the not knowing if they were dead or alive. Not knowing if he would ever see either one of them ever again. He replayed the vision of their reunion every night before his mind took him into dream land.

Recently however, the sweet quiet dreams of another lifetime had begun to diminish into the nightmares of torment that someone, *or something*, was coming for him and those that he loved...the *WE* dreams had returned. Bits and pieces of the visions he had suffered on that fateful summer day when he and Mrs. Longpotts locked eyes, were beginning to creep into his consciousness on a regular basis it seemed.

At first he attempted to ignore the dreams and pushed them deep inside. However, no matter what he did, the darkness and anxiety that the time was most definitely upon him to face this challenge head on, had come. Benjamin knew his only choice was to look straight into the eye of his fear. He knew he had to get to the bottom of the whole experience, or go mad from the sheer terror that the vivid, rapid visions conjured in his mind...*and his blood*.

Oddly enough, he had not experienced any more visions from Mrs. Longpotts *(still referred to as the Mac Lady by the children)*. As an odd matter of fact, Mrs. Longpotts had become somewhat of a normal fixture in the household. She pretty much kept to herself and didn't really interfere with the girls much outside of her normal duties. Benjamin was grateful he didn't have to have regular discourse with the nanny. Usually only when she answered the door, and then Benjamin kept his head lowered, so as not to invite any stray nightmares to take advantage of his presence. She always smiled at him, and it always made him uncomfortable. He never told either of the girls about his experience. It seemed there was really no reason to do so.

However, today was like any other day, finding the trio lounging on a larger than usual pile of burlap covered hay in the McTish garden shed.

Granny must be getting ready to do something big with all this hay, thought Benjamin. He had noticed she was working on a new project of grafting certain trees together. *Wonder what she's trying to do with these? Granny and her plants, and now it seems trees are the story,* he thought absently, as he let it slide away.

School was nearly out and the thought of a long summer ahead with nothing special to do was burning into the wee noggins of the Muskydeers. After a long drawn out spell in the musty air of the warm garden shed, Mathilda broke the silence, "Well, there must be *some*thing for us to figure out already. I mean really, this is like a whole new pile of fun to have if you think about it. You know Bellie? We just came here last summer and then we met Benjamin and we just didn't know anything about this place yet," she held out her opened palms and shrugged her shoulders, as if to say, *What else could we do, right?* "And then school started so fast, but now it's almost summer again. So I say we just think of something that could be really fun. We need some money first..oh, I know...what about a lemonade stand? We could make lot's of money and then we could..." "We could what?" cut off Annabel.

Mathilda put her shoulders back in place and just stared at her sister, "Well, I don't know Bellie, why don't *you* think of something?"

But Annabel was way ahead of her, "I have been thinking and I think I have an idea."

With this Benjamin's attention became fully focused on Annabel. One thing Benjamin had learned over the past year, when Annabel had an idea, it was usually a pretty good one.

"So last summer, when we first moved in here, I was exploring up in the attic and I found a pile of these old maps buried in the corner under some old chest."

"Under?" quizzed Benjamin.

"Yeah, under, it was so weird. The edge of one of the maps was sticking out enough that I could tell it was a map, and it looked really old or from another land or something. It was so cool finding these. So I slid the chest as best I could and pulled out five maps."

"Bellie, how come you never told me about them?" asked Mathilda with a hurt in her voice.

"I don't know Tildie. It all just sort of happened and then I forgot about them. I was just looking them over and then something happened, I don't remember. Oh, wait! I think it was Mrs. Longpotts. She was coming up the stairs looking for me so I just grabbed the pile and put them in this crate that was up there, and covered them with an old quilt I found."

"Why did you do that Bellie?" asked Mathilda confused.

"I don't know," replied Annabel, "for some reason I felt like I had come across something that was a secret. I didn't want Mrs. Longpotts to take them away, so I hid them."

"Then you just forgot about them?" asked Benjamin.

"Yeah, like I said, I just hid them and ran down after Mrs. Longpotts and everything got so busy then. You know, moving in and school, all that stuff. I guess they just slipped my mind. So anyways, out of no where the other day, I started thinking about them. It was really kinda weird the way it just popped into my brain...but anyway, I had to go and dig them out again. I almost forgot where I put them, which isn't like me either, but, *whatever,* I found them. They're really hard to read but I tried the best I could. It looks like they are really old and they show what Grandlochcheshire looked like a really really long time ago, like a hundred years or something I think"

Her audience turned and looked at each other then back at Annabel, who was now leaning in closer as if she had the secret to life waiting to escape her lips. They all instinctively scooted closer into the circle they had now formed.

"It took me some time because there are a lot of strange words and markings, like a code or something, on some of the papers, things I've never seen before. Some of the words are written in some kind of old looking foreign language."

Benjamin's heart started to beat faster as his eyebrows slide up his forehead in amazed interest.

"Anyway," Annabel continued with her engaging story, "one day, after trying everything I could think of, Cubby came running into my room and jumped up on my bed, and you know how Cubby is when he's on the bed? So I had to get up onto the bed for a minute with him and I just happened to look down on the floor at the maps...and something looked different to me. I can't explain it, but there was something, *umm*...I don't know, oh this is going to sound weird, but there was something *tingly* about them is the only way I can describe it."

Benjamin nearly jumped out of his skin when he heard these words come from his friend. He thought it all sounded too familiar to his own experiences. Something he thought no one else on earth had knowledge of, but him.

"So I got Cubby out of the room and locked the door. I got really nervous and excited all at the same time that this secret was something *really* big. So now I'm on my knees, spreading the maps out on the floor, and I hear a noise, like just a little floor creak, at my door....it totally freaked me out at first, but then I just thought it was Cubby again. But then I heard him bark from outside my window down in the backyard and at the same time I saw a shadow moving under the door, so I know it was Longpotts."

"Longpotts!" agreed Mathilda with a nod.

"So I waited a minute until I think the coast is clear...I'm telling you, I didn't move a muscle or breath, it was so intense I thought I would die...and then I can tell I'm alone. So I go back to laying out all the maps and then I went and stood back up on my bed to look down at them again. I thought I could get a different look at them from up high for some reason, anyway, as I was standing up on my bed I realized that something in the corners looked like some sort of a pattern maybe. So I jumped back down and rearranged some of the maps in the way the colors and words seemed to go, then I got back up on my bed. And this time when I looked down I could see it."

Annabel paused.

"See what Bellie, what did you see?" chimed in Mathilda with bated breath.

Benjamin looked at Mathilda with a cold stare, then turned towards her sister and repeated her question to Annabel, who was now staring back at him with the same cold look, "What did you see Annabel?" The hairs on Benjamin's arms stood straight up and a major rushing tingle ran through his body. Before Annabel had a chance to answer he said simply, "It's the directions to the path from the farm isn't it?"

"Farm, what farm, what path, what are you talking about Benjamin? Bellie what is he talking about?" quizzed the very confused Mathilda.

Not as surprised as Mathilda at Benjamin's mysterious knowledge, Annabel calmly asked, "Benjamin what do you know about the path?"

Benjamin looked deeply into Annabel's eyes and could see that for the first time in his life there was no judgement. He saw his closest and most loyalist of friends looking at him with only acceptance. An overwhelming sense of relief overcame him and he said blankly, "The path that leads into the Gilley Forest. A path that has something to do with a tremendous tree...a tree with a massive door."

Both girls sat staring at him with mouths wide open. Nobody moved for what seemed like an eternity. Benjamin, feeling their growing anxiety at the depth of his statement, realized that if ever there was a time to trust someone it was now. He couldn't stand the secrecy any longer, and he couldn't bear the thought that his best mates might think he had gone mental, but he looked straight at Annabel and continued, "I've been having dreams. Dreams that began on the second day that you lived here. Dreams that started when the Mac Lady looked me when I was hiding in the bushes. They stopped for a while, but they're back."

Mathilda repeated in a stunned whisper, "The... Mac... Lady..." It seemed that all the girls needed to hear was that the nanny was somehow involved and it made all the weirdness acceptable. They had always felt somewhat uncomfortable around Mrs. Longpotts.

"Something's just not right with her," Annabel had said to Mathilda one day. Mathilda agreed. She couldn't put her finger on it exactly, but there was something peculiar in a more specific way than broad. Mathilda thought she resembled a Cheshire Cat with her big sneaky grin. "A cat who just ate the big fat canary," she had said to Annabel.

Annabel agreed. "Yeah, she's holding on to some secret, something weird, I just know it." She was certain of it.

Annabel looked at her dazed and obviously scared best friend and realized she needed to come clean to him.

"Benjamin," she said with a small moment of hesitation. He looked her square in the eye. And after a breath of a pause she just let it all out, "Benjamin, I know that you...*umm*...know things. I've known it for some time now."

Benjamin just stared at her.

"Don't forget I like to figure things out, I like puzzles and riddles. I'm really good at them. And honestly, you're not that hard to figure out," she said with a small smile. "I don't think you're weird or anything like that Benjamin. It's like you have that ESP kind of thing I think, or something like that. It's okay, I think it's totally cool. Really..."But before she could finish Mathilda jumped right back into the conversation, "ESP! You mean he can see ghosts and read minds? Oh how cool! Benjamin do you really see dead people?"

Benjamin broke into a smile and let out a chuckle and was freer than he'd ever felt. He took a deep breath, "No Mathilda, I don't see dead people. It's nothing like that. It's hard to explain. It's not something I've ever talked to anyone about."

With this Annabel returned to her senses and put her arm around Benjamin's shoulders to lighten the moment, "Bengie, my boy, we always knew there was something weird about you from the first time we saw you up in your room with your pervie binoculars spying on us!"

They all burst out into an uproarious laughing spell of rolling around on the great mound of burlap covered hay. After a moment of exhaustive emotional repose Mathilda asked, "Okay, so is anyone going to tell me what this path thing is already? Why do you know about this path from the maps Bellie, I don't understand?"

"Oh would you just settle down tike and let me..." attempted Annabel before Benjamin cut her off, "*Oh,* and by the way Annabel, if you ever call me Bengie again you'll see just how weird I can *really* be!"

This started a whole new series of rolling around laughter from the three Muskydeers.

"Okay, so here's what happened," began Annabel again, getting the others complete attention, especially Benjamin's. "Once I figured out that the colors and markings had a pattern and put them in order, something was still not right.

So I started to follow the old creases on the maps and realized there was something strange about the folds. They weren't in the usual rectangle shape that maps are in. So I played around for a while and tried different ways to fold them, following as best I could. And then, I'm not sure what happened, but out of nowhere when I put them all together in the right colors and markings and then the creases fit, it just kinda jumped out at me. Like I said I don't know how to explain it, but it was almost like in that 3-D movie we saw a couple weeks ago, things kinda just came ..*forward*."

Benjamin and Mathilda looked at each other with their mouths open, not blinking, then quickly returned their full attention back to Annabel.

"It was like a box raising up off the maps, a clear box outlined in a thin white glowing line, and I could see something through the top. So I jumped down and looked inside, sorta. I mean it's really hard to explain, but it was like some holographic map or something, with this kind of glow to it. I was totally freaked out, but I was excited too. It was like I just couldn't look away from it, it was all so bizarre. And then right in the middle was this path that was all lit up. Like when the bedroom door is cracked a bit at night, and the hall light outlines the door...the path had that kind of look. It was just so weird you guys. But then the path went right to this big tree deep in the forest. And I mean *big* tree! This thing looked monstrous compared to the rest of the forest. And it was like I was seeing all of this in my mind too, like a movie or something, cause I could...*umm...feel* I guess, yeah, I could kinda feel what it was feeling. Geez! I just really can't explain it."

"You don't need to Annabel," said Benjamin, "I know exactly what you are saying. I get pictures in my head, really fast usually. And sometimes there are sounds, but when it's really intense I get feelings too."

"And you've been dreaming about the tree in the forest?" asked Annabel in shock.

"Yeah," was all Benjamin could spit out.

"Well, this is remarkable!" shouted Mathilda, breaking the tension, while getting up onto her knees. "I say we go and get these maps and see if we *all* can see this path thing, or whatever it is. Maybe it's a treasure map...oh wait! I bet it's some kind of weird alien transmitter or something, who knows! It's just the weirdest thing I've ever heard. Or maybe my sister is just going totally mental!"

And so began the third round of stomach aching, rolling around, tears down the face laughter. So off they went, with shiny faces left from their laughing tears, in exploration of the mysterious maps Annabel had discovered in the attic of the cream and green house they called home.

The closer they got to their destination, the more the anxiety began to creep up in the back of Benjamin's mind. When they got themselves situated up in Annabel's room, certain of complete privacy, Annabel pulled the maps out from under her bed. She slid out a long dark old wooden tool box that had a big white piece of paper securely taped to the lid that clearly read,

PRIVATE, DO NOT DISTURB OR TOUCH IN ANY WAY

UNDER PENALTY OF LAW!

with a bunch of skull and crossbones drawn all over it. When she opened the box she reached in and pulled out her magical bundle.

Mathilda and Benjamin held their breath.

The maps were wrapped in a colorful beach towel tied up with a short piece of red rope. Everyone gathered into the center of the room and sat on the floor as Annabel unwrapped the precious cargo. She laid the maps out for the others to look at before she began her mysterious calculations of precise folding. Right in the middle of the third map, Benjamin let out a small, but clear and powerful, "Wait."

The girls just stopped cold as if their lives depended on it and looked at Benjamin.

"Annabel, let me see this map."

He never took his eyes off the strange markings on the corners as she handed the old yellowed parchment over to him. Once he had it in his hands he held up the corner with the tiny print of symbols closer to his eyes for examination. "Do you have a magnifying glass Annabel?" "Of course I do."

Snapping the dazed dark haired girl into action, she leaned back on her elbows, then rolled onto her stomach, to reach for the bottom drawer of her desk. She pulled it open and withdrew the glass, sat back up and handed it to Benjamin.

As he peered into the lens onto the corner of the map looking for something...*something he wasn't even fully sure of*...without warning, everything began to grow darker. It was like a strange sudden case of tunnel vision. His heart started to pound in his ears and his breathing beat in double time with his heart. Sweat beads poured down his forehead and the sounds of the girls fell off into the distance....*and then the ride began.*

Suddenly Benjamin was flung into a dark tunnel of speed and sound. The dense forest of trees was moving so fast past him that it looked like the movie effect of going into warp speed. It was like he was on a wild and crazy extreme ride at a carnival in his blackest of dreams.

The visions were alarmingly fast and Benjamin felt he could not stand the strain of the speed. When suddenly everything stopped and he found himself sitting inside...*Inside what?* he thought, *A window, a tube...a tube made of water, a water tube, a what?* He didn't know. Whatever it was, he found that he was surrounded in this clear apparatus that was at a slight angle downwards, about four feet off the ground. He could peer though the entirety of this glass like gel tube and look out into the forest around him. When he looked below he could see the illuminated path and little dots of colored light floating about. He almost smiled. However, when his visual search traveled over to his left, his heart nearly froze in his chest. There it was, the body of his deepest fear, the soul of his nightmares, the mysterious cloak of darkness....*that now had a face.*

There before his sight stood a majestic and breathtakingly beautiful woman, in dark forest green with piercing green eyes to match. She was wearing a glorious crown of what looked like dried moss and vivid yellow daisies upon her head. She smiled at Benjamin with her perfectly full ruby red lips and sparkling white teeth, and he couldn't breathe....literally...*he stopped breathing!*

For a moment Benjamin didn't know what was happening. He began gasping for air as he pushed out with his arms and hands onto the walls of the gelatinous sides of his confinement. The overwhelming dizzying drive to fill his lungs was all consuming. Blackness was beginning to take over when out of the corner of his vision he sensed something...*a light*. A bright light that called to him. Almost too delirious to move, he fumbled around pleading in his thoughts for relief. Try as he might he couldn't hold onto the beckoning voice enough to look in it's direction. When it appeared no release was in sight for Benjamin to motivate his lungs to expand, his vision became inundated completely with the little colorful dots of light.

Little by little the color orbs filled his vision, surrounding the chamber completely. In his moment of stillness before eminent expiration, he saw that the tiny dots of color had....*wings*. Benjamin smiled in his brain and a tear rolled down his cheek.

Within moments, the entire tube of transport was engulfed with these magical little beings. Benjamin heard a beautiful melody coming from somewhere and he turned his head slowly, as if underwater. Once he found the source of his calling, he realized with utter gratitude, that it was the sound of his own heart beating in his chest, as his lungs tore at the air and filled to capacity. Slowly in time his wits came about, and a colony of winged little light beings flooded his senses as he could finally see them with every part of himself all at once. He could only assume them to be pixies, or fairies, not unlike the old folklore he was raised with. He didn't know what else to think.

Benjamin began to smile again, for real this time. Instantly, the little dots of winged color dispersed off to the right and took Benjamin's attention with them. There standing before him, was the most majestic and awe inspiring vision of his life....*the magnificent Grandfather Tree*.

The trunk of the tree was as wide as his panorama view. A tree so old and enormous he believed a city could live within its barky flesh. However, the most inspiring was the brilliantly carved, and equally majestic, door. And even more outrageous to Benjamin was the calling coming from the bright and *tingling* vibration of the huge gold lock beneath the ridiculously large handle. A lock that looked like it would hold...*An old relic of a key. A key precisely nine inches long, with a tattered green ribbon hanging from the stem*, thought Benjamin with sheer amusement...*that quickly turned into fear*.

Without warning, Benjamin was pulled backwards from this vision as if on a long etheric bungee cord. He went flying back with the same force that had pulled him in. Benjamin thought he would be ill, when suddenly, as if by magic, there he was sitting on the floor in Annabel's room. Both the girls were staring at him with complete shock consuming their faces. Benjamin regained his composure and simply said, "Well, thanks for the eye glass Annabel."

Downstairs, sitting in her easy chair in the den, sat Mrs. Longpotts with her knitting. Without a word she set down her needles, stood up and walked over to the door; where earlier she had placed her chenille satchel with the old worn out leather handles. She bent over, which wasn't a large task for a woman so small in stature, opened the bag wide to capacity, and stepped inside.....*then disappeared into thin air, taking the chenille flowered satchel with her.*

Who who, I say! Now we're getting to the thick of things. I dare say when the vision of the Queen came into the picture I nearly had to run for cover. Let me warn you dear little ones, do not for one minute allow her immense beauty to fool you, she is as dark as she is striking. And her power is the strongest there is. Oh Me! Burr!....brings shivers to me spine right up through my noggin!

Oh, but wee ones, the Grandfather Tree....how delightful! There is nothing more spectacular than the Door to this ancient amazon of a beast. The Grandfather Tree is as old as the planet and just as wise. And so is his Door. It is an entry that cannot be gained without the truest of hearts and minds, and a wit to match. Oh Me! And least I forget the most important attribute to unlocking the secret...courage.

D.T

ps. I figure by now you know it is I, Dunston, doing the dialoging. Shouldn't have to remain so formal amongst friends I would think...so from now on just expect my two cents AND my two initials. Ha!

Chapter Seven

The Key

The girls were sitting across from Benjamin with mouths hanging wide open in utter concern. Benjamin attempted to continue his faux examination of the creases in the maps, but was losing the charade.

"Benjamin! Are you okay?" Annabel practically yelled, "What happened?"

"Yeah, what the heck was that Benjamin?" joined in Mathilda.

Benjamin finally made eye contact with the girls, and he could see this may have been too much for them to observe.

"Well, what did you see me do?" he queried. Benjamin often wondered what happened to him on this side of things, since he was always on the other end and had no clue.

"Do? We didn't see you do *anything* Benjamin!"

"Yeah, you didn't do anything, you just sat there like a doll," finished Mathilda and then added, "It was like you were a zombie or something, it was really weird Benjamin."

Annabel took back control of the conversation, "Benjamin, you were looking into the magnifying glass at the markings on the map, do you remember that?"

Benjamin nodded his head.

"And then you just sort of started to shake and twitch and the next thing, it was like you went comatose or something. I thought maybe you were having a seizure. You didn't move or anything. Like Tildie said, you were....I don't know, you were...*gone*. But your body was here. Geez, Benjamin it was so strange."

He looked back and forth at the girls then attempted to gain his senses and explain his journey.

"Crikey, I'm sorry you got scarred. I know you think I've gone mental, but this kind of thing has never happened to me before. This is all new for me too. I feel completely done over. I'm frightened out of my wits right now. Not so much from what happened, but from what I saw. Although I'm kinda getting used to these little fantasy trips lately. It's sort of what happened the first time the Mac Lady looked at me."

"What do you mean when the Mac Lady looked at you Benjamin?" questioned Mathilda. "What does that mean, I don't understand? She looked at you and you had a seizure?"

Annabel jumped in quickly to clarify, "No Tildie, he didn't have a seizure. I just said it looked that way for a minute, but it wasn't, right Benjamin?"

"Oh, quite right. I didn't have an eppy or anything like that Mathilda."

Mathilda sat back more comfortably in her space. Benjamin had no choice, he needed to explain everything.

"Okay, this is the best I can do. I'm just going to tell you guys everything that happened and you can decide for yourselves if I've gone completely mental. Because I haven't a clue to this whole thing."

So Benjamin recounted the exact details of his entire journey with the first visions from the Mac Lady and the garden shed dream, all the way up to the map. Leaving out only one small piece of the puzzle....*the Queen*. When he finished Annabel looked at Mathilda and then at Benjamin.

"If I hadn't of seen the 3D map thing myself I would think you were totally nuts. But what I saw was so bizarre and I don't know....*witchy magic* or something. I've read a lot of books that talk about these things, and seen TV shows you know? But I just don't know, there's some very unexplained things in the world....and this is one of them."

Mathilda, in her Mathilda way simply added, "Blimey."

"But you can't fool me Benjamin," said Annabel, "I know your leaving something out. What are you hiding? I'm mean really, at this point I think we need to get everything out in the open and see what the heck we're supposed to do with all of this. And *fairies* Benjamin, *really*? This is all starting to get just too weird for words."

But before she could continue in her questioning Mathilda barged back in the conversation, "Oh my goodness Benjamin, Fairies! I always knew they were real, I just did! I can't wait to see one. And you know what Bellie, you sounded just as looney talking about this weird light glass box thingie, and magic paths, so you should cut Benjamin some slack already."

With this both Annabel and Benjamin blinked in amazement, then took a deep breath and relaxed the tension between them. *After all Mathilda has a very valid point,* thought Annabel, *I did see something that I definitely can't explain, and I know I saw what I saw. I mean I saw a freaking holographic tree in the forest as real as anything in this room.* She looked over at Benjamin and suddenly she felt calm again. She knew in her heart that he wouldn't make any of this up, nor was he a looney *(or barking mad as he would say).* But she was definitely not going to let him off that easy, just yet. He was hiding something, something important, she just knew it.

"Okay, so what are you leaving out Benjamin?" spoke up Annabel, relentless.

Benjamin had an instant argument in his brain. How far was he willing to go into this abyss, and how willing was he to drag his best mates in along with him?

He had seen the darkness that had filled his night *and* day time terrors, and it had a name now.... *Tar Vigorn.* A name that had come to him when she smiled at him. A name that he will forever remember. *Tar Vigorn....Queen, Tar Vigorn.* A small bit of information that he omitted from his recount of events to his friends. That and the antique key he held in his possession. Benjamin sat with the weight of the world on his shoulders.

47

"Benjamin, you gotta know we're the three Muskydeers. It's always that way in the movies, ya know?" said Mathilda. "Always one for all and all for one. Is that the way they say it Bellie?"

Her sister silently nodded.

"So I say we just tell everything we know and figure out why the Mac Lady gave you those dreams and...wait! The Mac Lady, where is she? Maybe we should just go ask her what all this means?"

"Oh no Mathilda!" Benjamin burst in with urgency, " I don't think that's such a good idea at all. I'm telling you, this was the weirdest thing ever...well actually up until today it was anyway. But either way, she knew she was aiming it right at me, I just know it. So if she really wanted to talk to me she would have done it by now. No, I think it's best we figure this whole thing out by ourselves. You're right Mathilda, we are the three Muskydeers. That means we're in this together."

"So you're ready now to fill us in on the big secret?" grinned Annabel.

Again, Benjamin had to reflect for a moment that he was doing the right thing. Finally he had to agree with everything that Mathilda had said. After all, was he just going to deal with some forest queen with the darkest force of energy he'd ever felt, all by himself? Was he going to venture off to the Grandfather Tree... *alone?* And for *what?* He still hadn't a clue? *You would have to be a mad fool to go off in hunt of the most bizarre danger one could dream up...all alone.* So Benjamin looked at the girls.

"Bugger it! Alright mates, follow me."

Mathilda chuckled, she just loved it when he spoke British.

Once they were back in the garden shed, Benjamin went over to the far corner and picked up the stack of terra cotta pots resting there and moved them out of the way. Then he pulled back an empty burlap sack used as a rug to keep the pots safe from chipping, that laid on the floor. Under the sack was a loose floorboard that Benjamin was able to pry open at the edge. On his knees, he began to reach down into the musty space, but stopped and looked back over at the sisters; who were both on pins and needles wondering of the secret that was about to be revealed. Mathilda hoped in her heart that it had something to do with Fairies. *Oh, maybe he built a little home for them under the shed...how cool would that be,* thought Mathilda with a huge smile on her face.

Benjamin finally turned back to the floor hole and reached in. He retrieved an old rusty tin box and pulled it out into the open air. He sat the box on his lap and set the floorboard back into place. He got up with his treasure and walked over to the middle of the shed where the girls were waiting with deep anticipation at the center table.

"This came to me a couple weeks ago," he stated.

"What do you mean it *came* to you?" asked Annabel.

"I mean it just literally showed up. I was sitting here on the stack and...remember that rain storm a few weeks back?" They both nodded. "Well, I was just sitting here thinking about things..." "What things Benjamin?" asked Mathilda with true sincerity and interest.

"Oh, you know Mathilda....just things."

"Like your parents?" spoke up Annabel.

Benjamin blinked his eyes. "Yeah, like my parents," he answered.

The girls looked to Benjamin with deep empathy. They really didn't know much about his situation, other than both his parents seemed to have gone missing. Missing for a long time now. Neither one of them could imagine their lives without Claire and Edward, or Cubby for that matter. It was a very sad moment for the three friends as they had never spoken of this before.

"Anyway," continued Benjamin, changing the subject quickly, "I was just laying on the stack and there it was. I looked up and it was just hanging on that rusty old nail, like it had been there forever." The girls glanced over at the nail that Benjamin nodded towards with his head. Then he opened the box and pulled out the key. The girls could barely contain themselves.

"O-M-G! It's so cool!" shouted Mathilda, who was standing up on her toes to get as good a look as she could onto the potting bench where the key now rested.

"Wow, Benjamin! It looks like something from an antique store in another world or something. But I don't understand? Where did it come from?"

"I don't understand either," said Benjamin, "I'm telling you, it just simply showed up one day. I've never seen it before and then *POOF*, one day it's hanging in the shed. I never even noticed that old nail in the door jam before either."

Annabel turned back around to take further look at the protruding piece of rust stuck in the wood wall.

"It was just the weirdest thing ever. I seriously thought I was going mental for a bit," continued Benjamin, "I've looked at it and studied it for the past few weeks, and I can't figure out what the symbols mean. But when you said that the map looked like some old foreign language, I thought of the key."

Suddenly Annabel looked up at the air in front of her and they could tell her mind was working on a puzzle. "Benjamin, let me look at that."

He handed her the key.

"Wow, this thing is really heavy!" she said with a start.

"Yeah, it surprised me too." said Benjamin.

Annabel began turning the key around in her hand for examination, much like Benjamin had upon his first inspection. Mathilda was pulling on her sisters' arm to lower the relic closer to her so she could get a good look at it as well. As the light caught the key stem, as she moved it closer to Mathilda...there they were again....*words*.

"This is so strange," said Annabel, "Something about this looks so familiar to me."

Benjamin looked at Annabel with amazement, "What do you mean?"

"Yeah, Bellie, what the heck do you mean?" chimed in Mathilda.

Without warning Annabel nearly jumped through the roof, and took Mathilda and Benjamin right out of their skin.

"I got it! Oh my god! I'll be right back, don't go anywhere...Oh my god!" And out the door she ran.

Mathilda and Benjamin just stood staring at the empty space that had held their third party a moment ago.

"Wow!" said Mathilda, "What the heck is going on? Benjamin, let me look at it, okay?" but quickly added, "But I don't want to hold it or anything, I just want to see it better."

Benjamin understood her trepidation and lowered the key down to her level. "Don't worry Mathilda, I know exactly how you feel. I did the same thing when I first saw it."

Mathilda just stared at the key in complete amazement. "You know what, she's right. It looks like some old thing from another planet or something. From some other country for sure. Well blimey, this is really turning into some kind of blooming day here!"

Benjamin laughed at Mathilda's determination to use the slang of his upbringing. And of course he had to agree....no truer words had been spoken. They both had a joyful little chuckle in the middle of the garden shed while they waited for Annabel to return.

Annabel finally showed up with a bundle that looked like it was wrapped in newsprint, tucked under her sweat jacket. Benjamin's heart started to quicken. His eyes widened and he watched as Annabel came over to the center table and pulled out her goods.

"The minute you said something about that language, and the symbols, it reminded me of something. It took me a minute, but then it finally came to me. I found it mixed in with all the maps and I set it aside. Here it is."

With this, Annabel unwrapped a single aged worn out yellow piece of crackled parchment, very reminiscent of a treasure map.

"Bellie, is that what I think it is?" said Mathilda with great surprise.

"Well, that all depends on what you think it is."

"Oh my grandma's good gravy! Is that a treasure map of some kind?" Mathilda practically yelled.

"No, it's not exactly a treasure map. But it is a map, and it directs you to the big tree. Oh! I almost forgot, it's called the Grandfather Tree by the way, which seems to be the only bit that is in our language...which is really weird, but anyway, it's more than just a treasure map. It's..." "It's a flippin primer is what it is," interrupted Benjamin in awe.

"A primer, what the heck is a primer? And why are all these funny words written down here? Would someone please explain this to me already before I go completely mental!" said Mathilda with great enthusiasm.

"All right tike, just settle down and we can explain everything," said Annabel with a grin on her face, "Benjamin would you care to have the honors?"

Benjamin took the primer from Annabel and stared in utter amazement. He had been racking his brain for weeks, attempting to understand the series of words and symbols without one iota of understanding coming to him. And then here it is, the answer to everything, wrapped in newsprint, sitting right in front of him. He gathered his wits and calmly spoke to the girls without taking his eyes off the contents of the parchment in his hands.

"This is the code breaker. I believe this series of words down here are the body of the main language used. Then it looks like these over here are a way to arrange them to make sense, to give the directions. This is going to take some time to figure out. This is definitely a map to the tree, but what's supposed to happen when you get there is still a mystery to me."

Annabel broke in, "I just need a little time with both these pieces and I know I can figure this out. We need to get some paper and pencils, and a calculator I think, and we need to get to work. This is high priority top secret Mathilda, so I'm going to need you to swear your biggest oath of silence ever. You need..." "What do you think Bellie, I'm not a baby you know? I know what top secret means. You think I'm going to blow something this amazing? I'm not a plank you know."

Annabel looked at Benjamin with a complete loss on her face, and mouthed the word *plank* and shrugged her shoulders in question. Benjamin spoke under his breath. "It means fool. It seems she's becoming a Brit right before our eyes," he smiled.

Annabel joined him while she shook her head in amazement at the worldliness of her baby sister.

As they sat on the floor in the back of the garden shed with their tools of deciphering laid out before them, they each studied the map for clarity and some kind of clue as to where to begin. Finally Benjamin spoke.

"Look at this device, or whatever it is, that's in this garden. It's drawn like a wall of wavy lines that appear to have some sort of energy. I think it's supposed to be transparent, like a big window or something. I don't know, but a moving, or glowing, feeling comes from this drawing. It clearly looks like the entrance into the forest. And it definitely is in this garden. How bloody odd is that?"

He couldn't seem to take his eyes off this part of the map. Something about it seemed too familiar. Then Annabel jumped in. "Well, this first row is definitely the main language. See here how it is sort of like a list, like a foreign alphabet or *um,...*Oh! I know, it's more like in the dictionary when it shows you the origin of a word. Like when it shows the first part of a word and where it comes from, like a German word meaning one thing and then the second part comes from some old Latin word and then they were put together to make one word."

Thank god for her smarts, was all Benjamin could think, but simply said. "I think you're right Annabel."

"See how these words over here look like maybe beginnings to words," she continued, "or prefixes like the dictionary words? Then this list over here has combinations of these partial words. These must be the language. Then I think this stuff on the right is the actual directions to get to the forest and the Grandfather Tree."

"The Grandfather Tree, what a cool name" giggled Mathilda.

"But what's this whole bunch of symbols down below?" continued Annabel, "Benjamin, can you make this out?"

Benjamin looked hard as he peered deeper into the paragraph of symbols when he began to hear a ringing in his head, and he could feel himself beginning to be fray around the edges in his brain. However, before he could succumb to the pull, Mathilda put her hands up to cover his eyes.

53

"Benjamin! No dark tunnels right now please. We got too much to figure out, and we can't waste anymore time on warp speed time travel, or whatever the heck it is that you do when you go all stiff board mental on us!"

And they all burst out into glorious tension releasing laughter.

That Mathilda, she takes right after her sister she does, thought Benjamin. "Well done you, Mathilda. Quiet right."

Then it suddenly came to Benjamin, and everything was crystal clear.

"This is what we need to know when we *get* to the Grandfather Tree," he said in a whisper, completely soaked in the awe of the idea.

"What? Did you say something Benjamin?" asked Annabel as she was pulled from her deep concentration. Benjamin got up onto his knees and put his hands to his head, and looked around the shed for a moment in clarity at the meaning of this information. Then he sat back down on the ground with the others, still in a bit of a daze from what this could mean.

"Benjamin, what is it?" Annabel repeated.

Benjamin said it again, only this time out loud, so everyone could hear.

"This is telling us what we need to know when we *get* to the Grandfather Tree. This is the code that allows us to use the key and unlock the door. We need to figure out this language Annabel, we need to do this now. See, some of these symbols are on the key, and these are words that can only be seen under certain conditions. This means something. We need to figure out the code in order to gain entrance!"

Annabel just looked at him without saying a word. Benjamin, after hearing no response equal to the excitement he was feeling, looked up and saw Annabel looking at him intensely.

"What, what's wrong?" asked Benjamin, with his grin fading.

"Gain *entrance*...r..really? Are you saying that you want us to *go* to the Grandfather Tree? That's what you're saying, right Benjamin?"

Benjamin just looked at her with a blank face. And now everyone was standing. Then Mathilda jumped in, "Holy jeepers creepers! Are you kidding me

Benjamin? When are we going, wait, *where* are we going? Oh Bellie, it's the adventure we have been thinking of, can't you see? I mean really, first we have nothing to do, then you show us these maps and then Benjamin has this key. It sounds like it was already planned out and everything, just waiting for us! Oh, and Bellie, Fairies! You just can't say we're not going!"

Annabel looked down at her jumping bean of a little sister and said with authority, "Quiet Tildie. Give me some quiet to think. I need to talk to Benjamin about this for reals, okay?"

"Okay," said Mathilda somewhat deflated.

Benjamin took a deep breath and slowly blew the air out of his full cheeks.

"Well...yeah, I suppose that is what I am saying. I mean, Mathilda has a point. It's just too weird that this key shows up, and then these maps. And I've been having all these dreams. Why is this all happening to me? Why did her visions come to me?"

Annabel attempted to break into his ensuing tirade, "Benjamin, wait, I'm just saying...." "Why did the key show up here? Why Annabel? Am I just supposed to ignore all of this...and...*Bloody Hell!* I don't understand *any* of this."

Annabel stood completely stunned by her best friends outburst.

"You know what guys, this is just too much for me all at once. I think we should just stop right now, I can't think anymore. I feel like my head is going to explode right off my sodding shoulders!" As he stormed out the garden shed door the girls could hear him shout outside. "Bugger it!"

Mathilda and Annabel had never seen Benjamin act anything remotely of this nature before. They both agreed it was time to put everything away and think about it over night. They would talk about it again tomorrow after school. So they loaded everything back up in their special wrappings and put the primer, the notes and the key, back under the shed floor board in it's safe hiding place. The girls went home and took their secrets to bed with them.

Later that night when Mathilda couldn't contain her excitement, she snuck into her sisters' room and crawled in bed beside her. Annabel was not asleep either, and welcomed her little sisters' warm body next to her. She was going over everything that had happened that day....a *very* long day indeed. She still couldn't believe that all of this was really happening. *How could this all be?*

But she had seen what she had seen and now they were talking about going in search of this strange garden, that had a magical entry into the Gilley Forest, with a glowing path that lead to a giant tree. A tree with a magical door.

Oh! And did I forget to mention little colored lights with wings! What in the world are we getting ourselves into?

Mathilda whispered softly, "Bellie are you awake?" She didn't wait for an answer, and simply said with a large yawn, *"Ahhh*..I can't wait to see the Fairies already. Good night sissy."

Annabel couldn't answer her....she just needed to go to sleep.

"And you're sure Mrs. Longpotts never said a word to you about not being here tonight?" asked Edward to his wife.

"No, I'm telling you, she never uttered a single word to me about anything. I can't believe she's just not here," answered Claire.

"Well, maybe something has happened to her, have you rung up the hospital?" quizzed Edward.

"Edward, her chenille bag is gone, there are no clothes in her closet, nothing. I tell you she's gone. I mean how unprofessional is that?"

"Bugger me!" replied Edward. Claire just looked at him. "What?" he said with a snicker, "Since I've been back home the old language is creeping back in a bit more."

Claire's expression didn't waiver and she continued in her anger.

"I gotta say I really didn't see this one coming, she seemed so responsible. I mean she's been with us almost a *year* now. Her work was always done to perfection and she really helped out so much with the girls. I tell you, I just don't know what I am going to do without her. The girls have less than two weeks left before school is out, and I have that fund raiser I need to get started on for the company. This is really the worst timing to be going off in search of a *new* nanny."

"Well, there's nothing we can do about it tonight, and I'm totally knackered, so let's just hit the sack and deal with this tomorrow. I mean who knows, maybe she'll show up or something. In the meantime let's just go to bed already, I have a really big day at the office tomorrow."

Claire reluctantly agreed, and so off they went.

Benjamin laid in his bed wide awake. He couldn't even begin to wrap his brain around how much had transpired in one day. First the maps, and then Annabel's story of the dimensional path to the tree. Then his *own* journey into the glass tube.

And then of course there was...*Tar Vigorn.*

What torment was this? Should he have real concern for his life? Is he really under threat from this woman? He certainly wasn't interested in knowing what it felt like to stop breathing again. Once was more than enough for him. It just all seemed so absurd when he thought about it. Maybe they were all barking mad.

Maybe something was in the water?

He had read about whole towns of people getting sick from drinking water right out of the tap. Who knows? These things do happen after all. It seemed more plausible to Benjamin that the whole town had contaminated water as opposed to magical maps, and powerful dark queens. Except he knew that wasn't the case at all. His insides were tearing at his emotions, and his *senses* told him that everything he had experienced up to today, was a *calling* to him. For some unexplained reason, he had been chosen to take on this journey. Every part of his being was ignited with the reality that he was without a doubt making a sojourn to the Grandfather Tree.

What he was expected to do once he got there and figured out the entry...*if indeed he could figure out the entry*...and then who knows what? It was all a mystery to him. He had no explanation to his motives other than to *feel* it was preordained. It was laid out in the stars or something. This appeared to be his destiny, whatever that may mean to a fourteen year old boy.

I mean really, my destiny is to find an invisible energy field in a garden. Where this garden is I haven't the foggiest. And then follow the glowing path through the Gilley Forest until I arrive at the most enormous tree on the face of the earth. Then I need to figure out what 'magic' I need to come up with to actually gain entrance through this door. All along I suppose I will have to dodge this mystery Queen, who appears to have it in for me...why on earth I can't imagine, but I suspect that I'll find out, sooner than later. Then I put this peculiar key into the lock and behold! What? Behold what? This is just barking mad! thought Benjamin, as he laid in the darkness; save for the street lamp light reflecting onto his ceiling, making lovely dancing images.

Images that had now caught his inner, as well as outer, attention. And within moments Benjamin was sound asleep. A deep, peaceful cozy sleep.

Chapter Eight

The Truth About the Chickerings

*W*ell, *little ones, it's time to tell you what really happened to the Chickerings. We're getting to a point where this past information is needed in order for you to follow what is happening currently with the children. Oh, but I must add a little tidbit regarding Whispers, as we are at the juncture in our tale that needs more clarity. This will help you immensely with the entire story. So listen carefully, as we don't have all day to dilly dally about.*

To begin with, plain and simply put, a Whisper is a highly magical being that can travel between dimensions. They are relatively small creatures (as am I), but don't let that fool you, they are a profoundly formidable bunch. They stand close to three lengths tall (that would be feet to you, more or less, three feet tall), and are slight in build; not like the Gnomes, who are a stocky brood. They usually travel about on something. Take Chantilly Lily, she prefers a large floating colorful ball most of the time, however, there are exceptions. For instance, her main mode of transportation when she travels great distance is on the back of a majestic Blue Raven known as Jeno. Whereas Tsula, the Warrior Whisper, saddles a stout Red Hawk with the wing span of five and a half lengths.

He is simply a magnificent creature to behold. I'm referring to the Hawk of course...although I must admit that Tsula is unquestionably a rather glorious fellow himself. There are different families, or clans of Whispers, just as with the Gnomes and the Elves.

The Whispers are the ambassadors of Nature. By this I mean that they are the emissaries that keep the balance of the Forest in tact and safe from all harm. Each Station has it's domain. The clan of Botanical Whispers, like Chantilly Lily, uphold their position as preservers of the esthetics of beauty and color in nature. Chantilly Lily is all about the Roses...which is where I am heading with this dialog, so please keep up.

The Alchemists, like Briggins Jin, are exponents of the ancient sciences and chemistry in nature. We call him Briggs for short, although he does not like it very much, scrunches up his nose whenever he hears it. Then there are the Warriors, champions to the protection and healing of nature, of which Tsula is King of his clan. As I have already stated earlier in this dissertation, Tsula travels on the back of an outstandingly rare and mystical Red Hawk known to all as Mott. And, last but certainly not in the least, there is a far superior Enchantress who is a member of the higher Spiritual Evolution known as The Essence.

This etheric beauty somewhat resembles a wee elf...well, what in all the kingdom of Charlie am I saying! In actuality she IS an Elf. Well, all Essence Whispers are Elves, this one however spoke a pledge of fealty, and a magic bonding spell was used to transform her into the form of a Whisper. Her present post as charge of the Whisper Clan is to stand on behalf for the Purity and Grace in nature. The Essence Whisper is no one less than Princess Avenel herself, hailing from the Elfin clan of the Darmon. This is very big magic! Very extraordinary for a Princess from her lineage to stand in this roll. She is all things magnificent! She has the most glorious copper hair that cascades down about her back...it's simply splendiferous! Oh Me! I completely forgot myself for a moment, how rude of me, please forgive my impertinence.

Well, marching on. They are all powerful magicians and very sly, tactical little beings with the ability to lay force to any opposition. I suppose you could say that in a way they are all Warriors in their own right, as is their job, nay, as is their duty to watch and protect the Gilley Forest and the whole of her denizen. To keep safe all who dwell in the Forest from harm and negativity. They each are fixed with the knowledge of all things to do with the wooded lands and it's life giving energies. They are known collectively as the Guardians of the Forest

Whispers are capable of shifting through dimensions at will, in an instant. From the earths surface to below in the blink of an eye. Something I myself am quite envious of, but that's neither here nor there...well actually I suppose it is both here and there for them, ha! I made a little joke. Well, well. Oh Me! I almost forgot, the most important of all, The Shining Ones.

These are the Light Energies, the Sparks, that are the inherent core Spirits of all the living plants, trees and flowers of the Forest. However, I will have to make note to myself to render that esoteric explanation in further detail at another time. That topic is a bit heady even for me...and I know from what it is I am speaking of! Ha!

But alas, we are in mid conversation here and now, about the nature of Whispers and one Whisper in particular, Chantilly Lily, as I have already mentioned. Well, I dare say I have rambled on long enough, as is my nature to do. So let us travel back in time now, as far back as 100 years, to the little farm nestled on the edge of the Gilley Forest.

The story goes....

....that the Chickering family, a Mr. and Mrs. and their ten year old twin girls, lived on the farm all those many years ago and raised sheep. However, sheep are rarely mentioned in this story, for it was the rose garden in particular that had everyones attention.

Mrs. Chickering had a flower garden that was unsurpassed by any in all of Grandlochcheshire. She grew every kind of Delphinium, Fairy Bells, Snapdragons, three shades of Heather, as well as Foxglove and Hollyhocks...and then there were the Roses. Something special in the mulch that Mrs. Chickering used, which she kept very secret, resulted in the largest most perfect buds and flowers the likes of which no one had ever seen.

The scent that came from the garden was nothing less than remarkable. As a visitor walking down the road past the perimeter of the farm, you could catch the scent of roses as it began to permeate the air around you. The most lovely enchanting perfume swirled about and delighted your senses, and without thought a smile would curl upon your lips. To add to this experience the first sight of the garden nestled on the edge of the forest took ones breath away. The brilliant saturation of color almost knocked you over. Your entire being was flooded with the vivid, intense, almost dimensional color. Although it was the overwhelming aroma of sweetness that was dizzying and intoxicating, if not a little disturbing, all at the same time.

Mrs. Chickering's roses grew up and over the trellis and surrounded the boarder of the garden yard. The garden had a unique black wrought iron fence that enclosed it, with a big arched wooden trellis and an ornate iron gate that had little gold tinkling bells hanging from it. It was a very unusual design for a farm garden in these parts.

However, Mr. Chickering had a propensity for iron work almost equaled to Mrs. Chickering's uncanny way with fertilizers and seed it seemed.

At first Mr. Chickering began smelting and hammering and tinkering with the long thin pieces of iron that he had purchased from a traveling wares cart, that had been passing by on the road home from town. The crusty old merchant had claimed the stack of iron had come from the original rail ties that had been used to build the tracks for the Skeffington Union Rails. The train tracks were meant to lay between the three counties of Callum, Backtum, and Stansbury and straight into Grandlochcheshire. Then continue on out of town, by route though the Gilley Forest, and end in the center of Ethington, on the other side of the Gilley Forest; thus joining the commerce of the two areas and creating prosperity for all the merchants.

However, an unimaginable tragedy had befallen the Skeffington Union Rails heir, with the mysterious disappearance of his two youngest children, Connor and Shelbe. They were never found, and the tracks were never finished. To this day the dormant tracks lay through the counties of Callum, Backtum and Stansbury, and straight through the center of Grandlochcheshire, where they stop dead at the entrance to the Gilley Forest.

One day, almost without thought, Mr. Chickering picked up a piece of the metal and turned it around in his hands for a moment. He studied the dark line, feeling the cool smoothness of the tie, admiring the richness in the depth of the many subdue rainbow of colors that shone in the light. A small grin started taking shape on his face. A compelling thought occurred to Mr. Chickering, "I must build something of...*distinction!*" he finally announced, out loud to no one.

So he began the rigorous process of melding the rails together by adding a beautiful ornate shape he twisted from the smaller pieces, and placing them between each stave. After several days of building, he stopped for a breath, and looked around for a moment at his work. Mr. Chickering realized, quite suddenly, that without fore thought, he had fashioned a very unusual, but equaling appealing, fence length. So taken by his creation, Mr. Chickering continued for several more days, hammering and smelting, until he had built another piece of equal measure.

Early every morning for twelve days, Mr. Chickering began his deeply driven labor, that did not waiver for one single moment, until the sun left the sky. Until on the final day, when the iron staves ran out, and he stopped to look at what he had done, had Mr. Chickering realized, quite by accident again, that he had built an inclosure, save for a small entrance opening.

When Mr. Chickering stood back to admire his creation, all at once a brilliant thought popped to mind. *I'll build a garden yard for Mrs. Chickering!* Except it wasn't a thought at all. For as Mr. Chickering stared into the yard that backed up against the Gilley Forest, what he saw, without exception, was an entire garden in full perfect bloom and bud standing before him. *Well, that's peculiar....the beautiful roses. I don't....I,* was the fleeting, and already fading thought Mr. Chickering had, as his balance quickly became unstable. His head starting ringing as he reached into the air to steady himself. Everything went dark for a moment.

He gasped, and then the feeling left him almost as suddenly as it had come. However, he was now on the ground, propped up on one arm, staring up into the iron enclosure! He could see the sunlight dancing on the long shafts of grass on the patches in the yard. *But, but the flowers,* a small thought nagged for a very fast and ghostly moment. *What...I... the garden. What just happened? The rosebuds...I smelled them.*

But there were no roses in sight. As Mr. Chickering looked about with a vacant glance, a dark feeling of foreboding attempted to infiltrate his mind. He came back to himself with a shock, shook his head, and thought, *Heavens! Too much sun and work.* And the images he could swear were there only moments before started fading out of reach. The grassy yard returned, as did Mr. Chickering thoughts regarding his brilliant new idea of a rose garden. He simply knew without question, that the conditions here were perfect for growing flowers, especially roses. Mr. Chickering had always loved roses.

So Mr. Chickering continued his labor for several more days, using the odd pieces and iron scraps that were left to form a sweet little gate and latch. Then he took some of the wood he had cleared from the edge of the property, a few weeks before, that had been stacked next to the barn, to make the trellis. He attached the trellis to the side pieces he had formed doubling the iron to make it secure, and hung the gate. Mr. Chickering envisioned his wife's climbing peach roses growing steadily over the arch, as visitors walked beneath the canopy of buds.

And finally, on a Wednesday, at three o'clock in the afternoon, almost fifteen full days after he heated up the first piece of iron and swung his hammer, Mr. Chickering picked up an old piece of bark plank shaved from a tree trunk. With some left over green paint he had used to cover the porch rails and door to the front of the farmhouse, he painted the words on the inside smooth piece of wood, *The Enchanted Rose Garden.* He used some twisted jute and hung the sign from the top of the arched trellis...*and smiled.*

Chapter Nine

The Enchanted Rose Garden

For several days, Mrs. Chickering had watched in curious amusement as her husband, Mr. Chickering, had uncharacteristically begun his day at the crack of dawn. He whistled as he walked out of the front door, to travel over to the side yard that backed up against the edge of the Gilley Forest. At first it pleased her to see her husband so completely delighted with his new project. He seemed genuinely happy. However, several days into this sudden, and unusual routine, Mrs. Chickering began to notice subtle changes in her husband's appearance and behavior.

The most worrisome was his almost violent tossing around and muttering in his sleep. He would heave himself about their bed, and utter strange sounds in his uneasy rest. This frightening and bewildering behavior began to affect Mrs. Chickering's sleep now, as well. She lay awake at night anticipating the flurry of confusion and mysterious words coming from her unconscious husband.

One day, while the sun was at its highest, she came out to the side yard to offer him some cool strawberry juice. When she came up behind Mr. Chickering she found him muttering in a very animated way to, *Well, to absolutely no one,* she thought. *I just heard him in conversation with someone, but no one is here.*

She swore she heard him utter the name *Chantilly* over the drone of the falling hammer hitting the iron. When she questioned him about the unfamiliar name, he just continued to raise the hammer high over his head and pound away, as if she wasn't even standing there.

Mrs. Chickering would watch out the window that was above the farmhouse sink, that had a slight view into the side yard. Try as she might, she couldn't quite see what it was her husband was doing. One day a very uneasy feeling started to creep up over her shoulders as she listened to the now constant ominous clanging of the hammer hitting metal. A dark thought occurred to her, *he is like a mad man possessed by his creation!*

He had begun missing meals several days before, and now looked more drawn and tired than a corpse. *He only comes in when the sun goes down,* she continued in her thoughts. However, the real curiosity was that save for the smattering of times she caught him staring listlessly out the window into the Gilley Forest, when her husband was in the farmhouse with Mrs. Chickering and their two lovely daughters, Grace and Emeline, he was almost Mr. Chickering again. That is, up until the stars were the brightest in the night sky, and his tortured sleep filled the room with an uneasy and impending dread.

Then, early one morning, Mrs. Chickering lay in the bed next to her dearly loved husband and listened to his slow steady breathing. Beside herself with grief about the mysterious malady that had befallen him, she wondered what she would do if ever she lost him. When, quite suddenly, she realized that Mr. Chickering had slept soundly for the first time in two weeks! As she caught the thought in her mind, her husband began to stir. Upon awakening, Mr. Chickering looked at his wife and smiled. The warmth of this smile reached way down to Mrs. Chickering's toes and she burst into tears, and hugged her husband, right then and there; in the old Big Belly Oak bed that Mrs. Chickering's parents had given them on their wedding night, almost eleven years before.

That morning after breakfast, instead of rushing out the door, Mr. Chickering came to his wife, and with a very mischievous grin, held out his hand, winked, and asked her to close her eyes. Mrs. Chickering was dumbfounded, but willingly took his hand, closed her eyes and let him lead her like a sleepwalker holding onto her guide. He led her out the front door and over to the side yard. With childlike amusement, he cupped his hands over her eyes as he stood her before the beautiful trellis-gate. He leaned in very close beside her and whispered sweetly into her ear, "My darling Mrs. Chickering, the roses are in bloom," and released his hands.

What Mrs. Chickering saw before her was nothing less than astonishing, and shook her to her core. She stared in utter disbelief as a strange sound started buzzing loudly in her head. What she saw before her was undeniably the most magnificent garden she had ever seen! The garden was in full vivid bloom, with the scent of roses permeating the air around her. She saw butterflies flitting about, and there was Chantilly Lily floating and...*Wait, how am I... No, I can't be....Chantilly Lily, the Whisper? But this is my garden. I've planted every seed here. I..I don't understand.*

Mrs. Chickering had to steady herself for a moment and closed her eyes, *But the Whisper?* Almost instantly the spinning in her stomach stopped and the crazy dizzy feeling went away.

When she opened her eyes and looked up, she saw before her an empty garden yard, with the most unusual, and beautiful, wooden trellis, and an iron gate the likes of which she had never seen. All thoughts of mysterious phantom gardens, *(and Whispers)*, simply vanished, as if they had never occurred. She squealed with glee.

"Oh, Mr. Chickering, it is the most beautiful garden yard in the whole of Grandlochcheshire County. Thank you, my sweet darling husband!"

The Enchanted Rose Garden, how magnificent, she thought.

It took no time for the garden yard to become the primary object of attention in the Chickering home. Even Emeline and Grace joined in with the arduous labor of preparing the land for sowing. Every morning upon daybreak, the family would gather at the breakfast table to fill their bellies as quickly as they could for the long day's work ahead of them. Most times they would forget to eat again until sundown. By then it was as much as they could do to get themselves inside the farmhouse and prepared for sleep. And sleep they did. Deep, heavy, lifeless sleep.

Whereas the troubled and restless nights Mr. Chickering had suffered during his construction of the garden fence were a constant, the complete opposite was true now.   It was as if the entire family were enchanted by some deeply entrenched magical spell, cast on them by some old twisted dark crone in a child's fairy tale.

Of course it was not a dark old crone at all, only a Whisper...but deep magic it was indeed.

Chapter Ten

The Whisper

Dunston here again! Well, it appears our story is moving right along, bringing you closer to the present situation. Which I might add is truly exciting indeed! As I've already mentioned in our earlier colloquy, specific actions, such as profound choice, are capable of remaking one's life. To explain a bit further, there is a most powerful transforming energy known as Path Awakening. Simply put, all sentient beings have the mind to directly alter the course of their lives when pressed with an immense choice of evolution.

I mean to say by Charlie, that it truly is not a matter of good or bad, right or wrong. Oh, don't misunderstand me, there is obviously a difference between right and wrong, and they matter greatly, however, what I'm referring to is a choice directly related to Evolving or Devolving. And believe you me, as I stated before, it is most definitely a choice, Ha! Of course, it goes without saying, that one would hope one would stay the path of righteousness and honor, as opposed to anything else. Oh but Me oh Me... It seems to be the way of the world these days to have to challenge oneself to remain conscious and present. To be 'awake' in one's life...ahh...now that, my precious little beings, that is the true journey, isn't it?

Oh but Me oh Me! Before I go off on some long drawn out dissertation regarding the meaning of life, I should stop while I'm ahead, and get back to the business at hand. That business of Chantilly Lily and the Chickering garden for Charlie's sake!

Once we get clear on exactly just what did happened with the Chickering garden, and their contract with the Whisper, we will be current enough with our story to bring in our three adventurists. So let's to it shall we? Back to Chantilly Lily and the Enchanted Rose garden...let's see, I believe this is the page we need to land on. Ahh yes, this is it.

When we last took a look, the Chickering family was very hard at work building the garden to specifications....whose specifications one might ask? Well, there would be no answer other than Chantilly Lily, the Whisper of course. But you already knew that, didn't you?

Many weeks had gone by since Mr. Chickering had presented the Enchanted Rose Garden to Mrs Chickering. The entire family worked diligently around the clock tilling the land and preparing the soil for sowing, planting seeds and watering. Nurturing every little green bud popping it's head out of the ground. And always present, the Whisper, a constant fixture amidst the garden. Atop a large orange ball with pink stars imprinted upon the surface, balanced the Whisper known as Chantilly Lily.

She wore a beautiful green and blue layered tutu with a brown and white stripe long sleeve tee-shirt like top. Her legs were adorned with baby pink tights that had dark rose pink ribbon stripes that wrapped around her legs, and ended in her long elfish stocking toes hanging off the ball. She wore a top hat of aqua with dark blue stars on it. Her bright crimson locks stuck out like a mass of spun cotton from under the brim of the top hat. Chantilly Lily was a sight to behold. A miniature being of color and beauty, traveling about the garden on her balancing ball, three feet in the air.

There she was as if she had always been a part of their lives. For some unearthly reason it did not seem unusual, or strange, to the Chickerings. They somehow took it for granted that she was always a presence in their lives. Lives that now consisted of Chantilly Lily and the garden.

After taking a short break from the heat, Mrs Chickering got up from her seat on the front porch and headed out to join the others in the garden. As she moved toward the side yard she remembered she had wanted to get another bucket of sheep manure and turned to redirect her stride. As she walked the trail past the barn heading toward the pasture, she glanced up to see the huge white washed barn door open. She suddenly noticed what looked like a small burlap sack leaning up against the wall, just to the right side of the barn door. Her full attention now on the sack and it's contents, completely diverted her path and she went off to investigate.

As she leaned in past the open door to pick up the sack, something moved in her peripheral view of the barn. Mrs. Chickering froze for a moment to allow the sounds of the barn to become familiar....*or otherwise.* And then the sound in question came again. *What in heavens name is that?* thought Mrs. Chickering with a sudden jolt upright. She peered into the dark shadows of the cool barn. It didn't sound like a roaming sheep or stray rodent out on a mission for loose feed supplies. No, this was more like the sound of...*Footsteps! Oh! There it is again,* thought Mrs. Chickering with alarm.

Why this would disturb her was unknown to Mrs. Chickering. After all it could be any member of her family. But for some unexplained reason, she knew this wasn't the case at all. So she turned to face the inside of the barn and attempted to peer in deeper. However, the brightness of the day took her vision to almost blackness. She began walking slowly into the barn as she called out, "Hello, is someone there...hello?"

And as lightly and quickly as could be, but as certain, something *(or someone),* brushed up against her apron skirt. With her eyes still unable to focus in the darkness Mrs. Chickering gave out an audible gasp as she involuntarily raised her hands to her face for protection.

Looking down around her the darkness began to fade, and the contents of the barn came into focus. Save for the deep nooks and crannies present in any barn, that regardless of the time of day would remain in shadows, Mrs. Chickering could see her surroundings clearly. She saw no movement. Panic beginning to grip her, she quickly followed her feet heading out of the huge barn door. She did not skip a beat as she bent down to snatch up the mysterious little burlap sack. And without looking back she headed quickly toward the safety of the garden.

In the back corner of the garden stood Emeline with eyes wide as saucers, nodding as she listened with keen intent to every word Chantilly Lily was whispering in her ear.

Grace glanced up for a moment without thought. However, before she could put her head back into her work, she stopped and took a deeper look at her sister and the Whisper. *What's that all about?* she wondered. After a minute of inquisitive staring, Grace headed over towards her sister and Chantilly Lily.

"What has you two so captured in conversation?" asked Grace.

Startled from the interruption, Emeline gave her sister a glazed over smile and turned to walk away, taking the secret with her.

After a moment of shock at her sister's peculiar behavior, Grace looked up at Chantilly Lily who simply smiled at her. Grace turned to follow in Emeline's direction to confront the sibling.

"What's going on? What are you two up to Emeline?"

Still silence, no words, no acknowledgement. Grace began to feel a tingle creeping up through the core of her body.

"Talk to me sissy, please, you're beginning to scare me."

With that Emeline stopped the hoeing that she was diligently involved in, looked up, and peeked past Grace's shoulder to gaze straight into Chantilly Lily's eyes. The Whisper nodded at Emeline. Grace turned to look over her shoulder in the direction of her sister's stare and caught the sparkle in Chantilly Lily's smile. She quickly spun around to find not only her sister mere inches from her face, but Emeline was peering with great intent into Grace's eyes!

Grace's shoulders went up in alarm, and she inadvertently stepped back from the surprise and anxiety she was now feeling. Emeline pulled her sister back in closer to her, almost nose to nose, before Grace could fall over.

"What I'm about to tell you has to stay between just the two of us. I mean it Grace, a twin sister vow. You need to swear an oath that this stays with us. Can I trust you?" pressed Emeline.

Grace was beside herself with fear at the severe manner in which Emeline, her best and closest friend, not only her sister, but her twin, was conducting herself. She had never seen Emeline behave in such a manner in all their ten years of time together.

"Emeline if you don't tell me right now what is happening I'm going to burst! You have me so frightened I might just faint any minute. What is going on!" Grace practically screamed at Emeline.

Emeline quickly grabbed her sister's forearm and shushed her to keep quiet. She looked around to make certain her mother and father did not hear Grace. Once confident that it was just the two of them involved in the conversation, Emeline repeated her newly acquired information to Grace.

"Chantilly Lily was telling me about the place she comes from, and how there is this Queen, her name is Tar Vigorn, and she rules over almost the whole of the Gilley Forest. But the people in the Forest are quite fearful of the Queen. She told me how there are these other Princesses from some other part of the Forest, and I forget what she said they are called, but they have wings! And one of them rides bareback on a big stag, can you believe that Grace? A large white stag! She says they are great warriors Grace. But they cannot come up against the Queen alone. Chantilly Lily says the Queen is far too powerful, and holds too much magic! *Magic* Grace!

"She was telling me about some other land, I didn't understand really if she said it was deep in the Forest, or if she said it was below the Forest, which doesn't make sense, I'm just not certain what she meant, but she says the Queen is attempting every thing in her power to gain entrance into this domain. For some reason, again, that I didn't understand, this is the only place that her magic is stifled. However, the people are terribly frightened! Grace, Chantilly Lily said she needs our help to save the Forest people...and this other land. It's called Coranim. Doesn't it sound terribly beautiful Gracie, *Coranim?*"

Emeline looked around the garden to make certain no uninvited ears were lurking about. And by mere proximity brushed up against Grace's cheek as she came closer for the biggest part of the secret, "And something else Gracie."

Grace didn't know if she could bear any more secrets about a mysterious Queen and the land she wished to reign over. It was everything she could do to keep from crying...or *laughing*, she didn't know which would alleviate the ramifications of her sisters' words more.

"She also told me about those children from the train people, you know the ones whose little boy and girl have gone missing now for almost a year, the Skeffinton family....she knows where they are Grace."

Grace's breath stopped, she stepped back and looked coldly into her sister's eyes. She didn't blink. She stood motionless.

"She says they were taken away by that Queen, and she has them with her in the Forest," continued Emeline.

Grace stood with her mouth completely wide open at this information. *This couldn't be true. Could it?*

"Oh, Gracie, we have to help them. Chantilly Lily says that it is easier for children to go through the forest because the people that live there are small, so we would blend in better. They are called the, something...*Set*. Oh, I don't know, Chantilly Lily said so much to me so quickly, I just couldn't keep up. I do remember she said they were builders of some kind. She called them a *clan*, it's like a brotherhood, a family. Just like the Tartan Clans of the Scottish and Irish families. Either way, she said there are more than one clan, and that the Forest had other people who lived there as well, and..." Before Emeline could utter another single word Grace held up her hand.

"Stop! Please I beg you, just stop. I don't want to hear anymore right now. I need to think about all of this. If it is true that this Tar Vigorn has those children then we need to tell someone right away." But before she herself could utter another word, Emeline's face contorted.

"Oh No Gracie! You can't tell anyone, you swore an oath!" she pleaded. "Chantilly Lily says if we get anyone involved that it could be very bad doings for those children, and could possibly be the ruin of the whole of the Forest clans!"

Grace and Emeline stood staring at each other while Emeline's latest words hung in the thick hot air above them. After a moment in silence, they instinctively began pulling closer towards one another. They held hands as close as they could get, and with eyes wide as the face of the moon, they stared off into the Gilley Forest.

Chantilly Lily was nowhere to be seen. However, on the other end of the garden another mystery was showing itself to the Chickerings.

"Well, it was just the oddest feeling Mr. Chickering. I can't explain it, but here is this mysterious little bag of seed, and you say you know nothing of it's contents?"

"No my dear Mrs. Chickering, I do not," replied Mr. Chickering with a monotonous tone. "As for the barn however, I have heard the same footsteps myself upon occasion this past week."

Mrs. Chickering stood stunned, staring at her husband, "You know the footsteps I am speaking of?"

Mr. Chickering simply nodded.

"Why have you not made mention of this before?"

Mr. Chickering simply shrugged. Mrs. Chickering stood for a moment staring down at her husband, who was digging around the root of some plants that needed thinning. She pulled herself together and took control.

"Well, we need to get to the bottom of this. I refuse to live with the uncertainty that something, or *someone*, is roaming about my barn in secrecy. Then to find this peculiar little seed bag. I'm sure it must have something to do with the Whisper, but I have not seen her about this late afternoon to question her. She has never left seed for me before, so I am bewildered."

However, before Mrs. Chickering could say any other words, or think any other thoughts, she stopped abruptly and looked up. A small smile started to grow from her lips. As sure as she was standing there, instantly, and as distinctly as one could imagine, the magnificent and overwhelming aroma of roses permeated the air about them. Mr. Chickering stood up and put his arm around his smiling wife, and they both paused in their revery.

After a few moments, Mrs. Chickering turned about in the opposite direction, with great conviction and authority, and with the little bag of seed in hand, she headed towards the back of the garden. There she knelt down in front of the newly mulched area ready for planting. She began to sow her magical bag of seed.

All along Chantilly Lily sat cross legged on her orange balancing ball with the pink stars on it, three feet in the air behind her. Mrs. Chickering was now humming a little tune as she smiled, and day dreamed of gloriously large magenta colored roses.

Well, you wouldn't expect that anyone in their right mind could fathom that they held a magical bag of seeds now would you? Ha! I mean to say, magical seeds indeed. But plant them she did. Oh but Me Oh Me, Chantilly Lily was certainly up to her tricks. And not very much further did the Chickering's have to wait before the magnificent magenta roses were beginning to bloom...as if by magic, Ha!

The impeccably perfect, and unearthly, roses were the crowning glory of the entire garden. I mean to tell you that folks crawled out from every nook, cranny, hill and dale, surrounding Grandlochcheshire after word quickly spread of the rotundas magenta rosettes. Seems this was big news to the local towns people. And quite rightly so. No one had ever seen anything the likes of this garden, not to mention such unusual roses of this caliber. It was most certainly a serious enchanting to say in the least.

Oh it was a circus of events I dare say. Photos in the local newsprint, blue ribbon awards at the tri-county fair. And always Chantilly Lily fading in and out, as company permitted of course. Floating about like a queen, amid her regal magical kingdom. I'll tell you something, that Chantilly Lily is a sly little creature...as is the nature of a Whisper of course.

Oh, however, I can hear it now...but Dunston, we already guessed about the magical seeds, we want to know about the mysterious footsteps? It's the footsteps we're curious about. And what of this Queen Tar Vigorn? What be her powers that could hold the whole of the Gilley Forest, and her denizen in flux? Yes, I'll wager that is precisely what each and every one of you is thinking.

Well, I won't keep you in the mystery any longer. Wouldn't want to put our budding new friendship in jeopardy now would I? No by Charlie I would not!

To begin with, the footsteps would belong to none other than Gibbles, Sir Gibbles to be exact. He is a Brownie. A barnyard Brownie, to be exact yet again. And now I suppose your next question will be, what is a Brownie? Really, where have you people been hiding all of your lives, I ask you? Ha! Well, upon deeper consideration, I believe I will let Gibbles do the s'plaining himself. He is, after all an expert in the nature of Brownies, even given his youthful age of 572 years.

And as for Queen Tar Vigorn, 'thems a whole nother story', as they say, who ever they is. Haven't you often wondered just exactly who THEY is? Really, for the love of Charlie, I'd like to know myself, ha! Oh, but that's neither here nor there right now. I'm certain they are a lovely group of beings whoever they are. However, the truth is I'm not quite sure that this is the time to reveal the legend behind this austere and resolute Queen. You may not be prepared for such a force as Tar Vigorn yet. And by Charlie, you would be correct in thinking so. This Queen is no one to fuse about with. This is BIG magic!

Oh but Dunston, you say, we simply must know more. You say you need a little something to wet your whistle, and find yourself aching for the rest of the story? Ha! Well, here it is, a small glimpse into the journey of Benjamin McTish. However, beware of dark mysterious cloaks in your dreams little ones...and don't say I didn't warn you.

Queen Tar Vigorn is the biggest of Magic there is. This journey is all about Sorceresses, Wizards, Queens and Gnomes, Whispers and Vila. And of course *now you'll be wanting to know just what a Vila is. Well, I'll give you a hint. The two prominent Vila in our story are sisters, Princesses in fact. Sethina, the white one, rides bareback on a great white stag, (sound familiar?), called Rahm. And the blue one is Morel, of the Forest lakes and streams. They are each great Warriors, and serve as champions to the Forest dwellers. And that's all your getting from me right now regarding Vila. Our topic today is supposed to be of the nature of Brownies and enchanted roses and here we are, way ahead of ourselves. Except to say that Emeline was correct in reporting that the Vila each have wings. Sethina is capable of soaring high into the clouds, mucking about with the weather if she so chooses. While Morel's wings are smaller and covered in down, as is the entirety of her body, to help propel her through the water at a grand speed. Now that ought to WET your whistle for the love of Charlie!*

Oh Me! Well, this much of the story I am privy to know little ones, and I will share it with you. A great battle of wits, magic, and a powerful test of courage will be presented to you for your observance. Let me just say emphatically, this adventure is tantamount to the edge of your seat intrigue, steeped in mystery and drenched in life and death decisions. This isn't child's play. Oh no, by Charlie, this is serious business. Forces will be united, and a war will rage....maybe not the kind of war you are preparing yourselves for, but a very powerful battle none the less. Oh my sweet seekers of truth, there is, and always shall be, a dark and light present in all of life. Finding the balance is the key to a peaceful and full existence.

You will learn about loyalty. Alas, you will also learn about deception and longing, however, hopefully you will also gain insight into healing. And you will, no doubt, be presented with a moral to the story. What you take from this understanding is upon you.

You will have to decide what your choices would have been under the same circumstances we shall find of our trio en route. You will have to face your own inner conflict and fears, and decide if the choices made are a part of your own metal. Do you have what it takes to heal something? Be it an animal, a person...or a thought perhaps? What about a tree or a planet? How much courage do you truly have? How well do you really know yourself? Because THAT my precious, and dear little friends, is the very center of our story. Right here and right now I will ask you...How much courage do you have to be yourself?

Oh me! Heavens, here I go, once again, spouting off like some lone sage on the top of a mountain, with all the answers to life. It's just like me isn't it? Well, in truth, I have had enough experience with the knowledge of the way folks choose to live their lives, and it never ceases to amaze me the troubles we sentient beings can get ourselves into. Me Oh Me!

Well, I shall let this part of the story unfold for you to experience for yourself. Besides, too much information may make your noodle begin to swell, and we wouldn't want that now would we? Ha! Oh by Charlie we would not!

So let's get back to the introduction of Sir Gibbles into our equation, so we can get on with the heart of our story...that being Benjamin, and his two best mates, Annabel and Mathilda of course. And the journey to finding themselves, as well as their journey to Coranim.

So hunker down and let's to it then, shall we?

Chapter Eleven

Sir Gibbles

Gibbles sat high up on the rafters of the barn looking down at Mr. Chickering. He thought it might be fun to toss empty acorn shells left behind by the rats, at him. He delighted in seeing what Mr. Chickering would do. But Mr. Chickering merely swung his arms absently about his noggin, like swiping at flies. He had no concern as to what, or to whom, may be toying with him.

When it came to mystery these days, Mr. Chickering simply turned a deaf ear to things and went forward with his task at hand. He had come to realize that it was much easier to just accept all the oddities of the past several months, then to question them any further. Because if he really looked at everything with deeper eyes, the fear of the truth was more than he could bear.

Sometimes he felt like he wasn't in charge of his life anymore. Like he was observing from the outside instead of living it. And every now and then, when the burden of the mystery started to ignite his anxiety, out of no where something cheerful suddenly presented itself to take his mind off the fear and make him smile again. Thus was the cycle of life for Mr. Chickering on the little farm that sat on the edge of the Gilley Forest.

Well, I say, fun that was not, thought Gibbles. *Auk! What fun is there for me to have here, when no one replies in anguish?* He almost burst out loud in a chuckle at the recollection of unnerving the Mrs. the other day. *Aye, I nearly caused her the vapors from fright. The first to respond to my lovely mischief...what a delight.*

However, here he was now, sitting in the middle of this sunny day with no one to play with. He was going to have to do something about this arrangement. After all it had been almost seven days now that he had hidden himself in the Chickering barn waiting for his moment to present himself to the girls. However, steps had to be taken. See, there were rules to follow when it came to introductions.

It is not in the nature of a Brownie to reveal himself to grown ups. No, that was something that was definitely frowned upon in his culture. It was even considered unsavory among some circles of Brownie to share a glimpse of oneself to children. Fortunately for Gibbles, he wasn't of the same mind as any of these circles. Used to being somewhat of an outsider, Gibbles was considered a bit of a rogue, and he liked that just fine. The one thing that kept Gibbles in good standing within the community was his incredibly distinct and exquisite singing voice. There was none better in the whole of the Brownie world.

Clans of Brownies from throughout the Forest gathered deep in the moonlit woodlands to partake of his astounding performances. There one could find Gibbles center stage, theatrically lounging on a boulder, or dramatically propped upon a tree stump gazing up into the starry night, with the flames from the camp fires reflecting on his face and body. He lolled like a king, with his minion in the palm of his hands. With the reminiscence of an old Irish lilt to his tenor voice, his lamenting ballads echoed throughout the Forest; harkening all manner of creature to follow the sound and become awed in his presence. The custom in which Gibbles held his stature during these recitals gave way to the nickname *Sir* Gibbles. A name he very much approved of *(even though it was a bit of a joke to everyone else)*.

Upon the subsequent Thursday of every fortnight, Gibbles would perform his arias of old folklore and tales of the Brownie legends. In the last final phrases he would suddenly spring up with gusto onto his platform, causing his audience to gasp in emotional anticipation. One arm raised to the heavens at the optimum point of exclamation in his musical story, accentuating the drama, he had the crowd right where he wanted them....all eyes upon him. Then like a weary thespian who has given every ounce of himself to his craft, he would slowly fall back down into his draped repose, eyes shut, panting for air, completely spent.

Following the throngs of applause, shouting and the tossing of beautifully colored strips of ribbon *(as is the custom)*, Gibbles would head back alone to his current living arrangement. Scores of ribbons dangling from his palms, as he trudged the deep night, he would get back to work. Work consisting of playing tricks on the unsuspecting owners of which ever barn he was now accustomed to calling home.

However, this was a different situation entirely. This time he was working with the Whisper, which of course was a great honor and only added more celebrity to his status within the Brownie clans. Something Gibbles took full advantage of at every chance he was given.

Later that night, after a very uneventful day of minimal high jinx consisting of overturned buckets of milk and shutting windows every time someone opened one, Gibbles waited in the barn for Chantilly Lily to arrive. He was stationed upon an upturned crate in the middle of the barn next to a hitching post. Weary of the silence, he sat with his body leaning forward, elbow poked into his thigh, his folded palm holding up his chin. As his leg swung lazily back and forth, his absent stare landed on the beam of moonlight dancing upon the surface of stale water resting in an old rusty bucket. A mournful melody attempted to escape his lips.

Gibbles shifted his gaze upward to the full bright moon, peeking through a large gap in the barn roof. Then without warning from his brain, Gibbles began to sing. Before he knew it his eyes were closed and his lamenting fable was pouring from deep inside him. The trills of emotions echoed up through the rafters. A sweeter more melodic sound there was not in the whole of this tiny kingdom.

Then with a sudden start he felt a burning pain as if the tip of his ear were being twisted off. With a jolt of alarm, Gibbles sat up straight as wood, his eyes shot wide open, abruptly cutting off his mellifluous soliloquy. His mouth now fully prepared to wail in anguish, he stopped cold in his tracks to see Chantilly Lily floating right in front of his face.

"What must you be thinking Sir Gibbles?" demanded the Whisper. "You most certainly are aware that the power of your voice will infiltrate every living soul for acres surrounding us? We have not made your presence known to a single living creature, be it man nor mouse, and yet here you are behaving in so nonchalant a fashion. Well, one might wonder the seriousness you place the charge of duties ahead of you. Under these extreme circumstances I would have expected more from you Sir Gibbles...really I must say that I would indeed."

This reprimand from someone of Chantilly Lily's station was the worse kind of torment to Gibbles. In dramatic fashion, as was his way, he jumped down onto all fours and began scratching at the earthen floor in an attempt to portray himself digging his own grave, such was his humiliation.

"Oh dear kind Lady, thinking, I was not. There are no excuses for my despicable and reckless behavior. A thousand pardons be generated, aye, a gazillion your stateliness."

Chantilly Lily sat crossed legged on her ball looking down on the diminutive little Brownie groveling in the dirt, and a smile formed upon her lips. She was not a harsh being in the least and certainly was not in the nature of forcing her level of status upon the lesser. She could see that Sir Gibbles *(as she preferred to address him, as was her nature)*, was clearly apologetic for his actions. And really, when she thought about it, how could she blame him? After all his instrument was a gift, and a suburb and extraordinary gift it was indeed. *It was simply inside of him exploding to get out,* she thought to herself in genuine amusement. So she simply smiled at him. Gibbles sensing her withdrawal of anger stopped his mime, looked up and smiled back at the floating Whisper.

"Well, let's too it than shall we?" Chantilly Lily finally spoke. With this a pronounced seriousness crossed her face, "It seems we have to move things along sooner than I had imagined. The Queen is gathering forces to scour the northern woodlands for the information she lacks. As far as this world is concerned there is still some time, but alas, in our world time is moving quickly. Once she discovers this knowledge there will be no stopping her from entering Coranim. If that were to ever happen....well, my mind can not grasp just what that could truly mean to our world...or this one. At this moment the Grandfather Tree is protected. The Magic used to generate this illusion is great at present, however, eventually the spells cast will wear thin. But for now his secrets are secure. We need reinforcements. It's imperative that we get these children to Ashwald before our window closes. That is why I left those seeds for you to put in the hands of the Chickering matriarch. We must invoke all the creating energy we have towards the completion of all the Roses blooming in conjunction with the coming full moon, in order for the Gateway to manifest. I know we have the little ones on our side, Emeline in particular, but we must hasten our steps. It is a matter of great urgency we find ourselves now, my dear Sir Gibbles. I can not do this without your assistance."

Gibbles simply stared up into the Whisper's eyes. He could see the depth of her concern for her beloved Forest and it's people. He quickly jumped to his feet and stood at attention.

"My mission is your desire, and aim dear sweet Lady. Just ask of Sir Gibbles any thing and I shall perform my duties with exalting speed," he saluted the Whisper with a puffed out chest and as much bravado as would surprise anyone from a creature so small.

"Well done! I knew you were the right person for this task. Now here is the plan of events to follow...." However, before Chantilly Lily could finish her thought she suddenly became aware that they were not alone. Gibbles saw something change in the Whispers eyes, then he saw the shadow cast upon the wall directly behind her growing in size. They both were halted in their breath to see Emeline standing in the barn. The glowing waxing moon was like a beacon of light and brought her shadow into direct contrast.

"Is she awake?" asked Gibbles, as it appeared from the look in her eyes that Emeline was walking in her sleep.

"Of course I'm awake!" Emeline spoke, causing both in the party of secrecy to jump in their skin.

"Well, dear sweet Emeline, whatever are you doing out here in this very deep hour of the night?" quizzed Chantilly, attempting to remain calm.

Not taking her eyes off of the diminutive creature before her, with his blond hair and floppy burlap hat, Emeline walked closer in the direction of the pair, not unlike the action of a sleepwalker.

"I was slowly awoken by singing. Somewhere in the distance, it felt like the most saddest of lullabies. When I realized it was not a dream, I followed the sound. Is he for real Chantilly Lily? What is this manner of creature before me?"

Entirely insulted by the comment, Gibbles turned towards Emeline as if to charge enraged. The Whisper put her hand out quickly. Indignantly Gibbles shouted back, "Aye! Of course I'm real...how rude the little one is. Well, I never!"

With this new development before her, Chantilly Lily regained complete balance on her ball and simply smiled.

Oh my, things are really starting to stir up right now, bringing us closer to the present situation. However, I swear, every time I hear mention of the ruthless Tar Vigorn my skin crawls with fright. The thought of that dark mistress entering my beloved Coranim...burr!

So now Chantilly Lily, with the aid of Sir Gibbles, has infiltrated the young Chickering lasses into their plan. The girls follow along willingly of course, as Chantilly Lily is very persuasive when she wants something of someone. You just cannot stop yourself, it's something in her voice that pulls you by Charlie...right along the edge with her!

Emeline and Grace have begun to raise their level of enthusiasm regarding all the unexpected happenings within the realm of magic. I mean to tell you it can definitely pique the interest of most any ordinary human being. If you have never seen the power of a Whisper in action, it can be very captivating to bear witness the first time or two. The girls have also taken a great curiosity and enjoyment to Gibbles, as one would expect. Each member of this tight little group of Warriors (as I would prefer to refer to them, and rightly so I should imagine), hold extreme honor to be a part of something so profound as....well as saving the world as we know it.

I know you are thinking to yourself, oh my Dunston, isn't that a bit extreme? And yes, I would tend to agree that it may seem a bit extravagant a statement. However, the gist of my meaning couldn't be more true.

For all intents and purposes, these two little magical beings, with the aid of their tiny new friends, are on a trajectory towards holding back one of the most powerful forces alive. And with this comes the hope to protect the Forest and Coranim.

Why so important to guard Coranim you ask? Because my sweet little beings, Coranim is home to the most precious of jewels known....none other than the Heart of the Planet (I'll wait a moment for that one to sink in).

In order for me to get the urgency of this point across at this moment I would have to give up too many details of what is to follow, and where would the fun in all that be I ask you, Ha! No, no, you will just have to wait your turn for events to unfold. However, I will summarize by labeling the pertinent facts at this time. They are as follows:

One. The maleficent dark Queen is on a rampage to discover the secrets buried deeply in the Forest Magic. Two. The Magic can only hold out for so long, leaving Coranim completely vulnerable should Tar Vigorn gain entry. Three. The guardian of this entry, The Grandfather Tree, is presently protected, but vulnerable indeed. And D. Chantilly Lily, Sir Gibbles, Emeline and Grace, are setting up all circumstances to manifest the Gateway into another world, where they will use all measures available to them to prevent the demise of the kingdom.

And lastly, at some point in this very near future, the past and the present must be caught up as one in order to begin the path for Benjamin, Annabel, and Mathilda. With the aid of someone close to them, these three brave little souls will begin the journey into the cleverest, and most daring, crusades of a lifetime.

The future of the Planet lies in the ability of these three children to follow the synchronistic path laid out before them, to bring forth a Gateway from a hundred years past. A Gateway that allows the dimension of the world within the Gilley Forest to present itself with all it's treasures, as well as it's demons.

The Key to unlock the mystery is already in the hands of our young charge, Benjamin. Will he be able to understand the foreign language and mystical clues left for him by a distant and long forgotten legacy? Only time will tell...and quiet frankly little ones, there really isn't much time left.

Chapter Twelve

The Gateway

The little gold tinkling bells that were placed on the gate by Mr. Chickering on the day he presented the garden to his wife, had begun to chime in the wee hours of the night. Little gold bells that Chantilly Lily had handed to Mr. Chickering on a very hot spring day, as if in a dream. The chimes began their singing in the bright light of the full moon. And on a magical wave of a cool breeze, the sound wafted into Emeline and Graces' room. The sweet, soft smell of roses carried with the sound and surrounded the girls in their dreams.

Emeline sat up first, alert almost instantly.

"Gracie," she called softly, as she shook her sleeping sister laying beside her, "Gracie, it's time. Wake up."

Groggy, and really not willing to shift from her toasty spot among the sheets, Grace finally sat up next to her sister. "It's time for...w..what Em?" yawned Grace.

"It's time to go to the garden Grace. We need to leave now."

This statement from Emeline was like a splash of ice cold water hitting Grace's face.

"Time for...Oh my goodness...you mean it's *time!*"

"Yes, Gracie, we have to go. Get dressed quietly, so as not to make a sound. Stick to the plan Grace. Everything is going to be all right. Chantilly Lily is waiting with Sir Gibbles in the barn. We really need to move faster, time is of the utmost importance, remember Gracie?"

The past couple of weeks had been a flurry of secret activity for the girls. After getting over the shock of meeting the Brownie for the first time, Grace had accepted her path along side Emeline; and was more than willing to help the poor abducted Skeffington children escape from the clutches of the dark Queen. She had begun to feel a sense of security in the knowledge that there were others awaiting their presence on the other side of the Gateway, to assist in this quest. Others with powerful magical abilities...*and weapons.*

She could not bare the thought of those unfortunate children so lonely and scared after being ripped from their loving home. Someone needed to help them. It looked like it was up to her and Em to take on this undaunted task. Large as it may sound, she simply put her mind to rest, and trusted the Whisper would not take them into harms way. She believed in the plan. And right now they were sticking to the plan.

They had gathered a small basket of belongings to take with them, tucked away under their bed. They both believed that with the help of the forest clans and Chantilly Lily's expertise, this matter should resolve itself rather quickly, in as little as just a few days, so they didn't pack much. Mostly bread, apples and some sheep milk cheese made by their mother. As they shimmied out the window onto the porch, Grace hesitated a moment, then leaned back in and reached for the photo of her parents on the bureau. She shoved it into the bottom of the basket and ran after Emeline. They quickly traversed the hilly side yard with it's multiple gofer holes and sheep dropping piles, and made it successfully to the barn without attention.

Chantilly Lily and Sir Gibbles were awaiting the children with dramatic repose.

"Oh, you're here without alarm, I am so pleased," spoke Chantilly Lily in a hushed tone. Tonight the little Whisper was dressed in a long midnight blue cape, with a head dress of green ribbons and white daisies.

"We must proceed with exact actions and timing. Because you are being invited into our world it is imperative that protocol be observed with all caution. Once we are through the Gateway, time is of the essence for us to move promptly into cover. Sethina will be awaiting our arrival to tarry us swiftly to our safe domain. She and the others have already set up camp a fortnight ago. All the heads of the clans have gathered in union and deliberation. We will strategize our timing with all the Set clans.

"The other heads of the Whisper clans, as well as the Fairy, Elf and Brownie Chancellors will all be present. I am most urgent to meet up with King Tsula, the head of the Warrior clan of Whispers. To witness this great warrior straddled to the back of the most magnificent creature of the air, the heroic red hawk Mott, is simply breathtaking. His ability to infiltrate into enemy territory is unsurpassed by none. I am curious to hear of his plans to silence the Queen from our charade. We already have Briggins Jin calculating some theories and working with the Or'aut Set to come up with some sort of shield to deflect the darkest of magic. And I believe...."

Chantilly Lily cut off her words abruptly. Both girls just stood utterly dumfounded, staring at the Whisper.

"Oh, my," Chantilly Lily gestured with her eyes towards Gibbles and blinked. She took a deep breath and continued at a slower pace. "I suppose I have given you both too much information to gather in your uneducated worldly minds at present. Please, I would give you a moment to reflect, however, it is most urgent that we begin our stages of preparation as..." Emeline cut off the Whisper, "Who is Briggins Jim and what are the Or rot set?"

"It is pronounced Or' *Aut* Set little one, and they are the specialty metal working clan of the Gnomes. And Briggins *Jin* is another comrade in arms. He is the General of the Alchemist Whispers. He has a brilliant mind and a plethora of knowledge to do with all things regarding the science and chemical equations in nature. Truly his genius is all encompassing. With the help of the Or' people, they will come up with something of rare force to render us safe from the Queen...I am certain of it."

Then Grace stepped closer to the Whisper, and with the smallest of movements, and a tear in her quiet quivering voice spoke, "This sounds b..bigger than..than I had ever imagined. I am now wo... wondering dear Lady..."

At this point all eyes were upon Graces sweet frightened upturned face, with the reflection of the bright full moon that was peeking in from the gap in the roof in her big dark eyes.

"...we will see our parents again, kind Whisper...yes?"

And before another word could be spoken the powerful scent of roses permeated the barn. Without warning a sound such as never heard before in the presence of humans; a resonance, like the entire world being ripped wide open, shattered the silence. Grace put her hands to her ears and squeezed her eyes shut. Emeline turned her head to see Gibbles running towards the exit. She quickly spun around, picked up the basket at her feet and grabbed her sister by the arm, pulling her towards the open barn door. In moments they were all running for the garden gate, with it's twinkly gold bells that now sounded like the horns of the heavens blasting upon them. Chantilly Lily was instantly transported to the back of the garden where she waited for the others to arrive.

The moment was ripe. The time was now.

All the roses were in full bloom and surrounded the whole of the garden perimeter. Gigantic and unearthly perfect magenta, pink and orange roses, that began their eerie enchantment, as they grew instantly taller and thick, like a wall...*or more like a fortress.* The trellised flowers and vines surrounding the travelers standing in the middle of the garden, extended to a height far exceeding beyond their original home on the iron fence. The magnificent fullness of the moon was glowing so brightly, the girls had to shade their eyes to deflect the sheer intensity of it. The Magic was working.

The perfume of the flowers was nauseating and dizzying, Emeline had to keep her balance and her wits about her. Clearly she was going to have to take charge and get her sister through the passage as well. Grace could no longer do it on her own.

Emeline looked up to witness the mind shocking anomaly of Chantilly Lily hovering in complete stillness on her floating ball, not a hair was moving, while everything about her was a windy swirling madness...*the eye of the storm.*

However, Emeline's attention was quickly diverted to the cause of the windy upheaval, as she realized that directly behind the Whisper was a giant window-like energy of consecutive circles. For a moment she thought it resembled what a slice of a glass onion might look like, with all it's rings in tight order from large to smallest in the center. The entire window was roughly twelve feet high as well as wide. Then suddenly the circles began moving all at once, in a clockwise motion, and the whole thing looked like a whirlpool of water standing on end, spinning faster and faster, while the force of the winds created from this action rushed at the girls. Emeline saw Sir Gibbles speed past her, and at the last minute he turned to look back at her and wiggled his finger, summoning her to follow.

Emeline put her arms around her now, shell shocked sister, who was huddled as tightly as could be on Em's shoulder niche, and inched her way closer to the watery passage. The force of the wind practically peeled the clothes right off the girls and made it nearly impossible to move. The sound was deafening. When Emeline looked up again at the Gateway it looked to her as if the moon had descended right down from the night sky into the very center of the vortex of swirling circles.

And then suddenly, in one unsuspecting instant, everything became perfectly still. The winds were gone, the moon was back in the heavens, the climbing roses were laying upon the small trellis, and the beautiful sound of the golden chimes sang like a sweet lullaby. The whole planet seemed to slow down. Emeline, with Grace in tow, had now joined...*the eye of the storm.*

The Gateway was still moving in slow motion with it's crystal clear perfectly smooth gel like water. It had a thickness to it. An organic, alive pulse came from this space and a bluish white glow surrounded it. A small hum generated in Emelines head...a very inviting hum. As she looked all around above her at the expanse of this magical fluid entrance to another world, she began to smile. It felt like the garden was levitating, such was the floating stillness around her. All still but the Gateway, which called to her.

Her smile seemed a permanent fixture and she felt utterly and completely calm. The beauty and peace, or was it even *love* she wondered, emanated from this window to another world. Whatever it was Emeline couldn't wait to step through this austere invitation. When she looked back down through the opening she saw Sir Gibbles was on the other side, smiling at them. She smiled back even bigger than she thought possible.

It was like peering through a looking glass that has ripples in it. It magnified the saturation of colors coming from the other side. Everything looked brighter and more spectacular than she had ever seen before. She could see there was a path directly underfoot from the Gateway that lead into the Forest. The path was illuminated with tiny little dots of colored light, and the ground itself looked like it was lit up from beneath somehow. Everything glowed. Everything hummed. And as Emeline walked her comatose sister through the peaceful and beautiful clearness, she realized that the tiny little dots of light had wings. Emeline giggled with delight. The spectacular light show was all consuming and she sadly wished her sister could have witnessed all of this for herself. It was like nothing from a dream. It left her feeling speechless and....*at home.*

As she was stepping out onto the path, with her unending smile from the awe of wonder around her, she felt an uneasy moment of distraction from behind her. She turned in slow motion, as she was pulled out of her reverie of beauty, and saw her father running full force at the wall of light and water. Then the image disappeared. However, the sound of her father's voice echoed in a muffled outcry,

"EM-A-LINE...!!"

And then silence. And then darkness.

For weeks Mr. Chickering attempted to recalculate and duplicate the same circumstances as that fated night when he watched his beloved daughters walk through what looked like a glowing wall of spinning water, into another world at the back of the rose garden. He went over and over every minute detail.

First there was that enormous sound that had ripped him from his deep enchanted sleep, which still haunts him, and probably will for the rest of his life. As will the picture of his daughter looking over her shoulder at him with that strange smile. A smile that broke his heart, as it was the smile of pure joy.

And what was wrong with Gracie? Mr. Chickering thought to himself, *Why was she leaning on Em like that all hunched over? Is she injured, ill, what? Oh, I simply will go mad from the mystery of not knowing what has happened to my children!* Mr. Chickering thought in deep anguish. And the biggest kicker of all, gave Mr. Chickering a sarcastic giggle. *And where does one suppose that confounded Whisper is hiding? She is present in my life every day for months, taking her charge of my family, and now where has she disappeared to? What horror has she guided my wee ones into?*

Because the last time Mr. Chickering actually saw Chantilly Lily, it was through a hole in the world sitting on a floating ball welcoming his daughters into a nightmare. Her, and that mysterious little creature standing below her. *What manner of magic be this place?* he continued in his flurry of silent questions.

Then there was the woman with the long white hair, perched up on the back of what appeared to be a white stag. And had he really seen it, or did he just imagine it, but it looked to him like she had wings?

Wings! Goodness gracious! Big white wings, and she was sitting upon a huge white stag. How can this be so?

So much mystery, so many questions.

However, try as he might, nothing worked. He couldn't sleep, he couldn't eat, the only action he could muster out of himself was to sit on the ground in front of the back garden fence and stare at the roses still growing there.

Then there was his wife, who at this point was completely inconsolable. She was in a state of comatose almost equaled to his daughter Grace. At least that is what Mr. Chickering was beginning to realize.

My poor sensitive little Gracie. I'm sure this was all too much for her senses. She is not made from the same fabric as her sister Em. Even though they are twins, they are very different souls. He was certain that Emeline was the instigator in this journey into the Gilley Forest.

However, his wife hadn't witnessed the girls walking through the Gateway. She arrived at the garden in time to find her husband tearing at the bushes in the back of the garden, screaming their names. And now here they were, weeks later, the walking dead. Mr. Chickering simply planted on the ground at the back of the garden, staring into nothingness. His mind working over time in an attempt to unravel the clue to opening the passage to the other world that had swallowed up his daughters.

I'm missing something important. What is it? he continued with his inner dialog. Then one day, many weeks later, as he sat next to the spot where the water wall had manifested, he felt his heart lighten for a moment as he thought of his sweet girls. Suddenly out of the corner of his eye he thought he saw some kind of movement beside him. He turned to face the spot in the air, but shortly let the illusion go as hopeful thinking, and returned to his memories of happier times spent.

Deep in his thoughts of the love he felt for his little girls, he touched on that place that lives only in a father's heart of hearts and with this full love and innate conviction, he absently spoke, "I intend to find my girls. You are not going to stop me." No sooner did he say these words and feel the love that was a part of them, he saw it again, a small movement in the air in front of him. It was like the ripples in a stream or lake, when a drop of rain, or a stone, has landed on it's glassy surface....*rings*. A small undulation of watery consecutive rings, transparent enough to view the roses growing up the side of the fence behind it. Then as quickly as he saw it, it was gone.

"What was that? Did I really see that?"

It was reminiscent of the same stuff the watery porthole consisted of in his memory, on that fated night two months before. His heart began to beat a bit quicker and his breathing started to speed up.

"Dear Lord, what was I doing, what was I thinking and saying. What was different this time that it produced some kind of action? Please, I beg you, help me to see the answer."

So he sat in the exact same spot and attempted to recreate his entire energy, down to where he placed his hands. He focused on feeling the same feeling in his heart, and grabbed onto the picture of the girls in his mind's eye. Then he spoke the words again, remembering the exact sequence.

"I will..no no... I believe I said intend, yes, I am most certain of it! I *intend* to find my girls. You are not going to stop me."

And there it was, clear as day....a small ripple of rings in the air in front of him. This time he reached forward and poked his finger into the dimensional thick wave of energy that when protruded caused the ripple to expand. He quickly pulled his hand back and the tiny window of watery light disappeared for a second time. Mr Chickering tried to catch his mind before it left him. When suddenly a great calm rushed over him and he began to smile.

Then quickly as was the first response, his mind began racing in all directions at once, when he realized what he had done. He could not contain his excitement and sprang to his feet, and off he ran yelling at the top of his lungs for Mrs. Chickering to come outside. He ran up to the front porch and pulled open the screen door, still hollering with urgency. He tore through the farmhouse to the back room where he found his unstable wife, lifeless, sitting and staring out the window into the Gilley Forest.

"Mrs. Chickering I need you to come see this! It's something, it's something *Big*! I believe I have gained knowledge of the list of actions needed to manifest the passage to the other world. You must come with me now. I need you!"

Mrs. Chickering moved her head, as if in a dream, to look up at her now frantic husband. When Mr. Chickerings' words could finally get through her deeply felt pain, she blinked.

"What... is this... you are saying? Have you...have you found my daughters Mr. Chickering? Where are my Grace and Emeline...are they here now?"

Mrs, Chickering was on the verge of babbling when Mr. Chickering took her by her shoulders and yanked her up out of the rocker. He shook her till her head might snap off.

"My dearest love, listen to me, please. You must come back to your senses, I need your assistance. I have figured out the mystery. We need to prepare to enter the passage into the forest to go after our precious girls. Please I'm begging you my love, come back to me. I can no longer bear this solitude I have been suffering on my own. *COME BACK THIS INSTANT*!" he shouted.

And with this Mrs. Chickering looked up into her husbands eyes and tears filled her. She leaned her head in on his chest and put her arms around him...she was home now.

Mr. and Mrs. Chickering were standing in the back of the garden in the wee hours of the night, with their own little basket of supplies, to carry them into another world. After Mr. Chickering had explained in detail the events that lead him to his discovery, he was able to put the last key into the lock of mystery.

"What is needed to facilitate this entire excursion is this, my dear," he had said to his now alert and willing wife. "Well, actually, it wasn't too much thought to realize the full moon had played a huge role in this conversion, and of course the roses, which I am hoping will still hold their magic. Although it appears they are quite under the influence of enchantment as their blossoms are still in utter beauty. However, the main thing I will share with you right now is this; it suddenly came to me when I was looking at the oddity of floating water wheels in front of me. It became ridiculously obvious to me in fact, that tonight happens to be...*a full moon!* So the stars are with us my darling Mrs. Chickering, the stars are with us!"

Mrs. Chickering stood beside her husband and took a deep breathe in anticipation of what was to follow.

"Do you really believe this is going to work? I did not see this strange occurrence as you have witnessed, and it just sounds all so unreal to my senses. Yet my girls are gone, and I must believe we will bring them back, whole and in one piece. So do please begin the process Mr. Chickering. I am here beside you, and I shall center my mind with your words."

Mr. Chickering looked lovingly at his terrified wife, and stole a moment to kiss her forehead. The last bit of information came to him earlier that day when he touched the liquid illusion in the garden.

It was my words, he thought with interest. However, not just the words, he realized...it was so much more than that. It was the power, the motivation...the *intent*...covering his words that matter the most. When he placed the deep love of his daughters, and the unwavering intention to find them into one action...the passage appeared.

So now as they stood together under the brightness of the full moon, they waited with baited breathe for the events to unfold.

And unfold they did.

And Mr. and Mrs. Chickering walked through the same magical Gateway that their two daughters had themselves, ventured through two months before. As they stepped through with the same awe and admiration, they stopped and both turned around and watched as the world they had known all of their lives, disappeared in front of their faces.

They were never to see their beloved farm again. As this journey into another world of deep enchantment held them captive for the next 100 years.

Oh my, well here we are now, my sweet little adventurists, the point I have been promising you from the beginning of this eventful saga. The past and the present have finally caught up with each other. The two worlds are going to collide and that's when all the magic can truly begin. So as once was said by some long forgotten poet of yours.

'Fasten your seat belts....it's going to be a bumpy ride!' Or was it night? I always get that one confused, but never the fuss, either way, hold on tight.   D.T.

Chapter Thirteen

Making A Plan

The last two weeks had Annabel and Benjamin learning an ancient foreign language, deciphering a code and making a plan.

Both Annabel and Benjamin had searched deep within themselves for the understanding of the extraordinary puzzle placed before them. They each in their own way thought through the possible ramifications of the odd circumstances they mysteriously found themselves seeped in.

Benjamin vacillated between complete and utter fear, to the polar opposite of all encompassing exhilaration. He felt like everything he had experienced with his intuitive nature brought him to this place of a deeper understanding of the choices he needed to make in his life. He had more clarity in trusting what he was being directed towards. He felt he needed to follow where he was most unquestionably being lead.

He knew with every ounce of his being that something significant, something life changing, would unfold when he met the Grandfather Tree face to face. He knew this tree had intelligence and wisdom. It was a living breathing creature, with a treasure of knowledge locked inside. He knew the Grandfather Tree was waiting for him and he was ready to go. These things, these strange occurrences, all meant something, and Benjamin McTish choose to follow the path placed before him and see what he would find on the other side.

Annabel believed that everything had come to them in a specific, calculated order. She believed as Benjamin had stated, *'This all meant something.'* Mathilda's words still echoed in her brain, *'Like it was already planned out and everything, just waiting for us.'*

She was right, it was all laid out before them to examine and explore. She had to agree, this was no coincidence. Everything felt utterly choreographed and directed by an unseen force. A force that was far too powerful to resist. In as much as there was an immense aura of fear surrounding her decision, she knew inherently that she and her sister, guided by Benjamin, would make it safely to the Grandfather Tree. She knew, as did Benjamin, they were meant to do this.

"And besides," her baby sister had said to her, "don't you want to be a part of something as remarkable as finding a magical tree and little colored fairy lights?"

Of course no one needed to convince Mathilda of anything. She was picking out her traveling outfit the very next day. "I mean after all, if you're going to meet a fairy princess, you better dress the part," was Mathilda's logic.

So school was out and Claire was preoccupied with her fund raiser. She had given up on the hopes of finding a nanny any time soon, now that the summer holiday had begun. And at the coaxing of her husband, determined that the girls could handle their days with the help of Benjamin's grandmother should they need assistance. At least until she could procure the perfect replacement for Mrs. Longpotts, who, as she jokingly said to Edward, *Had apparently vanished, into thin air.*

And the children were planning the adventure of a lifetime.

"Benjamin, what's the big rush to get us over here?" Mathilda questioned, as they all walked into the garden shed single file.

"I'll tell you Mathilda, once we get inside and make sure that no one else is around."

"Well, who the heck would be around? There's never anyone round here cept us, Benjamin. You really are pearnoid," said Mathilda to her friend.

"That's par-*a*-noid twerp," spoke up Annabel with a grin on her face.

"*Whatever.* You know what I mean," Mathilda responded with a bruised ego.

"Oh geez Mathilda, I'm just kidding you. Sometimes you're so sensitive," said Annabel.

"Whatever," slammed Mathilda.

"So anyway, what *is* going on Benjamin?" continued Annabel.

"Well, I know this may come as a bit of a surprise, but I figured out where the garden is." He waited to see their reactions. Both Annabel and Mathilda stared at Benjamin, speechless. It took a moment to really sink in and then Annabel spoke first.

"Are you kidding me? Benjamin, how?....what?...really, are you joking?"

"Yeah, what's the deal Benjamin? How did you figure it out?" added Mathilda.

"Okay, so we've been racking our brains trying to figure out where this mysterious garden is. We've been looking for clues for two weeks now and nothing. We keep going over and over the whole primer and still nothing. Then finally it hit me."

"What Benjamin, what hit you already?" cut in Annabel.

"Yeah, what already?" echoed Mathilda.

"After getting tired of studying the primer, I happened to glance over at the maps sitting there. I just kept staring at them, not really thinking of them in particular and then I just got it. You were right Annabel in thinking they are maps of Grandlochcheshire from a long time ago. Actually 101 years ago!"

"What? How did you figure that out Benjamin?" asked Annabel in shock.

"See, the primer is just a close-up of a farm, it doesn't show anything around it other than the Gilley Forest, which is a long stretch of land, so it could be anywhere, even in another county. The maps are different, they sort of connect. When you lay the first map down and put the next two side by side below it, then the next two below these, you can see the whole lay out of the entire city and it's surrounding counties, it becomes one big map. And you can see that each page has a number in the bottom corners."

The girls quickly went to spread out the maps in the proper order. Sure enough there were the numbers printed on the bottom corners.

"But there are five pages Benjamin, and a year only has four numbers, what are the others? Let's see, there's 15 and 06, explain please," said Annabel.

"It's the month and day."

"But there's no month that is 15, I don't get it," said Annabel.

"That's because the month is second in a lot of old English writings. So you can see the first page has a 15 in the left corner, and a 06 the bottom right corner. The map just below it has a 1 on the right corner and there's a 9 on the left corner of the map next to it, making that combination read 19. The two maps below those have a 1 in the right corner in the map on the left, and the map on the right has a 0 on the left, making that combination a 10. So that would make it 15, June, 1910. That's 101 years ago exactly."

"Wow! Benjamin, I can't believe you figured that out," said Mathilda.

"Really, that is pretty amazing. But how does that show us where the farm is?" questioned Annabel.

"Well, I started thinking about Grandlochcheshire and what it was like a hundred years ago. What was happening back then? Was there something in it's history that was news or a scandal perhaps? This is a small town and families have lived here for years and years. Look at my grandparents, I mean they all originally came on down from Scotland I think they told me, a long time ago. But the McTish family has have been in this area for over a hundred years or something, and in this house, like 50 years. And your father's family has been here just as long my grandfather told me."

The girls both nodded to each other.

"So I was just staring at the maps and looking at the date and suddenly it came to me....the Chickering farm."

Mathilda looked at Benjamin with a frown on her forehead, "The Chickering farm? What the heck is the Chickering farm Benjamin?"

Annabel echoed her sister this time, "Yeah, what's the Chickering farm?"

"It's an old folk story around these parts. I heard it when I first came to live with my grandparents and completely forgot about it until last night in bed."

"What's a folk story?" asked Mathilda.

"It means it's like the local rumor, or story, of a family, or like a legend that gets passed down for years. You know like a haunted house in a neighborhood, something like that," explained Annabel.

"Oh, you mean like that story about the lady and the cats in that old house over by where gramps lived?" asked Mathilda, excited.

"Yeah, just like that."

"Oh, my goodness Benjamin! It was the creepiest house in the whole world! Really, I swear it was haunted with dead cat ghosts. You could hear them meowing in the middle of the night...*ahhh*!" added Mathilda.

"Wow, that is weird" said Benjamin. "But, this one is weirder. This one is about an entire family that mysteriously disappeared from their farm with no trace what so ever. They just simply vanished! *And* what's even more strange is that some other kids went missing back then as well. Something really weird was definitely going on back then," said Benjamin with wide eyes.

"Yikes! So you really think this is the same farm?" asked Annabel.

"I have no doubt," replied Benjamin.

"Wow! Really Benjamin, why?" asked Annabel, amazed at his certainty.

"Because the legend speaks about a special rose garden, and how brilliant these particular roses were. They were the talk of three counties and still are to this day actually."

"Roses? Okay, so what do roses have to do with anything, I don't understand?" queried Annabel.

Benjamin looked straight at Annabel, then down to Mathilda and back up to Annabel.

"Because every time I have a vision, especially like the one when the Mac Lady looked at me....they're always surrounded with the overpowering scent of roses. It fills my head to the point that I get nauseous and that's when the darkness comes. And if that isn't enough for you, the clincher is that the farm backs right up against the Gilley Forest."

The girls just looked at Benjamin. No one said anything until Mathilda finally spoke. "Blimey. Well Benjamin, how do we get to this farm, and when are we going?"

Annabel couldn't say anything yet. She was lost in the synchronicity that had been placed before them. How every single step was simply put one before the other. The Universe was definitely attempting to get their attention and she was listening now with all burners lit.

"I brought a current map of the city to see if we could gage the route and how long it will take to get there. There have been some definite changes with some of these roads, it's a bit confusing I must admit."

"Let me see," said Annabel, "You're right, this looks way more complicated. There's so many more icons and symbols for things"

"Hey, wait a minute you guys," jumped in Mathilda, "Don't you think that if we were supposed to look at a new map they would have left *that* one? Maybe we should just stick to the old maps and get going already."

Benjamin and Annabel looked at each other and grinned.

"Well, she's got a good point there," spoke up Benjamin, still grinning from the simplicity of Mathilda's comment.

"Of course I do," responded Mathilda, and then continued, "I mean really, what's the big deal? This isn't that big of a place, right?"

Benjamin shook his head.

Mathilda, satisfied with his response continued, "So I say we just figure out the best way to get to this farm... Hey! Wait a minute, how do we know the farm is still there? I mean that was a really long time ago."

Annabel looked over at Benjamin, "Oh wow, that's a really good question. I mean there's no way an abandoned farm would still be sitting around after a hundred years, no matter how cute and tiny this little town is."

"Actually, the farm is absolutely still in tack," said Benjamin.

"What!" cried Annabel.

"Yeah, my grandfather told me that there was some legal situation that prevents it from being taken over or demolished. The only thing that was removed from the farm were stacks of wood piled up next to the barn. I think he said that the family had cleared some land on the edge of the forest, and left these wood piles untouched for years. I really don't know all the details. All I know is that the barn and farm are still sitting there, the same as always, empty."

Annabel opened her mouth to speak when Benjamin cut her off at the pass. "Oh, bugger and blast! I can't believe it! I just remembered my grandfather told me that he had bought that timber from the farm at auction, like thirty years ago. He built this garden shed with the wooden planks left on the farm!"

They all quickly surveyed the tiny room they were standing in, each with a look of complete amazement.

"Well, I'll be gobsmacked!" was all Mathilda said.

"Benjamin, you mean to tell me that this is the same wood from the farm? The farm with the roses, and some secret entry into the Gilley Forest? The same farm that some family vanished from a hundred years ago, that has some mysterious deed protecting it? Are you freaking kidding me!" Annabel practically shouted.

Benjamin nodded his head, still involved in his own utter amazement at the meaning of everything in front of him.

"Yeah.....this is really getting weird," said Benjamin.

So the plans were in the making and the Muskydeers were becoming extremely restless waiting for their perfect moment. It was going to take a little finesse to keep all parental units from questioning what it was exactly that they were up to. They had to pack provisions, and not being quite certain as to what they were up against, made it a challenge to know just what they needed to stow away. They determined that with Mathilda's younger age it made sense to cart her and their supplies in the red wagon. They would bring Cubby along for protection.

They figured they needed food and water for at least four days. According to the map, they estimated it would take them a full day, into the late evening, to get to the Chickering farm. Then they needed to get through the passage, which was still a mystery to them. They weren't certain if it was visible or if something needed to start the thing moving. or if the primer explained it deeper. So they were uncertain of the timing included to pass the secret entry. It looked like it was a three day journey to the Grandfather Tree once they were through the passage however, but they were stumped as to what to expect.

Annabel broke the silence.

"I've been studying these words in the primer for weeks now and it's really something unique. It's so interesting to me, figuring this out, but I think I finally have a better understanding of this language. I mean, the way it's all written out here, it's not so hard to read because it actually has a bit of our language mixed in to explain the words. Who ever put this together must have figured someone like me was going to be reading this someday, I swear, because these words have a deeper meaning.

"It's not just what you see in print or the actual word only, you need our language to make sense of theirs. Like this word Mar ah, it means water breath, not just water or breath, but both. And it doesn't just mean water breath all by itself really, it needs to be placed with the Set or Fet to get the whole meaning. No wait, that's not it, sorry, Set and Fet only refer to earth or land. It looks like the word Set distinguishes the forest tribes, or families. But then there is this other word Fet and it seems to mean the same thing regarding families, only in a different place. And I know this sounds weird, but I think it means underground. So Set would mean above and Fet below. Where Bri represents the ocean group and Lac would mean lakes or streams. So the whole word would be Mar ah'aut Bri or Mar ah'aut Lac.

"Oh yeah, they have this word aut in almost all of them. And from what I can figure that word means gold or golden. So the actual translation of the word Mar ah'aut Bri would mean golden breath of the sea. And Mar ah'aut Lac would be golden breath of the lake. It's really something special. It's almost like poetry...or umm....Oh, let me just show you what I've got so far. Here's the list of words," and put the piece of paper she had written as a glossary of words in front of Benjamin.

or	metal/ore
Mar ah	water breath
Kor	blood/soil
Win	?
Til	land/soil
Bri	salt water/sea/ocean
Aut	gold/golden
Hew	chip/cut/stone
Set	forest/woodland, above
Lom	earthen
Fet	earth/subterranean, below
Lac	lake/stream
Ben	mountain
coranim	heart/spirit/life

"Now here are these main words put together to create one word. Or'aut Set. If you look at it literally it would say, metal gold forest, or the way I've translated it to be golden ore of the forest. But then here is the word Or'aut Fet. So that would translate to metal, gold, earth. So I'm thinking these are the same family of people only one is from the forest above and one is from..."

"Below?" cut in Benjamin with a sharpness in his tone.

"Yeah, I know it sounds looney. But what about any of this sounds normal? I think we need to look at things in a....Oh, I don't know, in the paranormal world or something. I mean really, does any of this sound like anything we've ever known or heard of before? No, it sounds like some fantasy movie or fairy tale. But I'm doing what I can to make sense of all of this without blocking us in. Just taking it for what it is right in front of my face.

"So if what I'm seeing is correct, there appears to be four main groups of people, forest, earth, sea and mountain. They have their own names and symbols to represent them. And there is something about air, but I haven't figured that one out yet. But they trickle down to basically two main groups, forest and earth. Or in literal terms, Set and Fet, above and below."

"Well, I for one think it makes perfect sense," entered Mathilda, "I mean after all, fairies live under oak trees and sometimes they live inside little fairy hills, so that's definitely under the ground. I think that maybe that's where the door goes, right to the fairy city....*underground.* I mean where the heck do you guys think the door goes to anyway, because it doesn't make sense to have a big door that goes nowhere?"

Both Annabel and Benjamin looked at Mathilda.

"How does she do that?" asked Benjamin.

"Tell me about it. She's just thinks outside of the box that's all. And, she's usually right. I think she may be on to something, because..." Mathilda butt in, "Hey, I'm right here you know, I can hear everything you guys are saying."

"Okay tike, I get it, sorry," replied Annabel, and then continued with her interpretation.

"Down here I figure these are names of people. There's a small list, but once I got the basic break down of the language, these just didn't fit anywhere, and they sound like names to me. I think they're the names of important people, maybe leaders or something, because they all have this odd symbol next to them. Like here, this looks like Sethina, and they have something to do with the forest because Set is next to it, but then there is this second marking. There are only three of these types of markings. Sethina, like I said is one, and Morel is right next to this one and it has the same symbol, so I'm thinking they may be related somehow. But then there's this one that kinda stands out alone, Tar Vigorn. And, it has a different marking next to it and it's written bigger, so I'm thinking this is the big cheese or the leader or something."

The moment Benjamin heard the name sweat popped out on his upper lip and his heart jumped off beat. He went a bit pale and held his breath for a moment. Anyone else would not have noticed this subtle change in his demeanor, but it was not at all lost on Mathilda. She frowned and looked up at Benjamin.

"Hey what's up with that name Benjamin? Your face went all wonky when Bellie said it."

Annabel looked up at her sister then over at Benjamin. "What are you talking about Tildie?"

"Benjamin. He started sweating when you said that last name, Tar something. It means something to him, just look."

"Benjamin, is that true? What does it mean?" quizzed Annabel.

Benjamin just stood there, attempting to unscramble his brain. Everything was moving so quickly and his mind was spinning. He didn't think this was the right time to tell the girls about the dark Queen. He just wanted to get to the Grandfather Tree in one piece. Then he would fill the girls in on the identity of the cloak of darkness...*Tar Vigorn*.

"It's nothing, really. I'm just feeling hot in here and everything is just overwhelming right now. You've done a smashing job with the language Annabel, brilliant really. There's no way I could have figured any of this out. Well done you. And Mathilda is quite right, that door must lead to some where. And I believe that if you have deciphered that the meaning of this word is below, then below it is."

They all looked at each other and took a breath.

"It looks like we're going underground mates."

Mathilda grinned from ear to ear and repeated, "Yup. We're going underground!"

Chapter Fourteen

The Journey Begins

The day was finally here. All provisions had been put in place and everyone was as ready as they were ever going to be for the journey ahead of them.

Benjamin had awoken that day with a lump in his throat. He suddenly wished he had no knowledge of secret keys and magical locks in giant doors. He wished his life was a life of simplicity. One where mothers and fathers had dinner parties and families went on vacations and the water sprinklers went off everyday precisely at nine am. But that was just not to be for Benjamin McTish. Suddenly he was leery about leaving his grandparents.

What if something happened? What if he didn't make it back? he wondered. They would not survive such a horror, not with the pain of his parents disappearance. However, as he held all of this guilt and trepidation, he knew there was no looking back at this point. He had to move forward now. He was following the direct path placed before him. One could only hope it was a path leading to a greater good for Benjamin.

He ran downstairs where his grandmother was waiting to say goodbye to him. He had told her they were off on an adventure around the town and would be gone all day.

Benjamin looked at his grandmother with her sweet smile, wearing her worn out denim garden over alls, matched up with shocking green rubber work shoes, and gave her a big hug.

"Oh my boy, my precious boy. You are so deeply loved Benjamin," his grandmother said.

Benjamin looked into his grandmothers' eyes with concern.

"Is everything all right Granny?"

His grandmother always said that she loved him, but there was something very different in this comment. He felt something different in her embrace. It was almost like she knew he would be gone for a while. Maybe quiet possibly longer than he had planned, truth be told; a possibility he didn't want to admit to himself. However, there was no way his grandmother could know what was going on. Benjamin couldn't seem to get a grasp on it, but something was up, and he simply stared at her.

"No my sweet boy, there is nothing wrong. All is perfectly right with the world. Would you care for a little nosh before you go?"

Benjamin shook his head. She looked into his eyes and then she continued, "I know you have been so terribly lonely and lost for so long my boy. It seems your life has been all sixes and sevens. Really, I'm so very grateful for the Wickcliff girls."

Quiet rightly, thought Benjamin in agreement.

"I just want you to know that your grandfather and I couldn't possibly be more proud of who you are Benjamin, of the type of person you have become. You're a good boy, and I know you will grow to be a good man. Just be safe Benjamin. Keep your head on your shoulders and remember you are a special boy and your courage is commendable. You can over come any obstacles set on your path. So off you go now, have a jolly good time of it."

And off he went.

The girls were waiting in the garden shed. They had all rations of food and water as well as supplies packed tightly in the wagon and were waiting for

Benjamin to join them. Cubby was noosed up to the wagon and ready to go.

"Finally!" said Mathilda with a blast of energy, as Benjamin entered the garden shed. She was standing next to the wagon. Her traveling attire consisted of a purple tutu with gold colored capri tights beneath. She added an aqua tee shirt that had the logo for *The Blues Billies* written across the front. She wore her old stand by comfy bright green Converse high tops, with the sparkly purple laces. However, she packed her soft baby pink ballet slippers that laced up her calves, just in case she was invited to dance with the Fairies. And even though it was summer she decided to bring along her green mittens with the blue stars on them and the matching stripe scarf. After all, it very well likely would be chilly underground. And of course she wore her round blue lens rock star sunglasses. Benjamin just stood looking through her, still deep in thought about his grandmother's odd behavior.

"Is everything okay Benjamin?" asked Annabel when she saw the look on his face.

"Huh? Oh yeah, I'm fine. It's just that my grandmother was acting kinda peculiar"

"What do you mean? How?" asked Annabel.

"I don't know, it was weird. I swear it was like she knew I was going to be gone for a while. Like she knew about everything," said Benjamin.

"Are you kidding Benjamin? How could she possibly know anything? Right?" asked Annabel.

"Right, she couldn't, I suppose. I don't know? Either way, she seemed perfectly fine with me going."

"Okay then, can we go now?" said Mathilda impatiently.

"Yes, Tildie, we're leaving now, right Benjamin?" asked Annabel as she looked at him.

Benjamin shook his head fiercely for a moment to release all concern and doubt from his brain about his grandmother and smiled.

"Yes indeed Mathilda. We're off."

And so the three best friends and their trusted dog left to seek out the adventure of a lifetime, towards a magic door that would lead them to an even greater magical underground world.

The beginning of the day went rather smoothly as they walked beside Cubby who was pulling the wagon with Mathilda sitting at the helm. They all felt excited with the start of their journey now under way. They found that the maps had given them very perfect guidance finding all the lefts and rights they needed to take. They seemed to be left to themselves by passers by, who barely glanced at the colorful trio being lead by a dog. When they traveled by a small country candy store they quickly voted unanimously to turn back and stock up on a few of their favorite sweets.

As they walked and walked they talked about all the possibilities that were before them. They laughed and joked, they even sang for a bit, lead by Mathilda of course. Every now and then they took a break and had some water or juice. Later in the day they sat in a park to have a bit of lunch where they discussed the different scenarios they could possibly encounter, just to be prepared. They stopped to give Cubby pee breaks from time to time, as well as their own needs. They had to admit that all in all it was a pleasant day of conversing and travel. The sights of the little town were exhilarating to the girls as they had not yet explored any remote parts of their new home. In reality, neither had Benjamin.

The day was going by and the sun was starting to find it's home lower in the sky. Slowly it was beginning to feel like a very long and daunting journey to the young trio. The newness and the excitement of this exploration was beginning to fade, and the overwhelming anxiety began to creep in. *What would their families do when they found them missing?* As the day moved past them, and the night was beginning to show it's face, everyone of the Muskydeers wondered if maybe they hadn't made a huge mistake.

"Wow, I bet Mom is going to be freaking out pretty soon, huh Bellie?" said Mathilda with a bit of a tear in her voice.

"Yeah, I was just thinking the same thing. She's going to lose it completely. But don't worry Tildie, I left her a note on my desk. So when she finally goes up there to get a clue, she'll see it. It explains everything, okay?" said Annabel with reassurance.

"What do you mean it explains everything?" asked Benjamin with alarm.

"Well, I couldn't just disappear with my little sister and our dog for four days and not let her know where we were going and how important this was," replied Annabel defensively.

"Annabel, if she gets that letter sooner than later, everything is a bust. They could even be waiting for us at the farm right now for all we know. All our efforts would be wasted. Why would you do something like that Annabel?" chided Benjamin.

"Geez Benjamin, I'm not stupid, stop worrying. She's not going to go upstairs for a while yet anyway."

"How do you know?" his anger aroused.

"Oh my god Benjamin! Well, first of all, she's working on her fund raiser and then she was meeting some people for dinner and said she wouldn't be home until late. And then my father will be on an over niter for his work tonight, so we don't have to worry about him. I told my mother we were having dinner at your house and she thinks we're camping in your back yard. Didn't you see the tent set up out behind the garden shed?" quipped back Annabel.

"Yeah," said Mathilda, "didn't you see it? We put it up early this morning out behind the shed so your grandmother wouldn't see us. You can see it from our house."

Benjamin looked solemnly at the girls.

"You won't believe it but Bellie put a timer on the camp lamp so it turns off later. And then she put piles of blankets to look like we were inside sleeping. She even took one of my big stuffed animals and made it look like Cubby was with us. Mom's never going to figure it out! She'll just look out the window and think we're there. How cool is that?" chuckled Mathilda.

Annabel continued in a strong defensive tone.

"See Benjamin, everything is okay. Your grandmother will think we came in and went straight out to the tent. Besides she really doesn't pay much attention to us coming and going. And you said she was okay with you leaving anyway, so I can't imagine there would be a problem from her. No one is going to know anything until tomorrow morning. And by then we'll already be on our way into the Gilley Forest. Everything is fine. Cept I just lied to my mother Benjamin, and I'm starting to feel really guilty about it, Okay?"

"Okay," Benjamin softly replied.

Annabel continued her tirade with a huge lump in her throat, "This has been a really long day Benjamin. And now it's starting to get dark, and we've been walking on this little deserted road out in the middle of nowhere, like, fore..EVver it seems. *And* we're still not even at the farm yet. So I'm just a little scared right now!"

Benjamin looked down at the ground and spoke in a guilty tone when he looked back up at Annabel, "Sorry mate, just a bit edgy I guess."

"Yeah, well me too Benjamin!" said Annabel backing down slightly.

Suddenly Mathilda cut into the discourse with surprise in her voice.

"Hey you guys, isn't that the fence we're supposed to be looking for up there?" Mathilda pointed up the road a way, while squinting for a better look, "It looks like maybe there's a sign hanging on the gate too. Maybe that's it?"

Both Annabel and Benjamin jerked around quickly and looked in the direction Mathilda was pointing. Sure enough, even in the growing dusk of evening they could see it, a farm fence thirty yards ahead of them. Benjamin couldn't take his eyes off of it.

"That *absa-bloody-lutely* looks like an old sign on an old fence Mathilda! Quick, let's get there mates!" shouted Benjamin with a spark of hope.

Annabel looked down at here sister when she caught up with the fact that they may actually *BE* at the farm and smiled.

"Good job Tildie! Way to keep an eye out."

"Thanks," smiled Mathilda back.

With that Benjamin got behind the wagon to lend a push to Cubby's pull, while Annabel ran ahead. Arriving first she yelled back at her quickly approaching cohorts.

"This is it! Oh my god! We're here!"

"YA WHO!" screamed Mathilda.

"Oh my god, we made it," continued Annabel in her jubilation, "Look here, it's really worn out, but you can see that it says," as she shined the flashlight beam directly upon the sign for clarity, " The Chickering Sheep Farm est. 1901!"

"1901!" repeated Mathilda with awe, "That's really old. That's like...way old. Gee, how old is that really sissy?" said Mathilda with a wrinkled up forehead.

"Oh geez! I don't know Tildie," replied Annabel too caught up in the confusion and excitement to give the answer, "But it's really old like you said."

However, Benjamin jumped in with the quick deduction, "It's a hundred and ten years ago mates."

"Wow! A hundred and ten years! Oh my Blimey!" responded Mathilda in shock.

"You said it right this time Mathilda, you said it right!" said Benjamin with a chuckle. The tension of moments before having passed, the Muskydeers had themselves a very well needed release of laughter. However, the uncertainty and excitement of discovery lie ahead, and the trio walked with a bit of trepidation down the little road that led up to the farmhouse and barn. They all had eyes as wide as saucers, scanning the fields surrounding them, looking for anything unusual. The moon was beginning it's rise and coming up into it's full pose for that evening, lending a bright light for the children to see where it was they were heading.

"Wow, this is so cool," said Mathilda as they approached the house.

"It's like it was frozen in time or something," observed Annabel, "Look at this Benjamin." She pointed over towards their left to the empty garden yard where she aimed the light on the little worn out sign that hung on the garden trellis. In broken up old painted green letters, the title *The Enchanted Rose Garden* was still somewhat visible.

They all stopped and starred at their surroundings.

"Blimey, this is really something else," said Benjamin, "I wonder what it is we're supposed to see here? Because right now it looks pretty abandoned. I mean there is no scent of roses, let alone any actual roses. This just doesn't make sense to me. I just don't know what we're supposed to do here."

"Well, why don't we go into the house and get out the primer and see if it can tell us anything," said Annabel.

"I'm tired and hungry," whined Mathilda.

"Yeah, me too" continued Annabel, "This has been a really long day. We all need some food, so let's go inside and look around a minute, and set up the camp lights and take a look at the primer. I know it will tell us what we need to do next. I have some notes, so we'll go over those and figure this out. Tildie, I'll set up the sleeping bag for you to curl up on, and me and Benjamin will take care of everything else. Okay?"

"Ooo-kay Bellie," replied Mathilda with a yawn.

"Let's go mates," said Benjamin in the lead. Not wanting to look away from the garden, still utterly confused about the absence of roses. *I just know the roses are important*, thought Benjamin, *Where are they?*

As the children turned and walked away toward the entry to the farmhouse, an unnoticed single perfect magenta rose, at the back of the garden, shown in the bright growing moonlight of the approaching full moon. By the time the Muskydeers were through the rickety screen of the front door, six more roses had fully bloomed in secret.

Once inside Annabel set up the sleeping bag for her sister to lay down on, and Benjamin got out the camping lamp. Before Annabel could hand her sister a sandwich Mathilda was asleep.

"Well, that's that," said Annabel.

"Yeah, looks like she was really knackered. It has been a really long day. I'm actually too wound up to eat right now Annabel, let's just take a look around okay?"

"Yeah, sounds like a good idea. Do you have the flashlight?"

"Yeah, it's right here. Let's go."

They walked through the rooms of the farmhouse, although there weren't many. Only a kitchen and two bedrooms besides the main living area, that held a huge smoke blackened fireplace. When they went into the room that once housed the Chickering twins, both Annabel and Benjamin held their breath. In the blue light of the rising full moon the room had a serene and magical quality to it. One could think someone was actually still sleeping in the bed, such was the energy emanating from this space. However, it was the spotlight from the flashlight that caught the attention of the duo, as it featured a name carved into the left front side of the big headboard...*Emeline.*

"Oh!" was all Annabel said.

Then Benjamin moved the guiding beam over to the right front side of the headboard and there was it's engraved mate, *Grace.*

"It makes it all so real, seeing their names like that," whispered Benjamin.

Annabel nodded in agreement, then whispered, "Why are we whispering?"

"I don't know, something seems odd in here."

Then before either one could have another thought, a loud audible deep sigh came rushing at them. *Someone is in the bed!* realized Benjamin in shock. Both he and Annabel had instant goose bumps and Benjamin nearly dropped the light.

Not being able to take their wide eyes away from the breathing movement of the tiny bundle in the large bed, Annabel grabbed onto Benjamins' arm, and they walked very slowly towards the seemingly sleeping mound of blankets. As they crept closer in silence, Annabel looked at Benjamin and motioned for him to have the light ready to use as a weapon if necessary. Benjamin nodded in understanding and adjusted the handling of the light to become a club. When suddenly out of no where someone jumped up as alive as could be, and stood on the bed facing the two, *eye to eye.* Benjamin dropped the light and Annabel let out a scream.

"Ahh! What is it Benjamin?"

Benjamin didn't answer as he was staring in stunned disbelief at the diminutive being with his hands on his hips standing before them.

"Well, it's about time you three arrived. I was beginning to wonder if Longpotts had done her job or not. Well, never the mind, you're here now and we can move forward. Time is of the essence, as it is under all circumstances. But we really are behind so let's move then shall we? Chantilly Lily will be waiting for us in the garden"

With this the little Brownie jumped down off the bed and turned back to look at the shocked couple. With a very wide grin on his face. "Looks like I got a good fright out of you, Ha! Well, at least not all is lost. Fun for Gibbles. Well, what are you looking at? We need to move now, have I not made myself clear?"

Benjamin and Annabel looked at each other and finally moved their feet in the direction the Brownie was now leading them, as clearly, he was in charge.

"Benjamin, did you hear him say something about Mrs. Longpotts?" asked a stunned Annabel in a low tone.

"You're bloody right I did!" whispered Benjamin back, *I knew there was something off about her*.

As they all walked into the main living area Gibbles tarried over to sit down beside the sleeping Mathilda. *Well, this ought to be a good one,* he thought with delight, prepared to scare the bejesus out of the wee lass. "Who who, here goes," he whispered.

Mathilda began to rustle from her sleep, sensing the fullness of the room. She had heard her sister yell, way deep in her dream, causing her to awaken. Mathilda opened her eyes while stretching, and there sat Sir Gibbles with his big grin only inches away, staring right down at her. Annabel became terribly anxious that Mathilda would completely freak out. But before she could say anything to warn her little sister, Mathilda opened her eyes to see the Brownie standing before her.

"Oh holy socks! Are you kidding me? A *Brownie*! Really and truly? I can't believe I'm seeing this. Tell me I'm awake Bellie. Please!"

Annabel looked at Benjamin in shock, and shook her head, "Are you kidding me? You know what this is and you're not afraid of him?"

"Afraid of what? He's just a Brownie, he can't hurt you or anything. Oh this is just the coolest thing I have ever seen! I think I'm going to pee my pants!"

"And there you have it," responded Benjamin, "Mathilda, how do you know about...*Brownies*, did you say? I mean what on earth do you read?"

Mathilda looked up at the stunned pair.

"Duh...have you heard of the internet? I mean, you can look up anything you want you know. I like Fairies and Elves and magic things, so I read about them. I can't *even* believe I staring at a Brownie right now."

"Well, this is no fun for me. I'm Gibbles the Brownie after all, and Brownie's are supposed to have fun!" said the Brownie to the room.

"Gibbles, is that your name?" asked a very excited Mathilda.

"Well, the impertinence of it all! Of course that is my name. *Sir* Gibbles if you really must know," responded Gibbles with indignation.

"Oh Wow! This is unbelievable! I'm sitting here talking to a Brownie!" was all Mathilda could say.

"All right then," jumped in Benjamin, "So we know you're a Brownie and your name is Gibb...opps, *Sir* Gibbles....fine. Now what are we supposed to be doing here, since I suspect you have the answer?"

Gibbles mused out loud, "How on all the Earth are you three supposed to be the Ones? I think maybe Longpotts got it wrong. Seriously wrong."

Benjamin had enough. First the insults and now there was that name again, *Longpotts*. He'd had it up to here with all the questions and no answers. It was time for a change in lead. "All right mate, I'm done mucking about here. I'm tired of being led on these wild crazy scenes against my will."

"Oohhh, nothing is ever against the will," interrupted Gibbles with a grin.

"Ahh! Enough!" continued Benjamin in anger. "First some weird old woman looks at me and suddenly I'm running through a forest while someone is chasing me...us...whatever! Then I have a trip down a water tube into a part of the forest that has the biggest tree on the planet with an enormous door. I have a mysterious key that just shows up at my house and now here I am following some old treasure map to an abandoned farm. *Where*, I might add, there is supposed to be a garden of magical roses. And now I'm apparently being insulted by a Brownie, who appears to be a knight or something. I'm done mate! I want some answers, and I want them now. Starting with Mrs. Longpotts, what does she have to do with any of this?"

Gibbles stood and looked at Benjamin, as did Annabel and Mathilda. He suddenly turned around and went over to the corner by the fireplace where there was an old crate that he dragged over and placed in front of the confused trio. He jumped up on top of the crate which placed him in closer proximity to the height of the others and spoke.

"First of all young man, I do not appreciate the tone."

Before Benjamin could defend the comment with another tirade, Gibbles put up his hand to halt him and continued.

"You must be privy of certain circumstances in order to continue, if we are to receive any help from you at all. My mistake for thinking you were aware of the importance of what it is you have been chosen to do. I suppose Longpotts did what she had to do so as not to alert anyone not scheduled."

"Not scheduled? What the heck does that mean?" cut in Annabel.

Gibbles continued in frustration, "If you insist on interrupting Gibbles, we shall miss our transport. And then all shall be lost. And Gibbles will be sent in exile sure enough. Although I suppose then it won't matter much, as the world will be forever lost."

Benjamin looked with alarm at his friends. "Lost? What the bloody hell are you talking about now?"

"Oh dear, this is worse than I had suspected. I mean the Chickering lass' were more than willing in their understanding, but this..oh fiddle fudge."

Annabel's eyes went completely wide.

"The Chickering girls! What do you know about them? I thought that the whole family disappeared a hundred years ago. Benjamin's right, this is getting crazier by the minute. We need some answers before I explode."

With this Gibbles jumped down off of his perch and headed towards the door. The children just looked at each other with complete frustration and a query of questions flooding their brains. Finally Benjamin yelled over to the exiting Brownie, "What the bloody hell is going on here? Where are you going now?"

Gibbles simply turned around and faced them, "My job was to wait and direct the children to the garden where the Whisper would be waiting. I fear I can not do more than prescribed at this juncture. I can only pray that Longpotts knew what she was doing, and that you three are the ones we have been waiting for. If not, then all hope is gone and that makes me very sad."

"The garden did you say?" followed back Benjamin with force. "Oh yeah, we've seen *The* garden. There's nothing there! All this mystery about the roses and it's empty, dead, nothing but weeds."

"What's a Whisper?" butted in Mathilda.

Annabel just simply stood looking at the tiny little man in the burlap hat, her resign to the confusion evident.

Gibbles stood in the doorway and looked hard at the three seemingly inept beings standing before him. He felt complete hopelessness. He believed Longpotts was certainly in dire error with these three fledglings before him. And yet, when he took a deep breath and looked deeper into the matter, he realized that all efforts had been made to get *these* three particular children to the farm. It just couldn't have been an error.

"Every thing happens for a reason," he absently said out loud to the room, as he knew this rule of fate to be a certainty, as did every other being in the Gilley Forest. So somehow he was mistaken in thinking any thing otherwise. After a moment of silence he finally spoke in a quiet tone.

"I ask for pardon of my insolence. It is not protocol for me to judge the matter inaccurate or not. My humble apologies. I was put in the charge of waiting for your appearance and to bring you safely to the garden. I placed the key in the hands of the young squire as directed. And now I shall do my sworn duty to deliver you to the Whisper. She will know what it is that is needed in this matter. Please gather your belongings and follow me to the garden. As was stated at the beginning of our meeting, time is of the essence." And he turned around and walked through the broken down screen door. As he had his back to them while exiting, suddenly Benjamin saw it sparkle in the moonlight...a small brass ring strung with an array of colorful ribbons attached to his waist belt, as it swayed side to side.

"The key, with the tattered green ribbon? *HE'S* the one who put the key in the garden shed? Is that what he just said Annabel?" cried Benjamin.

"That's what he said," she responded.

And suddenly, as if from a dream, the sound of the most beautiful singing began to fill the air. It was the saddest of laments sung in the most pristine of tenor voices ever heard. Benjamin began to shake. His head started to spin and before he could utter another word the powerful scent of roses filled the room and he went into blackness.

"Benjamin, Benjamin, are you all right?" screamed the girls, pulling Benjamin out of his darkness.

"What?....what happened?" he asked, as he realized he was lying on the floor of the farmhouse with the girls beside him on their knees.

"You passed out Benjamin. Just like that, *BOOM!* You hit the ground like a sack of potatoes," answered Mathilda.

"Geez Benjamin, are you okay?" asked Annabel, "That was ridiculous! First your standing right next to me one second and then the next, *crash* you're on the floor. You gotta stop doing this to us already. What's going on? Did you see something? Another tube, or what?"

"Did you smell the roses?" asked Benjamin anxiously.

"*ROSES!* What roses Benjamin, they're all dead, remember?" pushed Mathilda.

Oh I must be completely barking mad! thought Benjamin. "I swear mates, right after I heard the singing the scent of roses filled the room and it was lights out for me."

"Singing? What singing Benjamin?" asked Annabel with concern.

"You mean to tell me neither of you heard the singing either?" asked Benjamin with fear beginning to take over his senses.

"No Benjamin, we didn't hear any singing and we didn't smell any roses. I'm sorry," said Annabel flatly.

With this Benjamin looked out of the broken down front screen and there was Gibbles looking right back at him. They looked at each other for a stale moment and then Gibbles smiled at Benjamin and turned to walk away. And as he did, the beautiful music started again.

"There, that voice, it's *Him*! Can't you hear him, it's as plain as day?"

But then Benjamin realized that it wasn't really so much as plain as day as it was in the background, like an old style Victrola with the volume turned way down. Benjamin sat and stared at the ground in deep thought.

"Benjamin, I'm really getting scared here. I don't understand what is happening to you. You really need to say something that makes sense already or I don't know what will happen. Maybe we should just turn back and go home right now," said a very frightened Annabel.

Benjamin shot a look right up at her and then over to Mathilda, who had tears in her eyes. The instant reality hit him, that in as much as his best mates were beside him, for all intents and purposes, he was on this journey alone. He knew that what was happening was really only happening to him. *Why?* Benjamin had to find out. As Gibbles had said, everything happens for a reason. He knew with every single part of his being that it was indeed his destiny to go to the Grandfather Tree. So he stood up and looked at the sisters and spoke calmly.

"Okay mates, I'm as good as rain. Let's get our gear together and head out to the garden and meet this Whisper, whatever that means. We didn't come all this way and meet up with the likes of a Brownie to turn away now. So let's muster up our courage and stick close together and remember...." Benjamin looked directly into Mathilda's eyes..."It's one for all and all for one...we're in this together mates. Now let's go meet some Fairies."

"Now *THAT'S* all I'm saying Benjamin! I mean who in their right mind would give up the chance to meet little colored lights with wings?" responded Mathilda with a big smile on her face that mixed in with her tears.

Benjamin reached over and wiped her cheeks with the palm of his hand and Mathilda came back to life. Annabel half out of her wits, simply followed directions and began gathering up the sleeping roll and food. And the three Muskydeers walked out of the front door towards the Chickerings' Enchanted Rose Garden.

Chapter Fifteen

When Two Worlds Collide

As the three friends followed the Brownie out to the garden, suddenly something seemed...*strange*. Benjamin looked around the farm as they walked behind Gibbles, scanning the area for a sign of something out of place. He could just *feel* it, whatever *it* was. Letting his radar pull back a bit, Benjamin decided to simply follow the path placed before him, and relegate his fears to the deepest part of his mind. He needed his wits about him and he needed to protect these quirky American girls walking beside him. It was a personal pledge he had made to himself before they left on this journey.

As they passed the barn, Benjamin couldn't help but notice that something looked very familiar about it. Then without warning his memory saw the snippet of his previous vision from the Mac Lady. *He saw himself walking into the dark barn being lead by that melancholy voice, singing an old fashioned folk song.* It immediately all came rushing back at him. *Why it was Sir Gibbles all along,* thought Benjamin with surprise. There he was, clear as day, Gibbles warbling his lamenting ballads in his lonely state, night after night, waiting for Benjamin and the others to catch up with their fate.

Benjamin smiled in acknowledgement of this fact. Once something became clear to him it was a deep sense of freedom.

So he turned back and followed the Brownie right along with his best mates beside him.

"Oh, jeepers! Where's Cubby?" shouted Mathilda.

Annabel looked around with instant anxiety, "Oh wow, I completely forgot about him. Where the heck is he? Cub-by, come here boy, Cub-by."

Crikey, they're right, I don't recall seeing him for quite some time now. Where could he be off to? thought Benjamin.

Mathilda let out another big shout, "CUB-BEE!"

No response.

"Benjamin, I'm worried about him..." but before she could say another word the group was easing towards the side yard that held the garden and suddenly everything became stark.

"O... M...G," was all Mathilda could say.

And Annabel simply muttered, "I don't believe this. This is insane."

They all stopped a few feet before the beautiful black iron gate that housed the gold tinkling bells that were beginning to chime very sweetly in the small breeze of the approaching mid night hour. Above the magnificent gate arched a hand made wooden trellis that held the most perfect climbing peach colored roses any of them had ever seen.

Benjamin stared in an unattached disbelief. Something had clicked over in his brain as he had walked from the house to the garden, and he was now fully accepting the path laid before him. And with this acceptance came a deep and comforting calm. He simply knew to expect the unexpected. Such was the nature of this very extraordinary journey he found himself a part of.

"Of course. I should have realized mates, it's an *enchanted* rose garden after all. And I'm guessing from the looks on your faces, you are both seeing this too?"

And against all odds, the Muskydeers laughed, Annabel included.

"Benjamin, it's amazing! I've never seen anything like it. I keep forgetting that this is all like some big magic dream. I mean, even though I saw that weird

3D map thing, I still forget that this is what this is....*magic!*" said an amazed Annabel.

Of course Mathilda simply said, " It doesn't seem so scary to me. I like magic."

They walked through the now opened gate and looked about themselves at the complete and utter beauty surrounding them. The moon was on the verge of splitting open from fullness, while the immensely bright light shown on the entirety of the enchanted garden with a clear bluish cast hue. It was the perfect picture of enchantment anyone could ever have imagined. The aroma was intoxicating, with a bit of an edge.

"Gee, I feel a little light headed, must be all the excitement," said Annabel.

"Yeah, me too" said Mathilda. And then before anyone could have another thought in their minds, there she was right before them, floating on her big orange balancing ball with the pink stars...Chantilly Lily, the Whisper.

"Shazam!" whispered Mathilda in utter awe.

"I think we're gonna need a stronger word for this one mate," responded Benjamin.

"Mathilda, do you know what she is by any chance? I mean, ah, I'm guessing that this is what a Whisper is...but have you read up on any of these...umm...people and what they do besides float in the air?" asked Annabel, hopeful.

"No sissy, I never heard of these ones before. But I'm just going to plotz right here and now, I swear. Bellie, she's wearing a tutu!"

Annabel reached behind her little sister and tugged on Benjamin's arm without looking away from the Whisper, "What the heck does plotz mean?"

"You got me on that one mate, it's not British."

"It's Yiddish," spoke up Mathilda, "Miss. Levinsky, that cool lady from down the street with the pretty curly hair, is teaching me some new words. It means I'm going to faint."

Annabel and Benjamin just shook their heads and grinned.

"Yeah, well I'm right there with you Tildie." said Annabel in humor.

And with this the little lady on the ball finally spoke.

"I am most pleased to finally make your acquaintance most nobel travelers. I am the charge of the clan of Botanicals in the Whisper Kingdom. I am Chantilly Lily and I will be guiding you through the Gateway. I see you have met my most loyal aid, Sir Gibbles."

With this introduction Gibbles bowed his head.

"Yes kind Lady, yes we've met him *(in more ways than one,* he thought*).* We've brought the primer with us that got us here. We thought we might have a bit of a challenge figuring out how to gain access to the...*Gateway...*but it appears your timely appearance has saved us that problem."

Then Mathilda quickly added, "Are you a ballerina?"

"Why yes wee lass, from time to time I do partake of the beauty of dance, as is the nature of a Botanical Whisper."

"Cool," replied Mathilda, as she ran her hands around the hem of her own tutu, "Me too."

"Unfortunately, I must interrupt this lovely initiation to gather more knowledge of each other, as the time is rapidly approaching for the Gateways' manifestation. If one is not prepared for such an event as this it can tax the nerves, to say the least. So please listen with care to my directive."

The three Muskydeers got as close as they could to one another and the two older children instinctively put their arms around the youngest between them. The Whisper continued in her instruction.

"I need you to ready yourselves for the unusual alarming sound of the Gateway. Please do not fret, it is forceful for a reason. You will learn little ones, that sound carries an enormous amount of power. It can lift large boulders and move forests if necessary. Once the moon enters the central orb of the vortex you will feel the energy. But then when all is expended, all will subside. And the etheric window will invite you through and all will be..." the Whisper looked straight at Benjamin and smiled when she said, "perfectly right with the world."

Immediately Benjamin got a lump in his throat as he remembered his grandmothers last words to him...*'my boy...all is perfectly right with the world.'* *that's too much of a coincidence, how could she know this?* *What am I thinking? How is ANY of this happening?*

"I really need to keep repeating to myself, that all of this is happening for a reason. I just hope the reason is revealed sooner than later for the sake of my nerves," he muttered.

No sooner had Benjamin said this when the most alarming inauspicious sound came tearing with full force at the three friends. Instantly, Annabel pulled her arms up close to her head and covered her ears. Benjamin jumped out of his skin, but quickly came to grips and covered Mathilda's own hands already placed over her ears. They were all squinting from the massive winds that were beginning to circle them, and just as promised, the moon began it's full bright decent into the middle of what was now a wall of swirling energy before them. *What the...?,* was the only thought Benjamin had in his mind.

Then, as if by some great force of very deep mystery, the roses began their swift Magical assent up the perimeter of the garden, reaching to a height yards above the group's heads. When Benjamin could get past the intensity of being blown to bits, and the mind crunching sound of the world being ripped in two; plus the ridiculous sight of the garden growing beyond all possibility right beside him, he finally saw it clearly....*the Gateway.*

With it's stunning consecutive rotating circles of dimensional thick watery light, the Gateway grew with every sound of the unearthly clanging bells. The disturbing notion that the world was forcibly being pried opened was all encompassing. Mathilda could barely stay standing from the force of the gale blowing at them. Annabel could not seem to make herself heard over the immense ear shattering sound. Benjamin kept looking at her in question.

And then without a warning whatsoever...it stopped.

All movement decelerated down to a complete syrupy slow motion...*the eye of the storm was now upon them.*

"This is the most amazing thing I have ever witnessed," said Benjamin. "How is this happening? How has no one ever spoken of something like this ever before? This is brilliant!"

And then the light show of spectacular beauty and movement began to permeate the garden. The tremendous awe covered the three small travelers. Tears came to Benjamin's eyes as he found himself being invited into the Gateway. The beauty was in every part of their aura. They all looked at each other with wide grins plastered to their faces.

Suddenly Mathilda shouted, "Look Bellie! Oh look, there's the little lights waiting for us. They have wings Bellie, they have wings! It's the Fairies!" And she started to jump up and down.

"Okay tike, let's go meet the Fairies."

As they began their entrance they each could see the lit pathway beneath, and without fear they stepped through.

And as was done in the past by everyone who ever entered the Gateway, the three best friends turned around, slowly as if in a dream, and looked at their past standing on the other side of a watery glass of energy....*and then darkness fell*.

When the children turned back around to continue with their discovery of the pristine world of all encompassing beauty they had traveled to, the immediate confusion was almost insurmountable, as the overwhelming sound of war had replaced all signs of harmony.

All hell had broken loose, and before anyone had a chance to understand what was happening the Whisper was shouting over the din of destruction.

"We need to take cover quickly. The Blunt are coming. We need to move now!"

What bloody hell is this nightmare? thought Benjamin.

Mathilda looked at her sister and shouted, "Bellie, I'm scared. What's happening?" "I don't know Tildie. Please, don't worry, I know the Whisper will protect us okay?" replied Annabel, not believing a word she just said. She looked at Benjamin. "What is this Benjamin? What's going on? Did you see any of this in your dreams?"

Benjamin just shook his head. *I never saw this coming,* he thought. And before anyone could think or say another thought or word, a beautiful woman with long raven hair, dressed in a magnificent leather war vest, riding the blackest of mares, rode up stopping mere inches from the frightened trio.

"Are these the children?" quickly asked the stranger of the Whisper.

"Yes, we must get them to the camp immediately," replied Chantilly Lily.

The ardent Warrior looked down at the stunned clan below her. "Don't fear wee children, I will get you to camp without incident. I swear."

Benjamin looked up in awe at the warrior before him.

"Who *are* you?"

The woman smiled at him. "I'm Emeline."

Annabel let out an audible gasp. She looked at Benjamin and shook her head in utter disbelief.

"This can't be happening Benjamin. I just don't understand."

The Whisper broke in, "I'm sorry to say there is no time for any discussion right now. Please take heed and follow Emeline. She will lead you directly to safety." And with that the Whisper disappeared into thin air.

"Oh holy cow! What the heck was that?" shouted Mathilda. And suddenly the Brownie grabbed onto her arm.

"You most certainly understood Chantilly Lily, we must not squander one more moment. Let's be off!"

And on the other side of the Gateway, in the darkness, stood the loyalist of friends, the Wickcliff dog, barking at the strange configuration that just swallowed up his friends.

Chapter Sixteen

The Time Ripple and the Path Tender

The children sat under the most beautiful canopy tent constructed from ribbons of orange, red and pink, with hand dyed fabrics of green and fuchsia. Overlaid on top of the fabric was an intricate design of hand spun gold embroidered flowers. A flurry of activity ran circles amidst the campsite outside the tent, and the children listened with astute interest. Soldiers, warriors, cooks, and Chancellors, every type of Forest dweller available, were bustling with deep concentration and intention. All were curious of the three children from another world.

Emeline was pacing back and forth deep in thought while waiting for the Whisper to return. The light from the tall ornately carved brass cauldron fire pit, glowed upon her skin, showing the depth of her immense beauty. Benjamin couldn't take his eyes off of her. *How is she here right now?* he thought, *She should be at least a hundred or more, but she doesn't look any older than her twenties. This is just too bloody bizarre.*

Actually what Benjamin found even more bizarre was the identity of the Forest dwellers. He had set his mind open to face something unusual, especially after meeting a Brownie and a Whisper. But nothing could really prepare him to walk through a camp of Fairies, Elves and Gnomes.

Really, Gnomes, thought Benjamin.

"It's like walking through Diagon Alley, like our own personal fantasy movie. Although, I do suppose the chaps who write those stories need to get their ideas from somewhere...may as well be reality it appears!"

And the girls giggled.

Suddenly Chantilly Lily appeared in the tent, floating on her transporting ball and the children flinched from sheer surprise.

"Oh sweet Whisper you're here, have you located the Path Tender?" spoke Emeline anxiously.

"No, I'm afraid not. But I have placed word about, so her presence should be with us in due time," replied the Whisper. Then Chantilly Lily looked over at the emotionally overloaded trio.

"As previously stated, you are all well and safe here at the home camp. I hope you find your accommodations adequate," she said.

The three simply nodded, still in shock from the complete turn of events they found themselves now a part of.

"Very well then. I do suppose the timing is proper for that discussion about who we are and why you have been invited here?" continued Chantilly Lily.

"Quite rightly!" said Benjamin, "I've got about a thousand questions I'd like to ask, but I'll just start with one right now." He looked back and forth between the two, very different women before him. "First off, I thought I was being directed to find a path that lead to the Grandfather Tree, and now I..*we*...find ourselves apparently amidst a war of some kind. I saw nothing of this in any of my dreams. And secondly, almost more disturbing is the fact that a little girl who disappeared a hundred years ago, is apparently alive and well, and looking quite crackin truth be told. Could one of you please explain this to me?"

Benjamin looked straight at Emeline.

Emeline looked at Benjamin and then to the Wickcliff girls who sat on both sides of him with the same question on their faces.

"It's the Time Ripple," said Emeline.

"The Time Ripple, that's it, that's all you have to say?" said Annabel.

"If I may continue," Emeline spoke with a deep sense of understanding. "The Gateway appears as an invitation to explore another dimension of the world. Here in the Gilley Forest there are many dimensions of life and activity happening all at once."

"What the heck is she saying?" said a perplexed Mathilda.

"Yeah, I'm with my sister. You need to use a language that makes sense to us right now. Words like Whispers and Time Ripples don't translate too well."

Suddenly a small voice came from somewhere down below everyone's line of sight. Everyone followed the sound and out from behind the cauldron walked Sir Gibbles to the middle of the circle of conversation.

"If I may, dear Ladies of the Forest?"

"You may with pleasure Sir Gibbles." answered the Whisper, relieved. With this Gibbles proceeded to stand directly in front of the alert and waiting children sitting on the soft padded bench.

"Since I am privy to your world for my joy, seeking mischief to rally up my innards, I have become well versed on the state of affairs regarding the human race to date. After all I have been around the planet for quite some time now, although still in my prime for a Brownie at 572."

The children let out a gasp of shock in unison. Gibbles never dropped a beat, he continued center stage.

"And I have had the opportunity to watch..oh.. progress, as you humans would call it. *I* would say there is no progressing of any sort, save the middles on everyone. You are a rather roundish sort, to say the least. And when you aren't feeding yourselves, your lives seem to be taken up with other distractions. One beast in particular I have found to be incredibly powerful, is the all consuming delusion of entertainment, or more to the point, the telly.

"In my recent exploration of the human species I had a chance to witness this very perplexing device. I had an opportunity to muddle about with such a contraption, as was my search for mischief in a silly household I was visiting in Stansbury. What a nuisance I might add. And *what* a waste of precious time! I also would add that when you are not planted in front of this mind altering box, searching for your next euphoria, your off kilter in the world of voracious consuming of everything you can get your mitts on. Be it food, drink, clothing, entertainment, time....*approval*. Oh the poor state of the world....I feel all hope is lost."

Emeline cleared her throat as code to urge the Brownie back onto the tract of his long winded explanation of the idea of dimensional time.

"Oh yes, well never the mind about me. I did find however, that the modern world is far too noisy and polluted a place for the likes of a barnyard Brownie. Nothing frightens children so much anymore. They are living within such immense chaos and destructive sound circulating their beings at all moments in time, they care not for the clever pranks of someone such as myself. I am unnoticed. My work is obsolete now." Gibbles lowered his head towards the ground and let out a deep dramatic sigh. Then as only Gibbles could, he looked up and shouted, "But praises be, that I have my concerts and fans to keep me warm!"

Emeline shot another look at Gibbles when he turned his head to look up at the ceiling in theatrical reflection.

"Ah yes, back to the subject at hand. Children, when you have your telly tuned to one picture...Oh dear me, I'm not certain what you would call it."

"Station," blurted Mathilda.

"Oh yes, the wee lass is very helpful to Gibbles. So to retract, when one is tuned into one particular station, there are still a multitude of other stations to choose from as well, is this not correct?"

"Of course," responded Mathilda with a smile, while the other two nodded their heads in agreement, completely engrossed in what the Brownie was saying.

"Oh, I am most grateful to the wee lass for expanding my knowledge of such things. Onward then. So just because your attention, your focus, is concentrated on one place, or one station as it were, does not mean the others stations do not exist. They don't just go away. They are off doing whatever it is that they do. Correct?"

Again, another round of curious nodding heads.

"Well, see, simple it is. While you are in one dimension, other dimensions are going on around you as well, all in their own sense of time. You are simply tuned into your own space, your own reality. If you walk into another space, depending of your timing, you end up wherever that reality is at the moment. Simple."

Emeline jumped into the explanation at this point.

"To clarify, depending on where the full moon is placed in the sky seasonally, one walks through the Gateway at the precise moment that is happening for that particular dimension at that time. The calculations required to fully explain this are really not important for you to understand at present. All you need to know is that from the full moon in June through the full moon in July, all travel is in the present. After that the other moons represent sequences of twenty years, either forward or backward. It's challenging to explain. Just know that when my sister Grace and I walked through the Gateway it was just before the full moon in June, so we were pushed ahead eighty years to the year 1991, which technically makes us twenty years behind you. Which makes me thirty at present."

The children looked at each other with great concern and Annabel spoke up first. "So are we going to be a different age when we return home?"

Gibbles spouted with condensation, "Oh, don't be absurd lass, didn't you pay attention? You walked through the Gateway at the precise center of the year with the fullness of the moon at it's peek. That keeps you in the present time, both here and in your world."

"Where is your sister Grace? Is she a fighter like you too?" asked Mathilda.

Emeline looked down at the floor and then up at the Whisper. She took a moment to answer.

"I haven't seen Grace in six years now. We are not the same in continence and our thoughts are a different road. Gracie had much heartache without our

138

parents. At first she accepted our station here among the Forest people, believing that we were indeed helping the Skeffingtion children as well as the Set clans. But as the years passed and things got worse, Grace decided she needed to return home. When Chantilly Lily took her to the backside of the Gateway to prove to her once and for all...."

Emeline sat down and stared at the ground.

"What Emeline, what happened?" Mathilda asked quickly, concerned.

"We had been informed that our parents had found a way through the Gateway." Emeline looked up at the three small faces staring at her. "They..." she took a long pause then continued."Unfortunately, they chose a time to enter which took them to a different place. Where that is, we are not completely certain, but it is believed they entered in the present time for 1911."

"Which would mean they would be over a hundred years old right now," offered Benjamin's quick calculation.

"That is correct young squire," continued Emeline. "When Grace peered through the window to our family farm, she could see there was no life anymore. No one had been there for many years. She became destitute, and then ultimately resolute to find them. She began her journey ten years ago."

"But I thought you said you hadn't seen her in six years?" Benjamin questioned.

"I haven't" replied Emeline. "We happened by chance to cross each other's paths four years into her search. It was at the water falls of Thornton Berry Shire."

"Thornton...Berry...Shire" whispered Mathilda in complete and utter awe.

Emeline put a smile on her face at Mathilda's wonderment, "The wee lass is smitten with the attraction of magic is she?"

"Oh yes your Ladyness," spoke Mathilda with continued wonder. And the entire tent had a round of cheerfulness at Mathilda's use of titles for Emeline, as the little girl blushed with embarrassment.

"No need for formalities when it comes to me dear child, just simply call me Emeline. The only Lady in this tent right now is Chantilly Lily"

"Why thank you my sweet Emeline," spoke the Whisper with genuine flattery.

"Well, I have another question" spoke up Benjamin.

"But Benjamin, I want to hear about the Berry Shire and Grace," said Mathilda.

"I know Mathilda, so do I, but I need to understand something that was said, so give me a moment would you?" asked Benjamin pushing ahead whether she agreed or not.

Mathilda just took a deep dramatic sign and folded her arms across her chest, "Fi..ne."

Benjamin looked back at Emeline, "You mentioned something about the Skeffington children and helping them, what did you mean by that? Because as far as the records show, the children were abducted from their home and never heard from again. Actually, that's why the legend of your family is still so popular in town...not only the two Skeffington children mysteriously abducted, but then the entire Chickering family disappear as well. And it doesn't help that the farm cannot be legally touched, it really adds an impression to the mystery. It's a tale that's been spun out of control all these years later."

Emeline looked up at the Whisper and back at the three children before her., "It's an uncommon matter to hear of one's own life from the mouths of strangers, so many many years later. The farm, my family, now a local legend. All these long years later, to know that the home of my childhood is still sitting as when I left it. It boggles the mind."

Emeline looked back at Chantilly Lily and stared into her eyes. After a minute she looked down at the ground beneath her feet, as she leaned forward and rested her elbows upon her knees and clasped her hands together between her open thighs. She took a long minute and a deep breath, "I feel this is not the time to explain about the Skeffington children. There is so much more you need to learn about our world here to understand the circumstances of their disappearance. Be certain that it was under no equal situation as my family's exit.

However, I must ask the young squire to be patient. I must implore your good nature to trust in my better judgement in this instance when I say, now is not the time for these details to be revealed."

"But..." was all Benjamin got out before an iron clad Gnome came running into the tent shouting. "The Path Tender has arrived brave Ladies, the Path Tender has arrived!" and scurried out again.

Emeline jumped up and turned towards the entrance to the tent with obvious urgency on her face. The children jumped up in solidarity and curiosity to meet the mysterious austere woman. The camp was in a state about her appearance, and the children were floating on top of the buzz of excitement.

Suddenly the tent entrance flap was thrown open and the Path Tender marched forward with purpose. The environment in the tent was instantly charged by the crispness of the cool outside evening air carried in the wake of her powerful stride. Everyone in the closed quarters felt a shiver run over their skin, both from this rush of fresh air and from the anticipation of her arrival. When she pulled her hooded cloak off her head to reveal her face, there to the sheer and complete bewilderment of the children stood none other than *Myra Longpotts!*

Initially expecting the Path Tender to be a Gnome, as would indicate from her small stature, Benjamin's shock was evident, "Bullocks! Are you joking me?"

"Oh, holy ghost on toast, it's Mrs. Longpotts! Bellie, O-M-G!" squealed Mathilda.

Annabel simply plopped her butt right back down on the padded bench they had been occupying, "I definitely didn't see this one coming," she said with utter concession.

Mrs. Longpotts turned and looked straight at Benjamin.

"Well, Master Benjamin as I live and breath. It appears you made the journey quite nicely I see. You're all here as one safe collective little group. I'm very glad to have been of service."

Benjamin opened his mouth, but the only sound that came out was an undecipherable squeak. Mathilda looked back at the nanny who was now looking with intent down the line of children.

"I see the wee one here is still in charge. Quiet the enthusiastic little creature, with an innate sense of courage I must admit. Not like her sister here, no, this one is all brains and no fluff."

With this Annabel slammed her gapping jaw shut. Then Benjamin finally found his words, "Well, of all the audacity! It would appear that you are taking credit for getting us here. Well, the only thing I recall receiving from you was a nightmare. If it weren't for Annabel finding the maps and the primer, and for Sir Gibbles leaving me the key, we wouldn't be here. I think it rather rude of you to take all the glory for yourself."

The nanny looked at Benjamin and then moved a couple inches in his direction as she held her Cheshire cat grin. All three backed up as an involuntary reaction to this closing of distance between them.

"My dear young boy, who do you think left the maps and the primer for the Wickcliff girl to find?"

Annabel's jaw dropped open again in shock.

Mrs. Longpotts continued, as she began walking down the line of frightened, confused children, as a drill sergeant would his inept platoon.

"Who do you think planted the idea for the eldest child to get up upon her bed to observe the map from atop, as is the rule to deciphering the hologram, the *dog*? Who do you think directed Sir Gibbles to place the key onto the rusty old nail for you to find in the first place?"

The nanny moved in close to Benjamin and looked him up and down, and landed on his eyes. She spoke in a low tone, very concisely.

"And really...nightmares did you say?" She paused and looked deep into Benjamin's eyes, then continued slowly, "Well, I ask you...who else could have seen the visions you have seen and have the courage and foresight to interpret their meaning, and then take the fearless action as you have done?"

The Mac Lady did not back down her gaze. Benjamin was aware of his two stunned comrades standing beside him, but his immediate attention was completely focused on the small cloak enshrouded woman standing before him. Benjamin's mind was racing. *What had he just heard her say?*

Suddenly, without a preliminary explanation, the Path Tender smiled with true admiration. She placed her hands upon his shoulders and spoke without shifting her gaze to the group of Forest dwellers huddled behind her.

"Oh, he is most definitely the One, I have no doubt. I have been beside this child for his entire life and before. He is most assuredly on the Path tended for him." Then she turned around to face the smiles of the Whisper, the Brownie and the Warrior.

Benjamin stood in stunned disbelief. *Had he heard the Mac Lady clearly? Was she saying he was courageous? And did she say she had been beside him all of his life? What did that mean? And more importantly, what did it mean to be the ONE?*

He traced back his thoughts to the farmhouse and Sir Gibbles's comments about Mrs. Longpotts being in error of locating the *Ones*. He wondered then and he wondered now....*just who did these women think he was?*

"Benjamin, what does that mean, that you're the One?" whispered Mathilda.

"You know as much as I do Mathilda. I haven't a clue."

Annabel was speechless. She was still stuck on the complete attitude turnaround of Mrs. Longpotts. And she still had no idea what a Path Tender was. Finally after everyone had decided to sit down, Mrs. Longpotts spoke, "It is very evident that the children are perplexed, and quite rightly so. And since this has been an extremely long day, I wish to keep my dialog short. This is the simple explanation."

Chantilly Lily excused herself and popped out of the tent. Mathilda jumped from surprise. Then Emeline ushered the Path Tender to please continue.

"Every being on the planet has their own story. They have their own book of their entire life, from beginning to end. It is kept in the World Library of Identity. Upon awakening each day everyone is given a clean slate, a new day, a new

143

chance to master life. There are no rules. There is no right or wrong direction, as every direction leads somewhere. The path can change at the choice of each being and how they use the new day. In order to take on the challenges of life one must be fully alert and present every moment. Nothing happens by chance. There are no accidents. Everything is a reaction to your specific actions and thoughts. And in order to catch the synchronistic gifts placed on your Path, one must be paying attention. In order to make a significant contribution to the world you must be fully on your Path, whatever that path be.

"As the Path Tender it is my duty to guide certain individuals to their full potential. I make certain that providence appears. I do not choose the people I facilitate, nor do I tamper with their progress in one favor or the other. I do not give someone guidance that is not governed completely by their own story. I merely help them get to where they are supposed to be, when they cannot always see it for themselves. But not all choose to follow the path laid before them for whatever their reasons, as is their choice, and that is the way of life."

Mrs. Longpotts stood up and walked over to Benjamin. Once again she looked into his eyes.

"There is a Prophecy that has been written in the annals of the Elven world, foreseen by a powerful intuitive Medicine Woman known as Pajah Set. She comes from a very distant time. This ancient prediction speaks of a young boy from another dimension who will guide our people into freedom using a particular Magic that has not been wielded yet against our opposition. This portents of the end to our peril at the ruthless whims of the all encompassing power of Queen Tar Vigorn."

At the mention of her name, Benjamin went pale.

Annabel leaned in and whispered to Benjamin, "Queen! Wow, I knew that name was important, but an evil Queen, yikes!"

The Path Tender continued to speak, "And what is more important, it speaks of the courage and strength of this boy to deliver the etheric and physical healing that is needed to save the planet from ultimate deterioration. I believe this boy is you Benjamin."

"What? What do you mean, it's me?" asked Benjamin with a look of genuine overwhelming confusion. Without warning Annabel, finally coming to her senses, stood up and stepped forward in to the room.

"May I speak please?"

"Well, of course you may child," returned Emeline.

But before she could begin, Chantilly Lily popped back into the room. Such was the surprise from her sudden appearance that Mathilda let out a small cry, "Ahh!".

Emeline looked over at the Whisper and then back as the quivering children., "It does take some time getting used to her popping in and out like that. But you will take to it sooner than you may believe right now. Please Annabel, speak your mind."

Annabel smiled when Emeline said her name, as she was getting used to everyone referring to them as *the children* or *sweet girl*, she felt comfort in hearing her name. She stood before the others and spoke slowly and deliberately to her audience.

"I haven't know Benjamin that long, but I guess you already know that. But in the little time we have been friends, I have learned a lot about him and what he thinks."

Benjamin wondered where this dissertation was heading and sat quietly to listen.

"Benjamin has powers."

All four of the Magical Forest clan looked at each other then returned their attention to Annabel. Benjamin sat up at this piece of information.

"What do you mean by *powers* Annabel?" asked Emeline.

"Well," Annabel continued, "He doesn't really know that I know all of this, except I just told him a couple weeks ago that I knew he had ESP... or something like that. He knows I know about that, but he doesn't know that I..." she paused to look at Benjamin and finally blurted it out. "Benjamin can make things...*appear*."

"Are you barking mad! Annabel, have you gone completely off your trolley? What are you talking about, I can't make things just appear?" shouted Benjamin.

Suddenly Mathilda chimed in, "Benjamin, it's true. I seen you do it too. And you make things move," she added.

With this information the whole tent went into a collective gasp at the unexpected information?

"Benjamin, just listen to me a minute would ya?" continued Annabel. "It's like I was saying to you before, I know you have this power to see things in your mind, but you can make things happen too. Like saying, Gee it would be really brilliant if Granny made us some ice cream today, and then *BOOM* your grandmother walks in with a tray of fresh made ice cream for us."

"Oh but Annabel, you can't..." "Be quiet Benjamin!" shouted Annabel to her friend. "I know that sounds silly and little, but there are loads of other things. Like butterflies landing right on your shoulder, it's like you can make them come to you or something, and it happens all the time."

"Seriously Annabel, *Butterflies!*"

"And what about the fact that you smelled those roses, even though the garden was nothing but weeds when we got there, then *BOOM,* a magical yard full of roses?"

"Annabel, you can't possibly think I had anything to do with that, really I..." submitted Benjamin. "Benjamin!" shouted Annabel, getting his complete attention, "No, I don't think you made the roses grow, but you did know they were there. And you said yourself, every time you had a vision that you always smelled the roses. And I know this sounds really crazy to you and maybe if it only happened once or twice, I would think the same thing. But this happens all the time, everyday Benjamin. It's just something I've gotten used to, well, and now Tildie too, now that she knows."

Mathilda nodded her head in agreement, "Yeah, ever since I found out you can see dead people with your ESP whatever, I been watching and she's right...you do some really weird things Benjamin."

"You can't believe it's just some random coincidence, not anymore, not after all these things that keep happening? Especially after listening to the Mac..I mean Mrs. Longpotts, say that nothing happens by accident," added Annabel. She took a deep breath and looked up at the foursome. "It just got me thinking, listening to all of you today. After everything we have been through and all the weird things we've seen, the holographic map thing that I saw with my own two eyes, and Benjamin's visions and dreams. And the most bizarre was his water tube trip into the forest, that really scared us..."

Mrs. Longpotts's eye brows slid up her forehead when she heard this, but remained silent.

"...and then here we are in this place right now. This is because of him. He can hear things other people don't hear, and see things others can't. My sister is right, when he is deep in thought, things move around him. Not really big, but they move. Like the glass of water on the table shakes a little, or the pencil just starts rolling for no reason. Or one time, when he was thinking something really deep, he just kept walking straight and the stool slide out of his way, just a little, but it did it all by itself."

Annabel turned around and looked at her stunned best friend in the eyes for a long moment then turned back around to face the others.

"I have no doubt that he is the one you are speaking of. Everything inside me feels...well, *squiggly* as my sister would say, so I know it's true. I don't know how he is supposed to save the world, but if anyone can, I believe it's Benjamin."

Annabel finished and sat back down between her sister and her best friend, who simply looked at her and shook his head.

Finally Chantilly Lily spoke, "Well, this is most unexpected. I am usually privy to all certain knowledge of Magic amidst our tribes, but this is an unforeseen addition to our side of things. I must speak with Sethina right away," and the Whisper was gone.

Annabel perked up at the mention of Sethina as one of the other names she deciphered from the primer and smiled. It seems she was right on target.

Emeline looked at the Path Tender, "Were you aware of the depth of his abilities my Lady?"

Mrs. Longpotts looked over at the children and then back at Emeline, she even looked down at Sir Gibbles for a moment.

"I am fully aware of his strengths. However, my suspicions have been realized here tonight." She turned to look straight at Benjamin, "When I gave you the message that first day, what exactly did you see?"

Benjamin took a deep breath and then explained in detail, to the entire room, the events that occurred in his *We* vision. Mrs. Longpotts looked deep in thought for a moment. Then finally spoke, "That is the message I projected to him. But something is amiss."

"What about that dream you had right after that Benjamin? It was the weirdest dream ever, with a fish that had a cat tail, and then it got real scary with some dark coat or something. You gotta hear that one," urged Mathilda.

Mrs. Longpotts looked back at Benjamin, "What is the wee Wickcliff speaking of?"

Benjamin felt tremendous reluctance to share, but finally took another deep breath and coughed up the entire dream sequence as well. When he finished everyone sat stunned in the beautiful tent with the glow from the fire and night lamps upon them, and the Mac Lady staring at him.

"Well, this is beyond anything I could hope for! You are indeed very capable of seeing things my dear boy! And now I must ask the most important question of all, and it concerns your watery tube experience."

Benjamin perked up at the mention of the glass tube, he knew this wasn't going to be good. He knew where she was heading with this inquiry. His heart beat faster and he began to tremble.

"Benjamin, are you all right?" asked a frightened Annabel sitting next to him.

Benjamin couldn't take his eyes away from the Mac Lady. She looked at him and said blankly, "Have you met her?"

"Met who?" asked Mathilda, "What is she talking about Benjamin, who did you meet?"

Annabel touched his arm and whispered, "Benjamin, it's okay, you're safe here, these people are going to help us. Who is she talking about Benjamin? Did you meet this person? Tell Mrs. Longpotts what happened, okay?"

Benjamin finally pulled himself away from her stare and looked at his friends. He realized that he could no longer keep this information to himself. He felt tremendous guilt for having kept it from them at all. But he honestly had believed it was safer not to explain to them about...*her.*

He looked back at the tribe of women, and the little Brownie standing before him. All of them with the look of genuine concern and excitement all mixed into one emotion. He knew he should tell them everything. But Benjamin realized now, as he had when he lay on the floor of the broken down farmhouse, that even with all these powerful beings surrounding him, no matter what he told someone, or didn't, it really didn't matter because ultimately.....he knew he was in this by himself.

Benjamin looked at the waiting group, almost begging for the answer and finally said flatly, "I have met the Queen....and the Queen has met me."

"Well, this is a rather odd turn of events, I had not anticipated," and she marched out of the tent flap.

"Who's the Queen? What's he talking about?" asked Mathilda to no one in particular.

Emeline began to pace back and forth with excited intent, then stopped abruptly. She looked at Benjamin with tremendous admiration and excitement spilling from her every pour, "This is amazing! This...I don't know what to say. We need the heads of council to discuss the next plan of attack. We need this boy and his friends safely delivered to Ashwald. The prophecy is unveiling. I must speak with Sethina, did you inform her of the need for her council, Chantilly Lily?"

The Whisper nodded.

"Good, I must strategize with her and Morel this instant!"

Then she looked over at Benjamin, "We, the Forest clans and myself, even for my short years as part of this family, have been waiting for your appearance

149

young squire, you and your two comrades. I am proud to have met you and your friends. I look forward to being of further service to you on your Path. Aut'banda." She placed her hand on his shoulder opposite of her and bowed her head, then turned and rushed out of the tent into the darkness.

"What the heck does out band aid mean, and who's this Queen?" asked Mathilda to anyone who would answer.

"It's Aut' banda and it means Golden Bond or actually, My bond to you is Golden," replied Annabel absently, still with her mind in other thoughts.

Chantilly Lily looked at Annabel with surprise, "My dear child you have translated our language in truth. You are correct in the wording, Golden Bond, and your interpretation is simply beautiful. It means we are all bonded to this world and the lives around us. It means we are one union. The Golden Bond. Very well done my child, very well done."

And taking a breath she looked at Mathilda, "The Queen, Tar Vigorn, is a ruthless Dark Sorceress who is raging war against the Gilley and that is a s much as you need to know about her at present little one."

Annabel, still deciphering her thoughts looked at the Whisper and asked, "Chantilly Lily, who is this Sethina? Her name is on the primer and so is Morel. I figured they were related somehow because they had the same symbol by their names. And then there was that other one, Tar Vigorn. I got the idea that she was pretty important or something because of the symbol next to her name. I didn't get that she was some...well, ruthless Queen, geez! And Benjamin! Why didn't you tell us about this nasty Queen before?"

Chantilly Lily looked at Benjamin and could see his confusion and spoke first, "Well enough questions right now. We must put you all at rest for the night. However, I will tell you that you will be meeting both Sethina and Morel soon. And you were correct, again, in assuming them to be related as they are sisters. Princesses in fact."

"Oh, Blimey! Princesses. Oh this just keeps getting better!" squealed Mathilda.

No sooner had Mathilda said this when Sethina entered the tent. She walked straight over to Chantilly Lily without looking around.

The children stared in complete and utter disbelief. There before them was a tall woman with long snow white hair, dressed in a short white sleeveless tunic over white leather pants edged in white leather strapping. She had a bow sheath across her torso that was intricately designed with the inlay of white owl feathers, crystals and mother of pearl. She was a vision of white etheric beauty and power. And she had the most perfect full white wings adorning her back.

"Oh my great Aunt Petutie, she's an *angel!*" whispered Mathilda in awe.

Gibbles spoke up for the first time in the long evening, "Oh for heavens sake dear child, Princess Sethina is a *Vila*. It would be wise to keep your wits accurate around here. You don't want to be thought a fool now do you?"

Mathilda just shook her head in embarrassment.

Gibbles looked over at Annabel and continued, "And to be accurate, I believe I spoke of the *three* of you being the Ones when we had our first encounter at the farm"

Annabel looked at Gibbles blankly, as did Benjamin.

"Yes, it appears young Benjamin here is the boy the Prophecy portents, however, there is more to this divination that was not said out loud here tonight."

Benjamin and Annabel looked at each other than back at Gibbles.

"No, there is more indeed. The bond of loyalty is a very powerful force." then he paused for a moment before continuing. "Gibbles will follow the courageous Warrior's initiative to thank you all for your timely appearance."

And with this the Brownie swooped his arm across his body and folded into a long proper low bow, while speaking the words, "Aut'bonda."

Chapter Seventeen

The Blue Lady

The children awoke from their deep slumber to the bustling of the camp. No sooner did their eyes open when Chantilly Lily appeared on her ball in the middle of the tent.

"Whoa!" shouted Mathilda, still not accustom to the surprise.

"Yeah," said Annabel, "it's kinda like a cell phone going off all of the sudden. It really freaks you out for a minute."

"Oh great goodness Bellie, cell phone. Have you looked at yours to see if mom has called or texted?"

"Oh, you're right Tildie, no I haven't, let me see."

As Annabel crawled off of her low cot to get into her backpack, Chantilly Lily asked, "Is everything all right little ones? Has everyone awoken with a fresh mind?"

Collective mumbles of *hope so* and *yes*, came from the Muskydeers.

"Oh splendid. Emeline will be here momentarily to take you to the river to freshen, and then you will meet with Morel and Sethina to discuss your journey to Ashwald."

Annabel sat up onto her knees, "Okay, my cell phone is making the weirdest noises and it's not even connected yet, so I don't get that. But I'm not going to get any service out here."

Benjamin stood up and walked over to Annabel and bent down behind her, looking over her shoulder down at the tiny cell phone, "We'll, we *are* in another dimension after all. And if that wasn't enough we are pretty deep in the middle of a forest. What are the odds it would work?"

Annabel looked back at Mathilda, "Well I guess we'll never know. Hopefully she isn't freaking out yet. And I hope Cubby is alright. I can't imagine what happened to him." She looked past her sister with a far away thought.

Mathilda finally spoke up as the Whisper excused herself and popped out, "Yeah, I hope he's alright. But you know, he's a smart dog, I bet he'll just find his way back home or something. And moms will find him anyway, you know how they are. Maybe Sir Gibbles knows what happened to him?"

Mathilda paused for a moment and frowned, then she pulled herself together. "Maybe we should just wait for Emeline outside."

"Yeah, let's go," agreed her sister.

So the three children stood in a foreign land outside of their tent looking about at all the activity surrounding them. It was the most peculiar of sights to behold. As stocky Gnomes intermingled with Whispers floating about on all assortment of flying devices. They saw a very tiny man who somewhat resembled a native American, with his long suede pants and leather head band. He was walking beside the biggest red hawk imaginable. They were almost equal in height, maybe three feet, which made the scene even more absurd to the observing threesome.

"This is really something else," said Annabel with a laugh.

"Well, ein't that the blatant truth," agreed Benjamin with an amazed smile.

Mathilda was suddenly having a field day in fantasy land, and all thoughts of lost dogs vanished when she glanced over to the left side of the tent to a group of large oak trees. And much to her delight, there below was a little family of colored lights, hovering amid the wild daisies.

"Oh my goodness, this is just the most amazing thing I have ever seen in my whole life!" she said.

Benjamin and Annabel were so taken with the activity on the far side of the camp, they barely even noticed Mathilda was there, let alone speaking. So Mathilda decided to walk over and introduce herself to the Fairy clan.

As she got closer, the little colored lights became still until the etheric little creatures were completely visible. Mathilda sat down on the ground next to the group who were all looking up at her, "Hi, I'm Mathilda, I sure hope you don't mind me coming over to say hello. I been wanting to meet you guys my whole life!"

The Fairy standing in the middle of the daisy ring smiled at Mathilda, "By all means, you are most welcome. We have been waiting to meet you as well. My name is Veolette, Princess Veolette. I am the Amethyst Fairy and head of my clan." Then she bowed her head and the other Fairies followed suit.

"Oh geez, did you say Princess?" beamed Mathilda.

The Fairy nodded her tiny head.

"Wow! I was hoping I might get to dance with you sometime, I brought my ballet slippers just in case," gushed Mathilda, then bowing her head she quickly added, "I hope it was okay to ask you?"

"It is more than okay, as you say. We're Fairies, we like to dance and eat strawberries and have fun. It sounds like you like to have fun too, so we are in accordance with each other. When the time comes, we will invite you to put on your slippers and dance along with us."

Suddenly Annabel realized her baby sister was not next to them, "Oh no, Benjamin, where's Tildie?" Frantic for a moment she twirled around and yelled her name, "Ma-Till-Dah!" Then seeing her over by the big trees felt a quick sense of relief. "Mathilda, get over here now, we need to leave, Emeline is coming," she shouted.

"Oh-Kay!" yelled back Mathilda, then turned to the Princess, "Hey I got to go now, but thanks your highness. I'll see you again soon I hope. Wait until I tell my sister, she's not going to believe this!" Then off she ran to catch up with the others who had already begun walking.

As they strolled down the isle of tents looking at all the many distractions and unfamiliar rituals of the Forest people, Emeline was walking towards them.

"Ah, there you are, good day. I trust your sleep was gentle?" asked the Warrior in earnest.

"Yes, thank you kindly," replied Benjamin, while the others nodded in agreement.

"Well, it's time to be off," continued Emeline, "Our scouts have gone ahead and made certain the safety of our short travel. Morel is standing guard at the water's edge. Sethina will also be awaiting our arrival. I feel the time is advantageous for our departure. Shall we?"

They all proceeded to walk the narrow worn path through the trees.

The beauty of the Forest surrounded them. Benjamin looked up at the canopy of branches above him as the sun poured through the gaps and made everything, and everyone, glow with a vivid bright white aura of light.

The journey to the river was indeed a quick pace and a short distance. When they all came through the clearing to the sandy shore there stood the majestic Sethina, beside an equally amazing large white stag, with a hand made saddle upon his back. The children gasped in unison. The visual of the sun soaked river with all the rocks lining the visible bed, and the cool blue water running over the stones looked like something from a dream. It seemed this to be the only place in the whole of the forest with open sky. The light drenched this spot and brought with it a very welcoming warmth. The foursome stood huddled together near the forest edge, almost afraid to disrupt the beauty before them, until Mathilda whispered loud enough for her partners to hear.

"Shut the front door! Is that a blue lady?"

Both Annabel and Benjamin shifted their gaze over to the right of Sethina and there she was....*a blue lady*.

Morel stood in the shallow of the riverside. Her entire body was covered in soft blue down, that would have been undetectable had it not been for the overtly bright sunlight bringing each feather into view. The Vila have an etheric glow about them. And just like her sister, Morel also had a pair of wings adorning her back. Hers where much smaller in comparison, and covered in pale blue down. She wore a short azure gauze like covering wrapped about her muscular body. However, when she turned in the sparkle of the sunlight, suddenly it appeared she was wearing a long sheath like covering that rested upon the waters surface. It almost looked like she was standing in a slow swaying waterfall from her waist down.

The illusion fooled Benjamin's brain and he couldn't comprehend what he was seeing. There appeared to be movement about her. Not a distracting or kinetic energy, but the complete opposite, it was calming and etheric. Benjamin felt *enchanted* by Morel, such was her Grace. He couldn't seem to shake the grin from his face. One minute he could see the sheer strength of her swimmers legs, and the next she somehow gave the illusion that she was a part of the water.

"This is brilliant!" he said, still smiling.

Beside the tight compact blue wings upon her back, the other point of focus that caught Benjamin came from a necklace made of tiny river stones. They were all perfectly flat round and dark, with a thin white line contrasting across the face. Benjamin remembered seeing the same necklace on Sethina the night before.

Suddenly Morel looked at the rest of her guest and spoke.

"I am Morel, the Guardian of the Lakes and Streams. All the waters of the Gilley Forest are my domain and in my command. I am honored to be in your presence and look forward to doing battle with you."

"Battle!" Benjamin exclaimed, snapping out of his cushy revery, "What are you talking about? No one said anything to us about any kind of battle. I thought we were heading towards the Grandfather Tree. I really need to understand what's happening here?"

"Yeah, we agree. I'm not here to fight anyone. We just need to get to the Grandfather Tree," added Annabel

"The children have not been made privy to our plight," said Emeline to Sethina, "They were only shown the Path to the Grandfather Tree. They have no knowledge of our battle. It is our duty to inform them of all circumstances and to protect them at all cost. We need to assure the safest harbor for their solitary journey to Ashwald"

"Wait a minute, what does that mean, our solitary journey? We pop into this place in the middle of a war and are scurried off before we even know what is happening," spoke up Annabel. "We just hear about some evil Queen and now we're supposed to just go off into the forest all by ourselves? I don't understand?"

"Yeah, I'm with Annabel on this one mates. We really need to know everything already," added Benjamin.

Sethina walked away from the white stag and approached the children. Benjamin felt his knees go weak from the scent floating about the Vila. *What is that,* he thought to himself. *It's like dreamy or something.* Whatever it was it made Benjamin feel *squiggly,* as Mathilda would say.

"We have not formally met, I am Sethina, I am a Guardian of the Forest and my companion is Rahm. I am here with my sister to speak with you about the nature of your journey, and to give you the soundest direction we have for your safe delivery to the Grandfather Tree."

They all just looked at her. It was such a foreign situation to have a woman with large white wings address them, however, there was something very soothing in her nature.

"This is what is before you. Tar Vigorn has been on a deadly hunt for the Grandfather Tree for these past twenty years. His existence has been camouflaged with deep powerful Magic. However, the spells cast will not hold out forever. She knows he's out there somewhere and will stop at nothing to broach this entry into another world. She will forge ahead at all cost.

"At present this is the only time in the history of the dark Queen that her Magic has not advanced her position. Her powers are flawless. It is by mere chance that we were able to protect the Tree for this long. And that is only because his existence was not made known in the collective mind for many years. It was only knowledge for the Gnome of the Fet, and they have protected their thoughts from revealing his existence for eons. Until they needed assistance in the Aurorus Jungle did they even permit the Guardians exclusive details of his home. In as much as Tar Vigorn knows every leaf and rock in this Forest, the timing and placement of protection was perfection. The stars were with us."

Annabel looked at Benjamin then back at the Vila, "So this Tar Vigorn found out about the tree and has been hunting it down and what...*torturing* people, *killing* people, what? What does *'at all costs'* mean?"

Annabel looked down at her now huddling little sister, who was as close to her as humanly possible. Mathilda had tears in her eyes. It seemed that this was the precise moment that the idea of being afraid had finally entered her mind.

"Bellie?" she whimpered.

"Hush sissy, don't worry, we're going to figure this out, okay?" replied Annabel in a comforting tone. Then she looked back over to Benjamin, who had his all consuming fear written all over his face. This didn't help the situation.

"Benjamin?" she questioned.

He finally spoke directly to Sethina, "What is so important in this other world that she has warred against the Forest clans for...*twenty years?* I need to understand, because I have been pushed to come here in search of this tree. My whole world has been forever changed because of the visions and premonitions that led me to find this place. And why is it that we suppose the Gnome of the Fet would let us in to this world?" Benjamin looked at his friends and continued, "I have these girls here with me. They need to be safe no matter what. Why wasn't any of this shown to me before I came?"

With this last statement Benjamin looked straight to Emeline, who had remained silent all this time.

"It has been brought to my understanding that you did indeed know about the Queen and her abilities," spoke Emeline, "When you experienced your journey into the Extension Chamber it took you into the Forest to the Grandfather Tree. And she took this opportunity to show herself to you. Is this not true?"

Benjamin nodded his head. Suddenly he wasn't so sure it was wise of him to bring all of this up now. He had said nothing about the Queen's strangulation hold over him, and now he was stuck in his own set of circumstances and had no clue how to get out. "What abilities are you referring to Emeline? I simply said we had met," Benjamin said cooly.

Emeline stared deep into Benjamin's eyes. Beads of perspiration began to form on his upper lip and forehead and his breathing became audible. Benjamin held his ground hoping no one would notice him trembling.

Suddenly Mathilda started to tremble as well, "Bellie, I'm scared. What did she do to him, look how scared he is?" Mathilda started to cry. "Benjamin what happened?" she begged, "Oh Bellie I want to go home, I want Mom."

Annabel attempted to calm her shivering sister, but she would have none of it.

"Please Bellie, can we just go home now?"

Annabel shot a powerful look over to Benjamin, "Benjamin, what the heck happened? You're totally freaking us out!"

Finally he couldn't stand the insanity of it all and flatly blurted out, "She tried to kill me!"

"She *WHAT*?" screamed Annabel.

"Oh my g-o-d, She tried to kill Benjamin. I want my mom. I want to go home!" shouted Mathilda who was crying so hard she could barely see from all the tears streaming down her face.

"How?" demanded Annabel.

"With her mind," was all he could say to her.

Everyone was sitting by the waters edge, showered in the healing warm sunlight, bringing them into a deep mindful calmness. They sat for a very long quiet while, soaking up the gentle heat. Finally Sethina broke the silence.

"It appears the young squire is familiar with the dark energy of the austere Queen. And he is correct in assuming that our battle is not to be a part of his journey at this time. His precise directive is to arrive at the Grandfather Tree and to take on the challenge of...*thought*. If he is indeed the child of the Prophecy, I have no doubt of his success. Part of this journey Benjamin, is that you and your comrades must face this challenge alone. No one can assist you in your endeavor to gain entrance to the other world. This must come from your own intellect and courage. And ultimately from your heart." Sethina continued her words to a very attentive audience, "We, as a collective force, can govern the outer perimeter of your Path. Which means we will do everything in our power to see you safely to Ashwald, without interfering in your personal quest. As the war rages around you, you must hold your center resolute. You must become a Warrior unto yourself. Stay alert and keep a clever eye about you, as Tar Vigorn is a ruthless and extravagant opponent, as I surmise you have paid witness to. She is not without humor, dark as it may be. She loves nothing more than to toy with her adversaries. You cannot allow her to gain access to your mind, as you will be rendered incapacitated to her power, and suffer a great defeat. Then all shall be forever lost"

Everyone sat in silence, taking in the overwhelming weight of the situation.

A much calmer Mathilda finally spoke, "I guess it sounds like as long as we stick together, and we don't let her mess with our heads, or...umm...I guess, feelings, then we can beat her?"

Annabel smiled with a deep, heart felt emotion for her sister. An hour ago she was beside herself in terror and now here she was ready to take on the world again.

"That is a very perfect way to say it young lassie," replied Sethina, "You all are very blessed to have the loyalty of one another. The bond of Love between you is very present, this is something that is very foreign to the Queen. This is a most welcomed reassurance of your inherent abilities to master life. I have no doubt you will be victorious."

Emeline asked to be excused to have a private conversation with Sethina and the two walked away from the small gathering. This left the extremely curious children alone with a blue lady.

Morel looked at Mathilda, "It appears you have found your level footing again child?"

"If that means I calmed down, then yeah, I did. When I saw Benjamin freaking out about the Queen I just got so scared. And I really miss my mom right now," replied Mathilda softly. Then she spoke candidly, and with innocence, "What kind of person are you? I never seen a blue lady with feathers before."

"Mathilda, oh my god! Are you kidding me? You can't just say things like that!" reprimanded Annabel.

"Do not worry yourself lass, it is a question that one would expect of a human child," responded Morel.

"Sorry about that," added Benjamin.

"Again, no corrections are warranted. I will explain in a very simple way. I am blue because I am part of the waters of the Forest. My skin is down to protect me, keep me warm and dry, and help me glide through the lakes. My wings act more like a fin, and propel me at great speeds," then she smiled.

"I'm curious about your necklace," said Benjamin, "I notice that Sethina wears one as well, is it magical or something?"

Morel absently ran her hand over the necklace when Benjamin mentioned it; in deep reflection for a moment.

"It is a symbol for our clan. Because of our stature as royalty, it is our duty to protect our area of the Gilley Forest. Whenever a member of the Woodland Family is in danger, or in need of assistance, they place a smooth dark river stone with a simple thin white line marked across it's face near a Yew tree or a stream. Either my sister or I will find the stone and know our urgent assistance is required."

Interrupting Morel's explanation, Emeline and Sethina returned to the group with a strong sense of purpose.

"We believe we have a powerful diversion to keep the Queen at a query. Since there is no way to hide you from the Queen, then we need to disguise all of you and create a dozen other paths as decoy. It will buy us tremendous advantage."

The children stood completely boggled. Emeline sensing the confusion explained further, "What we will do is put groups of three Gnomes into the same cloaks, to resemble you. Then we will send then onto paths going off in every direction. We have the Magic to give the appearance of the illuminated Path. She will eventually figure out the true path, but it will give you more time. And time is what is lacking."

"And what happens when she discovers us?" asked Annabel.

"We are not certain. As has been explained, her magic knows no depth. However, the protection of the Path itself is of great advantage for you."

"What protection, what does that mean?" asked Benjamin.

"How is it that you do not know?" responded Sethina with surprise.

"All pardon m'lady," Emeline cut in, "Alas, my mind forgets that the children have not yet been made aware of any part of their sojourn from this camp."

"Well, no wonder all the confusion and fear spilling forward," said Sethina with relief.

Benjamin looked at Annabel and then down to Mathilda, and they all shrugged their shoulders and took a deep breath, hoping the news they were about to hear would alleviate some of their overwhelming anxiety.

"What is it?" asked Benjamin.

Sethina stepped towards the tiny trio and looked each one of them in the eye, and then came forth with the explanation that had been withheld from them.

"The Path cannot be broached by the Queen. Not at first."

Benjamin looked back at the Princess with intensity in his eyes. "Do you mean to say, she can't touch us if we're on the Path?"

"No, she can not," replied Sethina.

An enormous round of relief filled the Muskydeers, and they all released their pent up tension, and smiles began to appear on their faces.

"Whew! That's really good news!" said Mathilda elated.

"Oh my god! Well then, what's the problem? If she can't touch us on the path, we just stick to the path and get there fast," said Annabel.

"She said, 'Not at first' mates," interjected Benjamin. "She is saying the power of the path only lasts so long."

Emeline looked over at Sethina and then Morel, then back at Benjamin.

"We believe the power of the Path is impenetrable until you reach the Great Tree," explained Sethina. "You are invisible, no one can see the Path except you. However, the Queen's magic will gain her the site, once she figures out the correct travelers. She will be able to gage your every move. You will not be able to out run her once she knows of your location. We are not certain, in full heart, that her magic is not capable of destroying any part of the Path. We do believe, however, that the strength of the Path is unmatched at this time. Since she has not discovered the Path as of yet, we have no way of knowing the truth in this regard."

The children looked somewhat relieved.

"However," continued Sethina, "we do know that once you are at the Grandfather Tree you will need to step outside of the Path to perform your tasks. This makes you completely vulnerable to her whim."

Benjamin shook his head, "This is bloody unbelievable! I'm pushed and pulled into this....this place, for what? To be chased by the most powerful bleeding dark Queen on the planet, who wants nothing more than to wipe me off the face of the earth. Why is this my job? Why am I the one? What am I supposed to gain in my life by going through that door? Where is it going to lead me, because it better be something pretty brilliant at the risk of losing my life. AND the lives of my best mates!"

He stormed off down the riverbank by himself, while Morel kept him in site and floated the waters edge just several paces behind him.

"Wow! This is really getting to be something bigger than we had ever imagined," said Annabel. "I mean, Benjamin's right. Why are we here? And what happens when we get to the tree and hopefully are able to put the key in the lock? Is this Queen going to follow us in? Into where I don't know, but like he said, it better be something pretty amazing to put my baby sister's life at risk. I don't know, maybe Mathilda is right in thinking it's time to just head on back home now. We didn't sign up for any of this."

And from somewhere behind her came a familiar voice, "Oh, but you did lassie....you all did."

The sisters spun around and there standing before them was Mrs. Longpotts.

"According to your personal book, you most certainly signed up for this. Not only that, but you have the privilege of choice. You didn't have to make the choice to follow along and end up precisely where you are now."

The girls stood stunned and listened to the Path Tender.

"People always wish to put blame for their discomforts in life elsewhere, yet they always forget that it was they, themselves, that went along. Even if it is something that appears forced upon you, say even as a child being told to go to bed when you rather not. It is the child's choice as to how they will follow this rule placed upon them. Will they go willingly and with joy, trusting that the parent knows more about life at that present moment? Or will they go kicking and screaming? Which action do you think sets up the childs mindset in an uplifting process for his future? How well will this person take direction later in life? Will they see the fullness of life or the lack? These things are all a matter of choice. No one here is forcing you to do anything you do not wish to do young Wickcliff."

Annabel stood with her mouth open. Then she heard her sister say, "Wow! Well, there you have it," and she slammed her mouth shut and stared down at Mathilda with a look.

"What? It sounds pretty clear to me, what can I say?" responded Mathilda with a shrug. Annabel just shook her head.

Emeline addressed the Path Tender, "Are you ready to begin? Is everything in place?"

"Yes."

"Well, I have a question," said Mathilda, "Are we supposed to call you the Path Tender now or what? I'm so used to Mrs. Longpotts and Benjamin always calls you the Mac...." "Mathilda!" cut off Annabel quickly. "Oh, sorry, I mean to say..umm...ah, well, what should we call you?"

"The Forest people know me as the Path Tender, however, my name is Cotti Set. So if it is easier, then Cotti Set is more appropriate for everyone involved. Although I must admit, I am quite partial to the Mac Lady myself. Very clever indeed."

Annabel and Mathilda both blushed and apologized all over each other.

Cotti Set simply smiled. Mathilda smiled back, "Okay, Cotti Set it is."

Benjamin had rejoined the group after a much needed time out to himself. Sethina was speaking with Morel when she turned around to see what the commotion was, that had begun on the trail from the camp to the river. Everyone had turned their site toward the trailhead, waiting for the appearance of the noise maker. When suddenly a Gnome came running at them, completely out of breath and still shouting.

"She's found the West camp, hurry! Word has come from the West camp, she's found us...we must move now!"

Sethina looked at Emeline, and the two began to hasten their step towards the trail. Within moments Chantilly Lily popped in. As Emeline ran past her she shouted up to the Whisper, "Is it certain?"

"Yes, it is very certain," she replied with distress.

Emeline looked back over her shoulder at Benjamin, and they locked eyes. Then she turned back, quickening her pace to catch up with Sethina, who was now riding upon the back of the tremendous white stag. Sethina reached her arm down towards Emeline who grabbed on and swung herself up behind the Vila, and they rode off, disappearing into the thick Forest.

"Come children, we must go at once," spoke Cottie Set with urgency.

Chantilly Lily looked at the children staring up at her with wide eyes. Annabel had her arm around Mathilda's little shoulders. Mathilda was white with fear. Benjamin looked back at Morel, then back again at the Whisper and the Path Tender. "I know what to do," he said and walked back over to Morel. "How can I be of service young squire?" The Vila asked in earnest.

"This chamber I was pulled into, and the Gateway, both appeared to be made of a gel like water substance. I'm assuming this Travel Chamber is made of the same stuff?"

The Vila looked at him with deep interest and a smile began to cross her face. "Why yes, it is precisely a manipulation of water. I can spot the glimmer in your eye young Benjamin, I believe you have a request of me?" she said slyly.

"Yes, I'm wondering. If you are the charge of all the waters in the forest, then couldn't you be influential on the Travel Chamber as well?"

"Oh my, it appears we do have a very creative thinker among us. I see that the time you took for yourself this past afternoon has sparked some specific thought. What is it you would have me do? Keeping in mind that I could not actually become part of the Chamber, however I could manipulate the flow for a specified length and direction. So your request must consider the time sensitivity."

Benjamin looked out past Morel across the wide river. He looked up at the blue perfect sky, then back to her. "Yes, I believe I will require your assistance kind Lady. How would I contact you when the time approaches?"

"Oh, that is simple, just leave a flat river stone with a white line across it's face at any part of the Forest water, river or lake, and I will find you in an instant."

Benjamin smiled back at Morel and turned towards his friends, and began shouting as he started to run, "Let's go mates, time is of the essence, as it apparently always is around here!"

And accompanied by a stout Gnome dressed in battle armor and the nanny who was now their comrade, the three Muskydeers tore off through the thick Forest towards the fight of their lives.

Chapter Eighteen

The Gilley Forest

A circle had been formed. In this circle were four groups of three, all dressed alike, the children among them. Emeline looked up at Chantilly Lily.

" I pray this diversion assists us."

Then she hastened the group to move forward along the individual paths laid before them. With the help of the Elven clan of the Darmon, using a spell created by the master Sorcerer known as the Ghem, the enchanting to gain the illusion that all four groups followed an illuminated path was set in motion. To any outsider one might think nothing of the treble of cloaked Gnomes passing randomly in the Forest, but to the Queen, the path would eventually show itself and the battle would begin.

"Leg it Annabel!" yelled Benjamin, while he ran holding Mathilda's hand to pull her along, "Once we're far enough away from the camp we can slow down, but we need to clear this place as quick as we can! We need to keep a sharp eye and stay completely on the path. Let's just keep moving right now, and stay close to me."

"No worries about that," yelled Annabel as she panted, running behind her best friend and her baby sister.

"Mathilda, are you okay running this fast?" shouted Benjamin. "Yeah, I just want to get away from here. So run would ya!" she replied breathless.

And so run they did.

The Path was lit up in such a way that it looked like a moving platform in an airport terminal; lit up from beneath with a bright white bluish neon edge. The Forest was thick and only getting thicker, which meant impending darkness. After what seemed like hours of running with just a few breaks to catch their breath, the children began to slow their pace, until they finally stopped for some much needed refreshment and a chance to gather their wits.

Benjamin came to a stand still, let go of Mathilda's hand and unconsciously fell back to rest with his butt up against a tree that was protruding onto the Path. This is when the girls realized something was weird, as the wall of the Travel Chamber extended with Benjamin's form. Mathilda's eyes opened wide and Annabel's hand flew up to cover her gaping mouth.

"Oh my god, Benjamin, we're in some kind of stretchy clear tube!" said Annabel once the shock subsided.

Benjamin looked down around him and sure enough, all familiarity hit him and he jumped up, turned around and looked at the transparent wall before him. "Blimey! I didn't realize we would be traveling the whole distance in the Chamber."

"You knew we would be in this thing?" asked a stunned Annabel.

"Well, yeah, I did. That's what I figured out down by the river earlier."

"Oh really, well thanks for sharing."

"Sorry mate, I got to thinking about the way the Path was depicted on the primer and how it looked more like a tunnel than a path because it had curved sides. Then I remembered the tube that pulled me into the map, and just sorta put two and two together. But since it wasn't there when we first started I figured I got it wrong somehow. But I guess it becomes more visible the deeper we go or something....I don't know. I don't know how any of this works, but I feel way more safe enclosed like this than just out in the open to the entire forest."

"Yeah, well the way I heard it, she got to you through the tube anyway." added Mathilda.

The smile left the faces of her partners.

"Boy, she's got a point there Benjamin," spoke up Annabel.

"Well, I wish she would stop doing that already, it's really getting annoying," slammed Benjamin in semi jest.

"So now what do we do? It's getting darker and we need to be at the spot Emeline told us to be at, and I don't think we're anywhere near that yet?" said Annabel.

"I think you're right. Let's take out the primer real quick and see if it gives us any clues," replied Benjamin.

So they all crouched down on the Path with Annabel kneeling behind Benjamin, and laid the primer out before them. And there it was, like a virtual glowing 'you are here', right before their eyes.

"What the blasted?.....This is amazing, all it's missing is an arrow, ha!" shouted Benjamin.

"Wow! This is so totally cool!" agreed Mathilda.

Annabel just stared. Looking down on the primer, they all shared the disbelief as they saw a glowing Path, that apparently stopped at the precise position they were standing in the Gilley Forest.

"This is brilliant," reiterated Benjamin, lost in the magic for a moment, "Well, it looks fairly obvious that we are *right here*. And as you can see, we're not even half way there yet. So I suggest we get moving mates. It looks like it should take us the rest of the day and into the night to get to the meeting place we agreed on with Emeline and the others."

Suddenly Annabel tapped his shoulder without saying a word. Benjamin so involved in his excitement didn't really notice her attempting to get his attention and continued in his calculations, until Annabel thumped him in the head.

"Ouch! What the bloody hell was that for?" And he turned to look up at her over his shoulder. She grabbed him by the sides of his head and turned him back around to stare at the primer.

"Have you gone off your trolley or something? What is wrong with you?" Then she pointed to the bottom of the primer, and suddenly Benjamin saw it. Beside the glowing outline of the Path, the only other thing visible on the primer was the now ominously glowing name of...*Tar Vigorn*.

Benjamin's mind began to race. "The Queen!" he mumbled.

"Benjamin, tell me it doesn't mean what I think it means." Annabel asked with growing anxiety.

It was at this point that Mathilda finally caught up with everyone and yelled, "Oh holy jeepers! The Queen's name is glowing too! *That* can't be good."

Annabel repeated herself, "Benjamin, what does it mean?"

"It means we run mates, we run like hell. Let's get out of here!"

And with this Benjamin rolled up the primer, Annabel put the water bottles back in her back pack, and off they ran again. But in the back of Benjamin's mind he knew this was a fruitless labor, as there was no way to run from the Queen. But it felt better than waiting for her to catch up to them, so they ran.

As the night began to take the Forest into a deeper darkness, the children could look out for a few yards from the light projecting off of the Path. It was almost like a child's night light. It was a welcomed relief to not be in total blackness. Although Annabel had her questions about the illumination. "It feels like we're sitting ducks right now. We're in a big glowing tube in the middle of the dark forest for cripes sake! She could see us for miles around, we may as well have a search light on our heads."

Benjamin attempted to stifle the growing anxiety, "No, remember, it's only glowing for us, so to anyone out in the forest we would still be in the dark."

"Yeah, just like they would be," said a cautious Mathilda.

Benjamin shook his head, "Crikey...Thanks for *that* one Mathilda."

"Well, it's true," said Annabel. "But didn't Sethina say the Path would become visible to the Queen once she figured out which one we were really on?"

"Yeah, something like that," said an absent Benjamin. He was looking about at the dark expanse around him and thinking. It was time for him to go deeper into his mind to get a clue as to what to do. He didn't like feeling like a sitting duck, nor did he like running in the darkness; be it physically or in his mind, and right now he was doing both. "I need a minute," he said and he stepped a few feet ahead of them. He paced back and forth for what seemed an eternity to the girls, when Annabel cut in, "Benjamin, we really need to keep moving okay?"

Benjamin was so deep into his thought he didn't register what she had said.

"Benjamin?" she repeated.

Then he suddenly turned and jogged back to the girls. "I got it!" he said. "She's looking for a long path, one that keeps going deeper into the forest, right?"

The girls both nodded.

"Well, what if we get off the path and run along side of it for a bit? The path will disappear, and hopefully if she's on the trail at all, she'll just think the path ended and that it's the wrong one. Then we just hop back on a bit farther down the line." He stood before them with a grin on his face, proud of his idea.

"Seriously Benjamin, that's your big plan?" mocked Annabel, "I think it was made pretty clear that we shouldn't go off the path. At least she can't touch us while we're on it."

"Yeah, Benjamin, I'm afraid to leave the path," agreed Mathilda.

Benjamin walked up super close to the girls, "Listen, I know this sounds barking mad, but you gotta trust my gut on this. I think this is a good plan. Like I said, we just run right next to the path the whole time, so if something happens we just jump right back on..*boom*, we're right there!"

"Oh Benjamin, I don't know..." said Annabel hesitantly.

Then Benjamin turned his full attention towards Mathilda.

"Come on Mathilda, we can do this, we're the three Muskydeers ein't we? We need to give it a try at least. The primer showed the path going straight from here for a few miles, if we just stay the course we should be fine" said Benjamin appealing to Mathilda's sense of fearlessness and adventure, "Besides you've got a lot of bottle Mathilda, I know you can do it."

Mathilda tilted her head to the side and smushed her lips in thought, then finally agreed, "Well, maybe you're right Benjamin. If we stay really close we can get back on really fast if we have to. I think we should try it Bellie. We gotta do somethin."

And that was all Benjamin needed to hear, it was a done deal.

So, much to Annabel's consternation, the Muskydeers stepped off the illuminated Path and the lights went out.

After a moment of resurrecting their courage to move, they held onto each other by the backs of their shirts and packs, with Mathilda in the middle, then ran slowly, single file, in the darkness. Benjamin had calculated the proximity of the Path to their bodies. He reached out with his hand and could feel the side of the Travel Chamber stretching inward a bit. As long as he could touch the Path he felt safe.

In as much as the dead blackness of the Forest was almost as frightening as the thought of the Queen coming after them, they kept running.

After a while they all needed a break from the sheer terror of not knowing what lie ahead in the darkness, almost more than their worn out lungs and legs needed a reprieve. When they stopped and were quiet, the abstract sounds of the Forest began to play tricks with their minds.

"Wow! This is really creepy," said Annabel in the darkness. She could just make out the outlines of her companions.

"Yeah, what the heck was that?" asked a shivering Mathilda, when she heard a loud screech that made them all jump out of their skin.

"It's just an owl Mathilda, don't worry. We're fine okay?" reassured Benjamin.

The group became quiet and Benjamin used all of his energy to put his *feelers* out into the Forest to see what he came back with. And suddenly he felt a cool shift of air move past his face. Before he had a chance to think about anything, he was mysteriously yanked from the back of his shirt into the Travel Chamber, and found himself sitting back on his elbows, on the ground of the fully illuminated Path. Before he could utter one syllable, Mathildas' hand slammed across his mouth, and Annabel was kneeling down next to him with her finger crossing her lips to shush him. Benjamin was completely boggled. He was about to pull Mathildas' hand away from his mouth, when he stopped and realized that he was looking at a ghost hovering above them, outside of the Travel Chamber.

At least it looked like a ghost...or an apparition of some sort. Whatever it was it was visible enough to see that it was Tar Vigorn; or some frightening transmitted projection of her. Benjamin's eye's were wide, and he held his breath, as did the girls.

On the other side of the window, a discarnate energy that belonged to the Queen, sniffed around and waved it's arms about in search of a clue. Then something caught her eye down towards the ground. The children followed her line of site, and amongst all odds they saw in complete horror, that the little plastic tip of Benjamin's shoe lace was sitting outside the protection, *and invisibility*, of the Travel Chamber. Sweat flowed off of Benjamins' forehead instantly. Not one single hair moved on the inhabitants of the Travel Chamber, no one let a breath escape.

Ultimate fear had engulfed the three friends, as the phantom explored the space mere inches from them. The Queen stopped in mid descent to the Forest floor, suddenly sensing something in front of her. The unearthly eyes of the ghostly extension of the Queen put her hand forward, almost touching the wall of the Travel Chamber. She could discern something was there. And the children inside could see this clearly.

She put her face an inch closer and appeared to look eye to eye with Benjamin. Benjamin felt his heart stop and the bile rose as he prepared himself for her strangulation hold of death. He crammed his eyes closed to hopefully break the spell, however no torture came, as he suddenly heard a strange voice speak in a muffled tone.

"Your Majesty we have the Gnome!"

Benjamin opened his eyes, and the Queen's projection was standing again, looking off to her left into the darkness. Benjamin quickly moved his foot and the shoelace tip was swallowed up into the Travel Chamber.

The Queen whipped her body around quickly, and looked down at the absent space that had held the object only moments before. A sparkle came to her eyes, acknowledging her sense that something was most definitely there. She began to move forward towards the Travel Chamber when the distant voice came at them again.

"Your Majesty, we have found them!"

And in a split instant the Queen's vapor vanished without a trace.

The small group huddled together in the Travel Chamber, still afraid to breath. Finally Benjamin sat up, and breathing heavy with residual fear, he quickly pulled the primer out from his backpack. He unrolled the parchment and saw that the illumination of the Queen's name was no longer glowing. Everyone took a big breath again, and relaxed the tension.

"Oh Benjamin, that was so close!" said Annabel.

"Yeah," said Mathilda, "I almost peed my pants when she looked down at your shoelace. I thought we were goners!"

"Bullocks!" yelled Benjamin enraged, "How did you both know she was there? What did I miss?"

"I don't know Benjamin," said Annabel, "it was just a weird feeling like somebody was standing next to us or something, and then I felt this cold breeze on my body...." "I felt that coolness too!" shouted Benjamin in surprise, "But it was like she passed by or something. I can't believe she didn't see me standing right there."

"Well, I think a ghost can only see little bits at a time," offered. Mathilda.

"Why do you say that Tildie?" questioned her sister.

"Because it was like she was right on top of us when I felt her go by. That's when I grabbed you. I think it's like she can only move her head a little at a time or something. You know, like a dinosaur can only see what's in front of him. Maybe it's the same with witchy queen ghosts in the forest."

"Dinosaurs, what the heck are you talking about Tildie?" asked Annabel totally perplexed by her sisters analogy.

"You know, like in Jurassic Park, when the dinosaur got up close to the little girl, he couldn't see her. Only if she moved, then he knew where to look," explained Mathilda.

Benjamin jumped in, "Yeah, you may be on to something there Mathilda. Did you notice how she had to move her whole body to come down to the ground? Except when she heard my foot move she turned around instantly."

"That's because she turned her whole body, not just her head," said Annabel. "But what was that Benjamin? It was the freakiest thing ever. Is that what she looked like when you saw her before?"

"No. No, she was a completely solid person, like you or me. And she had plenty of movement that day, that's for sure. I think this was some kind of projection, a hologram, something like that. You know, some spooky forest witch kinda thing."

"Well, whatever she was, I hope I never see her again. I really think I peed my pants a little," said Mathilda with a red face.

"Hey I was just this close to wetting myself too Tildie. She was totally beyond scary. But you know guys, we really need to get caught up with the others. I'm sure they're wondering where we are," said Annabel.

"Yeah mates, we better be off. I suppose there's no need to run outside the Travel Chamber at this point. We better just get moving. And after looking at the primer again, it looks like we're close to the meeting point. So let's pull ourselves together. But all this talk about peeing, I think I need a little piddle myself. I'll be right back."

"Benjamin!" yelled Mathilda with concern and embarrassment mixed in.

"Don't worry, she's gone for now. Here you keep an eye on the primer. See her name is dull now. If something happens just yell out to me, I'll only be a quick minute, really." And he stepped outside the Travel Chamber and disappeared behind a tree.

When he finished, Benjamin came back and took the primer from Mathilda and rolled it up. "Well, like I said, it looks like we're pretty close to where we're supposed to be tonight, so let's not fanny about any longer and get to the others. I'll feel a whole lot safer with Emeline and Sethina around."

Running in the lit Travel Chamber, and knowing that the Queen was no where in sight, made it much easier for the three friends to run full out and get caught up with the others. In no time they had made it to the landmark set by Emeline as their meeting place. A small blue light, of consecutive circles, shone in the center of a large boulder, and the silhouettes of the Warriors glowed in complete familiarity.

"*Who Ray!*" shouted a very relieved Mathilda when she finally saw Emeline and Sethina clearly.

"You said it sissy!" agreed Annabel.

Benjamin smiled and took a deep breath. He had not wanted the girls to know just how concerned he had truly been. They all jumped off the Path and greeted their guides.

"Oh man, are we glad to see you!" shouted Mathilda.

"I dare to hope you have made it back to us without incident?" said Emeline.

The girls just looked at each other and their faces showed the answer.

"Oh, I see a bit of distress has entered the situation. As you are here now, I must guess that whatever it was has passed? What pray tell took place?" asked Sethina.

Benjamin looked up at the warriors sitting on their steeds. He paused for a moment and had a chuckle at the irony of the two women in front of him. *Well, how interesting is this?* he thought, *The epitome of good vs evil. Sethina all in white on an enormous white stag and Emeline with her raven hair and her majestic black mare. What a weird thing. Especially since Emeline couldn't be more good. I guess not everything IS as it appears.* "If you don't mind I just as soon get back to the camp and have the others around us instead of standing here in the dark," said Benjamin.

Emeline understood Benjamin's concern. She nodded and jumped down off her mare to assist the girls in climbing aboard.

Sethina lowered her forearm for Benjamin to grab onto. He just looked at her with a grin. "You're kidding right?"

"Well, you don't intend to run beside us through the dark Forest now do you? We do have a ways to go, and I doubt you could keep half the pace to Rham," she replied.

Annabel cut in, 'Really Benjamin? You have to think about it?"

Benjamin rolled his eyes and with that reached up and grabbed onto Sethina's forearm. She locked her arm around him, and without effort, swung him up around behind her. Benjamin was dazed at the sheer strength and power in Sethina's body. She turned around and whispered, "Women, particularly one with my heritage, have a deep strength equal to a man young squire, sometimes more. You would do well to get past your notion otherwise."

And they all took off with a jolt.

After settling into the pace of the rides motion, Benjamin began to feel like he was in a dream. He was on the back of a massive pure white stag, holding onto a Warrior with long white hair and piercing grey eyes. He could feel how small her waist was and how muscular her back beneath her tunic. Succumbing to the rhythm of the back and forth motion, he placed the right side of his face against the space on her back between her wings and watched as the Forest slid past him. Almost entirely a blur, except for the times when it was not, the experience felt surreal to Benjamin.

He was seeing an out of focus world whooshing past, and every now and then there was a sliver of in between that just paused and stood still...like it was some part of another world. And there, in that space of stillness he saw them, or what he assumed was a *them*. Energies of pure light that surrounded everything. Like glowing colorful auras around each leaf of every plant. And mingled in were the small dots of color, the Fairies. But there was something even more *alive* about his view. It seemed to Benjamin that the Forest was breathing. Breathing in time with the heartbeat he was hearing echoing in his ears...*the heartbeat of a Vila Warrior.*

Benjamin watched as the multitudes of color and light danced about, illuminating much like the Travel Chamber did. He felt completely dreamy and at peace, while his head moved in time with the breath of a Warrior on a fierce white stag known as Rahm.

Suddenly in the depths of his revery he heard a different kind of echo and he began to pull himself back into the moment. Then it hit him, it was Mathilda shouting. Benjamin raised his head and sat up to look over to his right and there was the glow from the campfires. They had arrived.

Benjamin swallowed and shook his head to bring back his awareness of what was in front of him. They jumped down off their rides and walked through the camp of Gnomes and Elves. All attention centered on the three children. When they reached the middle of the camp, there was a huge fire blazing, and everyone was already gathering to settle into the area. They all waited for the news of the Path. They all waited to hear what had happened to three of their own, who had not made it back to the safe location. They all waited to hear the boy of the Prophecy speak for the first time.

Sir Gibbles walked up to the group and asked the children to follow him to the campfire, where a small bench waited for them to sit upon. Mathilda looked around at the sight before her and started to clam up. She grabbed onto Annabels' arm for dear life. Annabel removed her arm from Mathilda's grip and put it around her sister's shoulders and pulled her in closer. Benjamin looked out as every eye in the camp was on him. When they sat down on the bench, Gibbles turned to the now silent crowd and spoke.

"It is time for introductions. As you are all most aware, the Prophecy portends of three children from another world entering our realm to lend assistance in our battle to thwart the campaign which the Queen has placed upon all dwellers of the Gilley Forest. And to ultimately face the Test of entry into Coranim."

Annabel looked at Benjamin when she heard the name Coranim, as this was the first mention of such a place other then the primer. He shrugged his shoulders and went back to intently listening to the Brownie.

"Plans have been directed to protect and guide the three on the Path to the Great Tree," he paused and looked down at the ground in reflection. After a moment he continued, "Alas, the product of war is death. And it's byproduct is...*uncertainty*. At present we are unknowing of the survival of members of the Til'aut Set clan. We now sit in anticipation of knowledge."

Gibbles then turned to face the anxious children. "Before you I give admiration of courage, to young squire Benjamin, and the wee lasses, Annabel and Mathilda, ordained by the Path Tender as the three children of the Prophecy."

An instant wave of energy and mumblings swept through the camp.

"Young Benjamin, I give you the clans of the Gilley Forest. Our ears are yours to fill." And he sat down on the ground next to the circle of the fire. Benjamin looked at the girls and thought Mathilda might cry any minute. Annabel put her hand onto his shoulder and nodded her head in approval. Benjamin looked back over the crowd staring at him and spoke, "Well, as you know, we all left the last camp in a bit of a rush. We ran for quite some time until we finally needed to stop and rest a minute. That's when we pulled out the primer to..." Someone in the crowd yelled out, "The Primer? Is he speaking of the Galohishdi? The boy's got the Galohishdi?"

The crowd began to stir. Benjamin stopped in fear of saying the wrong thing. He looked over at Annabel and she just shrugged her shoulders. Suddenly a voice came from behind him, and Cottie Set stepped out of the shadows. The crowd became instantly silent. The Path Tender looked over the hushed audience of forest clans. "It appears there are concerns among you in regard to the rights to the sacred text. This instrument of divination and information were placed under my charge to be passed on to the One given this Path. Are some of you doubting my ability to seek out and ordain this boy?" Cottie Set looked around as she waited for a response to challenge her. And it came.

"How can you be so certain he is the One? Mistakes have been made before," came the faceless voice in the crowd.

Cottie Set turned in the direction the words had come from, "Because I have seen a page in his Book," was all she said, and the entire gathering went into a shock wave of excitement.

Finally a Gnome of the metal clan, the Or'aut Set, stood up and addressed the agitated crowd, "How is it that something of such Divine nature was laid before you? A person's Book is supposed to be sacrosanct. What impending harm has the Path Tender put before us?"

An elevated murmur began to spread throughout the clans. Sethina could no longer stand the outrage and stepped forward, her voice booming, "I will not stand by idly while the honor of a great and trusted woman of stature is put into question! Yes, mistakes have been made in the past, which is precisely why extra precautions were the strong hold of our search this time. How the Book was viewed is a matter of great secrecy and safety for everyone involved. The fact is the Path Tender has seen something of this boy's life, and has been attached to his journey enough to trust he is the One the Prophecy portends. And least you still have doubt, then let me end this disruption with one last bit of notice to you. Rhe Queen has introduced herself to the young squire."

Well, that was all they needed to hear, a complete uproar ran through the crowd. After a few moments of gasps and murmuring questions being passed about, the Path Tender spoke again.

"I give my word, as the Keeper of the Path, and all that is holy in our world, I have committed no crime against our nature; or all that we hold sacred as Guardians of the Forest. Providence has led every step of this journey. And once we are able to make our way to the Aurorus Jungles of Coranim, all doubt will completely vanish. I give you my word. Aut'banda." As she spoke the sacred word, she put her fingers to her lips, then pulled away with an open palm.

This seemed to please the crowd of Forest dwellers, and all agreed to listen to what the boy had to say. Cottie Set turned back to Benjamin and nodded her head in a silent confirmation of his continuing dissertation. Benjamin looked at Annabel and took a deep breath and continued with deep apprehension.

"Well, as I was saying, we looked at the... *Primer?*" Benjamin looked to Cottie Set for affirmation of the proper word.

"It's known as the Galohishdi." whispered the Path Tender.

"Right, the Galohishdi...anyway, we saw that we had indeed run a fairly long distance. It was at this time that Annabel noticed that the Queen's name was illuminated, which of course meant that she was near by. So we decided to run out along side of the path to allow the glowing light to diminish, and give her the idea that this was the wrong path to follow. "

Suddenly Sethina stepped up in between the children and the fire, "You removed yourselves from the Path and journeyed in the darkness?"

All three nodded their heads.

"This is unheard of! Was it not made perfectly clear to you that the Queen could not harm you if you stayed the Path?"

Again, three nods.

"And yet you felt compelled to take the risk, believing it would diminish the Queen's curiosity?"

Benjamin spoke directly to Sethina, "It was my idea. The girls weren't really happy with it, especially after what happened."

"What happened?" asked Cottie Set with concern.

"Well...there was this cool air passing by, and then the girls pulled me back into the Travel Chamber, and the Queen's...umm...well, her projection was there."

"The Vapor!" Cottie Set was stunned.

The crowd responded in an equal shock of gasps. Then Mathilda jumped in, "Yeah, it was like a ghost or something. Only she couldn't move around real fast and then Benjamin's shoelace was still outside and then he moved and we thought she saw us. It's the scaredest I ever been in my whole life!"

"Did she see the Chamber?" asked Cottie Set quickly.

"No, that's when the voice called to her," said Annabel.

"The voice, pray, what does this mean?" asked Sethina.

Benjamin took back the conversation at this point, "She didn't see the Travel Chamber, but you could tell she had a sense that something was there. She was reaching out, and she would have touched the Chamber wall if the voice that came from wherever she was transmitting from, hadn't distracted her. The voice said, ..." Benjamin paused then finally just said it, "It said, 'We have the Gnomes your majesty, we've found them.'."

And with this news the entire camp became overwhelmed with disruption and grief. People were crying and wailing as the entire camp became inconsolable. Cottie Set and Sethina hustled the children up and Emeline lead them all back to the tent.

Once inside, Benjamin looked at Sethina, "I'm sorry to bring you such horrible news. I feel like if it weren't for us, these people would still be alive."

"Nonsense my boy! This is a war we are dealing with here. No one went into this blindly. They all knew the potential for danger, and went willingly. This is the nature of this journey we are all on."

"Young squire I am wondering the courage to leave the Path, how is it you came to this course?" asked Emeline.

Cottie Set cut in, "This is the courage and audacity that is required to beat the Queen at her own game. This is the daring that is needed to make change, to conquer the obstacles that lie ahead...*the Test*. This is the boy, the One in the Prophecy, and he will think like no one else has. And he will look around every possible way to discern the puzzles to gain entry into Coramin."

"There it is again!" said Annabel. "What is this *Coranim?* I saw the word on the Primer and couldn't figure out what it was."

The three Gilley women looked at each other in utter surprise. Cottie Set looked at Annabel and put her hands on her shoulders, "You say you saw the name of Coranim on the Galohishdi girl?"

Annabel was a bit afraid to answer, then nodded her head.

Cottie Set turned around to see Sir Gibbles entering the tent and before he could say anything she spoke, "Calm the troops, we are all returning. We have staggering news....*an omen*...that will change everything."

Sir Gibbles looked at the three women, "If you please, it was my intention to inform you that the *'troops'* as you say, are requesting the presence of the boy and the wee lasses. Seems they wish to make amends."

The members of the entire tent felt a great sense of relief, and Cottie Set informed Sir Gibbles to make the announcement of their eminent return. Annabel put her hand on Cottie Set's forearm, "Pardon me, but what is Coranim? We still don't understand."

Sethina answered, "Coranim is the land below. A most extraordinary and beautiful world belonging to the Fet."

"Below, you mean *underground?*" asked Mathilda. "Well, yes dear child, that is precisely what I mean." "I *knew* it!" responded a happy Mathilda, "I told them, when Annabel said that word meant under ground that the door in the Grandfather Tree must take us down to the Fairy city. Oh I can't believe this!"

Cottie Set looked at Annabel in shock.

"You translated the language of the Galohishdi to understand that Fet meant underground?"

Annabel nodded.

"Are you kidding me! She figured out the whole bloomin thing, didn't you hear her explain the Aut' banda word the other night?" asked Benjamin.

"The Aut'banda? What are you speaking of?" asked Sethina. Emeline interjected, "That was when I went in search of you Sethina, I gave my bidding of Aut'banda to the young squire as I left."

"Are you saying she knew the meaning of this word?" asked Sethina.

"Yes, I knew the word. Chantilly Lily said I spoke the truth in your language. Hey where is Chantilly Lily?"

"Chantilly Lily knows of your knowledge of the sacred language?" asked a bewildered Cottie Set. "Yes," was all Annabel could say, as she was beginning to think something was wrong.

"Where is she?" chimed in Mathilda.

"She is off on a very secret mission at present," answered Emeline. "She left the minute the last camp was dispersed. I dare say we shall not hear from her for a few days."

"Oh," was all Mathilda could say.

Benjamin finally spoke up, "So what is the big deal with Annabel learning your language, we thought that would be a good thing?"

"It is not our language she has learned, it is the sacred words of the deepest part of the Universe," explained Sethina. "From these sounds and syllables comes our language."

"I'm curious as to what you determined the word Coranim to mean young Wickcliff?" asked Cottie Set.

"Well, I think it was something like..ummm...*Spirit*...and, and *heart* I think...Oh! wait, I remember, it was Heart, Spirit, Life. But it had another symbol next to it like some of the Aut words, so when I put everything together that I had learned I think the translation was "Heart of the Earth" or "Spirit of the Earth. Is that right Cottie Set?".

The Path Tender stared in utter disbelief. She could not fathom that this girl had not only figured out the sacred text, but also understood the beauty of the meanings.

"Yes child, you are very correct. And right now I believe it is best that we leave before the others determine us unworthy of the pardon they are bestowing upon us. All will be made clear."

"Yes, all will be made clear, we must return now." added Sethina.

So everyone followed out to the center of the camp again.

Once the children were seated and the citizens of the Forest were completely silent, Sir Gibbles spoke, "Bixby of the Til'aut Set would like to address the assemblage, with your permission." And he bowed his head to Benjamin, awaiting a word. Benjamin looking completely ill at ease with the formality placed upon him, simply nodded. With this a Gnome of the Forest soil workers, the Til'aut Set, step forward to face the group of leaders.

"Our most humble apologies to all Chancellors of Freedom, for the disrespect held against the Path Tender. We, of the Forest, know of the tremendous loyalty and love held by Cottie Set. On behalf of all the clans of the Set, we...it's just that we....well, we have been so weary these many long years at the force of Queen Tar Vigorn. We all long for the simple times of yore. When we could till the land and carry pride for our efforts of a peaceful life. The past has shown us more than one charade, and to pin our hopes on yet another, who brought with his arrival the death of some of our own, was simply more than our minds and hearts could bear. Our powerful and sincere apology to the squire Benjamin."

Bixby faced Benjamin, bowed his head while placing his hand on his heart, then sweeping an open palm, said, " Aut'banda."

Benjamin sat in his discomfort until Gibbles cleared his throat and Benjamin looked over at him. Gibbles, somewhat irritated at the ignorance of the boy, gestured with his head to stand up and answer the still bowing Gnome. Benjamin realized his gaff and stood up immediately, put his hand to his heart, and repeated, "Aut'banda."

To this the rousing chorus of cheers spread throughout the camp. Then Cottie Set came forward, along with Sethina. The women stood side by side and all attention was square upon them.

Cottie Set began.

"As is known amongst our people, the Galohishdi is a sacred text that was designed with the Magic from a most powerful and noble energy residing in the history of the Essence clan of the Whispers; of which Princess Avenel holds her station at present, within the West camp. The Galohishdi was manifested as a guide for the rightful owner to glean insight into our world in order to follow the Path and face the Test laid before them. The Magic placed on this tomb is not of fickle character. This is a precise and calculated directive, lest it fall into the hands of a lesser adversary, the code can not be touched to gain advance in any manner."

The children sat in complete concentration of Cottie Set's words. Then Sethina took over the dialog.

"The Galohishdi appears as a map to anyone who holds the parchment in front of them. A simple map of the Gilley Forest. But to the rightful owner, the map becomes a learning tool of tremendous advantage. Prophecy states that when the map is in the hands of the true heir, all will become visible. But there is much more than guidance hidden in the Magic."

Sethina looked out at the hungry faces before her...hungry for momentum.

"We understood that the map had shown it's face to the children in respects governing the entrance from the Garden and the direct Path to the Great Tree. What we did not learn until moments ago, is that the map spoke its secret in full to the young lass, Annabel."

She waited until the importance of her words could work their way into the minds of the Set clans, and the other Forest people present.

Annabel looked at Benjamin then down at her sister. Mathilda whispered up to her, "Annabel, are they saying that you're the only one that can read the words? Not even Benjamin can do it?" Annabel whispered back, "I honestly don't know what they're saying. Only that it looks like I did something no one was expecting?

The crowd finally hushed enough for Cottie Set to continue where Sethina left off, "The sacred text shared the name of *Coranim* with the children."

A unified gasp ran through the camp.

"And the young lass not only deciphered our language, but she was able to read into the holiness of the energy they represent. She speaks the inherent truth of our words. This is the omen we have been seeking. The Prophecy is unveiling before us!"

Once again, there was no stopping the uproar. Only this time it was cause for celebration. Suddenly everyone was on their feet, jumping and swinging each other around. And before the three friends knew what was upon them, the music began and the bottles of Gnome spirits were cracked open, and everyone wanted to be near them. The celebration went into the wee hours of the night. They laughed and danced along with the Gnomes of the Set, and the Elves of the Darmon. The sparkle of the Fairies mingled in among the torches and the campfire light, added a new dimension to the scene before them. Everyone felt a deep connection, and a lightness, that had been absent for many years.

Bixby came up to Mathilda, "Would the wee lassie care for a twirl?" "A twirl, you bet!" she said, and off she went to dance with the soil working Gnome, who didn't stand much taller than she.

Finally, utterly spent, they left the affair when a respectable amount of honor would permit. Sethina bent down to kiss the forehead of the girls. Cottie Set put her hand on Benjamin's cheek and smiled, "Good eve and sweet visions young Benjamin."

And off they went, along with Emeline.

"Well Benjamin, looks like we made the right choice to come here," said Annabel on their way back to the tent.

Benjamin put his arm around her neck and said with a huge grin, "Ein't that the blatant truth Annabel! Ein't that the truth!"

And their laughs echoed through the trees and disappeared into the night sky. And they all went to sleep amid sheets woven with Fairy dust, and all minds at peace.

Chapter Nineteen

A Night in the Travel Chamber

The entire camp was floating on a high that hadn't been felt in many years. Everyone was intently working on their personal effort to see the children safely to the Grandfather Tree. A scurry of activity was bounding as the camp was being dismantled and heading towards the next secret destination.

The children were ready to step onto the Path and head out, when Cottie Set, Sethina and Emeline approached.

"I see you are ready to hasten your departure, well done," said Sethina, "I am pleased that the celebration last night brought us all closer. It seems we have a bond between us no matter the world we live. You have forever changed mine"

"Yes," agreed Cottie Set, "we each evolve according to the timing set on our Path and the people we encounter. This piece of providence has been a great Blessing to us. As you are most aware, this is a tremendous undertaking before each of you. It is not to be looked upon lightly. The course of the stars shall be forever changed by the outcome of this journey. A journey to another land. Oh! What magic you shall see."

"We never did find out what's so special about Coranim and why we need to be there. It's all so mysterious," said Annabel.

"Yeah, all this talk about magic and destiny, it's hard to believe we have anything to do with something so grand as helping save a land from destruction," added Benjamin.

"A planet....saving a planet," was all Emeline said, not completely present in the conversation.

The children looked at each other with worry.

"What does that mean?" asked Mathilda.

"It's simply too much to explain in this wee time. You wouldn't be able to grasp the complexity of it all at present. It is better to see it for yourselves," replied Cottie Set.

So the children took turns hugging the three women and saying their good byes, then turned to leave. Mathilda, holding her sisters hand, turned in between them and looked back over her shoulder and waved, "See you later tonight!" she shouted with a big smile and she blew a kiss to Emeline.

A great dismay came over Emeline as she grabbed the floating kiss. Something inside her felt this would be the last time she was to see the children along this journey. This realization scared her. What could it all mean?

She turned to head back towards the camp with a great sadness in her heart. She felt strange...almost out of her body. Something was heading straight for her and was about to change the course of her life, and the lives of those around her, and she couldn't put a handle on it.

Because of her many years as part of the Forest family, she had honed her ability to meld with the Forest energy. She heard the heartbeat of the Universe through the movement of the trees. She had an understanding of the connectedness each one shared with everyone and everything. It was this understanding of Energy and Light that allowed Emeline to trust completely the intuition she was feeling on a very deep level. Knowing that her world was on a trajectory of impending, and substantial, change made her feel utterly alone. She missed her sister Grace now more than at any other time in her twenty years of living in the Gilley Forest.

"Emeline, you'll be leaving now as well?' asked Sethina.

Emeline was shaken from her thoughts, "Yes, Chantilly Lily is waiting for me at Thornton Berry Shire. That's more than two day's journey from here, if I am to travel unscathed." She paused for a moment then looked deeply into the Path Tenders eyes, "I feel that I have been dishonest with the children. It is not sitting well with me."

"But my child, there was no need to tell the children of our recent knowledge. This is a crucial time in their journey and the added burden of such information would have set the scales on the opposite end. I give you my word, once we are situated at the Great Tree, I will inform them of our discovery. All will be handled with honor."

"And by then we shall have heard word from you in regards to the situation," added Sethina. "We will have more reassurance to offer them. Right now I must put my faith in the decision of Cottie Set to keep the children at bay from this news."

Emeline looked at them, still with a heavy heart, and bid them both, *Aut'banda*, then turned to leave on her travels to Thornton Berry Shire, to meet up with a botanical Whisper.

As the day passed the children enjoyed the freedom they were feeling in not having to run the entire way. They had a chance to really look around at the forest and take in all her beauty.

"The sun feels good," said Annabel.

"Yeah, it's brilliant that we're able to actually have a little sun here and there," replied Benjamin. "It's a pretty amazing world here. I mean there is just something about the way everything jumps at you with such intense color."

Mathilda agreed, "Yeah, it's really pretty here. Better than any place I've ever seen."

Annabel smiled at her sister. As they walked in their own little bubble of protection, every thing felt dreamy to them. The heat from the small patches of sun hitting their faces, and the shadows off in the distance blended in with the background and everything seemed all right...almost normal.

Annabel had her arm draped over sisters' shoulder and a smile on her face. Then suddenly her eyes opened wide when it finally registered to her, that she had been looking at a very serene man, sitting on the back of a chestnut stallion! The Elf watched as the children passed by, and smiled at her. Annabel began to smile back when it hit her. *Wait a minute, how can he see me?*

"Oh my god! Benjamin, there's an over there and he can see us! What's happening? What...Oh my god!"

Benjamin turned his head quickly and looked over at the Elf, who then smiled at him as well. "Oh this can't be good. I have no idea what this is all about...but...Oh, bugger it! I'm going to find out.

And with that Benjamin stepped outside of the Travel Chamber.

The sisters stood motionless, in shock, as Benjamin walked towards the intruder. The Elf dismounted and met Benjamin half way.

"Aut'banda," spoke the Elf with a small bow.

"There'll be no bowing till I know who you are! Are you alone?" asked Benjamin as he looked around the forest behind the Elf. "Why are you here? And more importantly, how is it that you can see us on the Path?"

The Elf stood upright and smiled, "I am alone Master Benjamin." "*What*...how do you know my name?" quizzed Benjamin. "Well, I would suppose that every member of the Gilley Forest is aware of your name by now. However, as for myself, I am Tannis from the Darmon. I was at the West camp and heard about your journey from Gaston, a Gnome of the Til'aut Set, who had been stationed in your camp the first night. We have all heard your story, Master Benjamin. So inspired by your courage, I took it upon myself to see if I may be of service to you, and your fellow travelers. I was most pleased to come upon you this beautiful morning."

Benjamin looked at the Elf, then turned back to the girls, who were still standing in the exact same spot as he left them. He threw Annabel a look of acknowledgement, that things seemed to be all right, then turned back to face the Elf, "You haven't told me how it is that you can see us on the Path. It's been our understanding that we are invisible."

Tannis looked over at the girls as well and smiled again, then he looked at Benjamin, "Master Benjamin, I am an Elf of the Darmon. We are the highest order of Elf on the whole of the planet. This means that our lineage not only dates back the furthest in the history of the planet, but it also means we hold the source of the Path in our blood. It was from our ancestry that the Path was forged, as a gift to the Fet people. We joined in union with the Fet and Set clans to repel the dark Queen. All Elves of the Darmon are linked to the Path, and therefore can see the Path."

Benjamin looked at the Elf for a few moments more. Then sensing that everything he had been told was true, he put his hand to his heart, repeating, "Aut'banda."

Tannis smiled, "Oh and this brave stallion next to me is Bits. We are humbled and honored to be of service."

They both walked back over to the Path and the girls and made introductions. The sisters could finally relax and took a deep breath of relief.

"So can you walk along with us in here?" asked Annabel.

"No, I am afraid that would not be most advantageous. As the Path is a part of my blood, it would begin to meld with my essence."

"What the heck does that mean?" asked a very confused Mathilda.

Tannis answered with a smile on his face, "It means that the Path could become distorted with my energy. It means that I could become part of the Path and unable to separate out again."

"You mean you would just turn into the Path, you would disappear!" asked a shocked Mathilda.

"Not exactly, but along that idea," answered Tannis. "In actuality, the Path would become something a bit different. I really can't explain much as it has never happened. We inherently know, as the Darmon, that entering the Path for any extended amount of time would change both the Path and the Elf. I am able to brush my energy against the outer sides for a brief moment to re-energize myself, but any further contact would cause an irreversible reaction in the Path. What exactly that is, is unknown and only supposed."

"Wow!" was all Annabel said, and Mathilda nodded in agreement.

"Well, if you don't mind we really need to carry on here. We've got quite a days journey ahead of us and we've only tapped the beginning so far," said Benjamin.

"Yes," responded Tannis. "So, if you don't mind I will just follow along here, amid the trees. The senses of an Elf are far greater than any. I will be able to know if someone, or something, is close by."

Well, that's a huge relief, thought Benjamin, but said only, "That sounds good to us." The girls both nodded in agreement. And so off the newly designed group of four went.

"Oh, and by the way Benjamin, the next time you decide to just jump off the Path to go check out some strange person following us, you're going to get clobbered. You scared us to death!" said Annabel.

"Yeah, he could have whipped out his wand and done who knows what kinda crazy stuff to you! I mean, holy cow Benjamin!" added Mathilda.

"Point made. Didn't really think that one through I suppose. I'll pay better attention next time, if there is a next time."

Annabel looked at her sister, "His *Wand* Mathilda?" "Well, I don't know, he *could* have a wand," replied Mathilda and they had a good little chuckle.

And the three walked along in better spirits knowing that an Elf of the Darmon, the most powerful clan of Elves, with or without a wand, was just a few short yards away.

As the day wore on and the little sun light that was permitted to show through the trees became smaller, the Muskydeers became weary of walking. The last review of the Galohishdi proved to remain dull of any uninvited presence. The uneventful afternoon had grown monotonous. The anxiety to reach their final destination was taking over. The shadow of the Elf was a never ending sense of safety and security to the children; but it seemed this journey began so long ago, instead of the actual few days it had been in reality. They were all ready to be on to Coranim.

"Benjamin, what do you think we'll have to do when we get to the tree? Everyone keeps talking about a test or something. What do you think it is?" asked Annabel. "I couldn't even begin to guess," said Benjamin. "All I know is they've all pinned a huge pile of pressure on me and I really hope I don't blow it."

Then without warning, or understanding, Benjamin stopped cold in his tracks. He couldn't move, he was frozen in concentration. His feelers seemed to be on high alert and the hair on his arms stood straight up.

"Benjamin, what is it?" pressed an anxious Annabel.

Benjamin didn't answer.

"Benjamin, say something!" yelled Annabel.

And then from somewhere behind her, somewhere outside of the Travel Chamber came the answer.

"Well, so we meet again, young Benjamin. And who are the lovely little ladies with you?"

With this the girls quickly turned around and saw to their left on the outside of the Travel Chamber stood a magnificent, breathtakingly beautiful woman, dressed from head to toe in a mossy green garment. She had rubies the size of quarters on her fingers, that matched the color in her full lips. Her eyes were the hue of sparkling faceted emeralds and her smile displayed perfect white teeth. She had a crown of orange daisy's and purple heather wrapped in green braided ribbons, surrounding the top of her head and draping down her back.

"I see you brought along some little friends to keep you company. How charming. You know Benjamin, I quite enjoyed our last visit, even if the Fairies did cut it short. But it appears we'll have more time to spend together now. So why don't you introduce me to your friends?"

Benjamin finally turned around and looked at the Queen. He gasped involuntarily from the sheer site of her spectacular beauty up close.

"Yes, yes I know Benjamin... it seems I have that effect on people. No need to be embarrassed," said the Queen cooly.

Benjamin shut his gaping mouth. Mathilda stood behind her sister peeking her head out in pure panic; but truth be told, she was just as curious nonetheless. Annabel took the stance of a mama lion protecting her young cub, and put her arm out to keep her sister corralled behind her. No one said a word. Then the Queen began to step closer to the group in the Chamber. She looked about, examining the wall before her.

"*Hmm*..So... what.. have.. we.. here? This seems to be very different from the Extension Chamber you were situated in on our first meeting. As you are most aware, I was quite able to get my hands on you....*more or less*. But this, this is something very different indeed. You know it took me a small bit of time, and maybe a little bit of ...Oh, let's just say, persuasion, to locate the true transport. And now here we are. Face to face." And she reached her hand out to touch the side of the Travel Chamber.

As the tips of her elegant jeweled fingers grew closer the Chamber began to creak and crackle. Benjamin saw a small spark pop. Tar Vigorn noticed the peculiar sound, however, before she had a chance to react to the strange perplexity occurring, she continued to reach forward without hesitancy. Suddenly a bolt of sinewy electricity from the side of the Travel Chamber extended out to grab her finger tips, like the ground pulling lighting out of the sky in a storm. The Queen was completely taken by surprise as she was instantly thrown backwards onto the ground several feet away.

The children stood stunned and frightened from the sound *and* the visual of the released energy. It was like a huge invisible hand came off the side of the Travel Chamber and forcefully repelled, then pushed her away. Tar Vigorn was enraged.

"What madness have you provided for my wrath to devour! Do you not know who it is that you are dealing with? I am the Queen of this Forest......And you are *TRESPASSING!*"

The children drew closer to each other, terror running through their veins. Mathilda let out an involuntary audible gasp. The Queen quickly latched onto Mathildas' fear. She ate it up. She leaned in very close, as close as she could come and pulled her entire sight right in on the frightened little girl. Mathilda stood utterly frozen with the Queen's face mere inches from her own.

"So it would seem I am not to gain entrance at the moment...but give... me...time. My powers run bottomless, and I will proceed to pull every ounce of Magic from my bones and direct it straight at your hearts! Each and every one of you!"

Mathilda's eyes instantly became a river of tears and she visibly began fiercely shaking.

The Queen stood tall and smiled, "Well, I see my work here is done...*for now*. Sleep tight little ones."

And she vanished before them.

The moment the Queen disappeared, Annabel fell straight to her knees then collapsed back onto her heals while grabbing the quivering, sobbing Mathilda, and cradled her gently. Tears ran down her face as she attempted to sooth her baby sister, rocking back and forth. Benjamin came down onto his knees in front of the girls, he quickly pulled the Galohishdi out of his pack. The name was dull. The path showed that they had only a little ways to go before they arrived at the next meeting spot. Benjamin and Annabel just looked at each other without saying a word. Then suddenly a voice came at them from outside the Travel Chamber and they all jumped out of their skin. It was Tannis.

"Is everyone all right in there?" But he could see they were not. "I apologize for your surprise at the Queen's appearance. It was not in my best interest to alert you of her arrival."

"Not in your best interest? *Not* in your best interest! I thought that was the whole point of you being here!" shouted Benjamin. "You told us you would be able to warn us if anyone were coming. What happened?"

"The Queen is a very resourceful energy. As she said, her powers are endless. Her abilities rival any and all. My talents lie very deep as well, however, my energy comes from a well of highly evolved minds and emotions. Our motives for using Magic come from a different place than Tar Vigorn."

"Are you saying you use your magic for good and hers is for evil?" quipped Benjamin sarcastically.

Tannis took a moment then replied.

"It is much deeper than that simple statement. However, the premise is close enough. I am able to tap into all the space around me. To understand the needs of the Forest and the dwellers there in. As Elves of the Darmon we are able to communicate through the use of our minds. Distance is not relevant"

Telepathic! thought Benjamin.

"If the Blunt had been drawing near, or a Gnome, or any member of the Forest, I would have been able to give you ample warning of their eminent arrival. The Queen however, comes from a deeper, older source of darkness, and she comes without a trace. Even though I knew when she was almost here, there was no time for signals, as both of us would have suffered irreparably. It would have been a tremendous loss."

"What are you talking about? I don't understand, what loss?" asked Benjamin.

"Of all of our lives."

Benjamin's eyes grew wide. "How?"

"Had the Queen known of my presence, she would have considered it a great conquest to have an Elf of the Darmon in her grasp. She would use my life to flush you out, and you would have granted her that bequest gladly. Your honor, Master Benjamin, resides in the same source that mine does. You would have risked your life, and the lives of the others, to help save mine. And in the end, we all would have perished."

Benjamin just blinked.

"I knew you were safe inside the Travel Chamber. There is no way for her to enter at this time. So I stayed behind my shield of protection and observed. As an Elf of the Darmon, we are the only inhabitants of the Gilley Forest that can keep hidden from the Queen. And of course the Fairies do have some advantages as well."

Benjamin thought about what the Elf was saying, "What do you mean, 'at this time'?'" he asked.

The Elf looked at the frightened children nestled together on the floor of the Path.

"The Queen will find a cunning way to remove you from the Travel Chamber, a trick...a dare...*a lie*. Or she will take the time it will require to wear it down. Whichever way she continues, you will not survive either manipulation. The Magic of the Ghem and the Darmon is most precious, and exquisite and as old as the Forest. However, dark energy has a way of prevailing in matters such as these, powerful is the source. Her Magic began at the same time as mine. We are equally matched. It's only our minds that set us apart...and our vulnerability."

Benjamin stood up and looked at Tannis through the glassy wall of the Travel Chamber.

"So what do we do now? Because if I am correct, we can't continue to the safe camp because we would lead her straight to it, and everyone there. And we certainly can't go forward on the Path to the Tree, that would lead her exactly where she wants to go. So now what do you suggest we do?"

Mathilda picked up her head, that had been buried in her sisters lap, and looked to the Elf with hope. Annabel just looked deeply concerned.

"Yes, it is clear that we will need to stay exactly where we are for the night. As I said, she cannot harm you if you stay on the Path...at least not physically."

"What does that mean, not physically?" asked Annabel.

Benjamin answered. "It means she can mess with our minds."

"Precisely," responded Tannis.

After a moment Mathilda sat up, in total control of herself, and looked at Benjamin. She looked back at her sister, then she stood up next to Benjamin, "Benjamin, we already know she plays dirty. So we just play dirty right back." And she gave a solid nod of her head to emphasize her resolute formidableness.

It took him a moment, but then Benjamin slowly began to grin. He nodded right in unison with Mathilda, who now had turned her smile to face her sister.

Annabel, now infected with the sly grin, stood up to equal her cohorts, her comrades in arms, "Oh...*yeah*..." she said smiling, "we can play dirty too! What do you say guys?"

And as if on cue they all shouted together, "All for one and one for all! Who-ha!" They began jumping up and down. Shouting and twirling about in ecstatic clarity.

The Elf of the Darmon stood quietly and smiled at the courage before him. He was ready to do his part in this masterful charade, "However, we must begin our plan as time is...." and he was cut off by a rousing chorus from all three children, "Of The Essence!"

And so it was, but the laughter felt so very good.

Mathilda kept a keen eye on the Galohishdi for the return of the Queen's light. Tannis, Benjamin and Annabel strategized, sitting just outside the Travel Chamber, around a small ball of light generated by the Elf's Magic.

"The most important thing I can see is to not let her get under our skin," said Benjamin, "Although that's easier said than done. She really knows how to hit me right between the eyes."

"Well, that's her strength Benjamin. We just can't act surprised or scared in front of her," said Annabel. "Tannis, what kind of magic can you use to help us?"

Tannis thought for a minute.

"Something you said earlier has brought clarity to my mind Benjamin, I believe our strategy needs to be that of illusion." "What do you mean by that?" asked Benjamin. "Well, I believe we need to implore the assistance of the Fairies to execute this maneuver. I've sent word to Vieolette to gather her clan and join our fight. I bid she keep secret our situation here. If any of the others even learn of this, their thoughts will only interfere, and drastically alter the outcome against our favor. We dare not take the chance to elicit their help, it would only begin a battle right here at the Path. This would add further delay in delivering you to the Great Tree in time, if at all. We cannot take the chance with such tremendous importance. No, we must do this on our own, with the help of the Fairies who possess a power that is required to manifest our charade."

Then something clicked in Benjamin's instincts and he began to catch on to what Tannis was planing and he smiled.

Annabel looked at him, "What? What are you smiling about?"

The conversation continued and the plan was laid out. The trio felt incredibly confident that it would work to perfection, and hit the nerve needed to rattle the Queen.

Benjamin and Annabel returned to the safety of the Travel Chamber and explained their mission to Mathilda, who squealed with delight at the ingenuity of their idea. It had come to Benjamin when Tannis had mentioned the Fairies. He remembered how the cluster of the Fairy lights pulled him to safety from the Queen's death hold while in the Extension Chamber. Apparently, as Tannis explained, a large group of Fairies can be extremely powerful. Three or thirty, size really doesn't matter with a powerful intention, it's the energy that's important, he had said.

Tannis awaited in the safety of his protection dome in the trees for the arrival of the Fairy clan. Everyone was situated in their places waiting. Waiting for Tar Vigorn to return.

Then Mathilda shouted, "She's coming, it's lit up..her name, she's coming!"

Benjamin softened his voice and yelled to everyone, "Okay, this is our only chance to make it safely back to camp without bringing the Queen along. Just stick to the plan no matter what, and remember, we are all in this together. We can make this happen. Now everyone, get into your places." Then he added "Aut'banda."

Tannis smiled.

With this, Mathilda sat down cross legged on the ground of the Travel Chamber. Her elbow resting on her knee, an open book before her on the ground; she lazily turning the pages as if she didn't have a care in the world. She thought, *Bellie and her books, thank god she brought one with her.* But before she went into her act she took a glance over to her sister and whispered, "Sissy, I'm scared, but I won't let her see me sweat!"

"I know you won't Tildie, you're the bravest person I know. And I love you so much tike."

Mathilda smiled deeply, then went back to her book.

Within a few moments Mathilda, seemingly alone in the Travel Chamber, heard the now familiar voice, and took a deep breath.

"Well, isn't this interesting? I expected you three to be miles from this place by now. I felt certain you would run screaming for the others in your little camp of misfits to come save you from the horrible Tar Vigorn." The Queen turned to look around the immediate Forest and saw that is was empty.

"However, I see I am mistaken. Gladly mistaken I might add. Oh I do love a good intrigue, so what game are we playing little one? Where are the others?"

Mathilda looked up from her book and said flatly, "They went home for a while." Then put her head back down and continued to flip the pages of the book.

Tar Vigorn began to move closer to the Travel Chamber and in turn, closer to Mathilda, "Excuse me little girl, I don't believe I understood you. Please repeat."

This time Mathilda didn't even lift her head, she simply repeated her benign statement, "They went home for a while."

The Queen looked about her again, and then back to Mathilda. However, this time the site of the mass of orange locks from the top of Mathilda's down turned head, being the only thing in her line of site, began to perk up her sleeping rage, "Child, I demand the respect I deserve. You *WILL* look at me when I am speaking!"

Mathilda looked up at the Queen, whose face was gaining a touch of red anger. "You can't demand respect. You either get it or you don't," then went back to her reading.

Well, this sent an icy chill through the Queen's blood and the rage spilled forward, "I will have you look at me when I am speaking!" A large crack of thunder and lightening hit the air high above the Travel Chamber.

Mathilda jumped in her skin as she looked up through the top of the Chamber to see the bolt, then passively looked over at the Queen. She was quaking inside, but she said nothing.

Suddenly the circle of Fairy lights floated over to the Travel Chamber just to the backside of Tar Vigorn, whose mouth opened wide with surprise.

The cluster of lights covered an entire section of the Travel Chamber from view. Before Tar Vigorn could interrupt the group, they quickly darted off into the Forest behind her. When she looked back at the Travel Chamber, there stood Benjamin.

The Queen was visibly confused, "Where did you come from?" asked the dazed Queen.

Benjamin looked at her and simply said, "Home."

"What do you mean, home?"

"You know, home, the place that I live...in Grandlochcheshire."

This time the Queen made no secret of her shock.

"Will one of you explain this to me this very instant before I begin breaking things!"

Benjamin had to hold back his grin.

"I'm not sure what you need explaining about, but Annabel and I decided to go home for a bit and see our folks. Mathilda came back sooner to catch up on some reading and that's all I know."

The Queen turned to walk away from Mathilda and headed closer to where Benjamin was standing in the Chamber. She looked him up and down. She stepped back and examined the clear wall before her. Because of the darkness of the night and the Forest, the illumination of the Path made the entire Chamber glow, and she could see them vividly. She walked back up to the Travel Chamber as close as she dared, and looked Benjamin in the eye and said very slowly and calmly, "I will only ask this of you one more time young man, tell me how this is so."

Benjamin looked over at Mathilda who looked up from her book as if completely unattached to every word they were saying, "What Benjamin?"

"Why don't you go get Annabel and bring her back so we can explain this to the Queen."

No sooner had he said this then the cluster of Fairies returned to the Travel Chamber and surrounded the entire outside area where Mathilda sat, and blocked her out completely. And through the massive haze of glowing vivid color, Tar Vigorn could hear the little girls voice, "Okay Benjamin, I'll be right back."

And with this the mass of light flew off, and the space that had held Mathilda moments before was now empty, save for an open book. The Queen let out a gasp of surprise, "Oh!"

"You see we can come and go from the Path whenever we choose. We're not trapped here in the least. This was built to keep you out. This was built to guide the children of the Prophecy. You have heard of the Prophecy haven't you?" said Benjamin slyly.

Tar Vigorn backed away from the Travel Chamber, her mind furiously working for clarity and action. She turned away from the Travel Chamber and looked down in the darkness and pushed her brain. She went into her deepest regions of thought to gain any information to regain control. After a few moments the corners of her mouth began to turn upwards and she slowly turned around to look at Benjamin. Benjamin noticed the dramatic change in the Queen's demeanor and his antenna started to twitch.

The Queen walked back towards the Chamber, closer to Benjamin. Her smile disarmed him. *She's doing it again,* he thought. *She knows how to get into my brain. Don't let her win Benjamin. Keep steady mate, do your job!* But something was different about the Queen's energy. Then it hit him,

She's figured something out.

He pulled himself together.

"Mathilda should be back any moment with Annabel."

"Mathilda and Annabel. How sweet," the Queen replied blandly.

Then suddenly the mob of Fairies floated over to the Travel Chamber and blocked out the largest view yet. And while the Queen's site was veiled from this space in the Chamber, Annabel and Mathilda quickly crawled out of their hiding place in the bottom of the Path, much like a magician and his apprentice.

Tannis had used his powerful Magic and connection to the Travel Chamber to create three small compartments just beneath the Path. Since it was an extension of the Path, it still held the light and protection for the children. They would lie down on their backs under the floor of the Chamber with the invisible barrier shielding them from view. When the Fairies fully covered the Queens' view, the one child still standing would give a small signal, and the hidden child would jump up, while the other laid down in their own compartment. The Fairies would dart off and the Queen would see the now returned child, giving the illusion of dimensional travel.

"Well, Mathilda and Annabel is it? So lovely to finally have a proper introduction."

The girls stood still, also noticing the change in the Queen's energy. Apprehension began to creep in.

"So you had a lovely visit with your parents did you?" asked the Queen.

"Oh, yes, it was good to see with them for awhile," replied Annabel.

The Queen began to pace back and forth beside the Travel Chamber, completely unsettling the children.

"*Hmm*, I see. And they are both doing fine today are they?"

"Of course" replied Mathilda.

"And how is Edward, that would be your father correct?"

The girls instantly lost their smiles, fear began to take hold of their brains, "Yes, that's our father's name, and he's doing very well, thank you," replied a controlled Annabel. Her mind going in all directions as to how the Queen could know his name.

Benjamin began to sense the hands of power exchanging. The scales were beginning to tip straight towards Tar Vigorn. *What new madness is this,* he thought. He jumped into the conversation in an attempt to take the advantage back, "What's with all the concern about the girls parents? We have more important things to do right now, so if you don't mind I think we'll just head on out of here for a bit. It was lovely seeing you again. Have a nice day. Hope to not to run into you anytime soon." And he started to turn towards the girls when the Queen was instantly next to the Travel Chamber in a heartbeat, staring him right between the eyes.

"Young Benjamin, sarcasm will not get you very far with me. You will learn to respect my greatness, or...you...*will...suffer...the consequences.*"

Benjamin stopped in mid turn and looked back at Tar Vigorn. In that moment he could see clearly that she had them. He stood straight up and faced her. They looked long and hard at each other, then Benjamin spoke blandly, "What do you know?"

The girls looked at Benjamin and felt a tremendous sense of confusion and defeat. *What was happening?* Never taking his eyes off of the Queen, she finally relaxed her pose and stepped back.

"Well, it seems I have just been given a lovely little bit of information that pretty much gives me exactly what I could have only hoped to gain."

The Queen paused for effect.

"It appears there is news of two travelers who have made their way into the Gilley Forest through the Gateway at the Chickering farm."

With this the Queen looked over at the girls and smiled, "It seems that Edward and someone named Braxton, have begun their own journey into our exquisite little world here. And I can't *wait* to meet them!"

Both girls instantly filled with terror and Mathilda began to cry, "Benjamin, what does she mean? Is she saying my daddy is here in the Forest?"

"Mathilda, don't say anything, not another word!" shouted Annabel. She looked over at Benjamin, "Benjamin, is it possible?"

He finally tore his gaze away from Tar Vigorn and faced the two best mates of his life and simply said, "It's true, I can feel it."

With this Annabel released her tears.

Tar Vigorn clapped her hands together in one huge slap and smiled victorious, "Now that we are all in agreement as to who is in charge here, let's get you all out of this tight little chamber and start giving me some answers, shall we?"

The girls stood frozen and looked back at Benjamin.

What to do, what to do? thought Benjamin, as he racked his brain for a quick instant, then suddenly it hit him. Benjamin quickly cleared his racing mind then called Tannis with his thoughts. As quickly as he said the Elf's name, came a clear picture of Tannis...and his voice was attached.

"Do not lose control of your senses, Master Benjamin. Help is on it's way. Be calm, I will not leave your side."

Benjamin attempted not to give anything away. He looked out past the Queen, towards the direction Tannis and the Fairies were hiding, as if he had a long thought on his mind. He quickly saw the sparkle of purple light coming off of Vieolette and knew the time was upon him to play his bluff, and milk the much needed time out of this unexpected and nasty situation. He looked back at the Queen and spoke calmly, "You know you never answered my question about the Prophecy. You *have* heard the portend...am I correct?"

Tar Vigorn tilted her head in interest, her smile never wavered, "*Ahh*, the Prophecy of Pajah Set. Please tell me they don't actually have you believing you are... *that* boy? You couldn't possibly believe that. You are aware they've found others before you, are you not? Other boys they swore were going to save the world and put an end to all my beautiful darkness. Can you guess where those young lads are now, young Benjamin?"

Suddenly Tar Vigorn disappeared from site, Benjamin looked up totally stupefied. But before he could take another breath, she instantly reappeared on the other side of the Travel Chamber behind him and whispered, "Boo!"

Benjamin let the surprise grab him, "Ahh!"

"A little jumpy are we?" hissed the Queen.

Benjamin turned to look at her, his face filled with anger and question. She continued with her masterful web of unnerving him.

"Let me give you a bit of advice dear boy. You'd be a fool to trust these imbeciles with your life. They'll recruit anyone they can use to gain information. The last boy who followed the directive of Cottie Set....well, let's just say, he's no longer following *anyone*. After all, how gullible does one have to be to believe in fairy tales? A Prophecy, ridiculous! I thought you were much wiser than that young, sweet Benjamin. I mean honestly, do you really see yourself winning anything against the likes of me? You're just a normal boy after all."

Benjamin contained his anger, however the questions started to arise in his heart. *She's right, how could I be the One? Why am I any different from the other boys who were told they were the ones?* But before he had a chance to delve further into his impending doubt, the voice of Tannis appeared in his mind.

Master Benjamin, the two boys that perished were always a question, she is not divulging all the information. There is much more than you have heard. You must not falter in the belief that the three of you are the children of Truth, or she will gain advantage. You are the Prophecy, I put my life into your hands in trust and certainty. Search your heart young Benjamin, and you will know the Truth. You can not hide from your Path.

Benjamin thought a moment, and once again a slow smile began to fill his face, disarming the Queen. Benjamin looked over at his friends, locking eyes with Annabel, until she began to smile with him. Then Mathilda wiped her wet face with the back of her hand and followed suit. The girls walked over to Benjamin standing on either side of him and held his hands. They all looked up at the now boggled Queen.

"What you don't know," began the boy ever so cooly, "is that the Prophecy was never about just one boy...it is about three friends. It also says that these three friends have a very powerful magic, the likes of which has never been wielded in the Gilley Forest before...a magic that stems from Love. But you wouldn't know anything about that would you Tar Vigorn...*Love?* It also talks about a boy who has the ability to make things happen...just by *Think*-ing them."

The Queen flinched, her smile gone. Benjamin continued with his own Cheshire Cat grin.

"Can you guess what I am thinking right now Tar Vigorn...*hmm?*"

Then in an attempt to get even with the Queen, and take back her power, Mathilda stepped closer to the Chamber wall. Leaning forward as close as she could get, she locked eyes with Tar Vigorn, "Better watch out, someone might drop a house on you," she giggled.

The Queen went pale as the thought occurred to her in that instant that Benjamin McTish may very well be the boy of the ancient prediction. However, before she had a chance to change her mind, a chestnut mare with a rider on his back was leaping high over the Travel Chamber and right over her head! The Queen swung around and looked as Tannis and Bits landed on the Forest floor a few feet away from her. A sly smile came back to her face.

"Well, if it isn't my old friend *Tannis*. I should have *known* you would be involved in this. And how are things in the Darmon these days?"

Tannis smiled back at Tar Vigorn, "You know perfectly well that I have not seen my home in many long years. But all this is about to change."

And with that the battle commenced.

The children huddled together kneeling down on their heals, as Tar Vigorn unleashed a bounty of rapid fire lightening bolts straight for the Elf.

Tannis deflected the spikes of energy while jumping over the Chamber on the back of the stallion. The Queen instantly joined Tannis on the other side, and the exchange of red tinged electrifying currents flowed out of the two Forest dwellers. Bursts of exploding trees and stumps resounded like canon fire. The trio in the Travel Chamber were shell shocked at the intensity and force of the magic flying between the Elf and the Queen.

Errant lighting was ricochetting off the sides of the Travel Chamber, causing the children to cover their ears from the deafening sound it made. The entire Chamber shook with upheaval. Small trees that were unfortunate enough to be caught in the line of rage pouring out of Tar Vigorn, burned to char in seconds.

The Travel Chamber was creaking and moaning, like a wounded animal. It swayed and pulsed with every outcry of explosive energy thrown it's way.

The Elf of the Darmon and the Queen of Darkness fought relentlessly. The Fairy clan dove in between the bursts of lightening to blind the Queen with their bright wall of color light. But the Queen would not be swayed.

Then, unexpectedly, Tar Vigorn halted her tirade and spoke the Magic she needed to surrounded herself in a misty haze of smoke...*thick, dark and ominous.*

Everyone watched in astonishment as she appeared to be completely enveloped in the self propelled murk. Then she magically emerged from the cloud of spinning grey fog, in what appeared to be a large halo of light surrounding her body. It looked to the children as if she were in a small version of her own chamber, like an elliptical force field; her own personal vibrating shield surrounding her entire body. And suddenly Tannis's magic was senseless. Instead, the powerful force of battle energy being heaved at her from all directions was bouncing back off of the protective barrier she now resided.

The Travel Chamber began to sound off an alarming vibration. It shimmied and shook with dramatic force. It felt as if the whole tunnel of light would collapse any moment. The sound engulfed the children, and threatened to take their sanity with it. Mathilda was screaming at the top of her lungs. Annabel was holding onto her little sister as she grabbed Benjamin's forearm and yelled with all of her might, "Benjamin, I think the Travel Chamber is falling apart or something! We can't just sit here!"

Benjamin's mind was a whirling dervish of confusion. He could not keep up with the tremendous acceleration of events. He felt an immensely deep disappointment in himself for bringing this amazing journey to this final conclusion. He looked up at the girls and just when he was willing to admit defeat, they all turned to look up as something flashed above them.

They had entered the eye of the storm.

The tightly nestled trio watched the activity around them in the syrupy silence of surreal slow motion.

First they witnessed, amidst the clouds of smoke and singed sky, as the belly of the chestnut stallion carrying the Elf of the Darmon, leapt over the slowly disintegrating Travel Chamber. They moved their gaze over to the backside of the Chamber where the steed landed with precision. All three children looked up at Tannis.

Tannis looked calm and resolute, he smiled at Benjamin. In that quick moment Benjamin realized the intention of the Elf and raised to his knees shouting, *"NO! Tannis, don't do it!"*

But it was too late. The Elf was leaping on the back of his faithful stallion, Bits, right into the center of the Travel Chamber.

Tannis turned Bits around to face the bewildered children. They all looked over at the Queen, who was now standing solo amid her enraged destruction. The look on her face was worth every bit of fear the children had lived in the past evening. Her eyes were wide with incredulous disbelief. She was steaming with a rage strong enough to fell the tallest of Forest trees.

Then she let out a scream the likes of which had never been heard in the existence of the Gilley Forest.

She flew like a lightening bolt of deep dark magic at the Travel Chamber, which shook with a husky primal resonance that alarmed its inhabitants. When the Queen realized that her torture was beginning to wax heavily on the object of her anger, she reloaded and pulled the trigger again. She reigned a full force attack on the side of the Travel Chamber. The walls were showing signs of dismantling. The glowing light of the Chamber began to flicker and the children could see that it would only be a matter of a short time before she would penetrate the protection shield. She would have them in her hands at her unwavering mercy.

They all knew no one would survive.

Tannis jumped off of his steed and closed his eyes. He stretched his arms out beside him and touched the sides of the Travel Chamber with his hands. Within moments the watery energy of the Chamber started to become more solidified. And without warning or thought...*the lights went out.*

After a moment the children, still in the darkness, realized there were no sounds surrounding them.

"Benjamin, where are we?" asked Annabel. "I can't see a bloody thing. But it doesn't feel like we're with the Queen anymore. Maybe..." And before he could say another word a small orb of light, generated by the Elf, was in the middle of everyone.

"Wow!" said Mathilda. "Where are we Tannis?"

"We are in between."

Chapter Twenty

Thornton Berry Shire

"What do you mean we're in between?" asked Annabel with dread.

Tannis looked around him at the walls of the Travel Chamber. He could see the damage incurred by the wrath of the battle. He closed his eyes and began making a deep humming sound. The children were lost for words. They all simply watched as the Elf of the Darmon proceeded to work his magic on the Travel Chamber.

Spheres of color light generated from the center of his body, showing through his tunic like Christmas lights under a piece of gauze. They rose in a repetitive order from lower in his hips, and continued on up out the top of his head. From red to green then blue and purple. Every color had a correlated sound, a note of music on the scale. Small white dimensional orbs of energy glowed and pulsed from his palms as they lay against the Travel Chamber walls. The humming continued and the colors changed and the Path began to light up in the smallest, tiniest of increments. Small, like a refrigerator light in the middle of the night, in the middle of a deep dark wooded forest.

After a few minutes Tannis ended his ritual and opened his eyes. The children looked at him in shocked dismay. Tannis was *changing*. He was beginning to fade. His body was taking on the appearance of the watery clear Chamber walls.

"Don't look so worried, I knew this was the only way to save the Path and remove you from the grasp of the Queen's control. This is my journey...*my* Path."

"Please explain what in between means," said Benjamin.

"Neither here nor there," replied Tannis.

Mathilda raised her eyebrows, "You mean we're like a shadow or something? Cause that's what this looks like. It's all kinda grey looking, don't you think Bellie?"

"Now that you mention it, yeah, that's exactly what it looks like. So how long do we stay here, and how will the others know where to find us?"

"They can't, we are undetectable in this state of being. However, we should be returning to a part of the Path that is much further ahead of where we left today. If my calculations are correct, we should be very near Ashwald."

The children looked at each other with wide eyes and smiles began to form on their faces.

"Are you kidding me!" said Mathilda with a laugh.

"How will we know where we are?" asked Annabel.

"We need to stay still for a bit," explained Tannis, "We need to let the Path regenerate itself from it's deep wounds. We will stay here the night, and by morning we will all see the light of day. And the Travel Chamber will once again be back onto it's hallowed Path leading to the Great Tree. I will not know until the daylight comes just exactly where we have landed, such is the outcome of time jumping in the middle of a battle."

Benjamin looked sadly at Tannis. "What will become of you Tannis? Will you just disappear?"

Tannis took a long inhalation then released it and looked at the three children standing before him with worry on their faces.

"As was explained earlier, I am not fully aware of what to expect, as this has never been executed before. Right now I am fully conscious and alert. Actually, my senses appear to be heightened by a great deal. It's quiet an extraordinary feeling." And he smiled with deep satisfaction, "No need to fret young brave travelers, I will keep a steady watch tonight. I will be able to listen for the Queen, or any other uninvited disturbances, such is the advancement of my awareness at present. So you all may receive the much needed rest that is required of your bodies and minds. Just sleep now."

And so they did.

On the other side of the Gilley Forest Tar Vigorn stood in her heaping pile of monstrous rage. The earthworms buried themselves as deeply as possible to escape the inhuman sounds generated from her howls of anger. The smoke from the burning timber was wafting through the Forest. It carried with it's steamy stream a Magic that called out to the darkness...*a message to the Blunt*.

On yet another side of the Forest, the gritty substance that *was* the Blunt, began to rouse as if from a deep lifeless sleep.

"The Great Maleficent Force is beckoning our duty to arms. We may not tarry. Let us ride to the aid of our Queen...*Tar Vigorn!*"

And with this the group of hollow encapsulated bodies, of unspeakably profound negativity, moved into action. They road off into the darkness in search of their siren, to feed on her anger.

The Forest clans of the West camp had been in a heightened mode of emergency ever since the allotted time had come and gone when the children should have arrived to the safe camp. Word had been sent that everyone was to begin the trek to gather all forces towards Ashwald. Everyone was working furiously to tear down the camp. Several members of the Darmon were gathered in discussion of Tannis and the Travel Chamber.

"Do we know what state he is in at present?" asked a concerned Elf named Shiyah.

"No, the only information has come from the transporting of fractured images. He is in a limbo we have not witnessed before," replied Lonagon, a male Elf who was also the chamberlain to the royalty of the clan.

A third, Jaspen asked, "Has anyone spoken with the Princess?" No sooner had he said this when a bright light shown to the left of the group, and they all turned to look. It was the Essence Whisper, Princess Avenel, floating in on her massive pure white owl, Dew.

"Is it true?" she immediately asked, to no one in particular.

A round of nods followed. The tiny princess looked out into the Forest past the clan of Elves, and her eyes began to glaze. Finally, after a moment of silence among them, the Princess pulled herself together and spoke, "I will have to relinquish my role as head of the Whisper clan, I must go to him immediately."

The other Elves looked stunned, it was like someone had just slapped them alert. Protocol among the Elves did not permit someone of Avenel's stature to sit in this position. The Essence Whisper is a transformed Elf for the duration of their station, however, this seat is never held by a Royal. No matter the tradition, or the rules, Avenel swore an oath, regardless of the dissent from her mother; when the Chancellors were distraught over an untimely, and somewhat mysterious death of Vena, the previous Essence.

It was assumed the Whisper, Vena, was swallowed up in a rupture of venomous rage thrown from the hands of the evil Queen during a tumultuous chase through the Gilley from Goats Mead Shire. An Essence Whisper is not allowed to fight or kill. In order to defend the Til' aut Set of the Shire, Vena reversed her enchantment and became a full bodied Elf again. But she was no match for the dark Queen. Vena's companion Gnome Deter, watched in horror as his liege vanished into a thick purple cloud of smoke.

Avenel and Vena had been like sisters in their deep long lived friendship in the Darmon. Even as her mother pleaded and threatened, Avenel considered it her duty to take Vena's place. Avenel transformed into the diminutive energy of a Whisper and left her home in the Darmon.

Now today, without hesitation, she was resigning her duty after nineteen years. The Elves wondered how this would be received.

She turned to Lonagon, "Ready my charger, I leave at once."

Lonagon gave a quick look at the others, then bowed his head and left to retrieve Avenel's coffee colored stallion, Chant. She quickly turned to the others, "Please inform the Chancellor of my leaving." Then she bowed her head and touched her heart. " Aut'banda."

A round of bowing came back at her. She turned towards the Forest and lowered herself off of the radiant white bird that had been her transport for so many years, onto the ground. She closed her eyes, took a deep breath and let out a low, full, steady hum. As the tone surged out into the ethers about her, she began to run full speed. With every powerful step lunging forward, her body transformed. In the blink of an eye, she had physically morphed from the wee etheric figure of the Whisper, to the strong full size body of an Elf of the Darmon. When she knew the exchange was complete, she slowed her gait every so slightly and let out a high pitched tone that echoed up through the thick trees. Within seconds Chant was galloping up from behind her. When he reached along side her, without missing a beat, she leapt up onto his back, and they rode off into the deepness of the night.

Chantilly Lily and Emeline sat along the waters' edge in the cove off the Fallen Leaf River. The sun would be coming up soon and neither had slept. The news of Tannis had not yet reached them, and would be a hard blow for Emeline once she learned of the children's whereabouts. However, right now they had a bigger concern in front of them. Two men from the other world had entered the Gilley Forest and were on their way towards the Shire. The women of the Forest were urgent to intercept their journey. Hopefully, it hadn't already been detained.

"Whisper, how is it we find ourselves in this place? How could these men be expected to survive the circumstances we are entrenched in at present? What will happen to the wee lasses if danger befalls their father?"

Emeline sat in her usual manner, leaning forward with her hands clasped between her open knees, as she sat on a fallen tree trunk. The golden glow of the firelight shimmered on the front half of her body.

"Oh dear child, please do not go into that negative place of thinking. Only blackness will follow you there. We need to be secure in our efforts and our strength to take care of this matter successfully. We can only pray that the Queen has not caught word of their entry as yet. Or, at the very least, she may not have thought as to their precise location."

"I think I will never forgive myself for not informing the girls of his presence. It was not our place to keep it from them," spoke Emeline with deep regret. "Oh there you are again. You know there was absolutely nothing they could have done about this unexpectedness. They are on their *own* Path. Let him follow his," said Chantilly Lily with softness. "Why don't you get some rest, the sun will show soon enough. I am alert to any activity coming our way, and will give you ample time to gather yourself for the greeting....sleep now child."

Emeline pulled herself down off of the log to lean up against it and closed her eyes.

Several hours later Emeline began to awaken from the brightness of the sun on her closed eyelids. She stirred slowly, not wishing to be pulled from the safe embrace of the suns warmth on her body. Suddenly she remembered where she was and bolted upright.

"Have I slept long?" she asked the Whisper with urgency.

"Not too long, but long enough. The travelers are rapidly approaching, we must ready for their arrival."

Emeline leaned over at the waters' edge and washed her face in the cool blue liquid. She sat back onto her heels while she dried her face, and looked around at the beauty before her. They were in the cove of Thornton Berry Shire, one of the most beautiful places in all of the Gilley Forest. Surrounded by the deep woods with a tall canopy of flowering shrubs, nestled with the abundance of red and black berries filling in its boarders. The privacy given from the thickness of the bushes made the space hidden, yet it was wide open to the sky immediately above. It was a safe haven, giving refuge to dozens of species of colorful birds, who all lived harmoniously in the tranquil space.

As Emeline looked across the waters' pristine surface, to the opposite side of the cove, a soft breeze moved lusciously towards her from the crisp, cool, lyrical water fall. Aqua and blue mixed in with the silver of the light infused tendrils of water splashing down from the stones that formed the wall. Boulders and rocks that were rich with glistening quartz of pinks and browns filled her senses. This was a paradise of its own.

Emeline heard some twigs snap to her left and looked over with astute attention. Chantilly Lily popped in right beside her when they heard a voice call out, "Cubby, Cubby, wait up boy."

A moment later the two women of the Forest learned what Cubby was. Bounding through the berry briar came a great golden dog who landed in three giant leaps smack dab in the middle of the cove. He began lapping and splashing about, so relieved by the coolness. The women smiled at the pure happiness exuding from the animal. Then his masters came into view. The two men stopped and gazed up at the bluest of skies.

"Wow! This is the first piece of heaven we've gotten since we began this trek. Look at that Edward...sky. And right above our heads. How fortuitous for us."

Edward was watching Cubby swim around the refreshing water and lowered his backpack off of his shoulders. He looked around and suddenly froze. Braxton released his pack as wel,l as he lowered his site to land on the two strange women before them. *Crikey, here we go*, he thought, "Don't say anything Edward, I'll do all the talking," he whispered.

He began to step forward and Edward inched along behind him, never releasing his stare from the little woman on the floating ball. Braxton looked deeply into Emeline's eyes. He stared hard, then shook his head as if he were in a dream and attempting to wake himself up.

"Hello, I'm Braxton and this is my friend Edward. And that ball of wet fur is Cubby," he said as the dog climbed out of the water to find the most perfect ray of sunshine to plop himself down in. "We're from the other side of the window in Grandlochcheshire. We're not here to harm anyone, or disrupt any Spirit.

We're looking for Edward's two young daughters, Annabel and Mathilda and their friend Benjamin. You wouldn't happen to have seen them would you?"

Emeline looked at Chantilly Lily, then at the now happily resting dog, with the hot sun baking on his back. She finally looked back at Braxton, "I am Emeline and this is Chantilly Lily, and we are both loyal friends of your children."

Edward jumped forward anxiously, "You *know* them? What do you mean you're their friend, where are they? Are they alive? Please, what has happened to them?"

Emeline put her hands up to stop him from overtaking her with his spastic energy, "Shush! It's going to be all right. I will tell you everything. The last time I saw them they were safe in the Travel Chamber on their way to Ashwald. The Vila and the Path Tender are guiding them, no harm will come under their vigilant watch, I assure you. Now, please, both of you sit down and we shall share our stories."

"Yes, it is very curious that you are both, or I suppose I should say the three of you, are here right now," added Chantilly Lily. "How is it that you were able to gain entry into this dimension? Most folk just wonder into the Forest and never know we are here. But you arrived on a different level, this has never happened before?"

Braxton stared in utter disbelief at the diminutive creature floating in front of him, "Blimey....what *are* you?" he whispered in awe. Then realizing his rudeness he quickly added, "Oh blast! I'm sorry, I mean no disrespect. It's just we've never seen someone of your kind before. Our world doesn't hold such magic as yours. And we have not seen a single being since we entered the forest back at the Chickering farm two days ago."

"So you came from the farm?" said Emeline. Something tugged at the back of her mind.

"Yes, you know that farm?" asked Braxton.

Emeline looked into his eyes, she suddenly felt a familiarity that made her nervous and relaxed her all at the same time. She smiled at him. She caught herself going off in her emotions and gathered herself by clearing her throat,

"That farm was my home a long time ago. I am Emeline Chickering..." She trailed off into her own sad thought.

Edward looked at Braxton and whispered, "She's barking mad mate, that would make her close to a hundred. Why are we wasting our time with this, I need some information!"

Braxton held up his hand to quiet Edward, "You know I think we'll take you up on that offer to sit down. I have a feeling this is going to take some explaining, and we are both pretty exhausted from the quick pace we have been keeping these past two days."

So they all sat on the waters' edge, all except Chantilly Lily who floated just a few inches off the ground to be closer to eye level with the others.

"So do you always have to stay on that ball?" asked a very interested Braxton.

"Only if I want to get around...ho!" and she let out a little chuckle. Realizing the joke only made her laugh, she continued, "It is the nature of a Whisper. I am the top ranking post of the Botanical Whisper, and as such my duties call me to scurry about in an instant at any given moment. It's just easier to remain floating. In truth, it has become second nature for me, although there are times I am partnered with Jeno, the Raven. Now, *he* is a sturdy ride indeed. I tend to commute with Jeno when in certain dimensions, but for the Gilley I prefer my ball. However, if it makes you uncomfortable I could step down for a bit."

Braxton looked horrified that he made someone so special feel so awkward, "Oh my word, I would have nothing of the sort. I was simply curious."

They both smiled and looked back over to Emeline and Edward.

"You said you are loyal friends to my children. What did you mean by loyal?" asked Edward.

Emeline looked up into the perfect blue sky and thought, *What am I going to tell these men?* She finally looked back at them, "I know it is difficult for you to understand how it is that I can be here at my young age. *That* story is for another time. Unfortunately we are very short on time at the present, so I will make my remarks in an edited fashion. As you are now aware of the power of the Gateway, you know how it is that the children were brought to us, with the aid of the Path Tender."

"And Sir Gibbles of course," added Chantilly Lily.

Emeline smiled nervously, "Yes, of course, and Gibbles as well."

"The Path tender, what the heck is that?" asked Edward.

Emeline was caught off guard by Edward's mannerisms, she smiled sweetly at him. "You...just now, when you said that, you sounded just like the wee lass. She is always asking questions in that same manner."

Edward looked at her, but chose not to say anything at that moment. *She knows my Mathilda's habits? In FOUR days, what is happening here?*

"There is an old Prophecy that portends the coming of three children from your world," began Emeline, "It predicts the journey into Coramin, the land through the Door in the Grandfather Tree. Part of this endeavor includes the battle of wits and courage produced at the Great Tree in order to gain entrance into the city of Na'Talom. And part of this Prophecy is about the saving of our planet...and the ruin of the dark Queen, Tar Vigorn." She stopped to let it all sink in, then she continued, "We...*all of us*...the clans of the Forest, believe your girls, led by Benjamin, are the children of the Prophecy."

Edward looked her straight in her eyes and his mouth began to open and close without any words or sounds coming out. Then finally he jumped up and began pacing back and forth until he exploded, *"Benjamin!...what?* Are you telling me that you lured my girls and their friend into this mess because of some old fortune tellers prediction! What on earth do you think they are capable of doing for you? They are children, they are not magicians, or wizards! This isn't Hogwarts! This is complete madness! And who the bloody hell is this Queen, *what's* her name? Why do I get the feeling that I've just entered into some warped version of a twisted old fairy tale, where the evil Queen eats children for breakfast? If she harms one hair on their heads, she will have my rage to contend with...and you haven't even begun to scratch the surface of what I am capable of when it comes to my little girls!"

Braxton jumped up beside his friend and grabbed him by his shoulders and shook him, "Edward...Edward!" Speaking under his breath he muttered, "Listen mate, I warned you before we left your house, this is not the world you are used to. I told you things would be very different and to expect anything that your mind could come up with in the realm of magic and sorcery. I think this little woman on a floating ball is pretty much proof of that statement. You need to relax and let me take care of the details. We have gotten this far, and I know Emeline is going to help us. I trust her."

Edward looked into Braxton's eyes, "What do you mean you trust her? She's one of them, why would you believe anything she has to say?"

"Because I had a dream about her the night before we left."

Edward squinted and scrunched his face up, stunned, "What do you mean you had a dream about her? *Her*, this exact her, or someone like her?"

"Exactly her...on a black horse in the middle of a battle," he answered simply.

After a moment of stark disbelief, the men regained control of their senses and sat back down on the sandy shore line of the cove.

"I know this is all so untoward, but may I please speak with you openly?" asked Emeline.

They both nodded their heads, and the Warrior continued.

"This is a very different world. The dangers of the Forest far out weight anything you could imagine. I know this, as I come from your world. Granted, I was only ten when I left, but I do know what I am speaking of. The children are on the sacred Path created by the great Elves of the Darmon, that will guide them directly to the Great Tree. When they arrive they will have a small allotted time to answer all the exams put before them. One by one the correct action will begin to unlock the coveted Door to Coranim. This is the land of the Gnomes, the Gnomes of the Fet. I do not know what the childrens' role is in the repair of the present deterioration of the earth, but I do know that they will know what to do when the time comes.

"We have been waiting twenty years for their emergence into the Forest.

222

During this time the dark Queen has run catastrophe at the expense of the Gilley inhabitants. She is on a quest to discover the secret location of the Great Tree in an effort to gain entrance into Coranim, where she will wreak havoc on the people of the earth. And we shall all suffer greatly under her tyrannical rule."

Emeline took a deep breath and looked down towards the ground, "Your sudden appearance was not calculated into the strategy of the Chancellors and leaders of the clans. Your presence has put a greater burden on the success of our mission. If the Queen finds you, someone will be forced to make the ultimate sacrifice." And looking back at the men for emphasis, "Would you have that be Mathilda or Annabel?"

The two men looked at each other with deep concern.

"The Whisper and I are here to run interference of your journey and guide you to a place we believe will keep you out of harms way. We must protect the Path and the children of the Prophecy at all costs. Do you understand everything I have said?"

The men sat in silence. Neither of them could speak. The importance of Emeline's words made Braxton's brain go round in question. Edward just sat stunned, as if he had been shot. After a few more moments of silence Edward spoke, "So I was correct in thinking we have entered into some parallel Universe, with the devil at the helm. What do we do now?"

"Could you please explain in a small amount of time, just how it is that you are here. I am befuddled," asked Chantilly Lily.

Braxton looked at Edward. Edward shook his head, turned up his palm towards Braxton and said, "Be my guest."

So Braxton told of their journey to the dimensional world of the Gilley Forest.

"It took nearly two days for Edward and Claire to finally realize that the girls were gone. Edward phoned to let me know of their disappearance and his leave from the office. I, of course, let him know he could take all the time he needed. Then he told me about the letter Annabel had left for them to find. That's when my interest piqued, because in the note Annabel mentioned the destination as the Chickering Farm." He stopped abruptly and looked at Emeline, "That just sounds so weird to say it to you like that. Is it weird for you?"

Emeline nodded, "I was starting to get used to it with the children, but yes, it is foreign to speak of my life, and my family, as if everyone had perished. To become a story passed down for a hundred years."

Braxton commiserated by nodding his head, "Maybe I should give you a small background on myself to better understand my knowledge of your world."

The Forest women both agreed.

"My father's company, Dagwood Corporation, is an old family run business. We specialize in energy technologies. The lineage of my name, *Dagwood*, translates to mean *Luminous Forest*."

Emeline smiled at this information.

"This has been a source of great pride for me, because I'm pretty much the 'black sheep' of the family. I am a *'new thinker'* so I'm told. I don't follow with tradition, and this has always rubbed my father the wrong way. I am an environmental advocate and I support the Forests. Where as my father just wishes for me to keep the status quo by keeping the investors and share holders happy.

"I'm currently in the process of designing a system to transform sea water into viable drinking water, without bringing more toxic waste into the formula. There are smaller companies taking this on, but the cost and the energy involved defeats the whole purpose. And the brine left from the end results of the system so far cannot go back into the sea, as it would kill off many species of fish. So this technology would change our planet in a very big way."

Braxton reflected on his last statement for a quick moment, then continued, "As a child I fell in love with the mystery of the Gilley Forest and the magic surrounding the tales of witches and fairies. I read everything I could get my hands on regarding the Skeffingtion Union Rails heir and his captured children, *(Emeline flinched at the mention of the lost children)*, and the unexplained disappearance of a family who lived on a farm that butted up against the Gilley Forest." He looked at Emeline and mouthed the word, *Sorry.* Emeline had a tear in her eye, but smiled at Braxton. This action, mixed with her remarkable beauty, warmed his heart and he continued further, "Through all of my research of the past...oh...twenty years or so, I learned about the different folklore and stories of Gnomes and Elves that were said to live in the Gilley Forest. Never heard mention of a Whisper, however," and he winked at the little woman. This time Chantilly Lily smiled. "Part of my interest took me into deeper realms of quantum physics, and the idea of dimensional worlds. I've read a lot about these sciences. I've also read pounds of science fiction. So I simply knew in my heart when Edward mentioned the farm, there must be a portal of transport located there.

"I mean it suddenly all made sense! The bizarre and sudden disappearance of your family, Emeline, and now the Wickcliff girls. *Who*, in their letter, said they were going to seek a *'window into another world'*, I mean seriously! So after a long dialog I finally convinced Edward and Claire that I could figure out a way to enter the portal. That's when Edward and I packed our things and left immediately.

"When we arrived at the farm we found Cubby holding vigil in the garden. There was an eerie feeling about the place, like we were being watched or something, and Cubby was jumping and barking at the air in the back of the garden. So I knew right away we were in the right place."

He took a deep breath and continued, "My many years of meditation and study of different philosophies added another level of knowledge of such occasions. I also knew we needed to project a clear and powerful spiritual intention to facilitate the manifestation of the portal. Well, suffice it to say...here we are."

After a moment in thought Chantilly Lily asked, "And what about Benjamin's family? How are they?"

Edward picked up the story now.

"That's kind of an odd situation there. For some unexplained reason Benjamin's grandmother wasn't too concerned when Claire ran screaming to her that the kids were gone. She just looked at her and said, 'Everything was right with the world.' Claire was totally beside herself. She couldn't get the urgency through to her. However, it seems the old gal is somewhat of a mind reader or something, and didn't appear to be too worried about her grandson. Claire said she heard rumor about something to do with her *'abilities'* from a neighbor. Either way, you would think she would be more concerned about Benjamin disappearing considering her own son and his wife have been missing for...*oh*, I don't know, three years now I think."

Chantilly Lily's eyebrows ran up her forehead in piqued interest. Braxton interjected, "I believe the, *'old gal'*, as Edward puts it, is clairvoyant."

"Clairvoyant, what does that mean?" asked Emeline.

"It means she can see and hear things that others can't. She can kinda predict the future. They call it psychic or a seer"

Chantilly Lily opened her mouth, then shut it. Emeline looked at her, then faced the men, "Well, it apparently runs in the family."

Edward scrunched his face, "What does that mean?"

"Benjamin has the Site," said Emeline. "He can see future events as well. And he hears things in other dimensions. He has a very powerful gift."

Edward shook his head in disbelief, "Seriously?"

Emeline just looked down at the ground in her own thoughts.

Chantilly Lily asked, "And what of these missing parents?"

"I really don't know much about that. Apparently his mother and father are both scientist and they went off on excursions and neither has returned or had any communication with the family in almost three years now. It's heart breaking to think of," responded Edward.

Chantilly Lily shuttered at the thought. Braxton finally spoke, "So now that we are all caught up with the basics, what's next? How do we get to this chamber?"

"You are not going to the Travel Chamber," said Emeline. "What do you mean, we're not going to the chamber! But...." Emeline interrupted him, "You haven't seemed to grasped the severity of the threat we are currently facing. If Tar Vigorn even catches a breath about the two of you, all is lost. We are directing you to a safer place, that at present she is unaware of. And let me say, that keeping such secrets from the Queen is a particular feat unto itself. She knows every inch of these woodlands. The Forest clans have spent much energy and Magic to safe guard several of these places for our benefit. The Grandfather Tree has been the most auspicious of these. But there is another, his mate, that is on the other side of the Forest. We will be guiding you to this location in hopes that the Queen will not be on the hunt for you while she is embroiled in the battle at present. A personal request to assist with guidance has come from a formidable Warrior of the Whisper clan. It has given us hope that we will be successful in our endeavor to guide you both to safety. We are awaiting the arrival of King Tsula now, then we leave immediately."

"A King! Well, that should be interesting," said Braxton.

Edward jumped in, "You said Whisper clan. Does that mean he's...,"

But before he could finish his question, a dark grey shadow cast itself over the small group sitting by the waters' edge. Then a piercing cry of a hawk caught their attention. They all looked up as the sun was cutting in and out from the shadow of a profoundly large bird swimming around in the open blue sky above them.

"Wow!" said Braxton, "That's the biggest hawk I've ever seen. Bloody hell, his wing span looks about ten feet!"

"Holy mother of god! There's someone saddled to his back! Braxton look," said Edward in shock.

And that's when they both saw the Whisper. As the Hawk Warrior began his decent, another anomaly was presenting itself beside the little group.

Suddenly the water of the cove began to swirl like a strong wind moving across it's surface. Little caps of waves were beginning to churn and rise. The two men didn't know where to focus their attention at this point. Edward deeply enchanted by the site above him, returned his gaze, while Braxton now turned his complete attention to the whirlpool of water before him. His mouth hanging open, he watched intently as a funnel began to form and rise up out of the blue cove water.

Edward had his mind attempting to wrap around the vision of the small bare chested man, dressed in dark earthy brown suede pants, dismounting the saddle from the giant red hawk and walked towards them. While Braxton was now staring in utter disbelief at a blue woman...*with wings.* "Bloody hell!" was all he could say at that moment.

Emeline stood up and bowed before Morel speaking the words, "Aut'banda."

"Aut'banda sister of the Set."

King Tsula was now standing next to the others and produced the same ritual towards Chantilly Lily, "Aut'banda my comrade," she answered in kind.

The two men just sat completely boggled with their mouths open.

Emeline made introductions, "This is Princess Morel. She is the Vila of the Forest lakes and streams. All water resides under her protection and command. She is the sister of Sethina, the Vila guiding your children with the help of Cottie Set. And this is King Tsula, head of the Warrior clan of Whispers. His companion is Mott."

Both Morel and Tsula bowed their heads. Emeline continued, "This is Braxton, he is the friend to Edward, who is the father of Annabel and Mathilda. And with them is their traveling companion, Cubby."

The men finally closed their gapping mouths and nodded hellos to the two unusual Royals before them. Braxton felt a tingle run through his body when the Vila smiled at him, and wondered to himself why he was feeling so...*goofy.* Cubby was keeping a safe distance from the strange characters surrounding them. He wasn't ready to make friends with the likes of a giant red hawk.

Emeline spoke with urgency to Morel, "Have you heard word from either camp?"

Morel looked to Tsula who answered, "Yes my Lady, it appears there have been profound occurrences since you journeyed. The camps have dismantled and are gathering forces towards Ashwald. Tar Vigorn was able to reign severe damage to the Travel Chamber and Tannis was subjected to....well, I suppose he did the only thing he felt he could."

Emeline looked at Chantilly Lily with impending dread expressed on her face, "*What*, what has happened?" she asked with fear in her voice.

"He entered the Travel Chamber and transported it forward."

"NO!" shouted the Botanical Whisper.

Emeline stepped back and began to pace in her usual way, "This can not be so. This isn't happening. Where are they? Do you know if they made it intact?"

These words sent Edward into a full riddle of anxiety, "What do you mean *intact?* What has happened? Where are my girls? Someone give me some answers now!"

Braxton jumped up and stood next to Emeline, "What are you talking about? Who is Tannis and why do you all look like the devil just appeared?"

"Because she has," responded Emeline.

The anxiety level went up several notches, and panic was about to take over when Morel spoke, "Please, keep your heads! We have information and we need to remain in our centers in order to visualize clarity. We shall not gain advantage over Tar Vigorn with doubt and fear guiding our thoughts and actions. Be Still!"

And with this everyone stopped pacing and moving about. They all centered their attention on the Vila, while Tsula was over at the fallen tree dragging it closer in, so everyone could sit. Braxton helped Tsula situate the limb, and the two men and the beautiful warrior, with the long raven hair, sat down and looked up at Morel. The two Whispers were beside them facing the Vila as well. Cubby and Mott sat motionless behind them.

Morel finally continued, "Tannis took it upon himself to follow the children to serve as protection and guidance. And thank goodness he did, because the Queen was able to discover the exact location of the Travel Chamber and the children. From what we can glean from the broken up transmitted communications to the Elves, Tannis, in his unrelenting fierceness and compassion, entered the Travel Chamber before the Queen could fully ravage the Path. They have been in shadow ever since."

Emeline let out a small gasp, "Oh..my."

In a tiny voice Chantilly Lily simply said, "Tan - nis."

Morel added, "Princess Avenel has stepped down as head of the Essence and has ridden off in hopes of finding them."

Chantilly Lily let tears fall from her eyes and in a smaller voice said, "Avenel...No"

Edward was about to implode from the sheer terror he felt from what he thought he understood Morel to say, "Are you saying she got to them? Are they dead?"

"No!" replied Emeline. "They are only in shadow." "What does that mean?" asked a very confused Braxton.

"It means we have no idea where they disappeared to when Tannis transported the Path," answered Morel, "Their energy is undetectable at present. No Elf of the Darmon has ever entered the Travel Chamber, so we have no template of action."

"So am I to understand that Tannis is an Elf? And he did something to the Travel Chamber to get away from the Queen?" "Yes," replied the Vila.

"And they aren't dead, they are just....gone?"

"Well, that would be a simple version, but....yes, that is the idea," said Chantilly Lily.

But before Edward could lose his mind completely and begin a new rant, Tsula spoke, "I have seen much from where I sit in the sky. The Queen stormed on her rampage after the disappearance of the Travel Chamber and her path of destruction is evident. She has spread fire and anger at every turn. And what is more important, she has awoken the Blunt."

Edward looked at the little man standing next to him.

"The *Blunt*....there's something called the Blunt. Oh, *well*, that just can't be good."

Tsula shook his head, "It is the call to war. The Blunt are ruthless and clever when it comes to sniffing out fear."

"Sniffing out fear?" questioned Braxton, "What are they some kind of monster or Forest demon?"

Emeline explained, "The Blunt is something that cannot be described. They are not of body nor soul. They are simply a gathered source of negative energy.

230

They are like smoke." "Smoke?" questioned Braxton. "Yes, they are transformed from the grey smoke of the Queen's darkest Magic. They are her greatest creation. She crafted them from the smoldering embers of trees that perished from her errant magic during battle."

"Crafted them, I don't understand," said Braxton.

"She used her powerful Magic to transform a charred, burnt piece of tree bark, that still glows red from her dark spells thrown in the heat of conflict. She gathers her powerful intent and drives it straight into the burned out tree stump and the vapors becomes encased in moss and decayed leaves. It becomes the Blunt. They are contained concentrated dark energy, and they feed on fear, it makes them stronger. They ride on the backs of the Gretch."

"The Gretch, bloody hell...that sounds worse than the Blunt," said Braxton anxiously.

"The Gretch are savage creatures that once were beautiful horses that freely roamed the country sides and made their home in the Gilley Forest. She trapped them in between the sliver of dimensions, in the under wave of energy. They are no longer of any world, they are death. And they are brutal in combat, for they tear and rip apart any creature caught in their path."

Braxton was stunned into silence.

Emeline stood up, all eyes were upon her. She looked up into the blue sky for a moment, "We must trust the others to take care of the Path and the children. Tannis has power and insight, he will find a way to reenter the Forest and the Prophecy will continue."

She turned around and looked back down at the faces staring up at her, "We need to follow our own path at present. We need to get to the Tay'lor. We must leave now." Then she walked away to gather her pack and supplies.

Tsula nodded his head in accordance and turned to ready Mott for their journey. Edward sat in utter disbelief of the circumstances he found himself in, frozen in fear. Braxton stood up before the beautiful woman of the lakes, something about her made him feel like a blushing schoolboy.

"I hope..."

But before he could say another word the Vila's face grew alert and she looked past Braxton into another realm of dimension. Braxton could see she was in a trance of some sort, however, before he could assist her, Morel evaporated right before his eyes. Like a giant blue water balloon that burst, letting all the water globules fall quickly from solid mass to puddle.

The only thing he heard her say right before she vanished was "Benjamin!"

Chapter Twenty-One

Water Ride

$\mathcal{B}$enjamin was standing outside in the sunlight. It had been a long night in the darkness. Actually, it was more like greyness, the word shadow had described it accurately. They had all finally fallen asleep as Tannis suggested, but Benjamin had awoken before anyone else.

Unable to relax his mind, he decided to get up and look around. Tannis was not with them, oddly enough, and it appeared they were no longer in the shadows, as Benjamin was clearly standing in the Forest. He wondered where Tannis had gone off to as he looked at the big gaping hole in the side of the Travel Chamber. Tannis had obviously left them alone for whatever his reasons, curious as they were. However, at this point he simply needed to be outside for a bit to regenerate. Benjamin didn't want to think that the worst had happened to Tannis, however, it was difficult not to. He hoped he would see his new friend again soon.

He walked out beyond the trees a bit and came upon the smallest of streams swimming past him. He squatted down to look deeper into the cool water. As he searched without direction, his line of site landed on a river stone with a thin white line down its face. The water magnified the beauty of the stone, and Benjamin reached into the chilly stream and plucked it up.

"Hey, I think it's one of Morel's calling stones, wow, it's brilliant."

He studied the smoothness of the thin stone with its perfect crisp white line cutting through the center. *How does this happen?* he wondered. *Just a stone in the river with a thin white line across its face? Is it calcium, or quartz or something...what?* He just didn't know.

He stood up and looked around the silent Forest before him. *It's just so beautiful here,* he thought. *Who would believe the perils hidden behind every shrub and bush?*

As he turned to head back to the Travel Chamber, he noticed little pockets of wetness surrounding him. The area was somewhat marshy, as leaves squished under his feet. He saw orange and blue dragonflies gliding in pairs in their geometric dance about the bits of water on the Forest floor. He smiled to himself at the simplicity and serenity before him.

Back in the Chamber the girls began to stir. Annabel was first to notice the sun shining and Benjamin missing, "Oh my god!....Benjamin!"

"I'm here," came the answer from the near distance.

"Where are you Benjamin? I don't see you. Is Tannis with you?" she yelled back into the quiet morning.

"I'm over here Annabel, don't worry, I'm heading back your way. I don't know where Tannis is."

"Bellie, what's all the yelling about? Where's Benjamin?" asked a slowly waking Mathilda.

"Tannis and Benjamin weren't here when I woke up. Benjamin is outside somewhere, but he doesn't know where Tannis is. But is looks like we're out of the shadows finally. Thank goodness, that was just too creepy," said Annabel with a shiver.

"Ya think! That was the weirdest thing ever. How about the way Tannis looked? What do you think will happen to him? Oh Bellie, do you think he just finally disappeared for real this time?" asked Mathilda, fully alert now.

"Geez, Tildie. I hope not. Oh my god, poor Tannis." Then Annabel shouted to Benjamin again, "Benjamin, do you think Tannis has faded away?"

"I've been wondering the same thing, but I just don't think that's happened. Hang on, I'll be there in a minute."

As he slowly walked back to the hole in the Travel Chamber, mindlessly turning Morel's small stone around in between his fingers, he stopped several yards away to look at the damage to the Chamber. "Crikey, how is he going to fix that?"

Then Benjamin noticed for the first time this morning that the Travel Chamber was somewhat visible. His eyes widened at the new discovery and what it could mean to their safety. He looked to his left to see how far the Chamber went into the Forest. It was like an old plastic tube, like an old worn out water bottle that wasn't so clear anymore, running the length of the Forest for as far as he could see. Benjamin stared in disbelief. *Where is Tannis? What do we do now?*

Suddenly his attention was interrupted and he began to sniff at the air, he thought he could smell...*smoke?* "What the bloody hell?" said Benjamin turning around slowly, following the scent. Then simultaneously he heard Mathilda, in the highest pitched scream, yelling his name, "Look out Benjamin!"

He looked up to see the grey shape of condensed smoke wrapped in sooty, wormy vines and moss from inside a charcoal grey cloak; perched up on the back of what he could only assume was a demon skeleton of a horse. Benjamin froze solid in his tracks. His eyes popping out of his head, his mouth wide open and dry as a bone, he stared into the abyss of the phantoms face and terror took hold of his mind.

Annabel and Mathilda were on their feet screaming at the top of their lungs, as only girls can do. Annabel began to yell for Tannis and with all of her might she focused on him with her mind. Mathilda was a complete frenzy of jumping, ear piercing screams. Benjamin just stood before the Blunt, in sheer panic. Then from behind him came the now too familiar voice of his nightmares.

"Oh Benjamin, sweet Benjamin, here we stand, finally, face to face. And how are you this fine summer morning? I trust you slept well?" spoke the dark Queen in her gritty cool syrupy tone.

Benjamin faced the Queen and stood straight before her. A small relief had grabbed him as he now heard the voice of the Elf in his mind. *Benjamin, I'm on my way, don't panic...just buy us some time.* Benjamin pulled himself together and rallied up his courage.

"Well, Tar Vigorn. I was hoping we wouldn't have to do this again, we just had so much fun the last time.   But I can see you're really quite persistent aren't you?"

The Queen simply smiled.

Benjamin spoke with the same coolness as the Queen, "So I wonder how our dance will turn out today? The last exchange was rather interesting don't you think? I hope you weren't too upset when we popped out of site right before your eyes?"

Tar Vigorn frowned incredulously at his tone.

"It seems you have mustered up an ounce of courage to speak to me in such an informal and disrespectful manner. Lucky for you, I'm much to excited to be standing here with you right now to fire back at your insolence. And from the looks on the faces of your little friends it's worth the insult. It also seems that my little temper tantrum caused some serious damage. It appears quite extensive...yes?" She didn't wait for a response and continued with her emotional attack, "Yes, I can see that it clearly has. I will say that I had not expected the Elf to take such drastic and enduring measures as he has, just to save the likes of you three. However, now that we are here, alone, it seems worth all my anguish at losing you for one night. Pity everyone had to suffer so. I'm saddened to say there are parts of the Forest that shall never recover from my unhappiness. However none of that matters now. I must say, if it weren't for the Blunt and their keen sense of tracking, we may not be standing here together right now. So you can thank them for our merry reunion."

Then she looked about as she spoke, "And where is the Elf? Has he been swallowed up by his own creation?" She snickered.

Benjamin stared into the Queen's eyes, his own rage brewing. Suddenly The Travel Chamber began to hum in a loud low frequency, and the girls looked about them in surprise. The vibration that shook the Chamber was subtle but noticeable and the sisters stopped their yelling and put their hands out to steady themselves. Annabel looked up at Benjamin and she didn't need to say a word, he knew she was in a total panic. He also knew Tannis was up to something and would take care of the girls. However, before he could think his next thought, Tar Vigorn bellowed in a tone that came from a deep source of darkness. The amplified ghostly echo carried up through the trees, "The Time Is Now! Take me to the tree or I shall kill all of you this very instant!"

As she said this dozens of birds fell dead from the sky, landing with a thud all around them. It sounded like a rapid succession of arrows hitting their target.

Thap, thap, thap, thap, thap!

In shock, Benjamin looked behind him to see three of the unearthly smoky cloaks sitting upon their demon steeds. The bile rose in his throat and the terror surrounded his brain, absently, Benjamin opened his hand and let the smooth river stone fall to the ground. The beautiful charcoal grey stone with the perfect white line, tumbled slowly end over end out of his hand, landing with a tiny distinct splash in the smallest of marshy puddles. At the same instant the pebble hit the mossy water next to Benjamin, on the other side of the Gilley Forest in Thornton Berry Shire, the Vila, who had been talking to the man from another world, heard the call to aid coming at her like a rushing freight train. She had never been pulled from her watery form with such an urgency in all her years. Nor had she felt the terror projected from the vibration of it's source with such a force as Benjamin's call.

Benjamin, of course, had not intended to alert the Vila, it was by sheer providence that the stone had landed in the puddle beside him. However, the vision of the situation traveled with the tiny splash, and Morel vanished in an instant, right before Braxton's eyes.

Everything happened all at once.

First Tannis appeared in the Travel Chamber, still in his transparent form, on his trusted horse, Bits. The girls swung around to see him riding full speed at them. They moved quickly out of his line of charge, and Tannis jumped Bits right through the hole in the side of the Travel Chamber straight for the Blunt. As he exited, the Chamber began to crackle and little patches of celluloid disintegration bubbled throughout the walls. Tannis road three circles around the Blunt so quickly, he could have turned them to butter, then road back into the hole of the Travel Chamber before the Queen could react.

And just when Benjamin thought it couldn't get any weirder, the ground began to shudder and it sounded like a massive earthquake was now descending on the stand off between darkness and innocence. Suddenly Benjamin looked down at his feet as he became unbalanced, and Tar Vigorn was so confounded she had no idea where to look first. And then it happened.

The waters of the Forest floor began to meld into one another, drawn together like little silver globs of mercury on a table. Quickly, each puddle joined forces until the water was rising around everyone in the little group. Without warning, the sudden mass of water pulled together into one large funnel of concentrated swirling energy and there before them stood the Blue Lady of the lakes, Morel.

Tar Vigorn was furious. "Morel!" she screamed.

Then she raised her arms to call the Blunt into action, however no one moved, it seemed they were unable to shift in any direction. Tar Vigorn looked at them completely boggled, until she saw it glimmer. A thin, almost iridescent strand of white light that had wrapped around the Blunt like a lasso, came into focus. The Queen raged in power, "TANNIS!"

She whirled her body around quickly and armed herself ready to battle the Vila and let loose with a spike of lightening that cracked the ethers around her.

ZZZAPP!

Water tendrils jumped up to meet the errant strands of lightening. Then in one large roar of sound all the water on the Forest floor gathered into one giant flood, bringing Benjamin along in it's wake and heading straight for the Travel Chamber. Morel slid in behind Benjamin as the water began twisting like a corkscrew into the tunnel opening.

Suddenly Mathilda and Annabel were wading right behind Benjamin as they all were carried off down the Travel Chamber like a giant water slide.

Attempting to keep herself from being sucked under, Tar Vigorn looked up into the sky and howled, "I Want Death!"

And hundreds of birds fell dead at her feet. Trees exploded all around her, and a path of fire opened up a black doorway before her. She stood before the dimensional entrance and took several deep breaths then screamed, "Ready My Charger!"

And from deep in the Forest came a pounding of hooves, riding faster and faster until Tar Vigorn turned slowly to look up at the panting animal standing before her. Slathered in the heat of fury and fierceness, he was pure white with deep red eyes and a small knotted twisted black spike coming out of his forehead. A spike that was said to transform poison water potable and heal wounds inflicted by Magic.

The Queen jumped upon her savage unicorn and road off to follow in the direction of the water tube. As she sped off she flung a ball of glowing red light over her shoulder towards the still entangled Blunt and released the Magic binding them. The smoky demons caught up to their Queen at full speed.

The children were rushing through the Travel Chamber at such a dizzying speed that Annabel began to panic. She attempted to grab onto Mathilda as she whirled past her, but her grip was too slippery and Mathilda let out a "Whoa...oo!"

All three of them spun round and round the curve of the Travel Chamber like being flushed down a drain. Parts of the walls were dismantling and water was spilling through the holes, but not enough to slow down the travel of Morels' Magic. She swam behind them with her tight blue wings guiding her through the rapids.

Finally Benjamin could make out something up ahead in the very near distance, "Morel, what is that?" he yelled to her.

"It is the Great Tree, we are there young Benjamin."

Benjamin couldn't believe he had heard her correctly. He strained to keep a steady view of what was in front of him, but the force of the tide carrying them was overpowering. He thought it looked to him like a wall of tree bark, and they were rushing straight for the side of the massive trunk. Benjamin became concerned, "Morel, how are we going to avoid smashing into the tree at this speed?" shouted Benjamin over the din of rushing water. Then in his head he heard the voice of the Elf, *Faith, Master Benjamin, Morel is in charge of these waters. They will do as requested without exception. Let her guide you, and trust she can land you without effort or injury. I am ahead of you, awaiting your arrival. Sethina and Cottie Set are here, anxious to see you as well*.

So Benjamin relaxed back and enjoyed the ride of his life. He heard Mathilda squealing with delight from somewhere behind him and joined in with the laughter. And before he knew it, Annabel decided to let go as well, and with that the three children of the Prophecy arrived at their destination, soaking wet....standing before the Grandfather Tree.

Chapter Twenty-Two

The Test and The Key

Once Morel had gotten the children safely to the Great Tree she only had a small amount of time to merge back into the Forest floor and return to her watery home in the lake.

"My sister, your presence brings warmth to my heart," Sethina spoke gently to Morel. "My heart shines with love for you as well, dearest Sethina. However, I must not tarry, as my time is limited in this surrounding. I shall see you soon. Aut'banda my beautiful sister." "Aut'banda, sister."

The children were standing with Sethina, Cottie Set, and Sir Gibbles, just outside the gaping hole of the Chamber. A very faded Tannis stood within the mouth of the ruptured transport. They looked over to the left and saw a long line of Elves and Fairies chanting and humming as they faced the base of the Great Tree. The palms of their hands generating a bright white light outward towards the dark ancient bark of the Grandfather. Upon deeper examination, Benjamin could make out the newly forming barrier rising up the height of the tree. It looked very similar to the Travel Chamber in energy, and ran up the entire length of the gigantic tree, expanding out by ten feet. It generated a small vibrational hum, and felt like a fortress of protection to the children.

"It looks like your magic has secured our place here for the time being," said Benjamin, "But I gotta tell you we left the Queen in a pretty serious bloody rage. She wasn't too happy with me, and she certainly wasn't thrilled when Morel showed up to save the day. Oh, no offense Tannis, you did a brilliant job too. If it weren't for your heroic action we wouldn't be here in the first place. But that water thing was wicked!"

Mathilda jumped in, "Yeah, that was the best ride I ever been on!" and she laughed out loud.

"We had no idea what had happened to you that last night when you didn't arrive to the safe camp," said Sethina. "We sent out a search party and followed the trail of burning Forest to the spot where the Path was torn up. Then the Elves began relaying broken up transmissions from Tannis and we were able to decipher a bit of what had occurred. We were all surprised to learn that Tannis had taken it upon himself to be of service, and very grateful for his courage. None of us can still believe you were transported into the shadows. What an unexpected turn of events I dare say."

Cottie Set interjected, "This morning's exercise in escape will have the Queen raging on our heels. I would wonder she is not here as yet, however, we are prepared to go to arms."

She faced Benjamin square on, "Be forewarned young squire, Tar Vigorn will never surrender her position. She covets the entrance into Coranim. She will not rest until she has a victory.

"Benjamin, I don't wish to frighten you anymore than you are, however, you must know the Queen seeks revenge. You have eluded her grasp on more than one occasion now and this does not sit well with her ego. The damage she has unleashed on the Forest and it's inhabitants in this past few days is unfathomable. The poor Set clans will be repairing her destruction for years to come I'm afraid."

"I must say," came the little voice of the Brownie, "Gibbles is quite impressed with the durability and cleverness of the children of the Prophecy. The Elf has informed us of your ingenious idea to play tricks with the Queen. Oh I do love a good charade! I can only visualize her face when you each appeared and disappeared in the Travel Chamber, it must have boggled her but good! Well done you!"

"Yes, and speaking of tricks," said Annabel, "Tar Vigorn told us that my father and his boss are in the Gilley Forest, is this true?"

The Gilley women looked at each other with concern.

"Yes, my child, it is true," said the Path Tender.

Instantly Mathilda's eye's were flooded with tears and a little raspy whimper escaped her lips, "Da."

"How did this happened? Where are they now?" demanded Annabel.

Mathilda swallowed hard and asked, "Does T..Tar Vigorn know where they are?"

"No, lassie, she is completely unaware of their location at this time," answered Sethina, "We were able to intercept their path and guide them to a safe place buried very deep within the Forest. The Queen has no knowledge of this place, it is secured with exceptional Magic and has laid dormant for many long years. Emeline has run interference at Thornton Berry Shire and has collected both Edward, Braxton and their companion Cubby. She, along with the aid of King Tsula and Chantilly Lily, will guide them safely to Tay'lor. To the Grandmother Tree."

"Cubby!" screamed Mathilda, "Oh, Bellie, Cubby and our daddy are here together in the Forest."

Annabel couldn't speak.

"There's a Grandmother Tree? *Seriously?* Another tree? And where does *that* door lead?" asked Benjamin sarcastically.

Sethina gave a nervous smile and simply said, "Below."

"Yeah, that's what I thought," replied Benjamin. "There's another way into Coranim besides this one? So why was it so important to go through all of this ritual and insanity to get us to this door here?"

"Because it is written so in the Prophecy, and the Elves built the Path accordingly," responded Cottie Set. "This other entry has not been fully established as yet. It was placed there as a way for the Win and Set or that area to utilize when it was necessary. When it is complete it will open down into the Wizard city of Pancilet. The Elf of the Darmon will continue to keep the Magic fresh surrounding her whereabouts. There are only several of us who know of her home. Emeline is one of them."

"Who are the Win people?" asked Annabel, "I remember that name in the primer."

"Yes, child, it is written in the Galohishdi, it is in reference to the high mountain clan of Gnomes. Their main means of transport are flying machines, thus the name has the lineage taken from the wind."

Benjamin stepped up, "Oh, flying machines and wind people, well that's all very lovely, but has everyone forgotten we have a very angry dark Queen riding on our coat tails? And it's my understanding we can't simply put the key into the lock. So I suggest that since we know that Mr. Wickcliff and his boss are safe with Emeline, we better get on with this." Then he looked at Annabel and Mathilda and added, "I'm really feeling they're okay right now. Don't worry about them. You know how powerful Emeline is, and they have that warrior King with them. I'm sure they will take care of themselves."

The girls reluctantly nodded their heads, and a calmer Mathilda added, "Yeah, my daddy is pretty darn smart. He'll just knock that rusty old Queen right out of her shoes with his brains!"

Annabel gave a small smile.

Benjamin turned to face the group of Gilleans, "Well, what do we do now?"

"Now we leave you alone to take on the task of solving the tests put before you," responded Cottie Set, "You need full concentration and wit young Benjamin. You need to rely on your instincts and your friends help. This Path was created for you and you alone. Remember, if there is a question, then it stands to reason there is an answer. And all the answers lie within you Benjamin. Trust the Universe to guide you, and listen to the small voice inside that will let you know if you are heading in the most optimum direction. Don't worry about what is happening out side of the shield. We were fortunate that our Magic allowed us to create this barrier of protection. We had not planned for this fortuitous an outcome"

Benjamin swallowed hard and realized how grateful he was that they were able to do so.

"So clear your mind sweet young Warrior of Truth. You are the child of the Prophecy and your day has come. The time is ripe to fulfill your destiny. We are all here with you and believe in your abilities to master life." Cottie Set finished by touching her lips, then her heart and bowed, "Aut'banda."

Then Sethina stepped up and put her arm out across her body to reach Benjamin's opposite shoulder, "Master Benjamin, seeker of Light and Truth, I permit my energy to meld into your essence to assist in the facilitation of courage. Spirit's Speed, Aut'banda."

Benjamin felt a jolt of energy flush his entire being. He felt wide awake and alert...and most importantly, totally present. Everything appeared an octave above what it had been only moments before. Benjamin smiled, "I accept your offer of encouragement and trust. I will perform to the best of my abilities. Thank you all, every one of you, for all your kindness. I won't let you down. Aut'banda."

And the girls both touched their hearts and repeated with a small bow. "Aut'banda."

In an instant the group before them took a step back leaving the children magically placed inside the great barrier. As the children looked out past the protection wall, they saw for the first time that the whole Forest surrounding the Great Tree was filled with all the clans of Gnomes and Elves ready for battle.

"Oh my," said Annabel, "I didn't even notice them until just now."

"Me neither," said Mathilda.

Then Benjamin looked over at Tannis, who was standing within the barrier by himself, and suddenly it hit him, "Oh, Tannis, you can't go out there. And you can't stay in here, what are you going to do?"

The girls turned to look at Tannis now as well. Alarmed, Mathilda instinctively ran up to him and put her arms around the wisp of an outline that was the Elf, "Oh Tannis, we love you so much!" When she did this, little sparks of pink and green colored light popped off of his form and flooded the little protection Chamber they all occupied. Mathilda jumped back from the surprise, "Oh! Tannis it's so beautiful! How did you do that?"

"I didn't do it...you did. This is what your Love looks like when you gave it to me, and I let it shine through. So really, you are the beautiful one, little Mathilda with the happy eyes."

She began to cry softly and backed away to stand next to her sister.

"Since it is impossible for me to stay inside the protection while you proceed, I must remain outside the barrier. I do not know what will happen. I only know I have no regrets in any way for offering my service to the children of the Prophecy. No matter what happens to me, I feel glad that you will fulfill your destiny and enter the beautiful city of Na'talom, a place I have only dreamed of. You will conquer the task at hand, to assist in saving our world. I have no doubt in you, young Master Benjamin. Aut'banda."

Benjamin, with his two best friends beside him, all took a very regal bow before the Elf of the Darmon, who had saved their lives, and spoke in unison, "Aut'banda."

And with this they were alone in the barrier of protection surrounding the Great Tree.

"At least the three of us don't have to worry so much about being in the middle of the battle while we work out opening the door. I suppose that's one small victory," said Benjamin. And the girls nodded in agreement. Then they all took one last look out to the multitude of Forest dwellers surrounding the Tree and turned to head over to the massive Door that held all the Grandfather's secrets locked up tight.

"Well, here we go mates. Let's figure this old boy out. What do you say we go see what all the big fuss is about in this Coranim?"

They circled to the right of the enormous Tree until they stood in front of the most ornately carved majestic Door anyone could even almost think of imagining.

The Door itself stood about twelve feet tall. Carved leaves and vines twisted around each other and followed the border of the Door's edges. There was an inner carved moulding that repeated the border made from a different kind of wood. Across the bottom of the Door, as big as Mathilda, there were four large raised square panels. Each panel was edged with a gorgeous filigree engraved molding, and were made from four different types of wood; giving contrast to the Door. In the center of each raised panel was a smaller raised square that was carved with four tiny squares, two on top of two. In each tiny square was a symbol...a letter in the ancient foreign language.

The large rusted old lock, that resided just below the equally orange and brown patina Door latch, had a small tarnished metal faceplate right next to it. Running vertically down the center of this antiquated mechanism were four large colored dome buttons. Benjamin thought it looked like a prop used in espionage movies; when the protruding button on the device is depressed and blows up the world. He had a chuckle to himself when he realized that this may *actually* be the case for real in this instance.

Just above the last square panel on the right side of the bottom of the Door, there began a detailed carving of a flower stem, that ascended at a diagonal direction across the Door; ending near the top center with the large and spectacular image of, what else...*a Rose*. A single full perfect beautiful Rose bud. The three friends all gasped at the same moment in awe at the sheer perfection of this depiction.

The Door maker had used several different types of wood to lend depth and beauty to the Rose and her leaves. Thorns and berries intertwined the stalk of the lone bloom. One might think you could pluck the small round fruit, such was the likeness to truth.

Benjamin stepped back and took it all in, "Well mates, we better get started. Any thoughts up front?"

Annabel stepped back with Benjamin, "Well, we obviously need to push these buttons before we can use the key. But, I'm guessing we need to figure out the order of sequence first. These big panels are interesting. They all look identical, with the same four letters, or I'm guessing symbols, in blocks of four in the center. *Hmm*..I'm thinking right off the bat that each panel should represent only one symbol and we need to figure that out before we can do anything else."

"Wow! Annabel," said Benjamin in surprise.

"It's all the mystery novels and the computer puzzles, what can I say. Some things are just taken for granted. Like the symbols, there are four symbols and four main panels...so, I just figured we need to decide which symbol goes to which panel."

Benjamin said with a chuckled, "So glad you're on our side Annabel."

After staring at the big squares for a minute, suddenly Mathilda stooped down closer to the Door to get a better look. After a moment of scanning all the crevices before her, she absently began to hum. Within moments she thought she saw something flicker. She stopped humming, breathing and everything else, and stared at the surface before her...*nothing*. After a few minutes of continued searching her unconscious humming began again. And suddenly she saw it flash before her sight. *Was that a leaf carving deep in there?* she thought, but still nothing was there. Lost in confusion she let out a deep resonant long sigh and suddenly there is was, clear as could be...*a leaf impression*.

Shocked by the appearance, eyes wide, she shook her head, then the thought hit her...*it was my humming that brought it out!* She spoke up over here shoulder, "Hey, there looks like a shape right above this square panel thingie. I think it might be a leaf or something."

The other two jumped quickly and crouched down beside Mathilda.

"Oh my god Tildie, you're right! Look Benjamin, can you see it? Wow, it's so subtle I can't believe you saw it at all Tildie."

"Well I wouldn't have if I wasn't humming. Watch." And she went over to the next large panel and positioned herself just above the square moulding and began to hum a little tune. And just like the first panel another almost undetectable, but clearly recognizable, leaf imprint appeared.

"Crickey Mathilda," was all Benjamin could say.

Annabel reached up to run her finger over the depression, triggering the little block it was engraved upon to spin around, surprising her and the others.

"Oh geez! So it's a little rotating block with four sides with a different leaf carved inside each one. Wow, you can barely see the space between the block and the trunk...this is magnificent! Nice job Mathilda, I still don't know how you saw these. I have no clue what we're supposed to do with them, but I guess that's what we're supposed to figure out, huh?"

"It kinda reminds me of my molds, you know. Like the kind used with clay. Maybe we should fill em up or something?" offered Mathilda.

"Yeah, I could see that," responded her sister, "but what would we do with clay leaves, and where would we get the clay?"

"I don't know. It just looks like that to me. I mean it looks like something is supposed to go in there, so I say we just stick a matching leaf in there and see what happens." she replied with a shrug.

Benjamin and Annabel looked at each other.

"Oh yeah, I forgot, we've got the *'think outside of the box'* thinker with us...well, I have a feeling that's exactly what we're supposed to do Mathilda," said Benjamin. So he turned around and picked up several leaves from off the ground and handed them to his friends. One by one they placed the leaves into the depressed images engraved on the Door blocks. And one by one they all fell right out...all except one.

"Hey!" shouted Annabel, "This one stuck!" And they all honed in on the panel to see what would happen, if anything.

The square protrusion began to move, until it became a series of syrupy consecutive circles all spinning, incredibly reminiscent of the Gateway. They watched in amazement as the whirlpool of now liquid wood spun at a great speed like a striped toy top on it's side. Then instantly the goo morphed into one of the strange dimensional symbols and solidified onto its beautiful wooden home on the Door panel.

"Holy sweet peas!" whispered Mathilda, "What the heck was that?"

Annabel plopped down on her butt, "That was amazing, is what that was."

"But what does this mean now?" asked a boggled Benjamin.

"I haven't a clue," answered Annabel, "But I do know that we need to find some other leaves that will fit above these other three panels. Cause clearly they used different trees to make this door and they all seem to be represented here. Do you know what this one is Benjamin?"

"Yeah, that was an Oak leaf. I can't tell what other kinds of wood are used here, but there are only so many trees around this part of the Forest. So let's not fanny about, start collecting leaves mates, we're onto something important here!"

"Except how are we supposed to get leaves when we can't leave the protection barrier?" realized Annabel.

"Yeah, you got a point there," said Benjamin while looking deeper into the question.

"Hey what about Princess Vieolette?" asked Mathilda.

"What do you mean?" asked her sister.

"Well, she helped us before, maybe she'll help us again. We could just ask her to fly around and collect all the different leaves. Then she could just put them right outside the wall and we could reach out and get them."

"Brilliant Mathilda, brilliant!" shouted Benjamin.

So excited by their forward momentum, they all jumped up and quickly ran around to the other side of the Tree. They had been so wrapped up in their deep intellectual task, that none of them had noticed the battle had begun.

"Oh Benjamin!" shouted Annabel.

"The Blunt!" said Benjamin.

Gnomes and Elves were brandishing saber and sword. The clanging of metal hitting metal rang through the Forest. It appeared the Blunt had multiplied into dozens, and were raging full throttle against the Forest clans. Magic threw sparks of lightening that ricocheted off of enormous tree trunks, causing them to explode before their eyes. The children wept with sadness and fear.

"Oh Benjamin, the beautiful Forest..." said a very mournful Mathilda.

Flashes of colored lights and smoke engulfed the entire area surrounding the Great Tree. Horses pulled back onto their rear haunches, rising up into the air in defense. The skeletal demon the Blunt rode upon were busy tearing at fallen warriors. It was a horrific site. And none of them could see the Queen anywhere.

"Why isn't she here Benjamin? Do you see her anywhere?" asked Annabel anxiously. "No, no I don't," *What is she up to?* thought Benjamin.

The little dots of colored light belonging to the Fairies were mingled amidst the billowing smolder of fire and phantom. Mathilda saw the purple light of Vieolette in the distance, "Look, there she is!"

"Oh, we're never going to get her attention through all of this," cried Benjamin.

Then Annabel saw him. "Oh no, look, it's Tannis, he's dying!"

He was laying on the ground up against a big Oak tree. He was very fragile and almost faded clear. They could see his heart light still beating beneath his tunic. Sethina and Sir Gibbles stood guard over him, with the aid of several Gnome warriors. They watched as sparks slid off the Gnomes sword in defense of the weak Elf.

"Oh, Bemjamin, this is so sad," said Annabel.

Benjamin welled up and almost lost it. Then Tannis turn his head to look at Benjamin, and he heard the now familiar voice of his friend in his mind. *Why Master Benjamin, I see you just can not go about your business without me. Silly boy, your supposed to be working on saving the planet, not crying over me.* And he heard a small giggle. Benjamin smiled, then suddenly he realized he may be able to garner the help of his friend, one last time.

"Tannis, is it possible...do you have enough energy, to get in touch with Vieolette and ask her to do us a favor?"

"Oh dear boy, have I taught you nothing? You have the power within yourself to make that connection, you no longer need my assistance. Just relax your mind and open to the possibility that you have the ability to do so. Then reach out with your thoughts, as you have done so with me. Picture her in your mind's eye and she will respond. We are all connected in this way young squire."

Benjamin stood with his eyes closed and gathered a picture of the wee Fairy Princess in his mind's vision. Then he took a deep breath and heard his inner self say, *Vieolette, we need your assistance. Please help us.*

Suddenly it was like someone had turned a light bulb on right above his head, and the voice of the Fairy appeared crystal clear. *What is your bidding young squire?* Benjamin smiled deeply without losing the connection. *We need you to gather leaves from all the different trees surrounding the Grandfather Tree. We already have Oak, but we are in need of three others and we don't know which ones they are.*

Consider it done, responded the Fairy.

And just when Benjamin was about to open his eyes, Mathilda let out a scream that ripped at him. *What the bloody hell was that?*

"Look at her! O-M-G, just look at her!" shouted Mathilda.

And there, blazing and tearing her way through the crowd of darkness and grey smoke, came the contrast of pure white light and power. The clear sparkling etheric energy rode fiercely upon her stallion, high above the Gnomes battling on the ground below her. It was Princess Avenel of the Darmon, and following close beside her was her trusted aid, Lonagon.

"Holy macaroni! Who the heck do you think that is? Isn't she the most beautiful woman you've ever seen!" Mathilda was beside herself with giddiness.

"She's pretty amazing, I have to admit. I mean really, just look at her. I wonder who they are?" said Annabel.

Benjamin just stood, mouth wide open, captivated by the site before him.

She stood out like a bright glowing beacon, high upon her dark majestic stallion. Like a lone figure of Grace and Light, shining amidst the dullness of the tarnish of battle. He had thought Emeline exquisite, and Sethina and Morel both stunning, but he had never seen anything in his life as magnificent and awe inspiring as the mysterious beauty before him, with her crimson hair flowing wildly behind her.

"Bloody hell!" was all he could say.

You couldn't be more right mighty Benjamin, came the voice in his head from his Elfin friend, *But I give you fair warning young squire, be of no disrespect...that is my Avenel, my one true Love you are thinking about. And from the looks of things, it appears she has chosen to step down as head of the Essence clan to come and save the likes of this poorly old Elf. I'm one lucky sod as you would say Benjamin.*

Benjamin stood in shock. Then as the realization of what was happening began to percolate in his core, he let spring forth a boisterous howl that shook with a huge force. Both Annabel and Mathilda jumped out of their skin and spun around to witness their friend hopping up and down and hollering at the top of his lungs, "All Right Avenel! Yes, Thank you!"

Avenel rode hard through the battle of smoke and death, wielding her shiny sword that sparked with the light reflecting off of her pure illuminating aura. She tore through the Gnomes in armor, and grey capes of the Blunt, to arrive at the tree where her lover Tannis, lay dying. She floated off of her horse in one swoop to kneel beside the ailing Elf.

Lonagon now joined the Vila and the Brownie, along with the Gnomes, in protecting the small gathering at the tree.

"Oh my sweet dear Tannis, what have you gotten yourself into this time?" spoke Avenel with a smile. She held onto Tannis's almost invisible hand and smoothed the outline of his hair off of his forehead with the other. Tannis looked deeply into Avenels eyes.

"Your mother is either going to be grateful to have her daughter back, or furious that you brought shame onto the Darmon for breaking your oath to come to my aid. I have a feeling I know which emotion shall win out. She has never warmed to the idea of the two of us as partners."

"Shush now," said Avenel, "I will not waste this moment with you, the first I have shared in nineteen years, to speak of my mother's concern." And she knelt closer to him and put her lips to the trace that were his.

When she sat back she looked at his body. He was almost an outline of himself, a light bluish glowing shape of an Elf. She ran her hands down from his shoulders along his arms to his fingertips. He felt solid. Then she looked at his legs, "What are you feeling my love? You appear weak, yet your structure is very strong."

"I feel calm. I feel alert. I am certain I am dying, and I am grateful to look upon your beauty one more time."

Avenel shook her head and widened her eyes, "How can this be?" She looked up at Sethina who was staring down at the two Elves.

"My Lady, I feel something can be accomplished. My Spirit is not sensing departure as yet. Tannis has melded with the Travel Chamber, the Path, he has become an extension of that same Energy. The sacred Light and Water of the Chamber does not cause death. You of all people should understand this. It was forged from the Love and Magic of the Darmon. There is something we are not seeing here. Remember, not everything is as it appears. I'm certain you will feel the direction to take, and all will mend."

Avenel shook her head again and turned back to Tannis. She looked down and saw his heart beating with a green glow beneath his tunic. She wanted to cry, but she knew what the Vila had said was true. The Chamber would not distinguish the life of an Elf of the Darmon. Yet his appearance would suggest otherwise. She climbed into her thoughts. She felt the depth of the Energy of the Forest that she knelt upon. She heard the heartbeat of the trees and the movement of the wind. She went deeper and deeper inward, until finally a message came....from a most unexpected source.

It came from her mother, Brityn Set of the Damon.

My beautiful daughter, I have longed to hear your voice again. To feel you among the wave of our thoughts here in the Darmon, brings a smile to my heart. Avenel, Tannis feels he is dying, he appears to be dying...but ask yourself, where are his fatal wounds? What has smite him down? Magic, or dagger? Look deeper sweet child, what were his thoughts as he entered the Travel Chamber? If you look at what is not in front of you, clarity will find the answer you seek.

Suddenly Avenel looked up at Tannis and a smile came to her, "Tannis, what was your mind when you entered the Travel Chamber?"

"I only wished to advance the Path to get ahead of the Queen and protect the children. It all happened so quickly. It was not something I thought about. I just trusted that I was meant to jump into the Travel Chamber to make the transformation. I kept the thought of projection forward and becoming hidden in my minds eye, and leapt."

Avenel smiled deeper. She looked up at Sethina, "You are wise dear Vila. You are correct in thinking that the Chamber could not harm an Elf of the Darmon. It was not a part of the great Magic and Prayer used to create it."

She looked back at Tannis, "You projected the Path into the future and that in turn sent you into the Shadows to keep you hidden. Your form feels solid my love, because it is. It is the Shadow that still holds you captive, as your essence has not been able to catch up to your present. You long for your spark, which is why you feel death. You are part of the Travel Chamber in Energy, which is why you feel alert. Now you must release the Path from your mind and allow your past to catch up to your future, which is now."

Tannis looked at Avenel and smiled. He closed his eyes and began to hum. The light of his aura pulsed with the deep toning he was chanting. Avenel joined him and a globe of pure white light surrounded both of them. As the sound of the Elves grew in frequency, subtle, and not so subtle, changes began to permeate the Forest around them.

The enchantment took hold of the fighting and the battle began to slow it's pace and intensity, as both sides looked about them in wonder. Warriors searched the skies above the tall Forest with apprehension as the wind of the energy began tugging and pulling at them, while eluding them at the same time.

The children had all been standing like statues from inside their protective barrier, watching the activity of Avenel with complete awe and concern, when they suddenly felt something shift around them as well. They too, looked up at the air surrounding the Grandfather and heard it crackle, like a giant wave of electricity before a storm. The air smelled of dampness.

"Benjamin?" was all Annabel said.

They could see the lights of energy dancing off of the kneeling couple next to the tree. When the ball of protective white light suddenly appeared around each of the Elves separately present in the Forest, Mathilda let out a *"whoa."*

Then from somewhere behind them came a low thunder. The ground was beginning to move like a behemoth animal charging towards them. The sound was resounding off the Great Tree and growing in decibel when Benjamin finally understood where it was generating from.

"That's coming from the Travel Chamber Path!"

They could all look out of the protection barrier towards the part of the Path that was still connected to the space they were now standing in. Even though the Chamber had disintegrated in spots, the whole of the Path was still in tact. And because the children were still technically within the Travel Chamber, they could see it clearly.

Then Mathilda let out a shrieking holler, "Benjamin, What is that? It's coming right at us!"

He and Annabel just stared, not comprehending what it was that they saw.

It looked like warp speed and slow motion all at the same time. It was clearly the embodiment of the Elf and his horse rushing at them in a slow speed of movement. Yet the bits trailing behind them were moving at top speed to catch up. Like a slinky that has been stretched to maximum and then released. The front is complete and stationery, while the rest of the twisted perfectly matching loops spring forward at a quicker speed to combine with the lead. The sound that came with this illusion was like the echo of someone yelling from a passing vehicle. It came at them quietly, from the distance, then louder when it was in view, then lessened as the image passed the trio in the Chamber barrier protection. They all spun around and watched as the form of the Elf and horse jumped out of the barrier and headed straight towards Tannis.

They ran *SMACK*, right into the ball of white light surrounding the Elves under the tree. The brilliance that came flooding the Forest was like an explosion of pure illumination, like the core of an exploding firework, with sparks and sputters spilling out in all directions. The sound welled with the merging, while the Forest clans all stood silently watching the light show. The Blunt had pulled back into the protection of the darkness of the deeper Forest, such was the holiness of this effulgence. The children had tears in their eyes and suddenly

Benjamin heard the familiar voice once again. *Well, it looks like you will have the pleasure of my company for awhile longer it appears.*

And there, standing under the tree, was his friend Tannis and his horse Bits, in perfect living color.

Without thinking Benjamin began to move quickly towards his friend, but before he found himself almost entirely outside of the glassy protection Cottie Set threw her Magic and prevented him from coming out any further. Then her voice came booming at him, "Master Benjamin! Regain your senses this instant!"

And with this slap of reality, Benjamin pulled himself with lightening speed back inside the force field. He collected himself and looked back up at Tannis and they both smiled.

"Now get back to work Master Benjamin, you have a world to save."

Mathilda put her hands outside of the barrier to collect the pile of leaves left by the Fairies. "I hope these work," she said, as she passed them over to her sister.

Annabel looked up at Benjamin and he nodded back at her. So she began the process of placing leaf after leaf into the imprints. Until one mysteriously stayed in place! They all gasped and watched with refreshed awe as the transformation of the panel changed into yet a different foreign symbol. They continued the system until all four panels had both a leaf above it and a symbol upon the center.

"So now what Annabel?" asked Benjamin.

"Well, we still don't know what the symbols represent."

"Why don't you look at the Primer? Maybe it will give you a clue," said Mathilda.

"Oh for cripes sake! I got so involved with everything, I completely forgot that I had that...geez!" Annabel pulled out her pack and dug out the Primer. She sat cross legged on the ground in front of the panels. Benjamin and Mathilda, both joined her on either side. Peering over her left shoulder, Benjamin thought he saw something, "What's that Annabel? Don't they look like something we've seen before?"

"Yeah, it does sorta. But I can't place it."

Benjamin thought for a minute then it hit him, "It's the symbols that Sethina and Morel wear around their necks!"

"Holy cow! You're right Benjamin!" cried Annabel, "So how does that fit in with this I wonder?"

"Hmm," said Mathilda, "well, why don't we think of what comes in fours that would have something to do with the Forest. Then figure out what Morel and Sethina have that is the same as that."

"Okay, Tildie, good place to start," said Annabel.

So Mathilda began to list the things she felt would apply, "Well, let's see, there's trees and birds and rivers and lakes. There's *umm*...the ground, or dirt I guess, and sky. There's magic and Fairies...and.....

"Mathilda! Wait a minute, what did you say before that last one?" shouted Annabel.

Mathilda startled, paused and thought, "*Umm,* I think I said, lakes and sky...." "No, you said *dirt* and sky," interrupted Benjamin, "You said lakes and rivers, then you said dirt and sky."

"That's It!" shouted Annabel, "Of course, how could I have missed that, it's so simple!"

"What Annabel, what is it?" questioned Benjamin.

"Mathilda, you did it again. Benjamin, think about it, she said, rivers, lakes, dirt and sky."

Slowly the realization came to him and he smiled, "Well I'll be...blast it! Sometimes we make the simplest things so hard."

Mathilda looked at both of them still not understanding, "Would someone explain already before I lose my mind!"

Annabel looked at her sister and smiled with pride, "Earth, Water, Air and Fire. It's the four elements. And it certainly makes up the Forest."

"And better than that Annabel," said Benjamin with a sly grin, "Sethina is the Vila of the air and Morel the Vila of the water. Their symbols..." "Mean Air and Water!" cut in Annabel, "Oh my goodness! Benjamin, that's it, that's it! Now we just need to figure out the symbols for Earth and Fire and we're a huge step closer to unlocking this door!"

"Well, let's get to cracking the code on this Primer, cuz it's gotta be there somewhere," said Benjamin.

"I agree."

So they all went back to studying the quiz put before them. As Annabel was talking out loud in an attempt to decipher the code, Benjamin did the same internally. Then Benjamin noticed something that the others had not.

The name of Tar Vigorn was glowing.

Benjamin sat upright and looked around the perimeter of the Tree. He stood up and walked over to the opening to the Chamber Path, that not long before had ushered in the lost pieces of his friend. No vibrations, no sounds. He looked out into the Forest...*nothing*.

Wait, what was that? he wondered, as he saw a shift in the air in front of him. He stared and nothing moved. "I'm losing it," he said under his breath. Then he decided to walk the distance towards the right, in the direction of the backside of the Tree, to see what he might find. He looked over his left shoulder and shouted, "I'm going to explore here for a minute. I'll be right back."

Annabel so enthralled with her task barely noticed he had gotten up let alone said anything. Mathilda looked up at him quickly before turning back to her study, "Okay." The sisters took turns staring at the old parchment, then at the carvings on the Door and back again.

Benjamin journeyed passed the Great Door and headed towards the vacant dark side of the Grandfather. He looked up at the Great Tree and studied its cracks and crevices. However, he paid more attention to what was going on outside of the barrier. Nothing. No movement.

As he got further around he noticed something imbedded in the side of the tree trunk. He turned to face the Tree full on, hands in his pockets and stopped.

What is that? It looked like levers, two of them. "Well, this is interesting, wonder what these do? It looks like...wait, I suppose if it's some kind of power switch or something, I would imagine they need to be turned on." So he stepped up closer and seeing that they were both facing downward, he decided to push them upward.

In seconds he heard the girls yelling. Benjamin turned and ran quickly back around the expanse of Tree towards the Door. When he arrived both sisters were standing and shouting.

"Oh holy cripes! Would you look at that!" shouted Mathilda.

Annabel was yelling, as Benjamin rounded the corner, "Benjamin, look at this!"

And he looked up and saw that the Rose bud had transformed into a carving of an open flower. Each individual circular row of petals was slowly spinning in the opposite direction. The four lights on the faceplate next to the handle were lit up, and a small hum was generating from the tree.

"Oh Bloody Hell...did I do that?" he whispered to himself. "What happened?" he asked the girls.

"We were just sitting here and it just started. It was so totally cool Benjamin, you should of seen it."

"Yeah, it just started to open like it was blooming right in front of our eyes, and then that hum started. Something is definitely happening. Did you see anything over there?" asked Annabel.

"Well, actually, yeah. There was a faceplate with two levers and I turned them on," answered Benjamin.

Annabel just looked at him. She opened her mouth, but nothing came out at first. Then with growing realization finally came to her, "Oh my god Benjamin, I think you turned on the Door mechanisms. It didn't even occur to me that we needed to look any further than the door. I can't believe I didn't think of that first."

"Well, no need to beat yourself up Annabel. It's not like you've ever had to figure out a magical door before. It's cool. We're doing this together. I'm sorry I missed that opening up though. I bet that was something."

"Oh, something, doesn't describe it Benjamin. It was the coolest thing ever." said Mathilda with a huge smile.

Suddenly Benjamin remembered the reason he had gone roaming off on his own and looked down at the Primer in Annabel's hand,"Let me see that mate, would ya?" Annabel handed the Primer to Benjamin. The name flickered for a moment then went dull. Benjamin didn't like this. Something was up and he was beginning to think time was running out. "I'll be right back, I gotta talk to Cottie Set for a minute."

"What, what is it?" asked a curious Annabel.

"It's nothing, I just want to make sure the Blunt aren't back. I want to see if I can get a better idea on our time here. Don't worry, I'll be right back. You two try to figure out what the other symbols are. We need to open this door as soon as possible."

"Okay Benjamin," was all Mathilda said, as she kept her eyes buried on the Primer.

Benjamin headed back to the far left side of the Tree where he had left his friend standing earlier. Sure enough the Blunt were back. All the lights of the healing session had calmed back down and the battle had reignited. Benjamin attempted to locate Cottie Set amidst the crowd. He finally saw her and attempted to wave her down...nothing. Finally he cleared his mind and concentrated on the Path Tender and placed her clearly in his minds eye. Within moments her voice came at him. *I'm on my way young squire.*

And within seconds she was standing in front of him, with the protection barrier between them. Benjamin just threw it straight at her, "I just saw the Queen's name lit up on the Prim...I mean the Galohishdi a few minutes ago, and now it's dull again. I don't think that thing lies, nor do I think it's got a short or anything. I looked around a bit and I didn't see anything. But I just know she is out there somewhere near by. I mean there's no way her whole army is fighting here alone without her. Something's up."

Cottie Set looked sullen, "You are correct in assuming that the Galohishdi would ever show an incorrect account. If you saw Tar Vigorn's name glowing, she was present, or close enough. I too have wondered where she might be. It seems abstract that she is not fighting right along with her tribe. This is all very uncharacteristic of the dark Queen. But then again, when has anything like this ever happened before? She is up to something, I am certain of it."

Benjamin nodded his head in agreement.

"However, that is for us to handle right now Benjamin. As you can see, the Elf is himself, whole again. The Princess is a fearless and worthy Warrior. We are ahead in this battle at present, but there have been casualties keeping the Blunt at bay from the other side of the Grandfather. However, you need not concern yourself with the happenings of the Forest. You have a serious mission at hand and you must give of your full attention and insight to perform your tasks. We'll keep you safe and isolated in order to perform. The Queen can not get at you while you are inside of the protection barrier. She can not get inside of the Path that is still connected, even with it's damage. The Elves of the Darmon have reinforced her walls and it is much like new again."

Benjamin turned around and saw that the Path Tender was correct. The Path was beginning to glow like it's former self again. He could still see some of the dismantling and frayed edges here and there, but for all intents and purposes, it was healing quickly. Benjamin looked back at Cottie Set.

"Okay, I'll get back to it. I just thought you should know she's around here somewhere and I think she's planning a big surprise."

"Yes, I'm afraid you are correct. But how are things going with the puzzles? Are you making advancements?"

Benjamin smiled involuntarily, "Yes, you would be proud. We're really coming up with some amazing ideas. All of us. It's pretty astounding to say the least. I wish you could be there to see it."

The Path Tender looked at him and returned a sly smile, "Don't let it go to your head young Benjamin. It's supposed to be natural for you, you're the boy of the Prophecy. It was all laid out for your way of thinking. Now go...go finish the job you began and find Coranim. I shall see you again, soon. I promise." She turned on her heals and returned to the heat of the battle. Benjamin took a last quick glance around the scene in front of him. "How did I get here? How in all the bloody world did I end up in this fairy tale...*as the hero?*"   And he turned around and headed back to his friends.

"Benjamin, thank god you're back, you're not going to believe this," said Annabel.

"Yeah Benjamin, you're totally going to flip out. Watch this." And Mathilda picked up a handful of dirt off of the ground and pushed on the center of the symbol in the first panel on the bottom of the Door. A tiny little compartment popped opened and Mathilda looked up at her sister and Annabel nodded her head. Mathilda looked back to the now open compartment and placed the handful of dirt into the bowl of the opening. She shut the compartment back into the tree panel. In an instant the red light on the faceplate next to the door handle lit up. Benjamin's eye brows slide up his forehead.

"Blimey!" he said.

"YES!" shouted Annabel acknowledging the outcome of her calculated suspicions.   Then she went to the second panel and pushed open the tiny compartment and picked up the water bottle sitting out next to her and poured some water into the bowl and closed up the compartment. The corresponding button on the faceplate glowed blue now. Benjamin smiled, "This is brilliant you two! Have you been able to figure out the other symbols?"

"No, not yet, but I'm thinking we really don't need to because we know what they stand for. So we just try different elements in the remaining two panels and we should have it. Thank god you turned the thing on Benjamin, we would never have seen the outline of the compartments otherwise. That switched everything on, and we were able to figure this out.   Good work.   Oh, how is it going out there? Any sign of Tar Vigorn yet?"

Benjamin didn't know if he should tell them he saw her name on the Primer. He simply answered, "They're back at it out there, and Cottie Set said we needed to just get on with it here. Let's just do that alright? So if I'm understanding you correctly, we have earth and water. And this was verified because of the symbols for Sethina and Morel...hey wait, Sethina is air, what happened there? How did you come up with earth first?"

"We couldn't figure out how to put air in the bowl, but earth was easy, so we waited for you and started with that," said Mathilda.

"Okay, so we need air and fire yet, right?" asked Benjamin.

"Right," answered Annabel.

"Well, fire shouldn't be to hard, we have matches in our pack, I'll just..."

"It doesn't work Benjamin. When you close the compartment the flames go out. It doesn't stay lit long enough to be fire. I'm kinda stumped with this one. Besides I don't think we can use things from our world. The water came from the river, so I think that's why that one worked," said Annabel.

"Okay mate, well give me a minute...let me think about it." And Benjamin went to the deciphering place in his mind. He saw answers in detail when he questioned things in this manner. He paced and thought. He could see ways around something that otherwise might not present themselves. *Fire, how can we put fire into the bowl?* he wondered. After a few minutes he thought, *Maybe it doesn't need to actually BE fire. Maybe just something that represents fire. Like...oh, I don't know, it just needs to be...it needs to be....energy! That's it! It just needs to be the energy of fire.*

He went into his telepathic space and contacted Vieolette again. Then he waited a moment. The sisters stared at him, until finally Annabel asked, "What are we doing Benjamin? Why do you have that look on your face...what's up?"

And within moments of saying this, the purple twinkle that was the Fairy appeared a few feet away down the barrier. Benjamin jumped up and ran over to Vieolette. The girls sat dumfounded as to what was going on. Then Benjamin returned with something in his hand. He looked at the girls and lowered his hand for them to see...it was a charred piece of bark from a tree, it was still smoldering.

"Here you go mates, not actual fire, but the energy of fire. I figure it's worth a shot. I mean, even though it's not still burning, it is still active with that force and it's part of the Forest...it should work."

So Annabel took the smoking little piece of burned bark and opened the compartment on the last panel and placed the ember inside, then shut the bowl. Within moments the fourth light on the faceplate lit up, yellow. The Muskydeers smiled from ear to ear.

"Well, now for the hard part, *air.*" said Mathilda.

"Yeah, we tried blowing in the compartment and nothing. But I think your idea of using the energy of air, or something that represents the energy of air, is the way to go obviously," said Annabel.

Benjamin smiled, "I've got it mates, hold on a minute." He went into his communicating mind and sent out another message. He turned and walked down the side of the Tree a few more feet, and waiting at the barrier, this time was the Vila, Sethina.

"Thank you Sethina." said Benjamin.

"With great honor I do your bidding Master Benjamin," and she turned around and butted up against the barrier. Benjamin put his hand outside the protection and plucked the smallest of perfect white feathers from the under down of the Vilas' wings. He pulled his treasure back inside the protection of the barrier and bowed his head to the Villa Princess.

"Thanks again, you may have just helped us put the last piece into the puzzle."

Sethina smiled with every part of herself, "Oh what news this is Benjamin! We shall know very soon then if this is correct and the burden of keeping the Queen away from you will be squelched. I do hope this is the outcome you are seeking, as I am concerned about the Grandmother Tree and her safety as well. I may need to join the others soon." She bowed and left.

Benjamin returned to the sisters and handed Mathilda the feather. Mathilda's eyes lit up, and with her happy smiling face she took the baby perfect white feather, that had floated among the clouds and carried the wind, into the small compartment bowl of the third panel. The panel compartment shut and the final light, white, lit up. The children jumped up onto their feet and began clapping their hands and shouting.

"We did it Benjamin!" yelled Annabel.

"Oh my goobers, Benjamin, we did it!" repeated Mathilda, "That wasn't so hard." Benjamin chuckled.

Then they stood with bated breath while Benjamin pulled the old relic of a key with the tattered green ribbon, out of his pack and unwrapped it. Annabel walked up to the faceplate and pressed the lit buttons in order of the panels, red, blue, white, and yellow.

High above them the center of the Rose opened up more, to reveal a round piece of wood with an X marked across it's diameter. The children hadn't noticed this action, as they were too excited to use the key...*and missed the Magic*.

Benjamin put the key into the lock and turned it clockwise and made a quarter turn. They heard a distinctive click. Benjamin stopped and they all looked at each other. Then he continued to turn the key clockwise until he heard another click when it faced the bottom quarter of the lock. He continued turning until a third click sounded when the key was all the way in the left position. And then the final turn which brought it straight back up to the top and a final click. He looked back at the girls again and reached up and pulled down on the handle.

Nothing. No movement what so ever.

"What?" whispered Benjamin.

"What's happening? Why won't it open?" asked Mathilda.

"What's going on Benjamin? I know I heard it click on all four places in the lock. I don't understand," added Annabel.

Benjamin stepped back for a moment and looked back up at the massive Door. What was he missing? "What is not as it appears?" he wondered out loud. He looked and looked. *Wait a minute...when the Gateway opened up, it had the most bizarre sound, and it was loud. When Tannis was healing the Travel Chamber he hummed a specific sound that got really loud and forceful. There is always some kind of humming sound going on when something needs to be healed, or opened around here, Mathilda's discovery is proof of that. Even Sir Gibbles had a song that put me in a trance. Sound seems to be important in this dimension.* "But what sound, what could it mean? " Benjamin walked back up to the door and without much thought pulled the key out of the lock.

"What are you doing Benjamin!" cried Annabel, "The key needs to be in the lock!" "Really? Says who?" replied Benjamin.

"What the heck are you talking about now Benjamin?" asked a very confused Mathilda.

"Benjamin seriously, what are you doing?" questioned Annabel.

"We keep forgetting, this is another world. This is *magic*. I keep hearing Tannis saying, nothing is as it appears, so I'm thinking, sound has something to do with this. Don't ask me why, it's just one of my gut feelings. And besides, after Mathilda found the leaf imprints I know I'm right about this." Benjamin continued while he had their undivided attention, "Remember the key has some words engraved on it, something about these symbols on the panels looked familiar to me. I know I've seen something like this on the key. We need to figure out these words and say them to the door or something. I don't know yet. I just know we need to say these words, or *sing* them, and something will happen."

"*Sing* them? Wow Benjamin, that's really stretching. Here, let me see that key," said Annabel, taking the key as Benjamin handed it to her.

Annabel turned the key over in her hands, remembering the first time she held it. She knelt down on the ground and pulled open the Primer. She tilted the key so the words would appear clearly, and saw that Benjamin was right. These same words were written on the Primer. Now she just had to figure out the right words and sounds.

"So, looking at the break down of the language I did, I actually have more here than I thought. See here where I have the partial words written out? The word for air, is win. I couldn't figure out the air thing before, but Cottie Set said earlier that the Set and Win people used the Grandmother Tree. She said the Win people were the high mountain clans that used flying machines. So I think it's safe to say that Win is the word for air. But they have three different words for earth. One is Lom, which means earthen and the other is Til, which is land, or soil. And then there is Kor, which translates into 'blood of the soil'. I'm guessing we should use the word Lom because it actually has the meaning earth."

Benjamin sat up, "Annabel, the Grandfather Tree was a gift to the Gnomes, the Fet actually. How many clans of Gnomes live in the Fet? What are their names origin, like this one, Win, that means air?"

Annabel stared out in front of her vision for a moment, thinking, then got it., "Oh Benjamin, I get where you're going with this. There are four clans that represent the four elements. And since this is a door for the Fet, I need to use those words. Right on Benjamin! Okay, so let me see here. That means we would definitely use Kor for earth, because that is definitely a Fet clan. And the sea Gnome is a Fet and that word is Bri. The only other Fet clans are the Or people, which means, metal, or ore, and the Lom clans, which are the interior mountain people. I'm lost here, there are no words for fire or air in the Fet clans. The word *Mar ah* means water breath, so maybe we use that to represent both? I don't know Benjamin, I'm lost," and Annabel let out a huge sigh.

"Have you figured out all the words and symbols on the Primer?" asked Benjamin.

"No, not yet, maybe it's in here somewhere, let me give it another look."

"It seems you need to look for all the words, or names, that have the Fet symbol next to it. Don't worry about the others right now. Let me see the key. Maybe we should write down the symbols in order, then put the translations on top so we can match things easier."

"Thats a good idea Benjamin. Here why don't you put down the symbols and I'll keep checking the words for only the ones that end with Fet."

Benjamin drew out the symbols, while Annabel studied the Primer. Finally after another twenty minutes had passed, the crew began to get a little jumpy. Time was running out, they needed to get this solved now. Then Mathilda thought of something, "Hey, I was just thinking, maybe they don't have a word for air or wind down there because there's no sky."

Benjamin looked up and stared at Mathilda, then looked at Annabel. He went into a mind trick he does when he needs to *feel* if something makes sense to him. He suddenly had it.

"Mathilda, you did it again! We forgot, we need the *energy* of things, not just the literal meaning. Ore, metal, that represents fire. You need fire to melt the ore to create something of strength with it. And check in there Annabel, there must be something that translates into air, like breath or something that sustains them. You're right, they have no sky, but they breathe, so what do they breathe?"

Annabel put her nose to the Primer and ran her finger quickly down the line of words and letters before her. And then she saw it.

"Here! *Anim ah*. I figured it out! *Mar ah* means water breath. So *ah* would translate to mean breathing, or air. And then when you take Coranim apart, Cor means heart, and anim means spirit or life. So I put Anim ah together and here it is, it's on the Key! I think we have them all now!"

Benjamin picked up the piece of paper and read the strange words out loud to the girls, "Earth, Kor, Water, Bri, Air, Anim ah, and Fire, Or." He looked up at the sisters who were waiting to hear the decision, "Let's give it a try mates, what do we have to lose? And I think Mathilda should do the honors, after all she has the best voice here." He looked at Mathilda who lit up, and took the piece of paper from Benjamin. She stood up and faced the door.

"Here goes."

She took a deep breath and in her most pristine of perfectly pitched singing voices she chanted the words before her in the same manner she had heard Tannis use, "*Kor..Bri...Anim...Ah...Or.*" She repeated the words as she had heard the Elf of the Damon do. After the third round of singing the little wooden circle in the center of the Rose began to have movement. The children looked up and with each word sung sweetly, one section of the four triangle shapes within the X carved across the circle, indented into a strange uneven shape.

When Mathilda sang the word Kor, the lower triangle of the X sank back into itself and left an opening on the top of it. Then the word Bri caused the next triangle to the left to sink back and created an opening on the right side of it's space. The third note was Anim ah and the third piece of the X sank back and left an opening on the bottom. Then finishing with the last word and the last triangle space, which sank back, leaving an opening on the left side. When Mathilda stopped chanting, the three friends simply stood in complete awe.

269

Benjamin stared in disbelief. There in the center of the massive wooden depiction of a Rose, was the lock opening for the key. A big smile took over his face. "I knew the key could fit somewhere else."

And now here was a lock, but the door was far too tall for any of them to reach. Even if he hoisted Mathilda up onto his shoulders, it couldn't be done.

"What the heck do we do now?" asked a bewildered Mathilda.

Benjamin spoke quietly, "If there is a problem, then there is a solution." He paused for a long moment then got it, "Look around mates, there must be a ladder or a step, or something that will allow us to get up to the lock."

They all started to scurry about, looking for any clue to get them closer to the lock. They ran around to the other side where the levers were, in search of another protrusion to press. Then Benjamin stopped and ran back towards the Door, and the girls followed, "Wait a minute guys. It stands to reason that if the lock is here, the ladder should be right by. Everything seems to have been hidden somehow. Little compartments that needed something to happen first in order for them to be revealed."

They all began pressing on different parts of the Great Tree trunk and humming random sounds in hopes of igniting something. But nothing happened. No hidden chambers opened up. No movement what so ever. Benjamin spoke in a low voice, "What do we need to do? Let's think again for a minute."

Then Mathilda did it one more time.

"Maybe we just need to ask permission or something, like being invited into the Gateway?"

Benjamin whipped his head around and faced both Annabel and Mathilda. He looked at Annabel and shook his head with his palms up in the air and hunched his shoulders in question.

"Could it really be that simple Benjamin? Asking permission to enter?" said Annabel.

Benjamin stood, still shaking his head with a goofy grin on his face, "Well, I can't imagine why not!" So he walked over and took the key back from Annabel and turned to face the front of the Door. The sisters stood closely beside him in anticipation. Benjamin cleared his throat and spoke.

"Grandfather, it's me, Benjamin, Benjamin McTish. I'm here with my best mates, Annabel and Mathilda Wickcliff. We've made a grand journey to arrive here in front of you right now. We are told that Coranim is a most beautiful and enchanting world. We are told she needs assistance. We are asking for permission to enter the wondrous land beneath your honorable roots, with the intention of aiding the Fet people with their problem." Then he quickly added, "Aut'banda."

Once again, the Gilley Forest did not disappoint.

The magic of watching the perfect depiction of a Rose carved out of wood begin to move and slide down the length of the Door; to see it's thorny stem twist and curve to allow room for the descending bloom, was more than any of them could handle. It was completely and perfectly, awe inspiring. When the lock stopped at a height that Benjamin could easily reach, he stepped up and put the old relic into its home then stepped back.

The massive Door began to creek and groan, like a tomb being awoken from it's deep slumber a millennium later. It moved forward of its own volition and stopped when enough space was available for them to walk through.

The children quickly gathered there things and packed up their packs. Then stared up at the wonderment before them. Mathilda walked through first, followed by her big sister Annabel, who turned around and smiled brightly at Benjamin. He smiled back. Then he proceeded to follow his mates into the darkness. However, just before he stepped through he turned around, sensing something tugging at his nerves. He just couldn't shake it...*what was it?* Then he thought he saw a shadow, or shape, shift in the air outside of the protection Chamber, and he stopped. *What the bloody hell am I looking at,* he thought, as he was pulled right out of his reverie of awe and wonder.

There is was again. It looked like a piece of the Forest was......*overlapping itself.*

What the bloody hell am I seeing? And the strangeness began to gnaw at him and sent shivers down his spine. He looked deeper, then he heard the tiny breath escape her lips. *She's here!*

And as quickly as he realized the Queen was present, she came forward. She was a perfect chameleon, merging from the Forest background surrounding her. Her face looked like the bark edges of the tree she had been standing in front of, and her feet were the leafs and moss of the ground she stood upon. She stepped towards the outer protection of the Door.

"Oh Benjamin, I want to thank you for allowing me the pleasure of witnessing your somewhat clever techniques of problem solving. I've so enjoyed standing in the shadows as it were, learning all that I could on how to enter the Grandfather Tree. The Elven Princess has been challenging my mind shield rather relentlessly. She came close to picking me right out of the air here, but I managed to slip through her radar, popping out and back. The others aren't quite as keen on their senses. They knew I was around, but they could not determine where. And my comrades in arms have been keeping everyone busy on the other side of the Great Tree. This whole time Sethina and Cottie Set thought it was the other way around. My, my, what a shame.

"Oh, but imagine my surprise, to find that the talented little Gnomes have protected yet *another* Tree somewhere else in the Gilley Forest. I'm guessing it's on the other side near the mountain people, *hmm*? But I'll deal with that later. Right now I'm just standing on top of the world...well I suppose I am literally standing on top of the world, thanks to you."

And the Queen's smile turned into a grimace as her whole demeanor instantly changed, and she pulled herself as close to the protection Chamber walls as she could, "Have some fun while you can, young smart Benjamin, because it won't last long. I'm coming to get you...*all of you*. You will not make a fool out of me and live to tell," she hissed.

And before she could say another word, the massive Door began to close, and Benjamin stepped back into the entrance while the Great Tree shut the children of the Prophecy within it.

However, before the last bit of view was cut off to Benjamin he caught a glimpse of Sethina riding with her bow drawn, straight towards Tar Vigorn.

And then all was dark.

Chapter Twenty-Three

Na'talom

As the heavy Door slammed shut, the children could hear the last of the ensuing battle outside. A massive crack from the flawless magic thrown from the hands of Tar Vigorn, was the last sound taken inside with them.

"Do you think they'll be all right?" asked Mathilda to no one in particular.

"We can't worry about them right now," said Benjamin. "They're doing this for us and we've gotten this far, so I'm sure they'll be able to contain her long enough for reinforcements to come protect both of the Great Trees."

Even though he passed off his comments as positive, inside he knew otherwise. *I knew she was there. I knew it! Why didn't I do anything to shake her out of hiding? Now she knows everything and it's all my fault.* He hoped the words he spoke to Mathilda were true. But now here they were inside of the Grandfather in the dark, and it was time to get moving.

"Well mates, let's get some light in here and see what end is up," said Benjamin.

"I already pulled out the flashlight," said Annabel as she turned it on.

They all looked around at the smooth polished interior of the room they were standing in.

"It looks like a waiting room with no chairs," observed Mathilda.

"Yeah, it's all shiny and big. Do you see anything Benjamin? Oh, wait, look at this," said Annabel. She held a beam of light for a moment on each beautifully carved gold framed portrait, hanging across the wall. Some were of Gnomes and some were of different unusual landscapes. "Oh wow, these are amazing!" said Annabel. "I wonder who they are? Do you think these are places in Coranim Benjamin?"

Then Mathilda jumped in, "Hey look, there's one of Cottie Set, and she's with some old woman. Wow, look at her, she looks like some old witch!"

Benjamin took the lamp from Annabel and swung it around the perimeter of the room. His mind wasn't on the paintings. He was tangled in thoughts of understanding why his new friends, and people he didn't even know, had died to protect them and get them safely to this place. What was so special about Coranim? Then the light landed on an opening in the wall.

"Oh holy Sweet peas!" said Mathilda, "That must be the way down."

Right above the entrance was a plaque that read, Na'talom.

"This is it," said Benjamin. He stepped forward and peered through the doorway. There was a landing and a staircase leading down into darkness. On the wall next to him were large torches, and on the floor next to the wall was a pot of goo. Benjamin stepped through, took down a torch and dipped it into the bucket of slime, then he looked around for the way to light it.

"Here," said Annabel, as she stepped back to make room for him to see. She picked up a long piece of grey stone that had a small bit of flint laying in the groove, and next to the two stones was a basket filled with dried leafs. Benjamin handed the torch to Annabel and took the stones from her. He put a small pile of leafs in the groove and swiped the flint on the long porous stone and a tiny spark flew off. He attempted it several more times until it caught, then he blew onto the embers until a small flame rose off of the stone. He nodded to Annabel, who then touched the tip of the oil soaked cloth to the fire and instantly they had a bright light.

"Wow!" said Mathilda with surprise, "I never seen anyone do that before, cool."

They looked around the small space of the little separate entry to the stairwell. The walls were smooth, just like the entrance room. The darkness leading downward looked endless.

"Let's go," said Benjamin. And they all stepped down. They descended the beautiful stairs of variegated slate in silence for the first half an hour until Mathilda spoke, "Do you think they know we're here? I mean, do you think someone will greet us or something?"

"I don't know Mathilda," was all Benjamin said.

Annabel had let Benjamin's attitude slide long enough, she finally had it, "So Benjamin, what's up? Did something happen? You clammed up the minute we got into the Tree and it's been long enough. We need to talk already cause I'm hoping we're getting closer to the end of this hike and we need a plan."

Benjamin marinated in his silence a minute longer, then finally spoke, "Yeah, something is wrong. I knew the Queen was near by and I didn't do anything about it. I even saw her name lit up on the Galohishdi, I could feel her presence, but I didn't follow my instincts and look deeper for her. And now she knows everything to open the door. All that secrecy and tricks to keep her from finding the way in, and I handed it to her on a silver platter."

Annabel was shocked at what Benjamin had revealed, "You knew she was there the whole time?"

"No, not the *whole* time. That's my point. I knew she was up to something. I told Cottie Set, but by then her name went dull again, so I couldn't figure out what she was doing. If I had just sat still for a minute and thought further I could have seen it. I just kept feeling her around and I didn't do anything about it. Now she not only has the entry here, but she knows about the Grandmother too. So now I guess it all depends on what happens in the battle. If they can hold her off and the magic is strong enough to keep the tree protected, then maybe I haven't blown it completely. But Cottie Set said that the other tree wasn't a total fortress yet, so I hope Tar Vigorn doesn't just decide to go find it. Although, I don't think she heard that part of the conversation, so we may be safe. I just don't know."

"Isn't that where my daddy is, at the other tree? Do you think she'll find him? Oh no!" cried Mathilda.

Annabel stopped and grabbed Benjamin's arm. They all stood in silence for a moment. "Think about it real hard Benjamin. What do you really see happening? Do you think our father is in danger right now? Can you send a message to Cottie Set or Sethina and find out what's happening? You were getting really good at communicating with them, maybe Tannis? Try Benjamin, do something!" demanded Annabel.

So Benjamin sat down on the step below them and cleared his mind. For some unexplained reason he felt he was able to go to that clearer level in a much more efficient and quicker way here than in the Forest. He took a deeper breath and without warning he found himself being approached by a foreign voice.

Tis that ya boy? the odd little voice questioned.

Benjamin jumped a little and was afraid to answer, what if it was a trick of some kind? He began to get nervous and his breathing quickened. Then as if his thoughts were being read the voice continued.

Dun't ya be blockin me owt boy, ya be needin my assistance. I be eh good friend ta Cottie Set. Them's me en tha portrait width hair en tha entry hall gallery. I be Esmerelda Fet. Come find me tha moment cha arrive en Na'talom. Dun't worry 'bout what is happenin en tha Forest...tis not fer ya ta concern yerself width. Tar Vigorn is not on yer coat tails at present, nor is she en tha knowledge of tha location of tha Granmather Tree. Edward be safe right now. An tell the wee lass thar be some Fairy clans eh wantin ta meet up width hair.

And the voice faded away and took with it a visual wisp of the face in the painting. Benjamin sat in complete astonishment.

"What, what is it Benjamin? You look scared, what did you see?" quizzed Annabel anxiously.

Benjamin stood up and turned to face the girls, "I just met Esmerelda Fet and she said everything was okay, not to worry about your father, Tar Vigorn is not near them. She's the one in the painting with Cottie Set. She told me to tell Mathilda that the Fairies were waiting to meet her." Then he smiled and turned around and began descending once again. Only this time he had a bit of a lighter load on his shoulders. He thought, *I guess there is nothing I can do about what has already happened. So I may as well make the best of what is right in front of me, and remember to keep my instincts on top of things from now on.*

While Benjamin was in his own thoughts Mathilda was in a spastic frenzy of joy, "The Fairies know about me? I can't believe this is happening. Oh my goodness, this is the coolest thing ever! Bellie can you believe it? The Fairies want to meet me!"

Annabel smiled, "Of course they do tike. Who wouldn't want to meet you?"

The children marched down the stairs for a bit more when they all began to notice that the walls appeared to be changing somehow. It looked to Benjamin as if he could see further down into the stairwell. *What is this illusion,* he wondered.

"Hey, it looks like the walls are glowing or something, up ahead," said Mathilda.

That's it, thought Benjamin. He swung the torch around and the walls did not vary in shadow. Then suddenly Annabel shouted, "Hey, there's a bucket of water on the stairs over on this side. What the heck is going on now?"

"I think we're supposed to put out the torch now. The walls appear to be illuminated somehow," answered Benjamin. So he handed the torch to Annabel who dunked it into the bucket to distinguish the flame. Instantly the three friends were standing amid a neon green glow emanating from the tunnel of stairs.

"Wow....this is totally cool. It's like being in a fun house when everyone glows under that light. Look, we all kinda shine," said Mathilda, amazed.

"Yikes!" said Annabel, "This is so weird! It's like we're shining and glowing at the same time, just like the walls, we're neon green. This is just so weird."

They could each see the detail in the walls smooth surface. Even through the haze of a green glow the many different colors and grains of polished wood were like a piece of art, or sculpture. It was truly breath taking.

"This is brilliant," said Benjamin. "We better keep a leg up. I can't imagine this goes much further, we've been hiking for hours."

After another twenty minutes of climbing down the stairs, the smell of moss and dirt began to permeate the air.

"It smells like the forest," said Mathilda.

"Yeah, we must be getting closer to the entrance finally," said Benjamin.

No sooner had he said that, when a light began to appear in front of them. It was the light emanating from the entrance city of Na'talom. Excited, they hurried down the last of the stairs. The three friends huddled closer together as they stepped out onto the platform landing. Vines and roots surrounded the exit from the staircase. Benjamin looked up behind them and saw that they were surrounded by one of the gargantuan root tendrils from the Grandfather Tree. "Crickey!" he said in disbelief. As he turned around to look down into the city before them, a collision was about to occur right before their eyes.

"What... the heck... are those?" asked a very confused Mathilda, as two extremely tall slender poles miraculously walked solo past their vision; while at the same time a large object whizzed by in the air just out above them, clipping the front pole. Then someone cursed and the machine swerved up and darted away. Suddenly a voice yelled into the ethers high above them.

"Pips! Confound you and that blasted machine! You're going to kill me one of these days!"

They all flipped their heads straight upwards in the direction of the utterance, and to their shock and delight, there was a Gnome standing on top of the poles. In actuality they were stilts, the tallest stilts ever imagined.

"Bloody hell...they must be fifty feet in the air!" said Benjamin astounded.

Annabel got woozy at the mere thought of being up so high on two small poles. "What on earth is he doing up there?"

Mathilda suddenly shouted while she pointed out across the city scape, "Look! Look at him, he's in some kind of wooden plane or something! It looks like a little flying submarine. Oh holy macaroni! That's the coolest thing I've ever seen!"

"Geez Tildie, at this rate I can't keep up with you. Every thing you see is cooler than the thing you saw before. But I have to admit, the flying submarine is pretty cool."

And with that the little man on the stilts realized people were standing below him and yelled down to them, "Oh fiddle fudge! I had no idea you were there, I'll be down in a jif."

Then the children watched in amazement as the stilts began to fold up into themselves from the top down, like a telescope; until they were lowered enough for the Gnome to walk over onto the landing of the tall station about thirty feet away from them. The metal platform was built in to the side of the dirt wall next to the roots of the Great Tree, on the outside of the city walls, along the outer cobblestone road. On the landing was a small lit structure that resembled a ranger lookout station. The floor of the platform had a hole in it with a retracting ladder that the stilt walking Gnome used to lower himself down onto the ground.

Off in the distance the strange flying machine could be heard buzzing about the darkening sky, with incoherent shouts coming from it's driver. The trio looked up and realized that the night sky was upon them and there were stars shining.

"Hey, wait a minute, how the heck are there stars down here?" asked Mathilda bewildered.

"How the heck indeed?" repeated Benjamin.

Annabel just stood shaking her head. And with that the little Gnome was in front of them, "Oh, hello there, pleasure to meet you, I'm Finley Heaton. I'm the Star hanger here in Na'talom. And *that* reckless old *coot* who nearly managed to successfully land me right on top of your wee noggins, is Pips. He's always fiddling about with one contraption or another. It seems he simply can not discipline himself to save his trials for the daylight, instead of when I'm right in the middle of feeding the Ginnies. Someday he's going to get one of us killed!"

"Feeding the Ginnies, what are Ginnies?" asked Annabel, stunned.

"The Ginnies! Well, my... Aunt... Thea. That's them up there, the Starfish. What did you think I was doing up there, hanging real stars?" said an equally stunned Star hanger.

"Starfish?" asked Benjamin.

"Oh for the love of Charlie! You don't know about Ginnies?"

The three shook their heads.

"Oh my, well this is an unusual situation. But I do suppose if you come from the Gilley Forest you more than likely would not know what a Ginnie is."

"We don't come from the Gilley Forest, we're from Grandlochcheshire," said a proud Mathilda, then added, "I'm Mathilda, this is Annabel and that's Benjamin."

"Not from the Gilley Forest! Well, this is all very untoward. I dare say, I have never heard of this Grandlochcheshire, but I'm sure it's a perfectly splendid place to live, even if they don't have Ginnies. Actually the scientific name is Ginelly Radialus. We call them Ginnies here, it's much more personal." he replied, then mumbled under his breath, as he turned to walk away, flagging his arm for them to follow. The children quickly moved single file after him and within seconds smacked right up against each other when Finley abruptly stopped on the stairs to continue his dissertation.

"Well, the Ginnies are subterranean starfish that hang from long stringy tendrils of cartilage that are rooted deep in the upper earthen sky. The root tissue actually grows through the ground on up to the earths surface, and attached on the opposite end is a large brilliant flower that collects the sunlight and regenerates the Ginnies cells to radiate, making it possible for them to glow. Of course they're not really a fish at all, but a splendid little creature native to our world here, they just look like Starfish.

"When I feed them and sing to them...*ooh*...how they love to be sung to...well they simply sigh and coo, and then they glow. I walk about on my leg extension poles and nurture my sweet little Ginnies, it's my job and a rightly good job it is. And when I'm finished, well, as you can see for yourselves, it gives the illusion of a starry night sky here in Na'talom. Isn't it simply breathtaking?"

"It certainly is," replied Benjamin, and the girls nodded in agreement.

They were now standing on cobblestone stairs that lead down to a cobblestone road that went as far on either side of them as they could see;

following along a very tall stone wall that looked like it surrounded the perimeter of the entire city. There appeared to be other intermittent watch tower stations positioned on the outside of this perimeter up against the earthen wall, besides Finley's platform.

From the elevated spot they were standing the children could look out above the massive wall and in through the grand entrance at the huge expanse of the quaint little city of Na'talom. They could see off in the distance, in the center of the city, a large tall structure was erected with a huge purple metallic dome. A dome that appeared to rotate around in it's holding, letting the reflection generate a spattering of crystal like colors bouncing off the immediate buildings and sky. It was like a giant aubergine disco ball. They all had wide eyes and open mouths and no one said a word, as they gazed out at the serene and quiet city laid before them.

Finally Finley lead them down the rest of the cobble stairs and in through the impressive elaborate main entrance of the city.

An ornate arch, chiseled from limestone, span the upper opening, roughly about fifteen feet high, ending in exquisite side columns. A superb, hand forged wrought iron design piece, about four feet in height, hung with big thick rusty chains from the arch. Both end columns featured the most magnificent gigantic stain glass lamps, hanging from massive twisted iron hooks. The candle light shone through the array of colored glass making the whole experience enchanting. The three friends turned their heads in every direction taking everything in as fast as they could, such was the pure magic of the fairy tale drenched scenery before them.

Cobblestone roads and shoppes with beautifully colored signs announcing the wares and services held within. All the boutiques had spectacular window displays filled with treasures for the eye to feast upon. The foursome marched slowly past all the finery that Na'talom had to offer.

A confection shoppe called *LoLo's Sweet's,* had white lacy doily painted edges around the entire border of the big picture windows in the front of the shoppe as well as the side windows leading into the entrance. The door had a red lace shade pulled down in the closed position and the sign in the window read, *Sweet you later.*

There were exquisite pink and orange checkered silk drapes lined in an outstanding old gold silk, pulled to the side by large mossy green and bright blue braided tassel tie backs, in all of the windows. The name was in a beautiful hand script lettering of shiny gold foil. And smack dab in the center of the main display window stood a remarkable enormous strawberry cupcake on a gold pedestal. Huge, juicy, bright pink and red strawberries, topped the piled high pink frosting.

Mathilda let out a deep sigh, "Strawberry, my favorite."

A tailor shop with a hanging sign out from above the entrance, was of a large needle with a piece of thread going through the eye, on the other end the thread spelled out, *Finnigan's Stitchery,* in faux stitch markings. It dangled from a black wrought iron silhouette of an old fashion tailor's sewing machine. They had a short stout mannequin in the window dressed with a partially made mens evening jacket, exposing the layering of materials Finnigan used; showing the details of how well the coat was made.

The completed right side, and upper left shoulder of the dark teal wool jacket, hung over a crisp white shirt with a high collar and a green and orange striped thin tie looped in a bow around the neck. Shiny gold buttons with black obsidian centers trailed down the front of the completed side of the coat. Grey and black striped trousers ending with a chartreuse green flared cuff with little gold embroidered stars, hung on a glossy polished wooden valet next to the displayed coat. The finishing touch were a lovely pair of dark blue goat skin lace up ankle boots, paired up with orange and green stripe socks to match the neck tie.

There was a musical instrument shoppe called, *Schnellhound's.* The upper border of the windows were old parchment sheets of music. A single perfect Stratavarious violin was perched high upon an overstuffed pillow of deep purple velvet, that rested upon an equally exquisite wide worn out charcoal marble slab, with chiseled fairies etched around the bottom half. Rich thick magenta velvet drapery lined in a deep forest green silk, hung on the side of the windows, held back by huge ornate gold tassels.

A flower shoppe with an old white washed wooden Dutch door, had a little hand-painted wooden sign hanging from a rusty nail. The rustic little piece of worn out white wood was attached with a sparkly silver ribbon that had tiny white embroidered daisies on it and tied in a bow. The red lettered sign read, *Felicity's Garden*. However, simple as the sign was, the windows were something else.

A billowy red and white, thinly striped valance shade, with a pink lace ruffle, adorned the tops of the windows. With the side panels of white with yellow polka dots being held with tie backs made from the same red and white stripe as the valance. It looked like summer had exploded, such was the abundance of floral life on display.

Little dark blue pots painted with bright yellow moon faces, held orange and black spotted green orchids. Tall pale green whicker pedestal baskets let fronds of wild purple and blue berries fall from it's lip. Old rusty buckets of snow white daisies stood upon tiers of varying sizes of wood rounds. There were enormous long trumpeted funnel type bright fuchsia colored flowers, that had long neon yellow protruding filaments coming out from the center. They hung down in a bunch, such was the abundance of them. Attached to the top of the threads of filament was a round flat button like surface that was home to the Gents, which were tiny beetle like creatures with purple and orange stripes.

Huge colored flowers, the likes of which the children had ever seen or imagined, had mesmerized and captivated their senses.

"This is spectacular! Simply brilliant!" said Benjamin.

"There are just no words to describe it!" said Annabel.

And Mathilda simply said, "Ho..lee...Moses!"

There were stain glass street lamps that hung from forged wrought iron hooks on the sides of buildings at every corner. Windows with soft yellow lights peeping out from behind lace curtains, spilled from the silent homes they were now passing. Everything was still and quiet, with exception to the distant drone of the small aircraft with shouts of cursing echoing from Pips, and all the children could do was giggle.

Benjamin finally asked Finley, "I don't know where you are taking us, but I am supposed to meet up with someone called Esmerelda Fet. Do you know her?"

"Do I know her! Oh young man, everyone in Coranim knows of Esmerelda Fet. She is the most knowledgeable Medicine Woman in the planet. Maybe even *on* the planet! She is a fierce Warrior and strategist as well as a cunning and powerful Light Sorceress. I dare say, there is not another being in the world like Esmerelda Fet."

Benjamin looked at the Gnome and smiled. Things in Coranim were looking up.

The city was beginning to change as they walked further. They were coming into a more rural setting on the outer edges. Little fenced in gardens began to appear and the sound of crickets became abundant.

"Where are we going?" asked Annabel.

"We're heading towards the outer West perimeter of Na'talom. This is where Esmerelda Fet lives, just up ahead there." He pointed to a light coming from the bottom of another thick root tendril.

"She lives in the tree root?" asked Mathilda, confused.

"Well, don't be ridiculous child, she lives under the root," responded Finely. "You see the roots of the Great Tree go far and deep. We have built our city outward from the center of the Grandfather, living amongst the outer edges of the great tendrils. Some of our Wizards and Sorceress have made their homes closer to the inner border in order to utilize the threads of concentrated Energy from the Tree. You'll see soon enough...Oh, there she is."

The children all looked up ahead to see the great Medicine Woman standing by a little rickety fence with berry bushes following the slatted boundary.

"She looks old," said Mathilda.

"She looks wise," said Annabel.

"She looks like she knows me," said Benjamin with a chuckle. The girls looked at him and smiled.

As they approached, the wise old Sorceress held up her lantern, and smiled a deep warm welcoming grin. The three children of the Prophecy relaxed. And for the first time in all this long and tumultuous journey, they finally felt safe.

"Welcome, welcome, Aut'banda!" showered the great woman of the Fet, blowing kisses from her lips and fingertips. The three friends couldn't help but smile. Without thought, Mathilda rushed up and put her arms around the woman's waist, hugging her with all her might, "Oh Esmerelda Fet, you remind me of my grandmother."

The old woman put her arm around Mathilda's shoulder and cupped her head to her bosom, stroking her hair, "Ah, A'm so very glad of that me sweet lassie."

Annabel almost began to cry. "She's right, you feel so familiar to us, it's weird. I mean, I feel like I know you already."

Benjamin just looked deeply back into the ancient eyes that were now staring into his. He heard her voice in his head, *A'm so glad I have lived long 'nough ta meet ya, young squire.* Benjamin took a deep breath and his shoulders softened and he felt like he could sleep for a week.

Finally Finely spoke up, "Well, if everyone is complete with introductions, I will be off. From the looks of it, I'll be needing to give a little encore to the Ginnies on the West side of town tomorrow's eve. They seem a bit lack luster tonight. I wonder what could be happening up top?" Benjamin flinched. "Whatever it is, I do hope it is accomplished soon, as it truly reeks havoc with my precious starfish down here. They're such sensitive little creatures. Well, I must be off. Before you know it the sun will be shining and I'll just be laying my noggin down on the feathers." He looked at the children and gave a slight gentlemen's bow, "Well, it's been a pleasure to meet you, and I hope you enjoy your stay here in Na'talom. It would be a pity to miss some of our best resources before you tarry off to do what ever it is that you must do. Good luck. Charlie's speed. Ta Ta."

The children shouted Aut'banda's around and giggled as they watched the little Gnome return in the direction they had come.

Mathilda spoke up, "What does he mean before the sun shines? How can there be sun down here?"

"I was wondering the same thing myself," added Benjamin.

Esmerelda Fet pulled her arms in big circles around, as if gathering chickens and said, "Come chil'ren, let's be gettin enside. Thar be plenty oh time ta share all tha mysteries of Caranim tamarrow. Right now tis very late, an tha Ginny's lose thar light en a wee bit. Ya'll want ta be fast asleep by then."

And so they all turned towards the little gate and marched into the front door of the little underground home of the greatest Medicine Elder alive.

Chapter Twenty-Four

Esmerelda Fet and Dunston Tibbitts

The children awoke from a much needed deep and peaceful sleep to the smell of fresh baked berry pie. They had curled up on two small hay filled mattresses laying in front of a wide berth river stone fireplace. They were wrapped in hand knitted lambs wool blankets and soft chenille sheets, with big feather stuffed pillows for their heads. They each sat up wiping the sleep from their eyes, and suddenly remembering where there were, became excited at the joy of seeing Esmerelda Fet mixing something up at the sink counter.

"Good morning Esmerelda Fet," glowed a very content Mathilda, as morning salutations came abounding from her two partners as well. The old woman turned and looked down at the shiny faces of the three children before her and smiled. The reality that these were the children of the Prophecy hit her, and she knew that her world would be forever changed.

"Why, top of tha morning ta ya," responded Esmerelda, "I know thar be much ta discuss taday an many thins ta see hare en Na'talom. But I be thinkin maybe tis best ta keep thins simple fer a day er two. Too much information can make yer noodle swell. Ha! I got that one from Dunston, he be tha Keeper of tha Books, ya'll be meetin him soon 'nough. He be a clever little chap, always with tha sayings an quotes. I always liked thad one 'bout tha noodle. Anyway, if'n ya feel tha strong enough ta ask me somethin, than by all means ask away. If'n not,

287

than I say we eat some of this hare barry pie, ya width me on that?"

Mathilda shouted, *"Pie!"* and Esmerelda Fet giggled and turned back around to serve up the buttery pastry. In the meantime, Benjamin and Annabel were having their first look around the space that the Medicine Woman called home.

Finley had been correct in describing the curious abode as under a root. Clearly the massive tendril that tapered down from the Great Tree, ended with the visible narrowing tip that was the roof to Esmerelda Fet's home. Small threads of rhizome branched off in a multitude of direction growing across the earthen ceiling. Varying sizes of glass containers that hung from rusted wires, encasing the free hanging strands of root, covered the ceiling. Some of the jars had amber liquid filled half way saturating the filaments, some had moss; and still others held a green syrupy fluid that dripped from a small tube stuck up in a spliced section of knotted root.

There were rows of herbs and roots stuffed tightly into sealed jars lining every available surface. The counter tops, next to the cups in the open kitchen shelves, and the worktable in the middle of the room. A worktable that was saturated with all things magical. A large black cook pot, jars filled with various parts of what looked like fish bones, butterfly wings, and cocoon casings to Benjamin. And loads of flower petals and parts in baskets. In addition a huge wooden bowl filled with little chunks of black and silver ore, and quartz, from pink to green, sat spilling with shiny color.

There were bird feathers, leather twine, gauze, ointments, tinctures, and charcoal. Candle stubs with their black sooted snippet of over used wick sat on stacks of books; with the drippings stuck to the bindings and trailing off the edge of the table onto the floor. The windows housed multiple decanters of brightly colored liquids of orange and red. Mingled among them were short fat squatty jars of clear honey in varying shades of amber and gold. Bundles of tethered dried flowers and herbs hung from above the windows.

Piles of books were a close second to the display of medicinals. Stacks of magic spells and directives and botanical medicine leather bound volumes filled the mantle; while little pots with sprigs of herbs sat on top of the uneven piles. What could be seen of a huge carved gold leaf mirror that sat on the mantle, leaned up against the river stone chimney behind everything. And magnificent wrought iron lamp sconces with blood red glass, hung on either side.

Looking into what he could see of the little nook that was the bedroom; on the opposite side of the main room, Benjamin spied a large four poster bed made from dark wood; with a red, black, green and blue crocheted quilt covering the lumpy mattress. At the bed footing, in a pile of purring fur, lay a gigantic fat fluffy black and white cat making soft snoring sounds in between motor purrs. There was a small rectangular window right above the bed with diamond cut clear leaded glass. A simple drape made from burlap swayed ever so softly in the morning breeze. From the window on the right side of the room hung several crystal stars that played with the light streaming in. Peaceful chimes that hung outside the window gave a musical beauty and grace to the moving sparks of multi colored reflections.

The night table on the left side of the bed, was of rustic structure and had small tree branches for legs. At home on the table was an ornately carved silver candle stick with what looked like eons of melted wax two inches thick around the base. And trailing off was a collection of drippings down on the floorboards. He saw a tall slender decanter with cobalt blue liquid contents and an equally tall goblet made with little bubbles of different colored pieces, like marbles, embedded into the glass. An open book plopped down on its pages so that the worn out brown leather covers were upward, lay next to the candle. And a picture of Esmerelda Fet and Cottie Set; a copy of the painting in the grand entry to the Tree, stood motionless in a hand forged bronze metal frame.

Benjamin joined Annabel and Mathilda, now standing in the kitchen.

"Hare ya go wee ones, take this bit of tea an head outside, we can rest our souls at tha table," said Esmerelda Fet, as she handed each one a plate with a large slab of pie, and a small cup of something rich and dark.

Mathilda had her nose in the steamy scent coming up from her cup and without thought looked up to the surprising blue sky above, "Hey, there's sun shining! I don't understand."

Annabel looked up into the faux sky of the underground world and nodded in compliance with her little sister, "She's not the only one, how is this possible?"

Benjamin stood and studied the outer walls of the city. He looked out as far as he could see and by any other standards it looked like a normal little town in any part of the globe, sky and all.

"Woll thar be rh bit of an explanation, but I could keep it simple fer ya" responded the old woman. "Ya see, tha Gnomes are wee clever little task masters. Tha minin an buildin thay do is very imporant work, that be necessary en keeping tha earth runnin properly....," Before she could finish Benjamin butt in, "Keeping the earth running properly?"

Esmerelda Fet realized there was a deeper understanding needed here and took a deep breath, "Woll...it seems we need eh little expedition ta tha World Library of Identity. Ya'll be wantin ta meet up width Dunston much sooner than I anticipated." Then she stopped and looked out at her beautiful countryside, keeping her thoughts close inside. Benjamin could see that she was in a deep quandary about how to explain the evolution of an entire race of beings to the likes of three young people, who had never stepped a foot outside of their own back gardens until a few days ago.

"The World Library of Identity, that sounds rather interesting to say the least," urged Benjamin, "I'm very curious myself as to how there is so much light down here. But, I'm a bit more curious as to why I...*we*...were brought here in the first place. I keep hearing about how I'm supposed to save the planet. It looks fairly safe from where I'm sitting right now. We really just need some answers. None of this makes any sense. Can you just tell us the truth Esmerelda Fet? We need to understand what is happening to us, and how we're supposed to help."

Esmerelda looked at the three stunned children before her and realized the deep complexity that boggled their minds. She looked Benjamin in the eye, then let her sight fall upon him and studied his aura for a moment. Then she smiled, "Woll blast me buttons, ya got me on that one! So hare it be wee ones. I'll use a language ya can foller.

'Thar be an old proverb comin from up en yer neck of tha world, it says, 'As it tis above, sew it tis balow'. The Gnomes of Coranim reflect a direct correlation ta yer world above. They be havin thar Scottish an English heritage, just as ya do. All the clans of beings are represented en this hare warld as woll, although we ain't usin no labels down hare, ya can be certain of that. The life of the Gnomes has remained, an is lived, as tha basic an truest incarnation of each culture. They have taken tha best of each philosophy, an custom, ta live en tha most truest of sense. En 'nother words, are traditions, are world, comes from a time en tha beginnin, before all tha wars an battles an industry wiped tha true essence of tha planet away.

"Tha great Targanoe war put an end ta any struggle an dishonor among tha Gnome of Caranim. The Gnome live en eh highly evolved spiritual an mental state of Grace. I ain't sayin thar ein't any snits from time ta time, ore disagreements, just look at Finely an Pips! Thay be a real pair of old coots! No, what it simply means is we all tend ta put are differences behind us an concentrate on tha wholeness of life. We all work t'wards tha greater good of tha planet. We ware put hare ta nurture an protect tha Heart of the Planet. An right now, tha great Mother is ailin.

"The poisons an toxins along with tha chaotic mental an emotional state of tha world above, has begun ta seep enta tha crust, an has shifted energies en a very big, an nearly irreparable, way. Tha damage is extensive children. Tha Gnomes are workin at rh dizzyin pace ta rectify tha sitchuation...but thar losin tha battle."

The children sat glued to every word the Medicine Woman spoke.

"Woll, than ya mix en tha relentless rage of Tar Vigorn en tha Gilley Forest an her endless brutal attempts ta infiltrate are pristine lovely world down hare an ....woll, ya've got yerself one heck of a mess!" She paused to smile. But nothing could change the look of dread plastered all over Annabel's face. Esmerelda absently put her hand out and stroked Annabel's chin in the most gentleness of manner, and looked in her eyes, "Shush up little mind wee one... Ya never stop thinkin do ya?"

Annabel opened her eyes wider in surprise at the discovery made at her expense. She involuntarily reached up and cupped her hand around Esmereldas' wrist, and let the quiet tears slide down her cheeks.

"Garl, ya have tha ingenuity of eh great analytical discover'r. Ya be sew capable of bushels of creative taught. Don't ye be so fairful. All tha answers be en ya, buried deep. But not too deep fer ya ta reach them. Ya have tha stamina an tha ware width all ta release any iota of knowledge thar is. Yer truly brilliant! Tis all en ya...just waiting ta spring forth. By Charlie, Let It!"

Annabel began to breath heavy from the emotion she felt at the Medicine Woman's inherent and personal understanding of how she worked, as her tears streamed. Mathilda looked at her stunned sister and picked up her free hand and held it tight. Then she looked up at the Medicine Woman with wet eyes.

Esmerelda Fet now spoke to Mathilda, "Ya be a wee firecracker ein't ya!" And Mathilda jumped in her skin, with the same wide wet eyes as Annabel. "Yer all excitement an bravado! Ya have eh peculiar way of lookin at thins ya wee clever lass....Ha! No, I dare say not much can take away yer power, ya stand most erect en yer resolute...Woll done ya! Ya have eh very deeply lived sense of curiosity, ya simply can't quell it. Ya just need ta understand it all. Ya t'ain't afraid of nothin. Ya simply march up ta any foe, be it man, beast are word, and dare it ta face ya...Ha!" Then she paused again and kinda clicked her head sideways as if hearing something from another realm then looked back at Mathilda with a visual sincerity, "An ya hold tha biggest love I have ever felt, bar none." Esmerelda Fet looked back at Annabel, "Cone-sider yerself lucky garl. Tha wee lass places all of hair best parts en yer trust. I've never beheld eh more unwavering show of love from one human being t'nother."

She looked back at Mathilda, "Ya just keep on loving that hard wee sparklin one. Yer aura is filled with yer smile. Thad's gonna be gettin ya pretty far en tha world."

The sisters both had tears streaming down their faces, but never took their gaze off of Esmerelda Fet. Then the old sage turned all her attention to Benjamin. However, before she could say anything he cut her off at the pass, "You're not going to find any deep well of strength or knowledge in me. Nothing special here. There's nothing that you can pull out of your magic bag that can pin any kind of medal on me. Oh, I suppose you can tell me of my deep wounds over my parents disappearance, or the loneliness I've lived for most of my life. But that wouldn't be such a feet. And I don't cry that easily. So before you go and waste your time and pretend that I'm made of something I'm not, let's just get a move on with the day and meet up with this Dunston character. We've apparently got a planet to save."

The Medicine Woman looked long and hard at Benjamin until he began to squirm a bit. She didn't have a smile on her face like she did when she studied the girls, she simply stared him down. Benjamin started to become very uncomfortable from the intense way Esmerelda Fet was gaping at him and not saying a word. Finally, as if in a trance, she spoke, "Yer loneliness, as ya be callin it...tis palpable. I ein't never witnessed someone who insists on standin so alone. Ya wear yer talent like a badge of dishonor....like tis somethin ta loath, rather than rejoice en. Ya think thar could be no other livin soul on tha whole planet that bares tha same burden ta tha curious way ya find yer thoughts be a travelin. Da ya really think yer tha only one who has tha site boy? Tha only one who dreams en reality, an has visions? Ya be receivin messages from tha Universe, an yet ya choose ta block everythin, an toss it aside, as mearly tha ramblings of yer crazy mind!"

All three of the children blinked in unison from the peculiar manner in which Esmerelda Fet was now speaking to Benjamin.

"Let me tell ya somethin, it ein't so special as you be thinkin. If'n thay wonted ta, anyone could open up thar grand minds ta tha possibilities of 'seein'. It ain't some big mystery. Tis not some circus magic act fer tha love of Charlie! It just be awareness boy. It'd be trust, an more importantly, it'd be courage! Ya, that's right, it'd be takin courage ta trust yer instincts an listen. Listen with an open an clear mind an heart. But not ya."

Then Esmerelda Fet sat back a bit and shook her head. She took a deep breath and looked back at Benjamin, and slowly a smile began to creep upon her face. She leaned forward again in closer to Benjamin and said slyly, " Maybe ya should sit down with yer *granmuther* sometime an see what she be thinkin bout all of this nonsense." Then she sat back righteously and giggled.

Benjamin felt the wind get knocked out of his gut, "My grandmother! What do you know about my grandmother? What does she got to do with any of this?" Benjamin was charged up.

"She's got everythin ta do width it boy!" answered Esmerelda Fet with gusto,

"Why she's ware ya learned it all from en tha first place! If'en ya don't believe me, why don't ya just ring hair up en thar wee noggin of yers right now. See if ya can be makin tha connection....go ahead, I dare ya!"

Benjamin sat bolt upright with his mouth hanging open. *What was she saying? That his grandmother could predict outcomes and had visions? How could this be true? How could he live under the same roof and not know this about her? Why had she always made him feel like something was wrong with him when he would share something of his premonitions with her?* But before Benjamin could get any further in his thoughts he was slashed with the intrusion of Esmerelda Fet's voice mingled in his own mind. *She warn't thinkin ya be strange boy...she be thinkin how miraculous it t'were that she warn't sew alone en hair own world of foreign thoughts. Only ya scared hair off when ya clammed up an stopped sharin what was going on with yer visions.*

Then out loud she simply said, "Too bad. Ya could be so much farther en yer evolution had ya trusted, instead of runnin so scared."

Benjamin stood up abruptly and headed quickly for the little opening in the rickety fence and tore off full speed down the road. Both girls jumped up and yelled, "Benjamin!" but Esmerelda Fet put out her hand and motioned for them to keep quiet.

"He be owl-right wee ones. He be figurin out who he be right now. Wo'll catch up with him an head over ta see Dunston."

The day was wearing on, and the three friends walked slowly down the little country road following the old sage, heading towards the World Library of Identity. Once again they took in every bit of wonder they could land their eyes on. Everything was lush and alive with color. Birds sang in the trees and the sun was miraculously shining. There even appeared to be clouds. And floating among the mysterious billowy mist came the drone of an engine. Mathilda searched the air above her in anticipation of catching another glimpse of the peculiar flying machine. And truth be told, she was hoping to get another good chuckle out of Pips' expletives echoing through the air. Finally she spotted him, "Oh, there he is! Look he's doing loop d' loops! Wow, that's so amazing!" shouted a very happy Mathilda.

Annabel bopped Benjamin on his shoulder with the back of her hand and pointed in the direction of the flying machine. They both shaded their eyes with their cupped palms and squinted upward watching Pips' show of daring.

"I swear, it looks like a giant wooden flying fish, it's the weirdest plane ever," said Annabel.

"He's really got some bottle doing all that dare devil stuff," said Benjamin, now calm from his morning upheaval. If there is one thing he had learned, it was not to hold onto things for too long...it just made him crazy. He found that when he couldn't let things go he missed out on something special, or fun, that would inevitably always show up. It was a mystery of life he had witnessed one too many times. Oh, he still held every word Esmerelda Fet said in a neat little compartment ready to be dissected at his whim. He wasn't going to forget what she had said. But he wasn't two fisting the emotion and anger any longer. Enough time had passed for him to regain his balance and get back to what was right in front of him. He didn't want to miss a single, extraordinary, magical thing. And that couldn't happen if he wasn't paying attention and focusing on the present moment.

"Ow, ya ein't seen nothin yet! Pips be eh right old magician he is. Tis an ingenious inventor. He be comin up with tha most miraculous contraptions, I dare say. Tis eh right darn good artist too. Ya should see his paintins. Woll, actually, now that I tink bout it, ya already did. Thad be all his handy work up en tha entry gallery."

"Oh, those were amazing!" said Annabel with surprise, "I really thought they were something special. Are those paintings of places here in Coranim?" "Absolutely!" responded Esmerelda Fet. "Wow."

"Wo'll have ta get ya over ta his place in eh day ar two. Tis worth tha hike ta see tha splendor of his imagination. He's converted his old barn enta eh studio an thinkin room. Thar's huge canvas' an paint buckets everywhere. He be usin colorful charcoal, an smudges all tha lines, an it be nothin less than amazing! Very life like too. But the real show be all of his experiments. He's got every kind of machine imaginable. But I be partial ta his sketchin...his thinkin process. He carries eh little book around width him ta jot down anythin thad might pop enta his noodle. He has calculations an mathematical configurations tha likes of never seen before. He be eh brilliant mind. An eh rightly well fun gentleman too! Loves a good two step!"

As Benjamin let his gaze drift over the rolling hills that were now beginning to diminish the closer they were getting towards the town, he couldn't help but wonder yet again, *How in world is the sun shining?* He decided to aim a new question at the old woman, "Esmerelda Fet, I'm completely boggled by this idea of the sun in Coranim. Will you at least give me a hint how this is possible?"

Esmerelda Fet smiled, then looked over her shoulder in his direction, "If'n ya keep yer eyes peeled, an look up along tha owter area, along tha upper walls ya'll be noticin somethin peculiar. Maybe ya can figure it out fer yerself. An tis only en Na'talom. Once ya leave tha city, thar be a real son...butt thad be eh story fer 'nother time."

So all three children turned their complete attention to the walls of the underground world. Then, for a brief instant, something flashed, like a light, or a reflection. Benjamin honed in on the area. He squinted and shaded his view then he saw it again, clear as could be, "It's a mirror!" he said simply.

"What, what do you mean it's a mirror?" ask Annabel, confused.

Mathilda attempted to peer around the frontside of Esmerelda off to the right of them, never letting go of the old woman's hand.

"It's a mirror, a bit back in that cave up there. But how does it work?" asked a very intrigued Benjamin.

"Woll simply put. Tha Gnomes have dug out eh series of tunnels that connect up ta tha earths surface, thad be leadin all tha way down ta us standin right hare. Than Pips, tha clever ol' bugger that he be, figured out eh mathematical procedure ta calculate ware, an whan, ta place large mirrors on down true tha tunnels. He considered tha time of sunrise an geographical location, all thad rigamarole, than tha old coot had hundreds of Gnome strategically position almost 500 mirrors, an voila! Sonlight! An when tha planet is en certain spins thar be a good glimpse of tha moonlight as well. Pips controls all the mechanisms over ta his place. Tis quite tha contraption."

Benjamin stopped walking and shook his head in disbelief, staring up at the small almost unnoticeable indent into the side of the dirt, with a mirror resting against the wall.

"And because of some of tha flora an fauna as thay call it, live en eh kind of contained type atmosphere down hare, thay let off eh bit of a mist, so thems be tha cloud cover ya be seein."

"Oh, it's like a terrarium," blurted Annabel.

"I don't have no knowledge of such thins, all I know is whan Finley feeds them Starfish of his, well, tis a right magical little world hare indeed."

"Yeah, we saw that last night," said Mathilda, "It was simply marvelous," she added with flair. And everyone had a little chuckle.

They had begun walking through the streets of Na'talom again, mingled among all the beautiful shoppes and boutiques. The Gnome of the Fet filled the little cobblestone roads, busy with their days activities. Suddenly a little scraper of a Gnome pulled up beside the group dragging a little cart along behind him, "Would ya be needin a lift Esmerelda Fet?" he queried the Medicine Woman.

Esmerelda Fet looked around at her companions and smiled, "Woll ya know, now thad ya mention it, I tink that wood be lovely. No better way ta see aur majestic city than by Gnome trolley. Hop en everyone!"

And the children did just that.

O-M-G! This is just so cool!" squealed Mathilda, as she jumped up into the rickshaw like carriage.

It was a rustic structure made with a sturdy wood cart base that had tall posts on all four corners holding up a perfect red and metallic gold stripe canopy, that had little scalloped edges hanging down the sides a wee bit. The children sat on small benches with over stuffed green and blue plaid cushions and held on, as the powerful Gnome picked up his rails and began to pull them along the cobble street.

"Where to mum?" asked the Gnome.

"We be off ta tha Library ta have a wee visit width Dunston, Cates."

"Very good mum," answered Cates, and off they went

They road past some of the shoppes they had seen the night before, and they all remarked in unison with a big, *"OOH!"* when they passed the floral shoppe.

"Yea, I be agreein with ya on tha one....she is eh beauty she is. Felicity truly knows hair world of botanicals. I think ya should go take a peek enside Benjamin. Ya might find somethin unusual ta occupy yer attention." Then she smiled.

That was odd, thought Benjamin, with a small grin of curiosity on his face. "Right then, I'll do that soon," he said back in sarcasm. And suddenly they were pulling up in front of the huge structure with the purple rotating dome.

"Hey this is the place we saw from the staircase when we first got here," said Mathilda.

"Yeah, it's even more impressive up close. Hey, is that a giant crystal or something? I mean, it looks like an amethyst, but how could that be, it's just too ginormous?" said Annabel.

Esmerelda thanked Cates for the ride, "Aut'banda Cates." "Aut'banda mum."

"Woll ya smart lass, thad be a very big amethyst indeed. Quartz like this are buried deep en tha earth. It took tha great ancestors 13 years ta dig it owt of tha ground en one piece, shape it, an polish it up. Than thay rolled it on en ta tha center of Na'talom an took another year ta create tha structure ta hold it. Tha World Library of Identity sits ba'neath her."

"Yeah, but how long did it take to get it up on top of the building? That's three stories high, did they use cranes or something?" asked Benjamin.

Esmerelda Fet looked at him with a sincere smile and simply said, "It took all of three hours to put it to rest, an they didn't use any cranes as ya be sa'in."

"Three hours! And No cranes? Are you barking mad? What are you talking about? That thing has to weigh a couple tons or something. How could a bunch of little Gnomes..." Esmerelda Fet cut him off, "First off, 'Ow'll be asking ya not ta

refer ta them as 'a bunch of little Gnomes', an secondly, thar be many ways ta move somethin of great stature besides machines an brute strength. Ya gotta think outside oh yer typical pattern hare Benjamin. Think. Whad be tha one constant that keeps comin back ta ya en regards ta movement?"

Benjamin looked down at the stair he was standing on, leading up to the grand entrance, and pushed his mind to calculate and lead him to find the answer to the riddle. Then he had it, "Sound," he whispered. Then offered, "The vibration of sound seems to be the answer down here."

"Oh, it not just be down hare laddie, but ya folks up thar wood't know ware ta begin ta harness tha true vibrations ta make a diff'ernce, if'n it bit ya on tha nose."

With minds full of wonder and questions the children of the Prophecy followed the old Medicine Woman up the grand marble stairs into the World Library of Identity. They came before an impressive entry of ornately carved wooden doors with gigantic metal hinges and massive bolts holding it all together. Surrounding the entire opening was a magnificent stain glass window with a width of three feet. Purple light emanated from the fractal reflection of the giant amethyst joined by the multi colors streaming though the glass of the entry; and gave the building the illusion of a sparkling alive energy.

Esmerelda reached up and pulled the impressive knocker towards herself and let it fly back to land on the grand door, creating an echo that resonated down the entry hall inside. Within moments the doors opened. The group entered and the doors shut behind them.

"Yikes, that was kinda strange," said Annabel.

"No, thad be *magic* lass," remarked Esmerelda Fet. And the children chuckled.

"It was like the Wizard of Oz," said Mathilda.

"Oooh, woll, I don't know thad one, but he sounds like fon."

They walked down a wide hall that was filled with plush rugs made with hand woven designs of moons and stars on deep blue backgrounds. There were several doors lining the walls on both sides of the great hall. As they passed by one of the doors on the right was open a bit and the children could see in.

They spied a mess of unmade sheets peeking out from a heavy woven cozy canopy and drapes framing the top and sides of the bed; that had the same theme of moons and stars sewn into the fabric, and held back onto the side posts with large dark purple tassels. There was a warm inviting fire burning from a deep brown quartz hearth that was the base of a black marble fireplace. The walls had a worn deep burgundy damask print and a magnificent crystal chandelier; dripping with amber teardrop cut glass, sparkled across the dark wooden coffered ceilings.

"Wow, I ein't seen nothin like this before," said Benjamin, "Is this Dunston royalty or something?"

"Dunston Tibbitts be no such thing! But his position as Keeper of tha Books be a privilege an on honor bestowed on not many. Since he rarely gets out much, he likes ta live in comfort...an truth be told, a bit of luxury..*hee hee*!"

"Where is he?" asked Mathilda.

"Oh, I would be suspectin he'd be downstairs at this time of day. We can take tha moving staircase over there."

And the children looked to the left where Esmerelda pointed, and there was another doorway that had the word *Stairs* in gold foil, with a black shadow, printed on the opaque white glass window.

Before they entered, Esmerelda Fet stopped and walked over to the other side of the hall, up to an enormous painting that hung above a resplendent pink marble hall table; with an even more impressive massive gold urn filled to almost teetering with an opulent abundance or orange daisies and pink roses, and stood directly in front of it. The children simply watched in wonder as to what the great Sorceress would do next.

Then, without warning, the Medicine Woman sang three calculated notes of music in perfect pitch. With this the portrait of the man standing in his study dressed in full formal attire; from an impeccable blue cut velvet waist coat to a top hat and white knee stockings with gold ribbons on his laced up black shoes, picked up and held forward the gold filigree tray that had rested on the table beside him, and presented a key.

Esmerelda Fet snatched up the little gold key and thanked the gentleman, who in turned nodded his head, while tipping his hat.

The children stood mesmerized. *"Whoa,"* was all Mathilda said.

Esmerelda Fet returned to the waiting children, and the doorway for the stairs, and put the key into the lock. When she did this the word *Stairs* magically morphed into the word *Down*.

"Down, I don't understand?" said Benjamin.

"This be a way of protectin tha Library from no gooders our intruders. If'n ya don't know tha secret an ya be makin an attempt ta bust through ta tha staircase, thats exactly ware ya'll end up...on a staircase. A staircase that be leadin ta noware..*Ha!* So wa're smart e'nough hare to know we be lookin fer tha way down...not tha stairs."

When they stepped inside they stood upon a big square, polished black plank, tongue and groove floor. The surrounding walls had an ornate mahogany wooden dado coming up half way, with a beautiful polished chair rail that separated the bottom half from the top. The upper half was covered in a gorgeous rich tone on tone cut velvet deep purple damask. The boarder of the ceiling were lined with a thick gold braid that let loosely hang big gold tassels on all four corners.

"It's an elevator," said Mathilda.

"Oh, I like that word...it describes it very woll...*elevation*. Woll, hold on ta yer britches, hare we go," said a happy Esmerelda Fet, as she pushed the correct sequence of buttons on the shiny brass face plate, to enlist the chamber to move.

And down they went, climbing almost instantly to an alarming speed.

"Where are we going so quickly?" shouted an anxious Benjamin, fearful they would plummet to their death from the insane speed of descending in a three story building.

Esmerelda stood back with her hands folded in front of her, wearing a big Cheshire Cat grin, "Down." was all she said.

Annabel couldn't contain herself any longer, "How far is *down* Esmerelda Fet?

This is pretty fast."

Mathilda simply grabbed onto to her sisters hand and looked around wide eyed. After a few moments, that felt like an eternity, everything came to a sudden halt! Annabel looked up and saw the shiny brass floor marker above the door, it read *1952nd floor.* Her mouth flew open in complete astonishment, "What...?" was all that finally escaped her lips.

"One Thousand Nine Hundred And Fifty Second Floor! How...are you?" was all that came from Benjamin.

"It must be a *really* big library," said Mathilda innocently.

And everyone loosened up their anxiety and let out a nervous laugh, including the Medicine Woman, who was having a good old time at their expense.

"Oh ya wee children, not ta worry. It all be fine. An yer right sweet smart Mathilda. This *tis* a big library. It has ta be if'n it holds a book fer every bein on tha planet."

"Every person has a book?"

"Woll of course, why da ya think thay be callin it tha World Library of Identity?"

"Gee, I really hadn't thought of that," said Annabel. "What exactly do you mean everyone has a book...a book of what?"

"Why of thar life of course!"

"What's in the books, Esmerelda Fet?" asked a calmer Mathilda.

"First of oll wee ones, ya have me permission ta be simply be callin me Esmerelda, don't be worryin yer wee noggins 'bout tha Fet no longer. I won't be taken no insult from ya. Tis more of a formality, an honor ya show someone else. Thad, an it makes clear if'n ya be Fet or Set clan. But wa're old friends now, sew no pomp an circumstance needed. Furthermore, I believe Ow'll be lettin Dunston do tha honors of explainin thins fer ya."

As they all exited the elevator they stood in an equally elaborate, and similarly decorated hall, as the one on the first floor. However, there were no doors, only a large entrance on the left. They could hear the pleasant sounds of chimes and whistles blowing and beautiful music. They all walked towards the massive doorway entrance and stood looking into an even bigger room.

As they walked into the tremendous space, they stood in the wide open walkway that allowed them to stroll past the long aisles of the library on their left. Row after row of bookcases filled the room as far as they could see. At the beginning of each row was a work station with a table and a reading lamp; and various supplies and gadgets hanging from the shelf above the table. On the side of the table was a large clear tube that ran from just above the tabletop on up to the ceiling; and it's counterpart went from just below the tabletop to the floor, with a big wicker basket sitting next to it.

On the wall over to their right, was a built in bookcase, which ran the full length of the room, filled to capacity with leather bound books of different color bindings in magenta, green, blue, teal and brown, all grouped together accordingly. The wooden shelves were thick and painted with vines and pink roses. And the lower half of the built in shelves had closed cabinets that were painted with large aqua diamonds across the entire front. In each alternating diamond cabinet was a painting of either a quarter moon or a star. The backdrop to the large aqua diamonds was a deep cobalt blue with yellow stars on the surface; which was replicated in the upper crown and casings of the cabinets as well. A tall ladder with wheels on the base footing was attached to a brass rail connected almost at the top of the bookcase; as well as each of the separate free standing bookcases in the main body of the room. They rolled along the ground allowing the Gnome to climb up to any part of the shelves, and bookcases, to reach whichever tome he so desired.

The low ceiling had a hand painted mural of the night sky, filled with all the constellations, which magically moved about, as if the earth were spinning on its axis. It appeared as real as looking up into the dark heavens on a perfectly deep and still night, with the beauty of the twinkling stars to mesmerize and dream upon.

The floor was made of thick wide oak planks, that were covered every where with the same dark blue rugs as in the main halls, with the moon and stars woven in. And there he sat, smack dab in the middle of the wide walkway with the built in shelves behind him, facing the main library rows of books, Dunston Tibbitts, the Keeper of the Books.

He was perched high upon his hand forged metal stool, with a magenta leather tufted cushion, and little steps around the bottom rung. His stocking feet were dangling down and he was situated in front of a wooden podium. The ornate stand was held together from post to platform with an artistic two tone metal sunburst. And a humungous leather book was open and propped upon the reading surface with Dunston's face buried deep in it's pages. A glass lantern hung from the ceiling above the podium, offering enough light for the Book Keeper to read by. Sitting beside the tall podium, on a shorter small silver metal table with scalloped edges, and little silver quarter moons painted in glitter and bright red enamel painted legs, sat an enormous pink and fluffy strawberry cupcake. Without fore thought Mathilda let out a small sigh..."Strawberry, my favorite."

And with this Dunston turned his head up from his deep concentration and looked at his strange guest, "Oh my! Well, I suppose I should have expected you today. I've just been rather absorbed in my research here, that I plumb forgot all about the children of the Prophecy...well forgive my impertinence," spoke a surprised Dunston. Then he hopped down off of his roost and headed over towards the little group of visitors, "Dunston Tibbitts, at your pleasure."

'Ha! Woll, it certainly is our pleasure," responded a laughing Esmerelda, "It most certainly is."

"Oh me, well I suppose I twisted that one around. The pleasure is all mine of course. I've been looking forward to meeting you all for quite some time now."

The children all smiled and Mathilda stepped forward to shake his hand, "Hi, I'm Mathilda." "Oh Me!" responded Dunston. "And that's my sister Annabel, and that's Benjamin."

"Hi" they both added.

"Well," said Dunston, "and that's that for the introductions. So let's be off to it shall we, I don't have much time to dilly dally about at present. As you can see, there is much activity going on in the Library today. I wonder what could be happening up top, as it seems to be the inception of all the commotion." As he said this everyone began to notice the curious activity the Book Keeper was speaking of.

The children stood in awe as they watched as every so often a coiled up spring from behind the books would jump forward with a white gloved hand attached. The hand looked like a cartoon, with four round bulbous fingers and a fat thumb, that would push a book out from the shelves to tumble as if performing swan dives and turning summersaults; landing into the waiting open gloved palm attached to a spring mechanism in the cabinets below. The hand would pull back in, and the doors would shut.

Then there were others going in the reverse, from the lower cabinet springing up to a higher shelf, where another gloved hand would magically appear and snatch the flying book out of the air and place it in it's new home on the shelf.

Some books were glowing either green, blue or red while beeping and buzzing. Others were making whistling sounds, and still others were moving about; pinched between the magical thumb and fore finger of the white gloved hand to another group on another shelf.

Suddenly a different, more distinct alarm, sounded off, and a book up high on a shelf behind them floated off it's place and remained in the air, glowing a bright white neon while ringing loudly. It wasn't a harsh sound, Benjamin thought, *actually, it's not so disturbing as one would think with all the bells and whistles going off.* It was quite symphonic and pleasing.

Dunston turned the minute he heard the individual alarm and slid his movable rail ladder over to where the book hung glowing. He scurried up the stairs to pluck the floating book out of the air. He brought it down to his podium and absently spoke, "Excuse me..I need to mark a Remake. It's very important...no mistakes..."

He turned and put his foot on the hydraulic pedal at the base of the podium stand, which instantly lowered the book platform to Dunston's level. He removed the large brown leather book he had been studying, and put it in a cabinet two doors over to the left behind him. Then he placed the curious ringing glowing book upon his now lowered station, and began writing furiously on it's pages.

After a short moment he efficiently closed up the book and took it over to the end aisle workstation directly across from his podium. He took a big rubber stamp that was sitting on the little wooden work table, and pounded it squarely in the white ink; then he slapped the top of the brown leather of the glowing book with the imprint. Then he held the book under the opening to the wide pneumatic tube that was just above the tabletop, and away it was instantly carried; straight up and out of site through to the next floor above, on it's way to it's new home. He closed the ink pad and turned to walk back to the ever curious stare of the three friends.

"What the heck was that all about?" asked Mathilda first. The others nodded in agreement.

"Oh Me! Well, I needed to respond immediately to that alarm, and send the book up to another level because of the type of Remake."

"Remake, what does that mean?" asked Annabel.

"Oh, well that would take some time to explain at the present, suffice it to say it's very serious business keeping the markings of a Remake accurate. They don't come along too many in a day, but are a pleasure to keep track of I dare say. I will wonder of that person's Path from this day forward...very curious indeed." And Dunston smiled with a far away glint in his eye. Then he came back to himself. "In the meantime, we are here to discuss your books I believe, and keep to the present moment....yes?"

The children just stood in complete confusion. Finally Esmerelda Fet entered the conversation, "Book Keeper, the children are not aware of tha nature of our visit hare t'day. Thay not be privy ta tha details of tha callin...thay be needin some assistance ta take tha burden of secrecy off thar wee noggins. Could ya be givin us eh bit of direction, an maybe answer eh couple questions fer young Benjamin hare? It would help thins move along en eh more abundant manner."

"Oh Me! Well, this is all so untoward, however, this is a very unusual circumstance we find ourselves I dare say, and I will certainly oblige accordingly," spoke a slightly shaken Book Keeper.

First he walked over to the low cabinet directly behind his podium, took a tiny gold key out of his vest pocket and unlocked the door. Then he pulled out a massive black leather bound book. He turned around and placed the book on his reading platform, then put his foot on the hydraulic pedal at the base of the podium which instantly raised the station. He climbed back up onto his seat; using the little steps attached to the bottom rung, and began furiously scanning through the pages, while scribbling notes on a pad. When he finished his intensive jotting, he shut the book and lowered himself off the stool. He hit the pedal at the base again, this time releasing the platform; reached up, grabbed the book and put it back into it's own cabinet and locked the door.

He then walked down the bookcase cabinets to the left and stopped in front of another cabinet, and pulled out yet another key from his vest pocket. He unlocked the door and pulled out a small metal rack of tiny silver tubes hanging from itsy hooks on two levels, top and bottom. It was reminiscent of a dry cleaners, with bold black numbers on the metal frame above each tiny hollow hanging tube. He pulled it out almost three lengths.

"Wow, how thick is that the wall!" spoke a stunned Mathilda.

Dunston looked back at Matilda and simply smiled. He depressed the green button that was positioned on an inside panel of the cabinet and the mechanism began to churn and move along it's track, not unlike the clothes assembly in a dry cleaners. Dunston held his thumb on the green button until the number he was waiting for appeared, then he stopped the device and pulled the little mysterious tube off of it's hook. He turned to the main body of the library and put the little hollow tube to his lips and blew. A most beautiful note projected into the air.

"It's a whistle!" shouted Annabel. This time Esmerelda put a grin on her face.

The children waited in anticipation to see what magic would occur next, and they weren't disappointed. From behind them, in the deepness of the main library came a book, a green leather bound book, floating it's way to the Book Keeper. Dunston reached up and snatched it out of the air, and set it down on his lowered podium station. Then he repeated the process two more times until he had three books, all green, resting on his station. He slid his tall stool out of the way and motioned for the children to gather around the lowered platform. They all huddled in close to get a good view. Dunston opened a book and looked up to Benjamin and nodded, "This one's yours. Let's see what we have here."

As the children looked over the shoulder of the Gnome, it was clear that the book was written in the same foreign language as the primer, and made no sense to them whatsoever. As Dunston glanced through the pages to get to the present time, he would pause and read a line or two, then hoot and howl, "Oh Me! What a clever chap you are. I would love to have seen the look on Tar Vigorn's face when you disappeared right before her eyes! Brilliant!"

Benjamin noticed that the edges of the pages seemed to have a variety of glowing colors generating from them, "What's all the colors about? Like that white one, why is it glowing so brightly?" asked Benjamin.

"Well, the colors keep the events and the years in sequence, you know, past present, etc. The white one is this exact moment, today. And I'm headed that way now. I just wanted to fill myself in on some of the outcomes of your actions, as I have looked upon your book before, during one of your Remake markings."

"Remakes! I've had Remakes to my Path?" asked a stunned Benjamin.

"Oh my yes you clever boy, you most certainly have. How do you think you have ended up here in Na'talom? Not many would have taken the information given to them by Cottie Set and done a single thing with the knowledge. Actually most would not have been open enough to even receive the message in the first place. You have taken certain, precise steps along your journey, that have given you the advantage to be awake.

"When one is present in their life, they are more apt to decipher the bits of information being whirled at them. They are more equipped to discern the truth from the mumbo jumbo. However, to take action on that discovery is truly a monumental step in that beings' evolution. Oh, you most certainly have had Remakes Master Benjamin...you most certainly have. And I must say, well done you!"

Benjamin sat back for a moment then felt Esmerelda Fet staring at him and looked up her way. The old woman winked at him and smiled, and he heard her voice in his head, *Yeah, woll done ya, my boy, woll done.* Then she nodded for him to focus his attention back down on the open book before them. And Benjamin complied.

"See here, if I flip past the present into say...next week, or two months from now, a year, it will show what the probable outcome is according to your present trajectory. However, nothing is written in stone as they say, only the present moment. The thought you are having this very minute will create your tomorrow. It will determine the next step on your Path. It can effect a situation three years from now. Master Benjamin, an outcome can change in a breath...it all depends on the intention and motive, as well as the action of the being in question. Will they keep to the course laid out in front of them, or will they shift their compass to follow an internal voice? What external action may cross their Path and create an opportunity for them to respond...*or not?* So according to what I see here now, this very minute, whatever it is that you are seeking will show itself to you today, and change your Path immediately. It will put you into a whole new dynamic as they say."

"What does that mean, whatever I am seeking? Other than trying to understand why I was brought here, and how I'm supposed to help, what could I possibly be seeking except answers?" said a very disappointed Benjamin. He was counting on the Book Keeper to give him more sound advice.

"I can't give you that answer Master Benjamin, it is for you to figure out for yourself. I can simply say that according to your Path today, some...*thing*....of, well, relatively great significance it would appear, will present itself to you today. And you will, without question, follow it's lead and change the course of your present direction. It's as clear as can be, look here for yourself if you don't believe me. Without a doubt, your destiny shall shift today, I'm certain of it."

Benjamin sat back in deep frustration, and now shock, from the Librarian's words. *What on earth could he be talking about? What is going to change my life so dramatically?...today!* he thought deeply. And before he had a chance to explore further he was ripped from his intense thoughts to the sounds of multiple alarms ringing madly all about them, *"What the bloody heck...?"*

And with this they all noticed the words on the pages of Benjamins' book beginning to gather into one big swirling commotion. And before any of them could react, the two closed books, belonging to Annabel and Mathilda, began to react in the same alarming sound. Colors were sparking off the bindings, and a cacophony of maddening sounds ensued.

"Oh Me! This is remarkable! What?...Oh dear, where do I begin?" shouted Dunston.

"What's happening?" Benjamin shouted back to the Book Keeper, over the growing din.

"Why are the other books changing colors like that?" yelled Mathilda.

Without thought, Annabel instinctively reached for the shaking glowing book siting beside Benjamin's. As she clutched it to her chest, an instant image was shot into her consciousness. She saw, *her father and Emeline digging in a dark dirt tunnel....then the image shifted to a view of a deep jungle from high above....then in an instant, she was someplace else, and there were hundreds of bubbles in the air.* Before another image presented itself, the sacred tome was being ripped from her arms. She opened her eyes to Dunston, who was shaking his head, and now holding her book. Mathilda looked at her sister, "Are you all right Bellie? What the heck is happening? What do we do?" she shouted, as anxiety began to spin.

Esmerelda Fet pulled the two young girls up next to her and motioned for Benjamin to help Dunston gain control. Benjamin looked at the Gnome for direction. Finally Dunston acquiesced and stood up with the book in his hand. He motioned for Benjamin to follow him. He gathered the remaining two books, as he and Benjamin, headed towards the bigger work station at the end of the bookcase in front of them.

"There should be several other books ringing with that same alarm and glowing white as well. Look down every aisles until you spot them, then call me immediately. Don't delay, we must be quick and accurate!"

Benjamin moved with great speed, as he ran down the wide walkway, scanning each aisle for any floating glowing white ringing books. Then he spotted one, "Here, Dunston!"

The Gnome rushed over to the row of books and climbed up his movable ladder and snatched the singing book from the air. And before he was down off of the last step, Benjamin shouted at the appearance of yet another. The Gnome ran after the alert. There was a final call and a third book was claimed. Once the Book Keeper was certain there were no other books in question, he gathered at the worktable with Benjamin, and laid the six glowing, ringing books side by side.

"What's happening Dunston?" asked Benjamin anxiously.

"It's a Group Remake," he simply responded.

"A Group Remake? What does that mean?" asked Benjamin.

The Gnome was too deep in concentration to answer him. Benjamin turned and looked at the frightened sisters huddled tightly under Esmerelda Fet's arms, while she held them close. He looked back at Dunston.

"I need to concentrate right now Master Benjamin, please just do as I say. The minute I have finished with my markings I need you to take the book I hand you and go over to whichever tube is lit up and send it on it's way." He paused then continued, "However, I must warn you...you may receive some random information along the way. Oh Me!....Well fiddle fudge, there's nothing I can do about that at present anyway, so simply do as I have asked."

The Gnome continued to speak to himself, "My Aunt Thea, I've never had so many in one group before. Three, no, four was the maximum...*Oh Me!*" Then he looked back at Benjamin, "Something of serious proportion is taking place and I need to catch up right away..so please, just do as I say." Benjamin looked back into the eyes of the little Gnome who was staring at him in shocked disbelief and simply nodded his head in assurance.

The Book Keeper opened the first book and a huge bright beacon of light projected onto his face. He closed his eyes instantly, and instinctively reached up and grabbed at a pair of shaded goggles that hung on a hook above the workstation table. He put them over his head and pulled them up to protect his eyes, then he began his intense scribblings. As soon as he finished, he closed the newly marked book and handed it to Benjamin, who snatched at it quickly and turned to find the pneumatic tube that was shining with indication. He spied the tube three workstation aisles away, and ran to deliver the tome.

As he scurried to the station he was instantly imbibed with, *a flash of Emeline busting through an earthen tunnel onto a cobblestone road.* He stumbled a moment from the sheer surprise of the vision, then regathered his nerve and continued his steps. He placed the book under the tube entry and up and away it lifted out of sight. He ran back to Dunston who immediately handed him another book. This time the transport tube was three stations further than the last one, and Benjamin ran as fast as he could, and carried with him another vision snippet. This time he saw, *Edward, doing battle with the Blunt.* He stopped dead in his tracks from the impact of this information. *The Blunt...Mr. Wickcliff!* But he was instantly shaken from his mind freeze to the sounds of his friends yelling at him to hurry and get back on track. He made it to the tube and released the book.

He now he had the third book in his hands and saw the tube just on the left side of Dunston light up, and ran quickly to send the tome on it's way. At the very last second before releasing the book, he saw in his mind's eye *a man he had never seen before talking to a woman he had never seen before, standing in front of a little cottage in the woods...a cottage that stood next to a massive tree.* Then poof, the book was on it's journey through the delivery tube.

Benjamin was now next to Dunston who was writing with intense fervor, staring through his shaded goggles into the blinding white light of the open volume. He finished, shut the book and quickly handed it to Benjamin without looking up. Then reached for the fifth of the six books without skipping a beat.

Benjamin took the book and looked anxiously down the row of workstations but could not see the lit tube. He scanned the Library in a circle, but nothing jumped out at him. He panicked for a moment and looked around the space wondering what to do next. Then he heard Mathilda and Annabel screaming at him, "Benjamin, down further, near the end...*run Benjamin, run!*"

And with this Benjamin snapped out of his immobility and took off running full speed down the long walkway into the shadows of the deep Library. As he ran he was given the image of, *Mathilda sitting upon a glowing white orb and she was singing. Then he saw her in a cavern tide pool wearing swimming goggles....she was talking to a dolphin!* Then poof, the images were gone, along with the leather bound text up the tube.

Benjamin had to pull all of his energy to gain the speed he needed to get back to Dunston, who he could see was holding up the fifth glowing book. He ran up to the workstation and bent over with his hands on his knees, taking in a huge deep breath to nourish his weary lungs. Dunston shook the outstretched book in anxious anticipation of Benjamin grabbing it.

Benjamin snatched the book from Dunston, and before he turned he caught the illumination of the very spot next to where he was standing. Thankful, he walked over to deliver the book, and in that one long moment he was able to glean a vision of Annabel. *She was sitting at what looked like a cockpit of a wooden submarine, that was dripping with water!* Benjamin shook the peculiar vision from his brain and released the book. Then he turned to face the Book Keeper as he was finishing up with the last of the six books. Everyone held their breath to witness the final deposit of the last delivery. What would happen then?

Dunson shut the book and looked at Benjamin. All the sounds of the previous whirlwind of ecstatic energy was on a low simmer now. Dunston paused with the last book in his hands facing Benjamin. He slid the protective goggles up onto his forehead, then hesitated for a small moment. He then took a deep breath and handed the last of the books to the boy of the Prophecy. Benjamin skipped a beat himself, then accepted the offered volume. He turned to seek out the direction of the lit tube, and much to his immense surprise and confusion, saw not one, but two transporting tubes lit up. He stopped in his tracks and turned towards Dunston.

"Which one?" he asked in complete earnest.

The Gnome stood silent, unwavering, Benjamin began to panic, then the Gnome finally spoke, "That is *your* book you are now holding Master Benjamin. Where do you wish to place it? The choice seems to be all yours at the moment. But wherever that be, you best be getting to it quickly, there isn't much time."

Benjamin looked down at the book in his hands and the visions came. *He was looking through the foggy lenses of aviator goggles out across a great expanse of jungle.* The image faded and in it's place came a clear vision of *him standing before a portrait on a wall, however, the image on the painting was not clear.* He opened his mouth, but absolutely no sound came out. He finally turned back and looked at his friends, still huddled in a lump. Then he looked back at the Book Keeper, then another snippet entered his mind. This time it showed him *coming through a deep thick jungle to an open clearing into a camp of tents with work tables*...then the vision melted away.

Benjamin was tingling, his heart was pounding and he looked out at the library and the two tubes, one was blue and one was pink. He looked back down at the sacred book he held in his hands, then without hesitation, Benjamin marched right up to the pink tube and released his destiny into the ethers above.

All the alarms had stopped and the Library was back to usual. Benjamin wiped his face and pulled himself together. Then he walked over to Annabel and saw that she was still visibly shaken, "What happened Annabel? What did you see?" he asked concerned.

The young girl stepped forward, out from under the protection of the Sorceress, and looked him square in the eye, then spoke in a bland unemotional tone, "I saw my father. He was digging in a really long dark tunnel. Then I was in a deep intense jungle, and somewhere else there were hundreds of bubbles filling the air."

Wow, I wonder if it was the same jungle I saw as well?

"Bellie, what's wrong with you? Why are you acting so weird?" asked Mathilda in a panic. She ran over to her sister and placed her hand in hers.

"It's the vision thing, it can make your noodle swell if you aren't used to it. It is a very perplexing phenomenon to see snippets of your life. Especially ones that you have not lived yet. Oh Me! Don't fret wee lass, I dare say she shall return to her former self in no time at all. Such is the nature of the work that I do. And in speaking, I should like to take this moment to thank young Benjamin for his valiant efforts to assist me in containing the alarming urgency of a *six sided* Remake. Well, I mean to say, *Six*...unheard of!"

Benjamin looked at Annabel and walked up to her and put his arm around her shoulder, "Now you know what it's been like for me mate. It's quite frightening at first, but you kinda get used to it. You'll be right as rain in no time, I swear. And if it makes you feel any better, when I was carrying one of the books, I saw Emeline breaking through a dark tunnel and landing on a cobblestone road. So I suppose that was part of the same vision. We know they're together, so let's just assume they make their way here somehow...I mean it looked like the exact same road. So I think they make it to Na'talom."

Annabel snapped into her breath, as her eyes swelled with water, and looked at Benjamin. After a moment she smiled and wiped her tears, the color coming back to her cheeks, "Okay, Benjamin," was all she said.

Benjamin didn't see any reason to bring up the part about her father coming up against the Blunt.

No, Benjamin decided he would take that vision with him to his grave....*and so it was to be.*

Chapter Twenty-Five

The Grandmother Tree

Emeline, slow down your pace a bit, Edward can't catch up," yelled Braxton.

"The Queen won't slow down, you can bet on that. Just keep up, I believe we're nearly there. The sooner we make it to Tay'lor, the safer we shall all rest," returned the Warrior.

Chantilly Lily spoke as she traveled beside Emeline, "Oh, dear child, I do hope we can still count on the anonymity of the Grandmother Tree. The Elven of the Darmon have assured her secrecy for so many years. However, with all the upheaval of recent events, I am concerned for the timeliness of our retreat into obscurity."

"Well, there's nothing we can do about it right now anyway," countered Emeline, "We have no other choice but to keep to the plan and pray that the Magic is still in full tact and that no one is looking for us yet."

The travelers marched endlessly into the deepness of the Gilley Forest as dusk was approaching. They had run for three days, nonstop, save for several small rests to gather strength and nourishment. Then it was back to the maddening pace of *do or die,* as their mantra to keep them moving. Cubby was keeping up, but the weariness was beginning to show, even for him.

"Look! Up ahead," shouted the Warrior Whisper from his perch high above everyone, "The Grand Tree is in sight!"

"Oh praise the heavens! We are safe," released Emeline.

"We're here...seriously?" asked Edward panting for a reprieve. "Well, it would appear so mate," responded Braxton. "Well, let's not fanny about and get there already. I'm about to keel over completely," shouted Edward with a new burst of exuberance. Braxton chuckled and slapped his friend on the back in camaraderie, and they marched on in tandem with a new spring in their step.

Emeline spoke to Chantilly Lily, "I will wonder how it is that we have made it all the way here from Thornton Berry Shire without a single notice. I can only assume the armies are otherwise occupied. The battle must be strong, or the Blunt would have been on our backs by now." "We all agreed it was in everyones best interest for Tsula and myself to remain here with all of you," spoke up Chantilly Lily, "Our presence at the battlefield would have ignited curiosity, and the possibility of tracing our Magic was a risk we could not take."

As they approached the thick bordering Forest surrounding the Grand Tree, Emeline shouted above her head up to the King, "Tsula, how is her fortress? Does she appear solid?" However, no immediate response came forth.

They all stopped and waited to hear a return of the King's voice, but the stillness of silence smacked them in the face instead. A small panic was beginning to seep in, when suddenly the rustle of the tree branches alerted the small group to a presence.

"Be still," came the soft warning from the Warrior King, hidden among the leafs above. "What, what is it?" questioned Emeline in a low voice. Braxton and Edward could hear their hearts pounding in their heads and held their breath, eyes wide, waiting for the answer.

"The Grand Tree is not alone," he simply said.

"Not alone! Is it the Blunt?" Emeline asked anxiously.

"No, my Lady, it is not a Warrior. I came back to warn you of the situation. Please stand by quietly while I infiltrate the area for a closer look." "I shall follow along Tsula," said Chantilly Lily, "Maybe I can be a tool of understanding in this instance." And out she popped.

"So we just wait here to see who's out there?" whispered Edward.

"You heard the man Eddie, just sit tight. It doesn't appear to be the bad guys, so let's just wait and see what they have to say before we go off losing our heads. Agreed?" asked Braxton, masking his own anxiety. "Agreed." Then he looked at his friend and said sarcastically, "*Eddie?* Really?" And the two new friends shared a small nervous chuckle.

After another ten minutes went by, the anxiety had begun to fray the edges around the hidden group. Then the Whisper suddenly popped back in.

"Oh, thank goodness you've returned. I don't think I could have taken another moment of worry crouched beneath the briar. What is our situation?" asked Emeline.

When Chantilly Lily didn't respond immediately, Emeline became aware of the change in her demeanor. She stared deeply at Chantilly Lily and saw that something had shocked the Whisper. Something huge.

"Whisper, what is it, what did you see? Who are we up against?"

Chantilly Lily couldn't pull the words out of her mouth. She simply stared at Emeline, until the Warrior turned to face her full on, blocking out the men behind her.

"What has happened? What news have you for us that has given you such pause? Spill it now, or I shall seek out the answer for myself!"

Still the Whisper could not find the words. So Emeline pulled herself up from her deepest well of courage and tread straight in the direction of the Grandmother Tree. Edward and Braxton followed suit without saying a word, stunned by the whole bewilderment. As they came into the clearing Emeline pulled out her sword. She heard voices and could see there was a light up ahead. She smelled a fire burning and...*was that soup cooking?* Something about the aroma was familiar. *Why do I know this smell?* she thought perplexed. Then everything came into view.

As the group passed the far left side of the Grand Tree, they saw a small cottage nestled beside her. A cottage with candles glowing in the window and smoke coming out of the chimney.

What is this? thought Emeline in elevated confusion. She looked to the Whisper, "Have the Elven set up Guardians without our knowledge?"

Still no answer. The group scanned the area around themselves in the duskiness of the ensuing night.

"For whatever it's worth, it just doesn't feel threatening to me," whispered Braxton. He looked over at Edward and nudged his arm. Edward looked back and shrugged his shoulders. He had a quizzical look upon his face while he mouthed, *What's happening?* Braxton shook his head and whispered, "I haven't a clue."

They all stepped very slowly, and very deliberately, with clubs held tightly and arms raised in defense of any surprises. As they got closer to the cottage the voices from within became clearer. Looking down at the ground in deeper concentration, suddenly Emeline froze in mid step...*and held her breath.* She didn't move an eyelash. She had the look of immense confusion and pain, and was it....*longing?* wondered Braxton. Without warning, she looked up and headed straight towards the front door. Braxton and Edward were shocked by her obvious intention to enter the abode and caught up close behind her. Braxton reached for her arm, and just as she was turning to look at him the door to the cottage swung open. And out walked Grace.

The two women stood in complete stunned stillness. No one spoke a word. All eyes were on the lovely woman standing on the step. The woman finally spoke, " Em, is it really you?"

"Who is that?" asked Braxton.

Emeline could barely breath, then a small flutter stirred in her heart, "It is my sister."

"Your sister!" replied Braxton in shock.

The two lost twins rushed to each other and the embrace of love spilled forth. Tears welled in Braxton's eyes, he was speechless. And before either woman could say another word, unexpectedly, a very old man teetered out of the door and stood on the porch. He had a smile on his face and a twinkle in his eye as he looked up to speak to Grace. He halted in mid breath and stopped to look at the two woman clutching each other before him. He began to tremble as he reached up to his mouth, with his hand shaking, and tears instantly poured from his eyes. He finally let the words escape him, "Em? My sweet Emeline...can that really be you?"

Emeline stepped back slightly and let her hug release off of Grace's shoulders and slide down her arms, until she was simply holding the tips of her fingers. When the recognition reached her mind, she moved slowly past Grace, dropped her hands and walk towards the old wrinkled man. Her mouth hung open while disbelief filled her senses. And before she made it up the stairs to the old man, he was suddenly joined on the stoop by an equally old crinkled woman. Emeline took a deep breath and stared in disbelief. The old woman came up beside the old man, "Mr. Chickering, what is all the important business that needs tending to in this late of the eve? Come back in before you catch your death..." and her words trailed off as she realized the site before her, "Emeline...is...is that my beautiful Emeline?"

The Warrior walked up to her parents standing before her, with tears streaming down her face, and all the love that had been held deep within her for so many long years, "Yes, yes it's...your Em."

Mrs. Chickering began to sob, "Oh, my dear sweet child. It's you, it's really you! Oh, you've come home at last."

Mr. Chickering pulled his lost daughter into his arms while stroking her long dark hair, repeating, "My beautiful Emeline...home at last."

Braxton was in shock. The missing Chickering family from a hundred years ago was standing right before him...*how was this possible?*

Edward came up close behind him and whispered, "Is this for real? These two old people are her parents? Really? Like over a hundred years or something, *those* long lost parents?"

Braxton simply nodded his head. His heart felt complete joy for Emeline's inconceivable reunion.

She and Braxton had spoken of her sister Grace, and her lost parents during their last night in Thornton Berry Shire. He was filled with emotion at her happiness.

Grace looked up and saw the Whisper and smiled, "Chantilly Lily, it's so nice to see you again. And Tsula... Aut'banda." The King replied in kind and smiled.

"Well, this is simply astounding!" said Edward. "I don't know how this is possible, but here you all are and..." but he couldn't finish the words, as tears began to fill his own eyes. Braxton walked over to his friend and put his arm around his shoulder, "Don't worry Edward, we're going to find your daughters, really, we will. I just know they're fine, I promise." Edward wiped his face and shook his head, then suddenly his heart skipped a beat, as he looked up and saw the silhouette of two children standing in the door of the cottage.

"Annabel, Mathilda? Is that you...Oh dear lord!" And he started to run for the porch, but was stunted in his excitement as he realized that one of the children was a boy. The confusion rushed at him and he stumbled, stuttering, "No...not... Annabel..Mathil...."

Braxton came up behind him and cradled him to simply be still. Then everyone turned to see the two children standing on the porch. Emeline looked at Grace, but before she could say anything, the Whisper said it for them.

"Oh my! Connor and Shelbe!"

"Who's Connor and Shelbe?" spit out Edward. Braxton answered in a quiet tone, "The missing Skeffington children."

"What missing children?...but..." then the understanding hit him, "You mean the missing children from a hundred years ago? What are you saying? How can this be? Oh!...I'm going mad Braxton...completely barking mad!" He put the palms of his hands to his head and squeezed as if brandishing the thoughts from his brain. Then he turned broken and whimpering, and ran off to the other side of the cottage. Braxton let him be.

"What has happened? How are they here all these years later, still so young?" asked Emeline.

"When the Queen abducted them all those years ago she bewitched them to remain children," explained Grace, "It is a hellish magic to wield on so young a mind and body. As you can see they are subdued in behavior. She kept them next to her for many years then one day, quiet by accident, the guards lost sight of them. They found the opportunity to wonder into the Forest and hide. They ended up here in Tay'lor, under the protection of the Grandmother Tree."

"Hide, how could they hide from the Queen? She knows every inch of this Forest, save for the veil of secrecy on the smallest of areas," asked a stunned Emeline.

This time Tsula spoke, "Yes, it is as you say. The Queen is in great control of the forces of this Forest, but have you forgotten that she is not the only one with formidable power? There are others equal to Tar Vigorn in ability and strength. However, the dark magic is a mighty demon that brings with it a tremendous advantage. The Vila and the Whispers have worked in common with the Elven of the Darmon. We have been able to hold substantial wells of Light in the darkest of energies. It is simply a matter of who is more clever and daring. It is a matter of timing...*and intent.*

"The time came in an instant breath for the children to slide out of view from the guards. Then the protection of Light that is inherent in the Gilley Forest, guided their direction. The Fairies sang to them and left berries to nourish them. Until one day when they happened to cross my path. Their safety from the Queen was my concern, so I brought them to this place."

Everyone took a deep breath in shock. "*You* brought them here?" shouted Emeline.

"Yes," responded Tsula, "I was in the knowledge of the sanctity of these surroundings, and so I traveled with the little ones here, to this home. That is when I met the old people. They spoke about their missing daughters and how they had been guided on a path that lead them here. The Gnome of the Ben clan have been their Guardians. They built this place and have kept them safe and in secret for all these years."

Emeline faced the King, anger beginning to take hold, "How could you know of this and not share such information with me!"

"It was not my information to share," simply replied the King.

"I don't understand, what does that mean? All these years you have known of my family's position and have not given me one moment of peace in these regards?" returned a vexed Emeline.

"My gracious Lady, I did not perceive the old couple as your parents. The two Vila and myself were given knowledge of the Great Grandmother from the Elf of the Darmon. No one else. We are the Warrior Guardians of this Forest, it is our duty to watch and protect. We spoke a bond, an oath of secrecy.

"The old people had been here, in this home, for many years before I brought the little ones to them. Knowing you as the great Warrior, and the story of their young daughters, did not bring a familiarity to my mind of being one in the same. Children have been lost in this Forest many times before, as you well know. How could I perceive that they were speaking of you? And even if I had gleaned the understanding, I was bound by my word, and by Magic, to keep within me the sacred home of the Grandmother. However, I must let you know my dearest Emeline, that I am eternally grateful that I did not recognize them to be your parents."

She looked at the King in confusion. "The truth of knowing, locked inside of me, bound by honor, would have caused great pain and anguish each time I saw your face."

Emeline looked at Chantilly Lily for answers.

"I had no knowledge of this," she said, "However, Tsula, the King, is honorable and righteous. He would never do anything to hurt you Emeline...you know this to be true, child. I believe it is as he has spoken, he simply did not make the connection. He kept to his word, and his duty, as head of the Warrior clan of Whisper. It was never his place to speak of the matter to anyone...not even a fellow Whisper."

Emeline knew in her heart that Chantilly Lily was right. But the truth still stung. The thought of the possibility of finding her parents so many years before, and of saving the heartache endured by her sister to reunite with them was almost more than she could bare. All the years lived in between, all spent so utterly alone.....and even more to the point...*lonely*.

To be the only one of her kind, among the magical people of the Forest kept her at a disadvantage for so long. She loved the Forest people, that was not the question, however, she felt trapped in the see-saw of her courage to fight against the unjust, and her deep longing to feel love. Real true love, the love between a man and a woman. Or a woman and her family. She spent all these years as a Warrior, not as a daughter, a sister....*or a wife*. She was having a battle in her mind. Her anger was slowing, but her heart ached just the same. After a few minutes of silence she finally looked back at Grace, "I suppose I should be happy that at least you found each other. I would be disheartened even further to know that my parents suffered alone. At least they had the children for company, and then you came. How many years has it been sister, that you are reunited with our parents?"

"It has been a bit more than five years."

The shock and envy showed on Emeline's face.

"After we saw each other at Thornton Berry Shire, six years ago, I was able to capture the same path as you. The Fairies guided my steps until the day that I met Krinks, a Gnome of the Hew'aut Set. He was on a journey to visit his cousin, Fitz, of the Ben. We walked together and shared food and stories. He knew of the cottage and thought I might be safe here. He had no idea what joy he would hand to me. We have become great friends. You will meet him in the morning, along with his cousin Fitz. We have been working on a very big project together, and I will bring you into that discussion, but enough talk tonight." She put her arm around her sister's shoulder to turn towards the door, "My soup is well past done and the night chill is upon us all. Mother and Father need to retire and you and I have words to catch up on. And the first question I have for you, before another is asked," and she leaned in close to Emeline's ear while she peered over her shoulder, "Who is this lovely gentleman standing so close behind you Em? " she chuckled, " And what of his friends distress? Come sister, let us go inside and warm our bodies and our souls by the fire."

And so it was that the entire Chickering family gathered to eat soup and drink Gnome ale brought by their friend Krinks, in a little cottage nestled next to the sleeping Grandmother Tree.

Chapter Twenty-Six

The Entry into Pancilet

The two sisters stood outside the cottage in the early morning sun. "So what of the Skeffington children, what can be done to help them recover their lost pieces?" asked Emeline.

"I have searched this quandary for many years Em, we need a great Sorceress. We need Esmerelda Fet."

Emeline looked up in surprise at the mention of the name, "You know she rarely comes to the surface. How would we even get word to her of this atrocity? What about the Ghem?"

"Have you forgotten of whom I am speaking?" responded Grace with surprise. "I'm certain the Great Light Sorceress holds knowledge of this situation, as she holds knowledge of the entire Gilley Forest. Although, I have thought of the Ghem as well. However, it is even more unlikely we could enlist his assistance all the way from the Darmon."

"But Grace, he is of the Set. This is of his realm, much more certainly than that of Esmerelda Fet," said Emeline.

"Yes, but these are children from another world. They are not even children in spirit anymore. I am at a loss," responded Grace. She could see the distress in her sister so she immediately changed the subject, "Enough sad words, let's speak of something elevating.   So what of this man Braxton, I sense something between you two...are you in love Em?"

"*In Love*! Such words you speak! Why I barely know him. What would cause you to say something so absurd?" asked Emeline, with a soft red glow cast upon her face.

"Em. I'm your twin.   And even though we do not look exactly the same, I know your every expression, and I know of your deepest dreams.   I see the way you look at him and how you act.   And what is more important, I see the way he looks at you."

Emeline looked back at her sister. "What of the way he looks at me...what have you seen?"

Grace smiled, "There's something there, I can feel it.   It's a little seed right now, but I believe it will take full strides within a short time.   You mark my words sister...there *is* something there."

Emeline allowed herself to feel what this could mean...for about a breath... and then she shook her head in authority, "Don't be ridiculous, a *seed*... I have no time for this nonsense, let us speak of something else.   What of the project you mentioned?   I need more details about the business of the Grandmother Tree.   It is my understanding that she was never completed.   What have the Ben to do with this?"

"Very well Em...subject change duly noted," responded Grace with a big grin, "And the Ben have everything to do with this, along with the Lom and the Hew Set of this area.   At least they did until the war became all encompassing.   Now I'm afraid it is just Krinks, Fitz and myself.   It's been taking all our time and energy, but we have made noticeable progress. I will take you there the moment they arrive."

Braxton walked up from behind them, "Good morning Ladies.   What a wonderful sleep I had. After nights of being knackered unrecognizable, with little more than a half an hour here and there to regroup, I couldn't feel better than I do right now."

"Well, top of the morning to you sir," replied Grace, attached to a sly little smile and a wink to her sister.

Emeline, feeling very uncomfortable with her sister staring at her like a cat, just shook her head and let out an aggravated sigh, stood up, and walked back towards the cottage. Grace yelled after her, "We'll let you know the moment Krinks and Fitz arrive."

Emeline simply waved her hand over her shoulder without turning around.

Edward came up to join Grace and Braxton, "So what are we doing today? Whatever it is I hope it doesn't include a leg up... I'm wiped out. Although I must admit I had a brilliant sleep last night."

"It's the energy from the Grandmother," said Grace, "The Elf of the Darmon secured this entire area for three miles around. The energy is thick with Magic to camouflage and protect the vibration generating from the Grandmother from being exposed. It's been this way for centuries. The Paths through the Forest have a mind of their own. They guide the forces coming and going."

"So you're saying if you're a good guy you might end up on a path to this place?" asked Braxton in jest.

"Yes, I suppose you could put it that way," responded Grace, "The Gilley Forest is an entity unto itself. There is profound Magic in these woods. Depending on whatever time one steps through the Gateway, the Forest dictates which Path shows up to guide them. My parents came through back in the present time then of 1910, and were guided straight to the Grandmother Tree. It appears that the Forest knew the Grandmother needed Guardians, and directed them to come to her aid. It looks like you followed the same Path"

"How can that be?" asked a puzzled Edward.

"The sorcery of the Ghem and the Elven of the Darmon is not something to be explained. This Forest awoke at the same moment as the Darmon. As the Magic sprung forth and other elements began to manifest, the pool of power multiplied. Forces were joined and allies created. In every vibration there is always light and dark needed to produce a whole. Tar Vigorn was born into the darkness within 200 years of the first tree blooming in the Forest. She, and the great Medicine Woman Esmerelda Fet, came a few years apart, the Light sorceress being first. However, they are equals in strategy and ability. These three powers, the Darmon, the Dark and Light Sage, are the oldest and most potent.

"Then of course there are the Vila, who are a fierce resource for the Forest to employ as well. Especially in maintaining the balance of order. The Vila protect the Gnomes, as well as the Fairies, Brownies, and others. The Forest knows his entire history, forward and backward, in a blink of an eye. He knew of the ensuing war coming, and the parts played by both myself and my sister. The Grandmother knew we would all end up here eventually. And as it turns out it was the safest place for my parents to remain all these years.

"With the Gnomes it is about loyalty and family...*and honor above all.* They are workers. They have evolved Spiritually, and the Fet clans have shifted momentum in a larger way in their evolution; as keepers of the Heart of the Planet. The Set clans work close with each other. They all watch and protect the Gilley Forest and his inhabitants. They rely on the Vila and the Elf to help keep them safe from harm. The Gnomes have added to her secrecy by shielding their minds from interference. This is one of the clearest forms of strength the Gnomes have as their greatest advantage. This place, along with her mate, are the two largest fields of Magic in the whole of the Forest, not discounting the Darmon. Your path has led you to a one of these power territories. But there was a reason for that. Nothing here, ever happens by accident."

"You believe we were guided here from the garden on purpose?" asked Braxton in complete question.

"I believe you were guided here long before you ever stepped foot in the garden, Sir." Braxton sat with his mouth wide open, his shock evident.

Edward, getting past being shocked anymore said, "You called the forest He'?"

"Yes," said Grace, "The Heart of the Planet, and the Earth herself is female, the Great Mother. The balance of light and dark would dictate that the Forest be of male energy. In truth, this is a Forest of Warriors. Warriors are inherently male by nature, and the art of war is without a doubt a masculine vibration. The subtle energies of a persons eternal makeup have layers of male and female. The male core of all beings rests in the gut. This is the seat of the Warrior. This is the channel of energy that manifests action. That is why the Forest is the background for combat and strife. The male energy is strong. Whereas in Coranim, it is much more an energy of creation through thought, study, art, invention, these are dominantly female frequencies."

"Coranim? Where's that?" asked Braxton.

"It is the world below the earth's crust, beneath the Great Trees. It's the home to the Fet clans, and it is where the children have been guided."

With this Edward looked up into the eyes of the woman sitting next to him, "My children? Are you saying my children are in some underground world right now?" "Yes," was all she said, as two Gnome walked up to greet her.

"Aut'banda sweet Grace!" spoke Krinks. Fitz was beside him, "Aut'banda M'Lady."

"Aut'banda to you both," replied Grace, and everyone was standing up for introductions. Emeline joined them, "I am Grace's sister, Emeline, and you must be Krinks and Fitz? Aut'banda to you both."

And everyone followed suit.

"Oh this is so exciting," said Krinks, "We had no idea you would have friends with you today. And your sister, how wonderful!"

"Yes," agreed Fitz, "Grace has been speaking about her Warrior sister for many years now, I am so glad you are finally reunited."

The sisters smiled and grabbed each others hands. Everyone turned around when they heard the cottage door open and footsteps on the porch. The Chickerings had joined them, "Oh, good morn!" shouted Mrs. Chickering to the Gnomes. "Top of the morn to you as well mum," they responded in unison.

Mr. Chickering spoke as they walked towards the group, "So I suppose you will be showing these fine strapping lads what you've been toiling over so feverishly? It's about time you had some assistance."

"Yes father, I'm anxious to show them what we've been doing all these years," replied Grace.

"Well, no time like the present," said Braxton, "You've got my curiosity, I'll bite, what's this big project we keep hearing about?"

"Oh, you haven't told them yet?" asked Krinks.

"No, we were waiting for the both of you. And now that you're here, we shall show them together," said Grace, "Follow us." She led everyone over to the Grandmother Tree, around to the backside past the little cottage. They hadn't gone very far, when they all stopped before a door that stood roughly twelve feet tall. A most amazing and majestic Door, that was hand carved wood with the detailed design of a mountain engraved on it's surface.

"Holy buckets!" said Braxton, "I've never seen anything like it."

Edward added with a touch of sarcasm, "Of course...why not? A giant door in a giant tree. What else should we have expected?"

"So where does this door lead?" asked Braxton.

"It's leads to the North entrance city of Pancilet....in Coranim," said Grace.

Edward perked up when he heard the name Coranim, "The same Coranim where my girls are?"

"Yes."

"Well, what are we waiting for? Let's go!"

"We can't," said Emeline.

"What do you mean we can't? My daughters are down there and I'm going to get them and you're not going to stop me. I've followed you through days of relentless running, and done everything you have asked of me. I'm going through this bloody door and I'm going to find my girls...or you better give me one bloody hell of a reason why I can't!"

"It's not finished," offered Emeline.

"Not finished, what does that mean?" asked Edward.

"Just as she says, the construction is not yet complete. The stairway was only built so far before the war began and everyone was called to arms," said Grace.

"So you're telling me that a wall of dirt stands between me and my daughters now?" asked Edward with a sting.

"Yes, that would accurately describe the situation." said Grace.

"Oh, but if I may?" said Krinks, "We have been doing the job ourselves, and if our calculations are correct, and I'm certain they are, we should be breaking through any day now. More than likely within a forte night."

"Is this accurate?" asked Edward.

"Yes, it is accurate," responded Grace.

Emeline looked at her sister and then scanned the area around where they were all standing. "What of the protection? Where is the Key and the Test to keep the entrance locked from the wrong hands?"

"The key, a test, what is she talking about?" asked Edward towards Braxton. Before Braxton could answer Fitz entered the conversation, "The Key and the Test are specific to the Grandfather Tree and the Prophecy. Since the Queen had knowledge of such a place, the Door was reinforced with the Test and the Key. It was all a condition laid out in the Prophecy of Pajah Set. The Grandmother, however, is not common knowledge. Other than the Vila and the Whisper, no one knows of her...well, besides the Gnome of course. However, with the current state of affairs, it has been determined that the need to place a Test and Key upon the Door to guarantee it's formidable barrier from Tar Vigorn, is in order. It is my understanding that this be of the utmost urgent in nature."

"What? What is it? What has happened?" quizzed Grace anxiously.

The two Gnome looked at each other then Fitz spoke, "We have received word that the Queen presently holds the knowledge of the Grand Lady."

"No!...this cannot be so! How? What has happened?" shouted Grace.

"We received confirmation from the Darmon just this morn, relaying the final moments in battle before the children entered the Door leading to Na'talom." said Krinks.

"From who?" asked Emeline, as she said this she realized that neither of the Whispers were present. "Wait, where are the Whispers?" continued Emeline, and she began to pace back in the direction they had come, then quickly turned back around, "What is happening? Tell me this instant!"

"Em, calm down, let them speak. You're not helping matters," said Grace as she walked up beside Emeline and put her hand on her shoulder. Emeline took a deep breath and the sisters returned to the group. Fitz looked back at his cousin then turned to address the waiting faces, "The Whisper appeared this morning to verify the news from the Darmon. She left immediately with her comrade. Apparently Tannis and Avenel had transmitted the details to the Darmon, where Willow then contacted the Chancellor of the Ben." The Gnome edged up closer to the Warrior, "This is what we have been told." He looked her squarely in the eye, "The children made it safely intact to the Great Tree in Ashwald, they were able to perform to task and complete the Test to perfection."

"I knew they could do it!" responded Emeline under her breath. Edward butt in, "There's some kind of crazy test they needed to do to open the door...and they did it...in the middle of a battle?"

"Yes," said Grace.

"Blimey," said Braxton.

The Gnome continued, "The skirmish raged on the far side of the Grandfather, in an attempt to keep the Blunt and the Queen out of view of the children, allowing them time to perform their task. But alas, it was all a charade."

"Charade, why what happened?" asked Emeline, in high stress mode.

"It was the Queen's intent all along to use the Blunt to keep the others occupied, so that she herself could stand in the shadows and learn the secrets to entering the Great Door."

Emeline's face grew wide with shock.

"She exposed herself just before the Door closed on the children inside the Grand entry hall. She let the boy know she now knew the order of the Test, as well as the secret knowledge of the Grandmother Tree."

"How could you know this?" asked Emeline, puzzled.

"Because Tannis grabbed a transmission from the boy just before the Door shut. It showed him everything."

Emeline began to pace again. She went back and forth, thinking, steaming. No one said anything. The urgency spewing from the Warrior was enough to keep everyone in their place, waiting for her lead. Finally she stopped and looked up. "The children should have been through the Door, what is it, three days ago? Why are we just learning of this now? And why didn't the Whisper explain this to me herself?"

Krinks spoke up, "The Whisper is keenly aware of your passion for the well being of the children. She felt it was important that she and Tsula return immediately. She asked us to share the information with you, and to continue with the plan. It took longer to retrieve the Intel from the Darmon because of the nature of sending a transmission during a battle. Everyone is on high alert. The war is expected to gain in momentum with the current situation. All signs lead to the Blunt making their immediate journey to this part of the Forest in search of the Grandmother Tree."

Everyone stood in silent shock, then all hell broke lose. Suddenly it hit Grace and she became slowly hysterical, "The Blunt, coming *here*? Oh no, this can't be! What about mother and father! What will become of them? They can't fight....and..." Emeline cut her off before she had a chance to go further, "Gracie, stop! I can't think when you go mad...just stop and let us speak"

Braxton looked at Emeline, "What is it you need us to do?"

"I need everyone to just be quiet for a minute! I need to gather my thoughts." So everyone attempted to contain themselves to a point that Emeline could begin to strategize. After a moment she asked, "What of this plan you spoke of?"

The two Gnomes looked at each other in anxious anticipation of her response. Emeline was losing her patience, "Stop looking to one another and just spit it out, or I shall give you something to fear in this very instant!"

Finally Fitz spoke, "The plan is to take the Chickerings, with Grace and everyone else, and contain ourselves in the stairwell. The Ghem will arrive to perform the Magic and prayer to ensure the protection of the Door, and the entry into Coranim. He will set the Test"

Emeline let the words sink into her head. *The Ghem?* she thought, *Seal ourselves inside? What kind of madness is this?* But before she could say any thing out loud Grace spoke up, "Emeline, I know what you're thinking, but everything is not the fashion you perceive. The stairwell is nearly finished, truly, it is a work of art, *and* love. It has taken many years to create, and she is solid, and close to completion. There is ample room in the entry hall for all of us to stay inside while we work. We have plenty of provisions and....well quite frankly I don't see what other choice we have. I will not stand idly by and watch the demise of my family once again. A family that has lasted, through all odds, for a hundred years!"

Emeline looked at her sister. She looked at the two Gnomes staring up at her. She looked at the two scared men whose eyes were glued to her. Once again, she was the leader. Once again everyone was looking to her for the answers, and once again she would fulfill her role as the powerful Warrior that she was....*she would lead them all to safety.*

"All right, show me this stairwell you are so proud of. And the rest of you, get back to the cottage and start packing supplies. Think of everything we will need for a week. After that, we are left up to the hands of the fates. Go now!"

And she turned and walked straight through the Door of the Grandmother tree with her sister beside her.

Inside the cottage everyone was scurrying about attempting to pull together anything they felt would be necessary during their internment in the Grandmother Tree. The two Gnomes were expert packers and took charge of the food and water supply. The Skeffington children sat like little stuffed dolls, whose eyes moved back and forth, watching the activity buzz about them while absently swinging their free hanging legs. The Chickerings were gathering wood for burning. "This is so exciting!" said Mr. Chickering, "We're on to a new adventure. After a hundred years in the same place, we're traveling to new sites Mrs. Chickering. And we're doing it with both our daughters."

"Yes, Mr. Chickering, we have our Grace and Emeline by our sides. All is right with the world once again."

Edward was surveying the area outside of the cottage when Braxton walked out with a load of folded blankets to set on the growing pile of supplies ready to transport over to the Tree. "I really can't imagine we're all going to fit inside that

334

thing comfortably for an entire week," said Edward as he turned to see what Braxton had brought out with him.

"Well, maybe you should go check out this entry hall and see what kind of condition things are in. I mean really, it's the inside of a giant tree, how plush could it be?"

"Yeah, I think you're right. I'll go catch up with the ladies and see just what it is we're up against," and away he went to investigate the inside of the mysterious tree.

Grace was showing her sister all the efforts made in the entry thus far. "Well, this is magnificent Gracie, truly. You have done exquisite work here," said Emeline, as she ran her hands along the smooth polished wood walls.

"The Ben clan did all the work in the entry and most of the staircase, while the Hew concentrated on the digging and reinforcement of the tunnel. It wasn't until a couple years ago that it was left to me, with the aid of two Gnomes, to continue the construction. It's been back breaking work to say the least, but it's nearly finished. I swear Em, I dream about the day we burst through into Pancilet. I can't wait to see what she holds in store for us...the magical Wizard City of Pancilet!"

Emeline smiled at her sisters sentimental nature. They were heading further down into the tunnel when they heard Edward shout from above, "What on earth? I've never...well this is bloody brilliant!"

The sisters chuckled at his enthusiasm and Emeline called up to him to join them. He came rushing down the beautifully planed, and polished, wooden stairs until he caught up to them. "This is brilliant! Really, who could imagine such a thing as this?" he exclaimed with a wide grin.

"The Gnome of the Set, that's who," said Emeline, "They are very diligent and ingenious craftsmen. The design is very similar to the Grandfather Tree, so I'm told, I've never been inside. This entry was built to be used by the Ben and the Set of this area."

"What is that? The Set and Fet, and now the Hew and the Ben?" asked Edward.

Emeline chuckled and explained, "Set represents the Forest and Fet, Coranim. The Ben are the mountain clan of Gnome. The Win are the high mountain clan and the Lom are the deep interior mountain clan. The Hew'aut Set are the mason clan of the Forest. The Hew and Lom, with the aid of the Ben, are the architects of this passage.

"For centuries the only channel of travel between the Fet and the Set were through the tunnels built by the Lom, within the depths of the Badger Mountains. It was the only way in or out. Eventually the Grandfather was restructured as an outlet for the Set and Fet of the South area of the Forest. It has always been hidden and protected from the Queen. As Grace explained earlier, the Great Trees have been invisible to her....until recently. However, when she began to rage her masterful position, extra precautions were installed and the Door was locked, and the Test implemented. No one had used that entry in many decades. And now his mate sits here completely vulnerable. We need to remedy this situation as soon as possible. I just hope the Ghem can safeguard her before the Blunt show up"

"Wow! Well, so what needs to be done?" asked Edward.

"We were just on our way to find the answer to that. Let's go," said Emeline. And the three continued down the impeccable staircase with torches in hand.

When they arrived at the construction site they stood in silence and surveyed the situation. Unprompted, Edward walked over and picked up the pick axe and swung it several times, full force, into the earthen barrier in front of him. A massive pile of dirt and debris flew outward and landed on the ground in a heap. He knelt down and ground the chunky pieces between his palms. He stopped and looked back up at the women, "We may have lucked out. This is fairly soft, not too much slate or rock, at least not at this point anyway. If we put some muscle behind this and take shifts, I think we can pull it off. Do you know how far we need to go yet?"

"Roughly, 700 to a 1000 lengths yet. Which would be no less that a week or two using a woman and two Gnomes. However, judging by the improvement of one swing of an axe from a well bodied man, I'd say four or five days at most."

Emeline smiled, "That sounds good to my ears. Well, let's count the inventory of tools we have down here. Are there more to gather up top?"

"No, this is all there is," answered Grace.

"Okay then, let's organize what we've got here and get back to the cottage and start loading everything in. We need to create a bedding situation for mum and dad. And you were correct in saying there is plenty of room up in the entry hall to house all of us. Especially if we are taking shifts as Edward has suggested."

Edward took one last look around, "Well, it would appear we are prepared. So let's get this show on the road."

"Get the show on the road? What an odd manner of speech is the future." said Grace in awe of Edwards language. "Oh, no kidding, things have really changed since your time. It just means we're ready to get going," and he smiled.

Grace shook her head and returned the smile and they all hurried back up the stairs.

They walked up to Braxton who was standing next to the gathered supplies outside of the cottage, "Oh, hey, so it looks like we have everything we could pull together, and..." He stopped in mid sentence and took a double take, as the smiles on all their faces halted his thoughts, "Well, I'd like to take that as a good omen," he said with a huge smile of his own.

"Yeah, everything looks good in there," said Edward with encouragement., We really should have no problem getting things set up, and the work should flow pretty smoothly. The earth isn't too compacted at the present juncture. Hey, I'm just ready to get moving on the whole project. The sooner we get this thing done, the sooner I go find my girls." With this Cubby ran up to him, tail wagging. It was the first time in days Edward had seen him show any enthusiasm.

"That's right buddy. We got a plan, and it's a good one," and he rubbed the dogs neck with gusto.

Transporting piles by the armful everything was finally loaded into the entry hall. Make shift beds were laid for the elderly couple, as well as a nice cozy spot for the Skeffington children. Food, plenty of water, blankets, candles, all the necessary supplies to keep them as comfortable as possible for one week. And now everyone was gathered back at the cottage for a final sweep of the area. The men went inside to make certain nothing was left behind that could be of use. They let the Chickerings know it was time to head on out.

Emeline and Grace stood outside the cottage speaking with Fitz and Krinks.

"When is the Ghem meant to arrive, do you know?" asked Emeline.

"It was not stated as a precise time..." Suddenly Fitz was cut off and they all turned to see two Gnomes of the Ben walking up from behind the cottage, taking everyone by surprise. "Sandor, Harding, what is the news? Your arrival was not anticipated," said Fitz utterly surprised.

Braxton and Edward joined them as Harding began to speak, "We received word that a scouting party of the Blunt are heading North. It is believed the Queen is in a clear mind of where to take her search. A regimen of Set Warriors is gathering forces to come to the aid of the Grandmother. The Ghem is in route, but his time can not be established as yet. The Darmon is no less than two days journey from here. It would be logical to believe his presence to arrive in the wee hours on the morning of the morrow."

Emeline flinched. She looked at Braxton and he simply shook his head in concern, "So what is the tactic we are taking to protect the Grandmother Tree? Once we are all inside, how do you suggest we lock the Door if the Ghem isn't here? Your presence would alert me to the general belief that the Ghem will not make it here before the Blunt? Is this the case?"

"Your instincts are accurate, m'lady," replied Sandor. "Except," resumed Harding, quickly, "The Ghem has relayed a Locum to sustain the protection and lock the Door temporarily. Then upon his arrival he will move quickly to further the reinforcement and initiate the Test. It is thought that Sandor and myself, with the help of the Fairies, will sound the Magic and stand in protection until the Ghem arrives."

"You're kidding right?" said Edward.

"Oh, I assure you Sir, I am most serious," responded the Warrior Gnome in defense. Then Sandor added, "You are obviously mistaking our small stature as a limitation of valor and strength. May I remind you Sir, that we are Warriors of the Ben. We are the best that our clan has to offer. A Warrior of the Ben is a high honor and a title that is not given away without merit. We have fought in many a battle and have come up against the Blunt, successfully I might add, on more than one occasion. Our sole purpose is to protect the Grand Tree from falling into the hands of darkness. We are prepared to fight to the death to safe keep Coranim."

"Sandor is right gentlemen," added Emeline, "I've never seen fiercer Warriors than the Ben clan. I have fought beside many Gnome Warriors and have a profound respect for them all," She looked at the Gnomes, "However, aut'Ben, this situation is not simply just a battle. We cannot allow the Blunt to gain entry into this Door. It would be a monumental step towards the end of our world."

No one responded, faces were white with fear.

"What are the steps needed to begin the process?" asked Emeline.

Harding answered, "It is imperative that you have all your provisions in place and that everyone is secure within the entry hall. Sandor and I shall shut the Grand Door and place the Locum in the lock and speak the ancient words. This will hold the Door impenetrable for the night."

"The Locum?" asked Braxton.

"It's Magic that holds a temporary place. In this case powerful magic," answered Emeline.

The Chickerings had joined the group and everyone was gathered motionless, waiting to receive their next order. Shelbe looked at Mrs. Chickering, "Don't be sad, let me pick some flowers for you, that will bring you cheer." Mrs. Chickering grabbed onto the waif of a girl and smiled., "No need little one. We can pick flowers later. Right now we need to get situated in our new home tonight. Let's do that, all right? Why don't you and Connor come along with Mr. Chickering and myself and we'll settle in. We can have a cookie, how does that sound dear?"

The wee Skeffington child nodded her head in approval.

Grace added, "Yes, why don't we all get into the hall, so the Gnomes can begin the Locum. I don't think another moment should be lost in discussion." Grace paused to stare at the little cottage, as the others walked past her. This had been her home for almost six years. A home spent in happiness with her parents. A tear rolled down her cheek. Emeline looked back to make sure everyone was heading out, and saw her sister standing behind in silence. Braxton looked back and saw Grace's sadness, hesitant to keep up with everyone else.

"Just go ahead, help my parents and the children. We'll be right behind." Emeline whispered to him. m"Okay Em," said Braxton, with tenderness. Emeline stood still for a small moment and thought to herself, *That's the first time he's called me Em...* As she walked towards Grace, her thoughts continued, *I like the way that sounded.* She stepped up beside her sister and hugged her shoulders.

Grace shook herself back into the present and smiled at her sister, "So many changes in my life Em....*Our* lives. I never could have picked this existence if I had all the dreams in the world. Who would have thought that day back in the rose garden, when you and the Whisper told me about the Skeffington children, would forever change everything? This has been my home for many years now. We lived in peace during these last few years...and now everything is changing again." Emeline spoke softly, "But this time we are all together. I wouldn't have it any other way Gracie...I love you very much." "I love you too sister." They hugged each other, then turned to hurry and catch up with the others.

When they walked up to the entry of the Tree, there was a serious air of confusion spilling forward from everyone. "What's happening? Why are you all standing here? You should be inside. We haven't much time," said a bewildered Emeline.

Braxton faced Emeline and Grace and spoke slowly and quietly, "Apparently...the children...cannot...enter the door."

Emeline scrunched up her face and believed she heard incorrectly, "I beg your pardon?"

Braxton repeated himself and added a deeper explanation, "Yes, apparently the children cannot enter the Tree. We were getting things situated and your mother went to lead Shelbe inside and she wouldn't go. So I asked her what was wrong and she simply stared at me. I attempted to convince her, and assure her, that it was perfectly safe, but she wouldn't budge. Then Connor said the *'wall'* was blocking them."

"The *wall!* What on earth is he talking about?" spoke Emeline with an elevated anxiety beginning to swell. She and Grace weaved their way to the front of the little group and there stood the two Skeffington children with their docile disposition.

"Oh, Gracie, there you are," said Shelbe with a smile.

"Yes, Shelbe it's me. Why don't you go inside with the Chickerings, we all need to move quickly now. So let's just go inside okay?"

"Okay," said the little girl and she turned to enter the Door, but was stopped dead in her tracks.

"What is it dear? Why won't you go in?" asked Grace, as she stooped down next to the child.

"It's the wall Gracie, it won't let me in," responded the calm child.

Grace looked up at the others staring back at her in disbelief. Utter anxiety was mounting and Grace shook her head with an open mouth, and nothing to say. Finally Emeline stepped forward, "What on earth is going on here? I want..." However, before she could say anything else Sandor edged closer to the entry and stood next to the children. "Pardon me Miss, but did you say the *wall* was preventing you from entering the Door?" he asked.

The children both nodded their heads. Sandor looked back at the stunned faces behind him, "It's the Dark Shadow Magic," he said blandly.

"The dark shadow magic?" repeated Edward and Emeline at the same time.

"Yes," These children are bewitched with a deep evil sort of spell. They are from another world, and were made to live in this world with distinct stipulations. They cannot enter yet a third world in their state of being. They are ghosts, slaves of the Forest now."

He continued when he knew he had their undivided attention, "There are territories in the Forest that are walled off to dismantled energies. Watch."

Sandor turned towards the little boy who was standing closest to the Door and picked up his hand. He positioned the boys finger to point stretched out, then paused to look back into the eyes of everyone, making certain they were able to see his demonstration. The others huddled closer in stunned anticipation. The Gnome looked back at Connor and smiled, then he took the boy's hand and pushed his extended finger through the space that was the open entry into the Tree. The child's smile faded immediately, changing his expression to shock and pain, as he was literally shocked when a pulsing hot electric zap ran through his finger tip. The Gnome never looked away from the boys eyes while willing him with his thoughts to remain calm. As he did this he spoke very slowly and in the gentlest of tones to the others, without removing his gaze from the comatose child. "Please place your focus to the tip of the finger within the protrusion of the entry"

The others stood with gapping mouths in complete horror as they stared at the gray mildewed and decayed skeleton that was now the tip of Connor's finger.

"Stop! Stop it this instant!" yelled Grace as she pushed past Sandor and pulled Connor into her chest to cradle his confusion. A confusion short lived, as both children held tightly to Grace; while everyone else stood in complete stunned silence.

"So what happens to them now?" asked a bewildered Braxton, "Do they just live like this for the rest of their lives? They can't take care of themselves? They would starve..or... I don't know what happens? I mean, how do the undead ...*dead*... die?" he was beginning to sound hysterical.

Emeline looked at Sandor, "What of this matter? I know they are not themselves completely, but they are ...*something!* They are alive in some sense. I think maybe if..." However, before she could finish Sandor broke in, "The bewitching needs to be reversed in order to release their Spirits to peace. They are as you say, not themselves, but if they are not tended to, the hell that will follow is unspeakable. The dying undead is a fate not wished upon the worst of enemies. They need a great Wizard, or a Light Sorceress, with powers from the deepest well of Magic in the Gilley Forest, in order to distinguish this kind of evil. They can not enter the Grandmother Tree. And they cannot survive here by themselves."

"Well, this is insane! Completely bloody loopy!" shouted Braxton, "What kind of person does this to an innocent child? What kind of game is this Gilley Forest sorcery! Good magic, bad magic, fairies. Who are you people? Seriously? A crazy bloody Queen who steals the souls of children! What did they ever do to her?" Edward grabbed Braxton and shook him hard, "Braxton, stop! Just stop it! You're going a bit mental on me mate. This ein't going to help anyone. Just relax. We'll figure this out."

Then Fitz stepped into the middle of the group, "When Thaddeus Skeffington was erecting his railroad he planned to build it straight through the Forest. Now, under normal circumstances, his train should not have caused any interruption to the world we live here within the Forest. However, the Queen saw this as an infiltration into our realm, by bringing with the rails more technology as time progressed. More technology meant more people. More people meant changing subtleties of energy...energies shifting through mechanical and digital means. Devices that muck about with the auras surrounding everything. The etheric field of our world would be in serous jeopardy

"Truth be told, no one wanted the intrusion of the rail running into the Gilley Forest. You humans don't seem to grasp that the destruction on one plane of existence always seeps into the others. All dimensions are effected. The greater whole was at stake.

"The Set clans of the South set up obstacles designed to deter the continuation of the rails, but to no avail. And the Queen grew weary of the small attempts they were making. She grew increasingly angry at the audacity of men to mess about with something that wasn't his to do so. So she took it upon herself to put an end to the impending destruction of our world, and went into the other realm and stole the children away from Thaddeus.

"And it worked. He stopped building his rail. The remainder of his life was lived wandering the Gilley Forest in search of his children. He died in the Forest...in the dimension that is yours. However, his Spirit is unsettled, and is said to walk among the trees to this very day, sliding in and out of other dimensions. We don't know of his whereabouts at present."

Braxton and Edward were shocked beyond belief, "How...what...I mean, what happens now?" said a wearym and hopelessm Braxton.

"What happens is that we...," began Emeline, however, Edward cut her off cleanly. "What happens is this. I stay with the children while all of you get inside the Tree."

Not one single being moved. The stunned group stood with their mouths open until the reality hit them, then heads began to shake back and forth in rejection and murmurs followed. Braxton looked at his friend, "What in god's name are you thinking, Edward? You can't stay here. What about Annabel and Mathilda? You need....," but Edward stopped him, "I *can* stay here and I *will*. I couldn't live with myself knowing I left these innocent creatures to roam in hell the rest of their lives. What if, god forbid, this were my Annabel and Mathilda? I....I simply cannot stand around and witness this kind of injustice. It will be fine...."

"But Edward..." "No but Edwards, my mind is made up. Here's what we're going to do."

Everyone listened without saying a word.

"You and Emeline are going to dig until you are exhausted, and then you're going to dig some more. You can take shifts with Krinks and Fitz. Grace will take care of her parents and Cubby, and I'll stand watch up here with my new best mates, Sandor and Harding," he smiled down at the Gnomes, "The Blunt aren't going to find us tonight. I mean really, what are the odds they make it here before morning? Right?"

Braxton nodded in faux agreement.

"Right, so when this Ghem person gets here...he's like the all powerful Wizard of Oz or something, right? So he'll just do his magic on the children...," he turned to face Sandor, "That's what you guys said isn't it? That some super magician or witch, or whatever you call them, could release the children from this hell?"

Sandor nodded his head in silence.

"Okay, so he'll release the kids and then he'll just let us into the Tree. Then he'll finish up the big magic and prayers and whatever it is that he needs to do, and that will be that. And everyone wins."

The night was rapidly approaching. The Skeffington children were settled in Edwards sleeping roll in between two large root tendrils to the immediate left outside the Grand Door. Sandor and Harding had a fire started and stood with swords in hand, scanning the Forest out beyond the cottage and around. Everyone else was inside the Grand Entry Hall to the Grandmother Tree. The Door was nearly closed as Emeline and Braxton stood in the sliver of open space to speak to Edward, shadowed by the light from within. Emeline had handed her sword to Edward, "Edward, brave Edward. I'll collect this from you in the morning."

Edward stood looking at his friends, as he gripped the cool smooth handle while the blade hung down to the ground, a heavy extension of his arm, "Get the job done you two. I'm counting on it." He took a deep breath and looked at his friend, "Hey, just in case things don't go according to plan then..." he couldn't finish. "It's going to work Edward. And we're going to find them. Together, all of us, we'll find them. I'll see you in the morning," said Braxton with deep empathy.

Edward put his shoulder up against the Door and pushed hard ,until he heard the secured latch click echo inside.

Within a breath the sound of horses came rushing at them from behind the cottage. Edward turned wide eyes, staring into the dusky shadows and stuttered, "Is it?..."

"Sanc! It's the Blunt!" shouted Sandor.

On the other side of the Forest near the Grandfather Tree stood Sethina and Cottie Set in deep conversation, while a battle raged mere yards from them.

"I don't know how long we can hold out against the Blunt. The minute we distinguish one, three more show up in it's place. We need provisions, and the Gnomes are taking a terrible beating. We need to find a reprieve, no matter how small. It's imperative we lead this battle away from the Great Tree."

Before Sethina could respond to Cottie Set, Chantilly Lily appeared.

"Oh, Whisper! It is perfect timing. I would assume that your presence assures the safe delivery of Emeline and the two gentlemen?"

"Oh my heavens dear Path Tender, much has transpired in the days that I saw you last," replied the Whisper. The two women could see the worry on Chantilly Lily's face.

"What is it dear Lady?" asked the Vila.

Cottie Set's concern was clearly evident on her face, "Yes, tell us."

"The journey to our destination was made successful only to conclude with alarming news. Word came to us, through the Ben. from the Darmon that the Queen holds knowledge of the Grandmother."

"Sanc!" blurted Sethina in frustration.

"A war party of the Blunt has been scouted traveling North. All concern is for the swift action of the Ghem to protect the Door, by sealing it with the Test."

"The Ghem is traveling to Tay'lor?" asked Sethina, shocked by this new piece of news.

"I am not aware of the details in that regard. However, I do know that the plan is to secure the Entry Hall....*with everyone inside.*"

"What! How can this be possible? It is my understanding that the stairwell is not yet finished. Clearly they will be locked into their imminent death. How can this be the answer?" shouted Cottie Set.

Sethina looked around her at the battle and shook her head. She took a deep breath and then she spoke, "I feel my aid may be better suited elsewhere. I will ride to the duty of the Ghem."

"But how can you leave without notice? You are a pivotal Warrior in this battle," said Cottie Set, " Tar Vigorn has her eye upon you. It is by sheer luck that she has given us this small reprieve to stay on the outside of her reign of anger."

Sethina replied with a Warriors conviction, "She has given us nothing! We have rightfully taken this moment as our own. The Elf and the Set are doing commendable in containing her madness. I have stood still long enough. I remained passive, waiting to secure the safety of the children's father before I made harsh maneuvers. Well, the time has come. The children of the Prophecy are safe inside Coranim. And the others have made it to their destination. You are here Whisper, and I am needed else where."

They stole a glance at one another. Then Sethina knelt down, Cottie Set followed, and the three women intertwined their arms and placed their hands on each others shoulders enclosing a circle between them. They shut their eyes and began to hum in a low steady tone. A small white light began to generate from inside the circle, spilling outwards and surrounding them. The humming grew deeper in resonance and power until sparks began to fly off of them. From across the battle scene, in the middle of her smoky charred destruction, stood Tar Vigorn. She turned towards the now growing light and paused. Before she could think about what was occurring, Sethina jumped on the back of Rahm and began rising high into the sky above the thrashing and cries of the combat. Straight up through the murky grey smoke, she rose into the white clouds on the back of her splendid white stag. The Warrior Princess held her position amid the clouds, "I take back my power this minute!" She yelled into the ethers about her, "I do this in the name of Love and Truth. I do this for the safety of all the clans of the Gilley Forest. I do this for the children of the Prophecy!"

And with her final words she spoke the ancient language, pulling out an arrow forged from the Yew tree of her beloved Forest, she sent it flying into the billowy mist before her shouting, *"Rela Or et Bri!"*

Instantly the heavens opened up on the fighting below. Buckets of rain poured out of the sky, pummeling any lose embers of fire for the Queen to wield her dark magic upon. Lighting shot down in bolts of gigantic thick electricity, with multiple branches of the pure energy splitting off in all directions, scattering all that stood in it's path.

The Whisper and the Path Tender watched as the clashing of battle broke apart and cleared the area surrounding the Great Tree. And directly across from them they saw Tar Vigorn in a full rage.

The Queen turned and locked eyes with Cottie Set, then suddenly something took her gaze past the little woman. Cottie Set turned around and her eyes opened wide as she caught site of what held the Queen's attention.

Ever so small, like the unthreading of a side seam in a jacket, the light inside the protection barrier began to shine through the new tear in the field of protective energy. Cottie Set turned in complete horror and looked back at Tar Vigorn, whose clear bright smile was now transforming into the boisterous hideous laughter of evil victory.

The Queen shouted with a bitter sharp tongue, "Well, it appears this game just jumped up another notch Path Tender. Go! Take your moment to figure things out...if you can....as for me....Well I've got to go see a smith about a key!....*ahh ha ha ha ha*...."

Then she disappeared into the thick grey air.

EPILOGUE

The children strolled down the center of the cobblestone road in line with Esmerelda Fet. They peered into all the shoppe windows and spied many incredible wonders, while churning the days events around in their own silence.

"What's that over there, on the other side of the street Esmerelda? It looks like it says Cream and Honey's," asked Mathilda, breaking out of the quiet.

"Ow, thad be Honey's place. She whips up tha best frozen honey cream custard ya could imagine. Hair best bein strawberry with lavender honey."

"Strawberry, my favorite," sighed Mathilda and quickly added, "Can we go inside?"

Annabel spoke up in step with her sister, "Yeah, it looks really fun from here. Look at all the white balloons filling the windows. It looks like heaven on a hot day."

"Ow, thar be no better place on tha whole of tha planet on eh hot day like Honey's. Woll, it looks like ya be twistin me leg, sew let's head on over fer somethin cool an refreshin."

As they continued to walk towards the creamy sweet parlor, Benjamin held his thoughts close. *Something I seek will find me today. Something is going to change my path. What on earth could that mean?* He looked around the busy road without really noticing much, perplexed by all the images he was given in the Library; and by the snippet of information that came from his own personal book of his life. The buzz of the Gnomes rushing about and the warmth of the sunshine reflecting on his forehead, made him feel weary. He stopped for a moment in deep thought staring down the road, "Something I seek...." Then suddenly distracted, he turned his head to look at the store front beside him to the left. It was the floral shoppe. He noticed quite mysteriously that the little sign hanging in the front door window appeared to glow with a bright white aura for a moment. *Well, that's odd. Felicity's Garden,* he thought. "It's really like something out of a fairy tale," he whispered absently.

"Whot's that ya say laddie?" asked Esmerelda Fet.

Benjamin shook his head and looked back at the Sorceress, "Oh, nothing. I was just thinking that the flower shoppe is such an amazing site. I mean, all the color filling the windows...it's just...it's just brilliant!"

Esmerelda Fet smiled and the girls stopped to look over at the window display as well.

"It really is beautiful," agreed Annabel.

And before anyone had another thought, Benjamin was heading towards the little white Dutch door. The others willingly followed behind him, all engrossed in the majestic colorful array of beauty before them. As they crossed the threshold, the scent of the many distinct flowers filled their senses.

"Man, does it smell good in here!" crooned Mathilda.

"Who wee!" agreed Annabel.

Benjamin walked, as if in a trance, slowly among the aisles of wooden shelves and tables filled to capacity with everything green imaginable. He stood beneath canopies of large wide fronds dripping down from tall potted trees, that drew his view upwards, where he noticed the exhibit of paintings. As he walked on he admired the artwork hanging intermittently along the upper lavender painted walls. *Must be more of Pips' work,* he thought, as most of the painting were of landscapes.

And then he saw it.

At the back of the shoppe hanging high above a wooden counter that held receipts and pots, in a spotlight all it's own....*a portrait.*   Benjamin was immobilized before the painting. The girls finally caught up with him in the back of the shoppe. They looked up at the portrait and Mathilda smiled, "Wow, what a pretty lady!"

Annabel nodded, "Yeah, she's really beautiful, isn't she Benjamin?"

They didn't hear an answer from their friend. Finally, drawn away from the majesty of the painting from his silence, Annabel glanced over at Benjamin and a look of concern changed her smile, "Benjamin, what is it? Are you okay?" She could see the concentration on his face as he stared at the painting. Tears began to roll down his cheeks. She reached for his shoulder in question and comfort.

"I wonder who she is?" said Mathilda wistfully.

"She's my mother," said Benjamin in a whisper.

And the two sisters mechanically turned their eyes back towards the painting, stunned beyond words.

"She's wearing a necklace," he said flatly.

Annabel scrunched her nose, something about it seemed familiar, but she couldn't place it, "It reminds me of something?" Is it special Benjamin?

He finally turned to look at his friend and said, "It's the same river stone necklace that Morel and Sethina wear."

They all turned back and stared at the portrait in silence.

BOOK TWO

Benjamin McTish

And The Wizards of Coranim

Benjamin and his friends find themselves on a ridiculously amazing ride through all that is the World of Coranim.

From the enchanting magical city of Na'talom and the splendiferous flying contraptions of one, Pips P. Toggleton, inventor slash artist of the extraordinary, to the far off outer edge Steam Powered Metropolis of Pancilet; with the expanse of Aurorus Jungle residing in between. And always close by is their mentor and guide, Esmerelda Fet, the endearing but brash Light Sorceress. Amid the mysteries of the Aurorus Jungle, Benjamin finds himself confronting the most elusive individual yet, an Aboriginal Gnome Wizard known as Locke, who is able to tweak at Benjamin's psyche every chance he gets.

This journey broadens in scope with the addition of family members who find themselves in the Gilley Forest in search of the missing children. After a shocking encounter with the Dark Queen in her battle of monumental proportions with the Vila, we find Claire and Emmagene traveling with the Elves to their home in the Darmon.

Once in Coranim, the sites and bustling of the Wizard City of Pancilet is an overload to the senses, as great devices of transport wheel down the glistening cobblestone roads. Parasols and top hats dot the sidewalk strolls of the button gloved shoppers on their way to the nearest Pub for afternoon libations. However, all is not as it seems...nor is it ever, dear reader....there are a few surprises yet in store for you as you delve into the deep waters of Coranim; and the ever mysterious story of a family who appears to have some very deep secrets of their own.

Our journey begins exactly where last we left....in a Shoppe, in a magical little city in another dimension, and a portrait of a woman....a woman wearing the necklace belonging to a Vila...

BOOK THREE

Benjamin McTish and the
Hidden Caverns of Bristonbel

The McTish family is literally spilling open at the seams with Secrets.

Beginning with Owen and Emmagene, and a long held secret, that will shock the status quo in monumental proportions How will this revelation change the Gilley, and more importantly, how will it affect the Queen if she learns of the 55 year charade?

The Shire Clans are gathering forces for the battle of their lives, with the support of none other than the powerful White Sage, Esmerelda Fet, who may finally have her day with Tar Vigorn. And just how much danger are the Vila in? Can the secret they've held for centuries remain in tact?

In Pancilet, Mathilda is given a mysterious directive from an even more mysterious Wizard, that will lead her on a quest of a lifetime…to the Secret Undersea Gnome City of Rendahl. Her new friends grant her insight into some of the oldest secrets in Coranim…and beyond. While her sister, Annabel, accompanied by Pips, have ventured in the opposite direction and gone as far north as possible…north as in up that is… to the top of the Blue Peak Mountains and the Gnome City of Rowen. There they witness some of the most outrageous flying contraptions ever imagined, filling the skies. However, their excitement is short lived, as the toxic gas that has been infiltrating the Javerah has now presented its origin. It becomes a full out battle against time and the complete destruction of the magical world beneath the Gilley Forest. Can all the Scientist and Kor clans rectify this calamity, or is Coranim in its final days of existence?

Meanwhile, Benjamin learns more about the depth of his magical abilities, as he and Locke cast some spectacular spells. Along with Gwyneth, they travel the beaches to ascertain just how far the deterioration journeys up the coast of the Aurorus. Their search ends when they walk straight into another

McTish secret, that has long been held in check. Bursting to the fore front in one of the most climatic scenes yet, mysteries are being revealed…and it all takes place in the Hidden Caverns of Bristonbel.

So many secrets for one small family and their close group of friends. However, there is a clue to one secret that can be revealed to you at this time, dear reader, and that it this…Where there is a will, there is a way, and so it goes to assume, if there is a secret entrance into Coranim, than can it truly be safe when it comes to the devious tenacity of Tar Vigorn? Will the Dark Queen prevail? And who must die in order for her to win?

So let's pick up where last we left…Owen McTish and the Brownie are heading back to their home in the Gilley Forest, and a plethora of Secrets begins to unravel with the reappearance of a Bucklersman named Baldufore….

COMING EARLY 2018
THE FINAL ADVENTURE

THE SECRET TOMB OF LODDINGTON-
THE PROPHECY REVEALED

Made in the USA
Coppell, TX
03 January 2021